QUEST FOR THE SCEPTER

FIRST IN THE
SCEPTER AND TOWER TRILOGY

MARK E. FISHER

Extraordinary Tales Publishing

QUEST FOR THE SCEPTER BY MARK E. FISHER

Extraordinary Tales Publishing

P.O. Box 6196

Rochester, MN 55903

First Extraordinary Tales Publishing edition March 2019

ISBN: 978-1-950235-00-1

Library of Congress Cataloging-in-Publication Data:

Fisher, Mark E. | Quest For The Scepter / Mark E. Fisher 1st ed.|Printed in the United States of America

Contents

MAP OF WESTERN ERDE

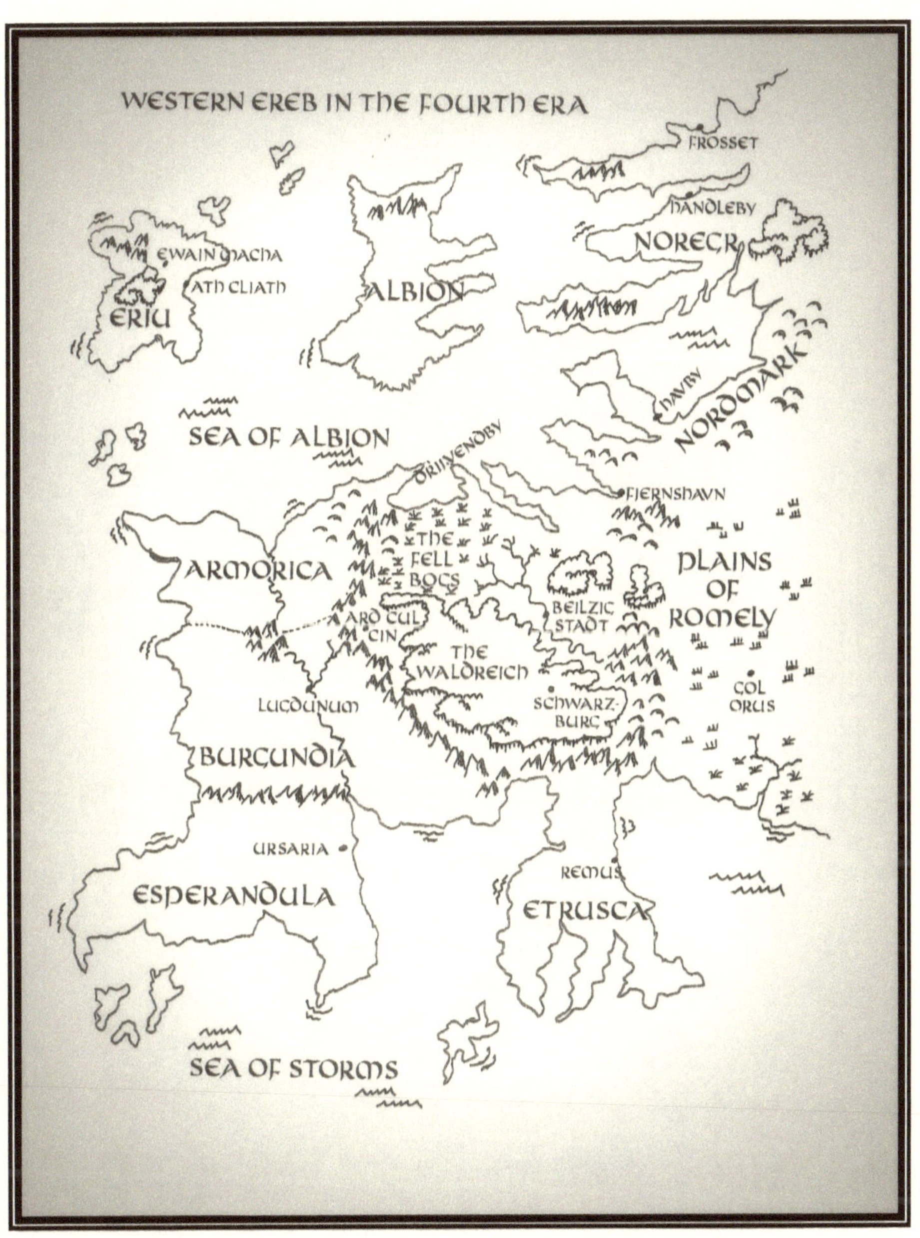

CAST OF CHARACTERS

- Angus mac Donaigh—King of Leinster.
- Blàthan—Captain of The Fair Winds.
- Brigid—Tristan's kindly aunt.
- Cairbre the Wise—Gray-bearded old scholar, Ériu's renowned expert in the ancient texts.
- Caitir nic Cathal—Tristan's longtime childhood friend, daughter of Cathal, the cooper.
- Camran mac Blàr—Short, voluble prince of Munster, member of the Company.
- Cé mac Colla—King of Munster.
- Connell mac Conn—The Ard Righ, or High King, ruler of Ulster and all Ériu, sitting in his palace at Ewhain Macha.
- Corc—Chief druid and advisor to King Connell in Ulster.
- Cowan mac Beisdan—Tristan's stern, unforgiving blacksmith uncle.
- Crom Mord—The dread idol inside which the Deamhan Lord now resides.
- Dermid mac Duff—Dark-bearded prince of Leinster, convener of the Council of Flaith, leader of the Company.
- Dieter Jäger—[DEE-ter Yager] Captain of the guards at Schwarzburg castle.
- Eacharn—Captain of the guards at Ewhain Macha palace.
- Egon—Silent captain of scouts for King Veit of the Naz.
- Elyon—God.
- Ewan man Ninian—Squire to Prince Neil mac Connell.

- ❖ Faolan the Traitor—[FOOL-an] Once Faolan was leader of the siòg, but Elyon banished him from Neavh. Now he's the Deamhan Lord, a foul spirit who lives within the idol Crom Mord.
- ❖ Faolukan the Grim—[FOOL-oo-kan] The Deamhan Lord's arch druid and a powerful sorcerer. Once he was Boiteag mac Clodach, a disgraced monk of Ériu, but the Deamhan Lord turned him to his service and gave him immortality on Erde.
- ❖ Violca—Roamer fortuneteller working for Yanko.
- ❖ Finnean mac Friseal—Red-haired archer, prince of Meath, and a practical joker and rhymster.
- ❖ Hedwig—Queen of the Pruss, ruler of Beilzig City.
- ❖ Joost—[Yoost] King of Drijvendby.
- ❖ Luag mac Laise—Axe-wielding lehbrágan and member of the Company.
- ❖ Lange—Spirit king of the ancient Saxians and ruler of Überhort Castle.
- ❖ Lutz—Chief druid to Queen Hedwig of the Pruss in Beilzig City.
- ❖ Machar mac Maon—Tall, silent, prince of Connacht and member of the Company. Sometimes called the Cloaked Rider.
- ❖ Maeve nic Connell—Princess of Ulster, sister to Neil mac Connell.
- ❖ Malavhìn—[Mal-AH-veen]—The siòg whom the Roamers captured and the only source of the crimson oil that can heal most illness.
- ❖ Ros mac Doughall—One of the Ulster candidates to be chosen to become the Toghaí.
- ❖ Searlie—Tristan's cousin living in Uncle Cowan's hut in Hidden Pines.
- ❖ Sem DeVliet—A guide who knows the way into The Fell Bogs.
- ❖ Siòg—[SHEE-owk]— A fairy creature who serves Elyon, from a race of angel-like beings.

- ❖ Thrag—A barghest in Faolukan's service, in whose presence all light dims and goes out. Some say he's like a bear or dog walking on hind legs, but no one has ever seen through the shadows and gazed upon his true form.
- ❖ Uta—A Prussio princess in Beilzig Castle.
- ❖ Veit—King of the Naz in the forest city of Hochnest.

PART I

CHAPTER 1

A MISSION

When Tristan squeaked open the door of his uncle's roundhouse, his cousin Searlie lay unconscious on the floor, her face yellow and wan, her breathing fast and shallow.

Aunt Brigid, her red hair sticking out in disarray, knelt beside the slight wisp of a girl. As Brigid faced Tristan, tears spilled down her cheeks.

"What happened?" He rushed to Searlie's side. "Where's she been?"

"Una's brother just brought her back. Then she collapsed. Help me get her into the bed."

He lifted his cousin, light as a shock of harvest wheat, and gently carried her to a bed of hide stretched over a pine frame. He knelt and laid a hand on her forehead. Cool. Clammy.

Her eyes opened. Their sickly yellow tint made him gasp.

Uncle Cowan's lean form burst through the door, bringing the smell of woodsmoke, hot iron, and the forge.

Tristan stood and turned to face him.

"Where you been, lad?" His gruff tone carried its usual accusation. "I was ready to fire the furnace, start the plow order. Needed your help, I did."

"I was cleaning up. Didn't you just say I could join the Beltane festival?" All day, Tristan had bent over the coals under the open-sided building beside the hut, holding the tongs, beating the red-hot daggers and swords until he could dunk them at last, hissing and steaming, into the trough. And all day, as his hammer rang on steel, snatches of music, laughter, and excited voices from the fair had drifted down the lane. Until this moment, he'd longed desperately to join the festivities.

"Well, I changed my mind, I—" Only then did Cowan catch sight of Searlie. He faced Brigid. "What's she doing in bed?"

"If you'll stop thinking about that forge for just one moment and come here"—her voice broke—"your daughter . . . she's dying."

Cowan gasped. Pain rumpled his forehead as he hurried to join them at Searlie's side. He stared at his daughter's limp form. "What's wrong with her?"

"This morning, Searlie and her friend, Una, traipsed off into the forest." Brigid lowered her head, shook it, and faced them again. "Ate a poison mushroom, she did."

"W–what kind?" Tristan held his breath.

"A witch's cauldron."

Tristan's eyes closed. A groan escaped his lips. He stared at his cousin, so frail and thin on the furs. Even eating a death cap would have been better than the deadly witch's cauldron mushroom.

"Back in Una's hut," continued Brigid, "they said she retched her guts till her stomach was like to come out."

Cowan's face, burn-scarred and beardless, turned ashen.

"Tristan," came a faint whisper from Searlie's lips. He dropped beside her. "I thought it was something else. It tasted so good. I thought it was safe." A spasm lurched her body, and her eyes squeezed shut.

He swept a hand through his jet-black hair, formed a fist, and pulled a painful tuft down across his mouth. How could this happen to Searlie? Sweet, always smiling Searlie, always melting Cowan's sour moods, bringing light into Tristan's dingy world. She was like a sister to him. His throat tightened.

She was a spring flower fighting for life in a sheltered nook, the withering winds crowding close.

His glance sought his aunt's.

Brigid pulled them both to a far wall.

Cowan faced his wife and whispered, "How long does she have?"

"I'm no healer, but I saw this once before. Two, three days at most." A tear-filled gaze crossed the room to her daughter. "I do not ken what to do for her."

Cowan paced to the hut's far corner, whirled, and returned. "Only one thing to do, and you know it." His face hardened. "Go to the Roamers' camp. For oil of crimson."

Brigid gasped. "B—but we do not send folks there anymore. Not since we lost two men there last year."

"What choice do we have, woman? The crimson oil—it cures everything." He slammed a fist into an open palm. "Tomorrow, I'm meeting an important customer in Portadown. He promises to bring me half a year's worth of business. If I do not get that order"—he shook his head—"soon, we'll be cooking the thatch on the walls. I canna go."

"Then who?"

"I do not ken."

Tristan's heart pounded against his ribs. He knew what he must do. But walk alone into the Roamers' camp? He'd heard the stories. The kidnappings. The witchcraft. The disappearances. The very thought seemed to darken the flames of the hut's central fire.

He glanced at his cousin, so lifeless and delicate on the bed, so unlike her usual perky self. "I'll go." He pulled himself to his full height. "Searlie can't wait. And Uncle needs that customer."

"Nay, lad." Cowan scowled. "You've never gone before. And I need you here. Must be someone else."

"You have no one else. Let me go." His uncle had always been too protective of him. Sometimes he wondered if Cowan simply wanted to keep him at the forge, fearing he'd someday strike out on his own.

Cowan scratched the back of his head, glanced once at Searlie's sickly pallor, and nodded. "I ken you're right."

Brigid faced her husband with narrowed eyes. "You will let him do this?"

"If the lad says he'll go, let him go."

Brigid's jaw tightened. She faced her husband with hands on hips, eyes on fire, and feet wide apart. "Works himself to exhaustion, he does. And this is how you treat him? That camp's full of thieves, tricksters, and ne'er do wells. And lately, the roads are not safe. Do not let him go."

"He'll be all right." Cowan faced Tristan and laid a hand on his shoulders. "But find someone at the festival to go with you. Maybe the baker or the druid? Tell them"—he grimaced in pain—"aye, tell them if they go with you, I'll forgive . . . aye, I'll forgive what they owe. Otherwise, I do not ken. Everyone else'll be busy."

"No one's going to leave the fair today, and you know it." Brigid stared at Cowan, but he waved a hand at her in dismissal.

Brigid frowned and stalked, muttering, to the pot hanging over the fire. She grabbed a wooden spoon and rammed it so hard into the brass kettle, Tristan thought it would go through the bottom. She stirred without mercy.

"Sometimes, lad," said Cowan, "you've got sense." He went to the corner, sent a suspicious glance toward the door, and pried up a floor plank. He fished around and pulled out a bag of coins. "The price for oil of crimson used to be three crowns. Now—who knows? You've got twice that much here. 'Tis much coin, lad. Many weeks' hard work over the flame. I'll have a good explanation for the spending of this"—he eyed Tristan with narrowed brows—"or you'll pay for it out of your hide. You ken?"

Tristan nodded. How often hadn't Cowan's fists slammed his ears for some offense, real or imagined?

Cowan started passing him the bag but stopped. He winced. Then he dropped it into Tristan's hands.

"You'll be seeking only the sìog. Only that one's got the crimson oil. The Sheachranahk have got her chained inside a special tent. And oh, me laddie, just being near her—well, 'tis enough to steal the breath from your lungs."

"Now do not be filling the lad with grand expectations." Brigid shook her ladle at him. "Or he'll succumb to her bewitching."

"And she's the one to do it, aye. But she's the only good thing in the entire camp."

"I'll be all right."

From her bed by the wall, Searlie struggled to face him. The firelight cast wavering shadows across her face, deepening her yellow pallor. "Thank you, Tristan," she whispered. "But be careful."

"I'll get the potion, Searlie. Then you'll get better. You'll see."

She smiled, but her eyelids drooped as if she hadn't strength enough to keep them open.

As Brigid wrapped some food in a leather pouch, her voice softened. "Such a good lad, doing what your uncle should have done. But, Tristan"—she shot him a piercing glance—"you're as handsome a lad as they come. The hucksters and their women will spend all their wiles on you."

He smiled. "I'll try to keep them off me."

"I ken you'll try." She huffed and resumed wrapping the food, muttering under her breath and casting an accusatory glance at Cowan. "Do not the men always try?"

"Enough jabbering." Cowan motioned toward the door. "Now chase yourself off. And take your dagger. You never know who or what you'll meet on the road these days. Rumor has it strange folk are abroad. When Airril came to pay his bill—and only half, mind you!—he reported a troop of lehbrágan marching on the Portadown road last week, and—"

"Sprites? Little people?" Tristan's hand froze halfway to his satchel. He gawked at Cowan.

"Aye. All dressed in red and green and prancing in broad daylight."

Tristan lifted his shoulder sack from a peg by the door and strapped his knife belt around his waist. He'd heard the sprites were coming out in the open, but in all the twenty years he'd lived, he'd only ever seen two, and that was last year. Both of them, each no taller than his waist, disappeared off the forest trail the instant he spotted them.

"Take this bread and cheese." Brigid shoved a bundle in his hands. "You'll not be returning till late tomorrow."

He thanked her, accepted the package, grabbed his cape, and stepped toward the door.

"Lad?" His uncle held up a hand.

Lips pressed tight, Tristan faced him.

"Rumor also has it"—Cowan's voice lowered—"that folk of dark intent also walk the roads, strange folk never before seen in these parts. And it's put quite a fright into those as have seen them. So take care now, hear?"

Slowly, Tristan nodded. But he was puzzled. What manner of person or persons stalking the roads could spawn such fear in otherwise sober-minded villagers?

"I ken you'll be all right. But just"—Cowan looked toward the wall—"just take care." His head down, Cowan crossed to a pedestal holding an idol of Goivhniu, the god of smiths. As he often did, he bowed before it, then shuffled to a straw mattress in the corner and slumped heavily upon it.

Tristan left the hut and grasped his walking staff leaning against the thatch. Tilting his head back, he caught the dying sun on his face. But for Searlie's plight, he would be smiling now. For the first time in his life, he was headed out on the road, alone.

Forests of yew and juniper surrounded the village, and as he breathed deeply, pine scent mingled with the smells of baking bread and roasting meat from the festival fires. He turned left and strode down the path between roundhouses, each large enough for a *feighn* of twenty to thirty family members. A short walk later, flute and *bodhrán* music, laughter, and boisterous conversation welled up around him.

The early-evening sun washed golden over a field bedecked with makeshift stalls, tents, and banners. Neighbors from Hidden Pines mixed with clans from nearby villages, everyone wearing their best tunics, kilts, buskins, and breeches.

Last night, Cowan had kept him at the forge so long he'd missed the hilltop fire. Of all the people in the village, he and Cowan were the only ones not attending. Events were now conspiring so he'd miss yet another Beltane festival—

Beltane, the harbinger of spring, when the druids said the Otherworld spirits came closest to this world and sometimes even crossed over. He shuddered. He only wanted the food, the dancing, and the music. Let the Otherworld spirits stay where they belonged.

But today, Searlie's fate lay in his hands. The festival must wait another year.

He walked the crowd, seeking one of the men who might agree to accompany him. At the edge of a circle of dancers, he spied the druid, a tall thin man in a white robe with a long, sober face.

"Oh, 'tis you." The man's lips turned up in a sneer.

"I've a favor to ask." He explained Cowan's offer to forgive the druid's debt if the man accompanied Tristan to the camp.

The druid narrowed his eyes. "Why should I help *you*, the one who stole the secret of writing without our permission? If I'd had my way, Brigid's brother would be headless in his grave for what he did. Never should we have let that traitor become a druid. And never should we have abandoned the old ways of oral learning, without all this scribbling on parchment."

"I–I'm sorry." Tristan grimaced. He hadn't realized how much the druids resented his learning what Brigid insisted her brother teach him in secret—how to write both Gaelic and the Common Tongue. "But will you not help me for Searlie's sake?"

"*Help* you?" A sly grin lifted the corners of his mouth. "Tell your cousin to greet Manannán mac Lir for me on her way down to the Underworld. Nay, I'll not go anywhere with you, Tristan son of *Torn*. You're as worthless as your father."

The scorn with which the man spat his father's name made Tristan wince. Would he never escape the shame and humiliation his parents had bequeathed him?

Sidling away from that rejection, he found an empty spot between bodies and peered out, searching for the baker. If Tristan saw Caitir, his only other friend in the village besides Searlie, he must tell her what happened. She needed to know. But he saw neither.

The dancers drew his glance into the circle.

With heads held high and hands planted on hips, two clansmen in plaid kilts jumped and kicked their legs to the beat of a bodhrán. Their boots stomped down in rapid succession, shaking the ground in syncopated rhythm. A wee man with wild red hair and a kilt to match pranced beside them, adding his fife to the music. Oh, what a spell the man conjured from his flute! How Tristan wished he could play like that. He closed his eyes as the music and the dancers' stomping beat swept him away.

The smell of fresh-baked pastry drew him from the circle. He wandered to a stand where the baker's wife—short, plump, and flour-dusted—sold apple turnovers.

"One pence for one tart." A wicked smile lifted hairy lips. "And, unlike others of our mutual acquaintance, me tarts are respectable and fully clothed."

Ignoring the insult to his mother, he asked, "Is your husband here? I've a favor to ask."

She eyed him warily. "What could the likes of you want with me husband?"

"I need someone to go with me to the Roamers to—"

"Leave." She lifted both hands, waved him away, and took a step back. "Chase yourself off. Me husband is not going to the Roamers. Especially with you. Now, or ever."

He stared at her in disbelief. "B–but Cowan said he's owed, and Searlie is—"

"I do not care. Cowan will get his shillings. Get yourself along."

He turned away from her, stopping as folks milled past him. His gaze found the trampled, muddy grass. No one here would listen to his request, would they? The druid, in particular, hated him. When, in this village, would he ever receive honor and respect? Nay, he couldn't waste any more time here. The only thing left was to go alone.

He strode quickly through the last of the festival, passing the round-houses, Cowan's hut, and the goat pen with its staved-in gate. On one side of the path, a low stone wall bordered a field planted with stunted barley, cabbages, leeks, and carrots. On the other, a few scraggly sheep and cows grazed in a stubbled pasture. Too few animals, even after a long winter.

Just last month, a wolf pack stole four lambs from the flock. A week later, a bear broke into a hut and killed a clansman's daughter. And this besides countless accidents, fights, arguments, and illness.

Was he imagining it, or were gloom, tragedy, and death crowding ever closer around them? He shook his head.

His buskins fell into a steady gait.

Pulling the bone whistle out of his tunic's inner pocket, he pressed it to his lips. Then he blew, forcing the instrument to release a few notes. He tried to recreate the jig he'd just heard.

Pounding feet raced up from behind. "Strangling the cat again, are we?" Caitir skipped up beside him, a grin on her face, a half-eaten chicken leg in one hand. She easily matched his height. He smiled at her long blonde hair bouncing with every step and at her slim gangly limbs, her ever-ready smile.

"'Tis not that bad. I'm getting better all the time." She was in such a good mood. How was he going to tell her about Searlie?

"'Tis so bad you do not need a sword in the woods. Your playing alone could kill a wolf." She flashed him a sly, sideward look with her green eyes. Mesmerizing, enchanting, green eyes. Then she bit into the chicken.

He stifled a laugh. "You exaggerate. And how can I improve if I don't practice?"

"You're leaving the fair? Is my laddie off on an adventure?" Her glance searched his bag.

"Caitir"—he shot her a worried glance—"I'm heading to the Roamers' camp for a healing potion. Searlie's in big trouble. She ate a witch's cauldron mushroom."

"Nay, nay." Her hands gripped the top of her head. "How bad is she?"

"Bad. Brigid says she's only got two days. And I couldn't find anyone to go with me."

"But on the road, alone? To the Roamers? 'Tis . . . unwise." She tossed the chicken leg into the field scattering some crows. "They say that's how Athairne and his brother were lost. Went by themselves to their camp last year and never returned."

"I'll be careful."

"But have you also heard the rumors? Una's brother heard from a friend of his cousin who talked with a woman from Mossy Rock who saw something on the road. Stood upright, it did. But 'twas not a man she saw. Neither was it a beast. Above the waist, the thing was mostly a wolf."

Tristan stared at her and shuddered. "A shapeshifter?"

"Aye."

"But they don't exist."

"Folks are saying they do. And they're on the roads. So let me come with you. I can shoot an arrow better than most men. I've naught to do tomorrow but make butter, and I can do that anytime. One of the children can tell Father where I've gone. Let him be angry. You need me."

He admired her pluck, but he shook his head. "Nay, Caitir. 'Tis not for young women to go traipsing off on a man's mission."

She skipped in front of him and began walking backward. "And how bold and full of ourselves we are that we willna accept protection from a woman."

"You'll be expected home tonight."

She hopped to the right and walked beside him. "Next week, Father's taking a wagon full of barrels to Áth Cliath. Let me go with you now, and you can help with the load. Considering these rumors, adding my bow to your wee blade would be wise."

"My blade is not wee. And Cowan would never let me go. Besides, your father doesn't think much of me."

"You ken you need me. You're just making up excuses."

They left the gardens and stone fences. Ahead, shadows from the setting sun stretched long over the forest path. This evening, those shadows seemed laden with portents.

The Black Pines Trail led to Ewhain Macha, and there, Tristan stopped at the entrance.

"Caitir." He grabbed both her hands and turned her toward him. "There's another reason you can't come with me."

She eyed him suspiciously. "What?"

"I could never put you at risk."

She pursed her lips, stifled a smile, and eyed the ground at his feet.

He cupped a hand on her shoulder. "I'll bring you back a trinket."

"I'm afraid for you, Tristan." She searched his eyes, worry in hers. "Return with naught but Searlie's potion. And yourself. Alive."

CHAPTER 2

THE ROAMERS

As Tristan fell into a steady walking pace, the forest silence enveloped him. Over half a day's journey separated him from the Roamers' camp. With any luck, he'd reach it sometime after midnight.

But he'd traveled barely half a league from the village when muffled voices approached. He darted off the trail, ducked behind a yew's spreading branches, and slid his dagger from its leather sheath—a foot-long blade he'd forged himself, good protection against anything but a sword.

"My lord, once we get to Ewhain Macha, you'll not be drinking yourself stocious again." The scolding baritone carried a note of frustration. "Sure and certain, I'll not have it."

"Ewan, Ewan, Eeeewaaaan." The second man sounded half cut. "I can drink a quarter my weight in ale . . . and still ou'fight any man alive."

How much that voice sounded like his own! If he could stand outside his own body and listen to himself, this was how he imagined he would sound. He squinted and moved a bit closer to the boughs, trying to hear the voice better.

Parting a hole in the branches, he peered through. Two men sat on horseback. The taller one swayed in the saddle. Obviously some kind of high *flaith*, a lord of lords. A vest of mail rings peeked out from a tunic decorated with red circles. Even on this moonlit forest path, the metal gleamed. His black stallion, too, wore a brass breastplate. From his baldric dangled a longsword. But the man's face was turned away from Tristan, toward his vassal.

"Do not fall off now. I canna keep putting you back up there." The baritone belonged to the mustachioed man identified as Ewan, the lord's squire. He rode a dappled mare, and over his back hung a bow and full quiver. His leather vest, also festooned with red circles, bulged.

"I . . . fall off?" The lord swayed far to the right, then to the left, then centered himself. "Never." As he lifted a wineskin high, he leaned further toward his vassal. The stream missed, splashed beside his hood and down his back. He tipped his head to catch what he could before lowering the skin.

"Be serious. We should be returning to Ewhain Macha." Ewan frowned. "I do not ken why we go now to Hidden Pines. I grant you, they *are* hosting the regional Beltane festival. If not for that, 'tis barely worth a traveler's nod."

"My bi'ness. Something I should 'a done long ago." He straightened in the saddle. "Important personal business."

"Nothing as important as the gathering of high flaith to discuss . . ."

Their horses carried them away, and silence dropped about him like fog after a morning rain. Tristan waited to be certain they were gone. He stood, took one step toward the trail, and then froze.

A shadowy figure, draped entirely in a black cape, glided down the path after the men.

A cold shiver rippled along Tristan's back. Something about the man was odd, not right. His heart pounding, he ducked behind the yew. A twig snapped under his foot.

The figure halted, twisted his head in Tristan's direction. Tristan stared between the needles, but the black hood obscured the man's features. The stranger raised his nose, like an animal, and sniffed.

Then the hood fell off, and full moonlight washed the face.

There walked a man with a close-cropped brown beard, large-boned eye sockets, overhanging forehead, and protruding jaw. But even as Tristan watched, the man's face was changing.

Bristles sprouted from his cheeks. The mouth bulged, stretched out, and formed into a protruding hairy muzzle. Its teeth grew down—aye, this was no longer a man—until they became knifelike incisors. Its nose became wet and black, like a dog's or wolf's.

It ripped off its clothes, shedding them at the trailside. All along its chest and arms, broom-bristle hair replaced skin. A mane of thick fur sprouted from a muscled neck. Where once human hands hung at its sides, jagged claws protruded from paws on front haunches.

Cold moonlight bathed it all.

Tristan's heart struck hard against his ribs. His breath came in short, frantic gulps. Still holding the knife, he put his hands on top of his head.

The thing before him was no longer a man, was it? It walked like a man, but everything above its waist screamed beast, shouted abomination. He staggered, grabbed a branch for support, knocked away needles.

It raised its snout to the air and sniffed.

He held his breath, feeling faint.

But the stalker merely pawed at its own muzzle and shivered as if recovering from some kind of painful blow. Then it loped down the path toward the warrior and his vassal.

Tristan sucked in air, tried to calm his racing heart.

A shapeshifter, here on the road to Hidden Pines? What manner of evil was this?

He waited until he was certain nothing else followed. Gingerly, he inched back onto the trail. The lingering scent of a feral, unwashed animal hovered.

He looked both ways.

Should he follow, try to warn the high lord and his vassal? Nay, they were well armed. And how could he ever get in front of that thing? Nay, his duty was to Searlie.

With far more caution, he continued the long hike to the Roamers' camp.

Strange folk were abroad, indeed.

By the time he reached the outskirts of the camp, nearly two leagues south of Ewhain Macha itself, the night was half gone. He encountered no man, creature, or anything in-between. At a rise in the trail, he paused to overlook the field where the Roamers had drawn up their wagons. Even this late, a hundred fires burned in the darkness, wafting the welcoming scents of cooking meat and burning yew his way. The shadows of men and women danced and writhed before the tiny flames. The music of their strange instruments rose to the hilltop, tickled his ears, invited him to join them.

He started down the dark slope, moonlight throwing shadows on rocks and roots.

Centuries ago, went the tale, the Roamers had arrived from distant Erdelstan. They landed a fleet of ships, transformed them into wagons, and made this isle of Ériu their home. But this new folk, so unlike the *tuatha*—the clans—of Ériu, was ever homeless, never settling in one place, always wandering from village to village, kingdom to kingdom, in search of new customers or, some would say, victims. For a few months each summer, they camped just south of Ewhain Macha.

The path ended in a flat plain, invaded now by the camp. He stepped out of the dark into crimson, dancing firelight. Flames seemed to bounce off the wood-sided wagons and the heads of a small crowd.

"Here, lad. Here." A wizened man with sun-hardened skin and fierce eyes, wearing loose, flowing pants and trailing braids, emerged from behind a wagon. His hand beckoned. "I've got all you need. Spells to bewitch a woman, make her wild for you. Potions to cure the sick. And whiskey. Laddie, have you ever had whiskey?"

Tristan shook his head.

"'Tis Beltane, lad, and no night for caution. Only two shillings a glass, and you'll be sorry in the morning."

"I seek only the siòg. Where might I find her?"

"Always the siòg." The man shook his head, gave Tristan his back, and trudged toward his wagon. "Always her." He motioned with one hand toward the center of the camp. Then the shadows swallowed him.

Tristan passed a group of men from Ewhain Macha, recognizable by the plaids of their tunics. Beside a raging bonfire, they danced to a bodhrán, a harp, and a flute, their eyes gleaming with a feral, untamed light. So mesmerizing was the rhythmic Roamer music that Tristan stopped to listen.

A woman in their midst—dark-skinned, dark-haired, wild-eyed—sang in a strange tongue. She threw her hips this way and that, wove her hands in the air, and winked at the men. So unrestrained were the shadows they threw against the nearby wagons, so crazed and intent was their dance, they appeared drugged. Perhaps by some Roamer potion?

"A woman for the young lad?" Appearing suddenly before him stepped a middle-aged man, a smile pasted on his face, and trailing wild, curly hair as black as night. "Of unusual beauty, with skills in bed to make a man cry with pleasure." Just beyond, a young woman peeked from a wagon window with dark, alluring eyes, long, winking eyelashes. She wet one finger with a slurp of her tongue and beckoned Tristan toward her.

"Nay, sir." He shook his head once more. "The siòg? Where can I find her?"

The man tossed his wiry mop and scowled. "Keep going in this direction. You'll see the light."

Tristan nodded and passed one pleading Roamer after another, ignoring their wiles and entreaties. Did no one sleep at night in this place? He came to a small tent where a lantern shone brightly through thin walls. A tall man with a brown beard and skin the color of burnt copper beckoned from the entrance.

"I seek the siòg."

"So it's her, is it?" The bronze man pulled on his beard with one hand and examined Tristan intently. "What do you want from her?"

"Crimson oil for my cousin. I have coin."

"Then aye, lad, this is the place." He grinned and opened a palm. "Three crowns. In advance."

From a leather pouch, Tristan plunked the coins into the man's hand.

"Wait here." He ducked into the tent. After a muffled conversation, a chain clanged and greater light issued through the tent walls. Reemerging, he lifted the tent flap and waved Tristan inside.

Tristan stepped through the opening. The sweet smell of incense permeated the room. A small slender woman sat at a table. Behind her, some kind of metal cone, punctured with holes and set atop a cluster of candles, shot rays of light behind her head onto the wall and into the room. The effect was dazzling, as if she were the light source.

As he approached, the shadows on her face receded, and he saw her features clearly.

Decades ago, she might have borne great beauty, but no longer. She appeared much like the other Roamer women, only older. Same dark complexion, but wrinkled. Same black hair, only thinning. Same dark eyes, but lined.

He winced in disappointment. It must have been the light display that so impressed Cowan. The siòg was merely a woman.

"What can Violca, the siòg, do for you, today?" Lines of weather-worn sobriety etched her face. "Your future? Perhaps a spell to harm an enemy?" A pleasant smile flickered across her lips. "Nay, for a handsome lad like yourself, you'll be needing a love potion."

"Only crimson oil for healing." Why hadn't his uncle told him the siòg's name was Violca?

"Crimson oil?" She narrowed her brows, her eyes examining him. Ever so slowly, she nodded. Reaching behind her into a box, she fished around and brought forth a glass vial filled with an oily pink liquid. "Here."

Tristan inspected the flask then looked at her. "I thought it would be redder."

She shrugged and reached behind her. He heard the popping of a stopper, liquid being poured, and she faced him again. "There. Greater potency now." The vial had become a dark, oily red.

"This will cure my cousin?" He accepted the bottle with raised eyebrows.

"Give her all of it at once. Whatever's wrong with her, she'll perk up right soon."

But as he nodded to thank her, he imagined—for just one moment—this woman as she once was. Young, vibrant, unbowed by time. A smooth-skinned face, unmarred by age or wrinkles. Bright smiling eyes, untouched by sorrow. Hair, ungrayed, gleaming black and full. For just one moment, he glimpsed a woman of great beauty, unaffected by time. A woman whose heart had been broken many times. Was that what Cowan had seen to think so much of this woman? But nay, his uncle was not the kind of person to sense such things.

He smiled, reached out, and, gently, his fingers slid across her face.

Her mouth opened in surprise. She grabbed his hand, squeezed, and held it. "Little have I to call my own." Her lips brushed the back of his hand, and she released it. "What I do have is a sense about folks that others don't. And you're different. Where do you call home?"

"Hidden Pines."

"Never heard of it. How much did Yanko charge you?"

Tristan told her.

For a moment, her glance drifted to the tent's farthest corner. Then, smiling, she spun toward him. "Wait," she said. Again, she reached behind her into the box, poked around, and brought out a tiny round case. She held it for a while, then faced him. "Take this, too. It's real magic. There's something about you. . . . I cannot let you go with just the oil."

He grasped the small brass case and traced the intricate circular etchings on its cover. Many years and many hands had tarnished and oiled its surface. "What is it?" He began to open it.

A hand shot out and wrapped his fingers like a vise. "Don't open it. Not now. Only when you really need it. Inside is tallow. A very special ointment." She gazed into his eyes, her forehead creasing, her grip tightening. "Now this is important, lad. The tallow is infused with a spell for use in battle. Not any fight, mind you, but one with spirits. Open this case, smear some of the grease on a blade, and your weapon can strike even the most powerful spirits. I'm talking specters here, lad. Creatures without bodies. But you can only use it for one blade, one battle. After that, the spell will depart."

Tristan stared at the canister in his open palm. "I don't understand. Why did you give this to me?"

"I don't know." Nibbling her bottom lip, she averted her face. From outside, the strange flutes began again, mixed with drums. "Aye, lad, I *do* know. Because you're different." She spun back to him, jaw hardening. "And I'm sorry, but Yanko's swindled you." He heard the sounds of the chain being kicked away under the table, as if in anger.

"Swindled?" His fist clenched, and his heart beat faster. "The crimson oil?"

"Worthless. I never do this, never. Yanko's going to beat me. But I don't care. I sense something about you. . . . I'm not the siòg you seek. I cannot let you go home thinking I am. Or that the worthless oil I gave you will cure your sister."

"She's my cousin. And the tallow? Also worthless?"

"Nay. 'Tis my most precious possession. Many years ago, another gave it to me in payment for a debt. And it *did* come from the siòg. I've kept it, waiting for the right moment, the right person."

She dropped her glance to her trembling hands then opened them.

"All these years, I fear I've done . . . only harm. Great harm. In all my travels, all the men who've come before me, wanting this or that, all for questionable purposes—I've seen too much, done too much. And with this mouth, these hands, I swindled them all."

She hid her hands under the table.

"The world does things to you, lad. Makes you hard and numb inside. Then you do things to others you wish you hadn't done. All for what? Some coin? To make Yanko happy so he won't beat me?" She shook her head. "This magic I've kept for so long—'tis useless to me.

So I give it to you. Because I sense something in you. . . . I don't know what. And perhaps, aye, perhaps, this will atone for some of the harm I've done."

Tristan thrust the case into his satchel. She said it was magic. But he'd always heard magic was evil. Yet if it came from the siòg, was it still?

"Thank you, Violca." He stood from the table, bowed, and glanced down at her. She'd just given him her most precious possession, hadn't she? "Give me your hand."

With a quizzical look, she raised her hand to him.

He bent over and pressed his lips to her skin.

Her eyes opened in surprise, a smile lifted her face, and she nodded.

Again, he bowed then walked toward the opening.

On the other side of the tent flap, he approached the bronze-skinned Yanko. "I want my crowns back. This oil is worthless." He threw the vial of fake oil on the ground.

Yanko stood with feet wide apart and grinned. "A refund?" He laughed. "Never."

"You've cheated me. She wasn't the siòg."

"So next time you'll know better, won't you?"

Tristan pulled his dagger from its sheath and pushed the point against the man's tunic, just hard enough to begin slicing through the leather. "The coins. *Now.*"

Yanko's hand jerked to his belt.

Tristan glanced down as the man reached for a knife.

CHAPTER 3

THE SIOG

Tristan clamped his free hand on Yanko's wrist and tightened. Years of working the forge had given him strength. The man cried out in pain and dropped the weapon. His hand shaking, Tristan shoved the point of his knife deeper into the man's chest. It cut through the tunic to bare skin. "My three crowns. I'll have them now."

His face somber, the man took a step back. "Did she tell you?" Aye." Sweat beading on his forehead, Tristan nudged the blade a bit farther.

Yanko backed against the tent wall. He looked side to side, as if seeking help, found none.

"The coins?" Tristan's knife cut a thin red line on the man's skin.

With widened, fear-filled eyes, Yanko pulled the coins from a sack at his belt and handed them over.

Tristan took them, hesitated, and threw one on the ground. "For the tallow." He backed away until he reached a safe distance. Then he turned and ran through the aisles between the tents and wagons.

When he was certain Yanko hadn't followed, he slowed to a walk.

Already, he'd spent an entire crown and hadn't even found the siòg. Cowan would be furious. He wouldn't tell his uncle about the tallow. But what good would such magic do him? Who ever heard of fighting spirits with a blade? Who'd ever even *seen* a spirit?

A bit later, he saw what he'd been seeking.

Four men holding clubs guarded a circle around a large canvas structure. From within radiated a strange, ethereal light, a brilliance that made Tristan's spirits soar and told him whatever was inside was good and honorable and pure. In this camp, it didn't belong.

He approached a small man, only four feet tall, sitting on a stool by the entrance. Red hair tumbled over his green tunic. A lehbrágan? Elsewhere on Ériu, they'd begun to live among men. But he'd never seen one up close.

The sprite's glance shifted continuously from side to side. "Can I help you?" His voice was high, like a child's, yet his serious tone announced that here was no youth.

"I'm here to see the siòg."

"What do you want of her?"

"Crimson oil. For my cousin."

"What everyone wants, of course." He held out an open hand. "Four crowns, in advance."

Tristan swallowed. A dear price, indeed. He pulled the silver from his bag and counted out the heavy coins.

The sprite slipped off his stool, reached a small hand into a wooden box, and brought out a glass vial of clear, heavy liquid. It sparkled by torchlight. "She'll make it from this."

Tristan accepted the tiny flask and waited. The sprite opened the tent flap, peered inside, and said something in a foreign tongue. Then he popped back out. "She'll see you now. Been a slow night. Take as long as you like."

Tristan pushed the canvas aside and stepped into an otherworldly glow.

Then he saw her. The most beautiful woman he'd ever seen, slim, smiling, sitting inside a bright halo, wearing robes of white ethereal light. The room smelled of fresh mountain breezes.

But around her neck hung a chain of dark iron. When bound to a creature of such beauty, it was ugly, out of place.

"Step forward, Tristan mac Torn, seeker of honor. Your uncle, he who worships Goivhniu, abuses your loyalty and trust. I bid you, of all people, to enter." Her words were like music, floating over the carpets covering the floor. They echoed in his ears like the chimes from musical bells. "Sit before me and ask what you came for."

He opened his mouth to speak, but no words came out. She knew what no one else could have known. How could he ever have confused the aged Roamer woman, Violca, with this otherworldly creature? He stared at this vision of light, then at the chain around her neck. "Wh–why are you chained like that?" Where the chain touched her, a dark shadow painted an obscene dark stain over her heavenly glow.

"Few have ever asked that. It shows a kind heart." She smiled, and it brightened his inner being. "Long ago the Sheachranahk bought me from Faolukan himself—the servant of the Deamhan Lord. Ach!" She shook her head. "Their names befoul my tongue even as I speak them. As long as the iron throttles my neck, the Sheachranahk—or Roamers as some call them—own me. And I must obey. Thus do I make potions for love or for healing for visitors like yourself."

"Has no one tried to free you?"

"Once, there was a young man. But when he came with sword in hand, they cut him down at the entrance."

"Does it hurt? That chain?"

"I've grown used to the throbbing." She stared at him so long and with such clear-eyed honesty, he looked away. "You came because you want oil of crimson for your dying cousin."

"I did." Again, her knowledge astonished him.

She reached out her hand. "The vial the sprite gave you. May I have it?"

He passed it to her.

She popped its wooden stopper then breathed toward the tiny flask. Breath left her mouth as a slow white vapor. It swirled above the vial, circled, and gradually settled inside. The oil instantly turned a clear bright red. Then she stoppered the bottle and returned it.

"Three drops, three times a day, for three days."

Tristan bowed low and put the flask inside his bag. "And that will cure her?"

"It will."

"I thank you, my lady. But is there something I can do for you? It grieves me to see you bound like this."

"Your compassion is touching. But unless you have a key to unlock this foul device, you should go at once."

"My lady, I know the inner workings of most locks." Tristan smiled. "I believe I can free you."

A sudden explosion of light erupted from her body and burst across the carpets. Her eyes widened, glowing with what looked like happiness. The brilliance stabbed through him with an experience of joy. A soft breeze, filled with the scent of pines, clear air, and spring mountain snowbells, washed his skin.

Then the glow, the breeze, the scents receded, dimmed, and gathered in a steady halo around her.

"You would do this for me?" she whispered. "You are able? But they will track and hunt you. When they discover what you've done, there is nowhere you can hide. They are relentless."

"I cannot leave you like this. Your captivity is not . . . honorable. May I approach?"

She nodded.

He fished in his pack for the two tools he used for Cowan's richer customers when they lost the keys to their strongboxes and came begging for help—a short metal rod with a hook and a flatter rod. He walked behind her to the locking mechanism, inserted the flat tool, and turned it slightly. With the other hand, he slipped the hooked rod into the keyhole, fished around until the three locking pins clicked into position, one after another. Then he turned with the flat tool. The lock snapped open with a loud click.

She grabbed the iron collar before it clattered to the floor. Then she held it in her lap, staring at it. A wide smile spread across her face. "Do you know how long it's been since this device has not burned my neck?" She gazed into his eyes.

He shook his head.

"Forty years. Much the life of a mortal man."

Then she leaned over and kissed him on the forehead.

Warmth shot through him, energized him. He wanted to sing. But he just bowed low.

She positioned the collar around her neck so it appeared she was still bound. "To keep them from catching you, I will wait until you are at a safe distance. Only then will I flee. But now I owe you something more."

"Thank you, my lady, but you have already given me what I came for."

"Nay, you deserve more. Come closer so I can touch you."

He had no fear of this ethereal creature. He stepped closer.

She reached out one hand and ran a finger over his upper and lower lips, her touch a warm tingling. Again, he smelled sweet, mountain snowbells. "Now you have the gift of music. Continue to practice your bone whistle. Soon, it will carry a song from deep within your heart that before you were unable to play."

He stepped back and bowed low again. "Thank you, my lady."

"Just now, as I touched you, I sensed something I cannot describe. Tristan, you are destined for great things."

He lowered his chin, his face growing hot. "Surely, you are mistaken."

"I am not. Come closer. You must have one thing more."

He again stepped before her. Now she ran her fingers down both arms until she held his hands in hers. Another rush of energy flowed up from his fingers, through his forearms, and settled, tingling with warmth, in his shoulders.

"Now you have the gift of fighting. I am loathe to make it easier to take a life. But for what I believe you will soon face, you must be able to protect yourself. Do not kill unless your life is threatened. Practice your chosen weapon, and this gift will be yours." She released his hands and smiled.

Tristan bowed low once more. "I don't know how to thank you."

"You fear it's magic, don't you? And you've always been told magic is evil. And it is."

He looked at her in wonder. Again, she knew his innermost thoughts.

"The magic of Faolukan is indeed evil. Because he draws it from a well of evil. But these gifts I've given you—they're not exactly magic, but the power of Elyon, focused and planted within the things of this world, and now, within you. So fear them not."

"Thank you, my lady. I had wondered. . . ."

She shrugged. "But a warning about these gifts. As with all of Elyon's 'magic'—for lack of a better word—when you use them in the service of what is good, right, and honorable, they will remain strong. But if you use them for your own ends or ambition, then what you have received today will weaken. And if you continue to pursue the wrong path, they will destroy you."

"My lady, I will use these gifts only for good."

"I believe you will. But that's not all. If ever there comes a time when you are in dire need, when everything you've tried is for naught and your life is in danger, call my name, and I will come—unless Elyon's affairs have led me elsewhere. But what I can do for you is limited."

Tristan's eyes widened. "How is this possible? To come to me wherever I am?"

"I am one of the siòg. Elyon created us to do his bidding, just as he made the lehbrágan. But long ago, the lehbrágan became worldly and lost their true natures. Only we siòg, and a few other races, retain powers that neither sprites nor men can wield. And those powers, Tristan, are what told me you are indeed special, and why I am able to come to you as no mortal ever could."

He nodded, not knowing if he completely understood.

"I will also tell you this. A darkness is spreading over Erde. I feel its presence even here in distant Ériu. Since the Deamhan Lord trapped me so long ago and sold me to the Sheachranahk, his evil has grown deeper, stronger. From the east, it comes. From Drochtar, the dark lands, where he reigns again. And unless someone stops him . . ."

"And this Deamhan Lord is behind it? Who is he? And who is Elyon?"

"Ah, you do not know?" She smiled. "But more of this matter should be learned from the lips of men, not from a creature like me."

"Thank you, my lady. But what is your name?"

"Malavhìn. Of all your race, you are the first to hear that name spoken aloud. Keep it secret, for it carries power. You must leave quickly."

"Malavhìn." He tried it out on his tongue.

"Aye. Now, may Elyon go with you."

He bowed low one final time, backed away, and left the tent.

Outside, he wove through the aisles of wagons, avoiding the hucksters, vendors, sellers of illicit passion, and the crackling bonfires where the men of Ewhain Macha danced, still mesmerized by Roamer music and potions. Eventually, he found himself climbing the heavily wooded trail up the slope away from their camp.

As he neared the top of the rise, he heard a commotion. He looked back toward the field. From the firelit wagons below came the noise of men shouting. Then he saw it. A bright, fluttering creature of light rising from the camp's center. It stopped several dozen feet above the wagon village, made a quick glowing circle, hovered, and then shot off in the opposite direction over the trees.

Malavhìn. She was free.

Below, men ran this way and that, shouting, gesturing. The scene was an ant's nest into which someone had thrust a stick and stirred.

He headed back into the forest. Though the night had entered the wee times and he was more tired than ever he could remember, he started for home. He hoped the crimson oil was as good as the siòg said it was.

Searlie only had one day left.

He increased the pace.

CHAPTER 4

HIDDEN PINES

Tristan hiked the Black Pines Trail almost until morning, but no one followed. As his buskins padded over the soft ground, occasionally snapping a twig, he pondered what the siòg had said about him. That he was special. That he would do great things. But surely, she was mistaken. He didn't feel special at all. He'd lived all his life in dishonor, and nearly everyone he'd ever known looked down on him. So how could a few words by a siòg change that? His only two friends, the only ones who'd ever shown him any respect, were Caitir and Searlie.

After he'd stumbled for the third time into a tree, he crept off the trail onto a bed of soft needles beside a rock face crowded with pines. He ate some of Aunt Brigid's bread and cheese. His eyelids drooping, he wrapped himself in his cape for a short rest. But the time fled, and when he woke in forest half-light, the morning had gone. He shot to his feet and hurried down the trail. What a fool he'd been to lie down at all.

By late afternoon, he had less than a league to reach the village. One turn and over the rise. From nearby, came the sound of an axe chopping on wood. The village was close.

He feared the Roamers would follow. He should never have told the Roamer woman, Violca, where he lived. What a foolish thing to do. Would she tell the others? Perhaps not. He kept to that hope.

He turned a corner, but a small crowd blocked the trail. What in Erde were they doing *here*? Village folk had gathered around something lying on the ground. Others clustered in groups, talking in hushed tones. He approached the circle of men and tried to sneak a look at the object of their attention but couldn't break through.

"'Twas a púca, mark my words." Artagan, the druidic physician whose skills most avoided unless they were near death, had spoken. After he'd learned only enough of the druidic healing arts to call himself a physician, the druids disowned him. "Look at the eyes, how deep-set they are. And the brow, how pronounced. This, they say, is what happens when a man walks too long in that particular kind of darkness."

"Ah, Artagan. He's just big-boned," spoke the tanner. "No one believes those old stories about shapeshifters."

"Then how do you explain what happened to the high flaith laid up right now at Cowan's? They say he's near death. And that a monster attacked him."

The tanner scowled and folded his arms. "And why aren't you there, physician?"

Artagan shuffled his feet and mumbled. "Wasn't called."

Tristan's heart beat faster. Was the injured man the same lord he'd seen wavering half-drunk in his saddle yesterday afternoon? And now the man was in Tristan's uncle's hut? Someone moved aside, and he stepped within the crowded circle.

In the center of the trail—a naked dead man. What looked like a sword-cut had nearly severed an arm. Another deep strike had punctured a lung. Two arrows rose from his chest. As he examined the corpse's face, Tristan's eyes widened. Deep eye sockets. Pronounced forehead. Jutting jaw. Close-cropped, brown beard. It was the same man—creature?—he'd seen yesterday who'd followed the lord and his squire.

"If he was a shapeshifter when he was killed," Tristan breathed the words, "why is he now a man?"

Artagan placed a hand on his shoulder. "If injured or killed, they revert back. Or so the old texts say."

"Artagan, you've read too much." The tanner smirked. "He's just a man."

Tristan couldn't take his glance off the dead man. Should he have temporarily abandoned his mission to warn them? But, nay. Searlie waited near death.

He turned his gaze from the corpse and pushed through the group to the path. He hurried down the way toward home.

The trail left the forest, and soon he walked between the stone fences bordering the village fields. The fair was over, the nearby village folk gone home. Women now tended the gardens, weeding, plucking early cabbages and leeks. Caitir bent to her work in the eastern field but looked up in time to see him. Clutching her half-full basket, she jumped the fence and ran to meet him.

"I'm glad to see you, Tristan." She hugged him.

"I got Searlie's potion."

"Looking tired, are we?" She smiled. "Did we have a good time with the Roamer women?"

"You know I didn't."

"But did you hear what's happened since you left? There's a nobleman staying at your house. Badly wounded, he is."

"I know. Back on the trail, everyone's gathered around his attacker's corpse."

"A corpse?" She smiled as if he'd offered her a blackberry pie. "Let's go see. Nothing like this has ever happened in little, old, boring Hidden Pines."

"Nay, Caitir. What about Searlie's medicine?"

"Of course." She raised one hand and dropped it. "We'll see the dead man later."

"Nay. I also got in trouble with the Roamers."

She frowned. "What kind of trouble?"

"I released the siòg from her captivity."

"You did *what*?"

"I freed her. But foolishly, I told one of the Roamers where I live."

Caitir grabbed one of his arms and whirled him toward her. "Tristan, we can't let them find you." Fear contorted her face. "The siòg, of all things!"

"'Tis possible the woman won't tell anyone. Last night and today, no one followed. At least not yet. But right now, Searlie needs this oil." He patted his bag.

Caitir nodded and followed him the short distance to his small roundhouse. Like many in the village, a few years ago Cowan had abandoned a group house for his own abode. But Tristan had been far happier when they all lived together as one feighn. As soon as Cowan became lord of his own house, he turned mean.

Outside the hut, Cowan was pacing, glancing occasionally toward the door. When Tristan appeared, he scowled. "About time you showed up. We got big trouble here, lad. Some noble's taken over me house. The man's dying, and his vassal says I'm not to beat with me hammers or fire me forge while he's there. Canna make a living again until the man dies. Let's hope it doesna take long."

"I passed his attacker's corpse on the Black Pines Trail."

"Well, this lord's nearly passed on, so bad are his wounds. Face about gone. A terrible sight. Brigid and the man's squire are tending him now."

"I got the crimson oil." He pulled the vial out of his sack and handed it to his uncle. "Three drops, three times a day, for three days."

Cowan shoved it into a pocket. "That'll be Brigid's task. How much did you pay?"

Tristan hesitated. How could he explain the lost crown he'd given to Yanko? He opted for the truth. "At first, a woman deceived me into thinking she was the siòg. So I paid a crown for something I didn't want. But then I found the right tent and paid four crowns for the oil."

Cowan's face blotched red. His hands formed into fists at his side. "*Four crowns*. And you squandered an extra crown!" He lashed out with a fist, hitting Tristan full on the right side of his head, stunning him.

Then came another blow. Tristan winced, tried to duck, but the fist smacked his left ear. He backed away. His ear rang, burned. Dizzy, he staggered back.

"Mister Cowan! *Stop*." Caitir rushed forward and stood between them.

Cowan shoved her roughly aside and landed two more blows before he backed off, breathing heavily. Cowan stared at Tristan, who cowered now with both hands covering his ears. Anywhere but on his ears.

He peered up at his uncle and winced. "I . . . I'm sorry." Then he backed away from further attacks.

"Tonight, you'll not step foot inside me house. I'll not be able to bear the sight of you. Besides"—he slammed a fist into a palm—"the lord and his vassal have taken over." He glowered at Tristan. "'Tis a wonder you got the oil at all." Then he stalked to the door, stepped inside, and slammed it shut behind him.

Caitir rushed to Tristan's side, threw her arms around him, and held him close. "You're bleeding." She led him to the well behind the house. The handle creaked as she drew up a bucket slopping with water. Her wet hands began wiping off his blood. Then she dried the wound with a corner of her tunic. "Is this what happens at your house?"

Tristan nodded.

"And you do not fight back?"

He peered into her eyes, so green and inviting. "I've been tempted. But I would never strike my uncle."

She smiled and stroked his right cheek with one hand. "You're a good nephew, Tristan mac Torn. Too good a lad to be living with the likes of Cowan mac Beisdean."

That afternoon he slept a few hours under the woodpile's awning to the distant sounds of goats bleating and lambs baaing.

Toward evening, Aunt Brigid brought him a bowl of stew. "Looks like we'll soon have a corpse on our hands. Sore wounded this lord is. Such injuries I've never seen. I canna stop the bleeding. Something ripped into both legs, near tore off an arm, and his face—oh, such a sight!"

"There was a dead man back on the Black Pines Trail. Some say he was a shapeshifter."

Brigid wiped her hands on her apron. "What's happening to us, lad? Sprites coming out in the open. Folk changing, and not for the better. Years ago, we never had the fights, the drunkenness, the anger we see in the clan today. Aye, it's everywhere. Now *this*." She threw up her hands.

"How is Searlie?"

"Much improved. I've given her two doses, and already there's some color in her cheeks. Since you brought the oil, she's not had a single spasm."

"That's good, aunt. I'm glad." Tristan closed his eyes and breathed deeply. "I wish I could go in and see her."

"You better not. Right now, he's in one of his states. These days, even your uncle has gotten worse."

"I just wish he'd treat me honorably. Not talk about me like I was a mistake."

She cocked her head. "Honor's important to you, I ken. He works you hard, too hard, and doesna appreciate you."

"The names he calls Torn and my mother—why does he do that?"

"I ken, lad. He's a harsh man, becoming more unfeeling all the time. But he said to tell you he didna mean to hit you like he did. You ken how he is about coin?"

Tristan nodded then touched the spot on his head where Cowan had broken the skin.

"Let me see your forehead." She leaned toward him, eyeing the wound. "I'll get some oil of pine."

Tristan winced. "I'll be all right." He hated the sting of her turpentine.

"Nay. We must kill any bad spirits that slipped in. These days the forest is full of them."

She hurried off.

While he waited for Aunt Brigid to return with her remedy, he wondered if she was not right. The siòg herself had said a darkness was spreading over Erde. And today, it seemed to have reached all the way into the tiny, remote, forgotten village of Hidden Pines.

CHAPTER 5

EWAN MAC NINIAN

After wandering the yard for a time in the gathering dark, Tristan again laid a blanket on the woodshed floor and shut his eyes. But sleep wouldn't come.

Then a low voice, often wavering, sometimes cracking, filtered through the thatch of the roundhouse wall. He recognized it as belonging to the high lord on the trail. He moved his ear closer.

"I've made a mess of it, Ewan." The voice had lost its timbre. "Haven't I?"

"Do not speak, my lord." The baritone was the squire's voice. "Save your strength."

"Don't lie to me, for I ken my time is near. I could barely draw my sword and land a few glancing blows, so stocious was I."

"A fierce beast it was, and you killed it, whatever it was. You couldna have known it followed us."

"It was up to me and me alone to stop the darkness. And now . . ."

"You did . . . your best."

"I've failed everyone. Myself most of all."

"Nay, my lord." Ewan's voice cracked.

"There's no denying it. I was supposed to be the Toghaí. Unless, there was . . . another."

"Another?"

"I've wasted my life, Ewan. On gambling. Drink. On wandering. And on wenches."

"'Twas not wasted." Tears choked the squire's voice. "You've done some fine things in your time."

"Name one."

Tristan heard only silence.

"Ewan, I'm so cold. I cannot feel my legs. Surely, the midwife knows the truth. Find her. Make her talk."

"Be still, my lord. You're raving."

"The midwife . . ." The sound of air being sucked into lungs. "I . . . I'm sorry." Then came rapid, desperate breathing.

"My lord?"

The lord gasped, expelled air, and then was silent.

"*My lord?*"

The bed rattled and shook as if Ewan was trying to wake him. Then came the sounds of a man weeping. Long, drawn out, agonized weeping.

Tristan rolled away from the wall, feeling like he'd violated a very private exchange. But just as he did so, Ewan said something he couldn't help but hear, "O Elyon, now who will save us?"

Tristan leapt from his bed in the woodshed and raced into the yard. There was no sleeping now. Not after hearing that.

The cry of a tawny owl broke the night and added to his mood, sounding like a creature, lost, wounded, and alone.

The full moon cast a silvery light on the pines encroaching the yard. He stared up at the bright orb, so full and warm and beautiful. But oh, so lonely.

The old legends, repeated at night by the fire, said Erde was an echo of another world, distant in time and place. Earth was its name. And the only thing Erde shared with this other world was the moon. Erde, they said, was similar, yet different. An echo of worlds—that's what Erde was. Now Tristan stared up at that bright, silvery disc and wondered if anyone living in that other place was right now staring up at that same moon and if they, too, had just witnessed the death of someone close to them.

Neil mac Connell, high prince of Ulster, had died tonight. Now his squire was in great distress. And what comfort could anyone give him?

The druids taught that an eternity in the Otherworld awaited the dead. A place ruled by the capricious Manannán mac Lir, the sea god. And that was a place Tristan surely feared to go. Was Prince Neil there now?

He thought about his aunt's words. Death and tragedy seemed everywhere in Hidden Pines. Only last month, Ailde fell off a roof, broke his neck, and died. There was also the bear attack, killing a child. And two months ago, Brianag died in childbirth, her baby stillborn. Last winter, the coughing sickness took Borgach, Baodan, Donaidh, and Teàrlach. More people gone to their graves in one year than anyone could remember. He knew them all, grieved for them all.

A sudden heaviness weighed on his chest. For the suffering, the pain, the loss he'd experienced here in the village.

What was worse, folks heard the same tales from other villages, even from Ewhain Macha and distant Tara and Cruachain. Now even his aunt, who'd lived far longer than Tristan's twenty years, seemed worried something was wrong with the very fabric of Erde itself. He'd heard the mutterings, the campfire philosophies, the warnings from amateur seers: *Drochtar is rising again in the east.* But when he asked what that meant, mouths shut, faces turned away, and silence reigned.

He sat on a boulder at clearing's edge and lowered his head into his hands. He didn't even know this Ewan, yet he felt the man's grief as if his own father, whom he'd never known, had just died. How long, he wondered, had Ewan served his lord?

He stood and gazed long at the moon. Finally, he returned to his bed and tried to sleep.

With the morning came Brigid bearing a bowl of oatmeal porridge, topped with milk and honey. "The lord died last night."

Tristan took the bowl and nodded.

"But Searlie's much better. She's sitting up, and for the first time since the fair, she's eating."

"I'm so glad." Tristan smiled. "Then the oil is working."

"Aye. If you hadna gone, I fear she'd be dead right now."

"What's Cowan doing?"

"He helped bring the body out of the house around front then left for Portadown. Ewan's tying the corpse to his horse right now. I'm thinking he'll be taking it to Ewhain Macha for a funeral. But he's mighty glum, that one. Didna keep him from eating half his weight in breakfast, though."

"Did Cowan say how long he'll be gone?"

"He'll return this afternoon. Then he said he'll be firing up that forge and you're to help. I'll be in the gardens. Check in on Searlie, will you?"

He nodded, and Brigid left for the fields. His morning was free.

When he finished the last of the porridge, he walked around to the front of the house. He must speak with Ewan and give him sympathy. Someone had to comfort him, however little it would mean now. He found the vassal tightening cords about the body.

"Excuse me," he said to Ewan's back.

The squire turned around and saw Tristan. Then his jaw dropped.

"You don't know me, but—"

"My lord?" His eyes were wide as a hand found the top of his head. "But this canna be. Oh my, oh my. And I havena drunk a drop of spirits."

"I'm sorry, for your loss."

Ewan stepped closer, his hands shaking. "How is it you're standing before me? Am I seeing things?" Tentatively, he reached fingers toward Tristan, tapped his shoulder, and drew them quickly away. "Sure and certain, you're as solid as me. You're not a spirit. Oh, my lord. Forgive me for thinking you were dead. I am so confused. But who's on the horse?" He whirled to look at the body draped across the stallion. "What's happening here?"

"I'm not your lord." Was the man delusional, his brain addled with grief?

"Ah, but you are. What joy! What relief! You're alive. You really are. You've come back. You're not a ghost. And now you'll save us!"

"Nay, Ewan. My name is Tristan mac Torn, and I live in this roundhouse with my uncle. I'm not your lord."

"But you ken my name. You sound like him. You look and move like him. My eyes do not deceive me. Aye, you *are* him. You canna play another game of hiding from responsibility with a ruse. I'll not fall for that again."

Tristan shook his head. "I saw you both the day before yesterday on the trail. I was hiding in the trees on my way to Ewhain Macha. Before that I never laid eyes on you."

The vassal burst out laughing. "What a trick. This beats anything you've ever done. Even beats the time when you painted yourself white with clay and laid at the bottom of that grave. I was so mad at you then. But I forgive everything. All of it. I do not ken whose body we've got tied up here, or even care, but—aye, what a trick!" He slapped his hands on his thighs and laughed, the tears running down his cheeks.

Tristan grabbed him by the shoulders, shook him, and stared into his eyes. "I'm *not* your lord! I grant you he sounded like me. I noticed that when I heard you both in the woods. I don't know what he looks like, but he's not me. You're stocious with grief, man, not thinking clearly. What about the creature that attacked you? How could anyone make *that* thing part of someone's ruse?"

Ewan stopped laughing. He peered closely at Tristan. Gingerly, he lifted the mop of Tristan's black hair. "Let me see your right palm."

Tristan extended his right hand and opened his fingers.

Ewan stared at it, and then closed his eyes. "I . . . do not understand. You are the same. But your hand. The scar is gone. And your hair? 'Tis longer. And badly trimmed."

"She means well, but my aunt cuts badly. My name is Tristan. I don't know your Prince Neil."

Ewan raised his hands, gripped his head, and shook it back and forth. "Forgive me. The resemblance . . . 'tis uncanny. But of course, I saw him torn apart. He couldna have escaped." He lowered his head, the grief obviously taking over again.

Tristan put a hand on the man's shoulder. "You've lost your lord, your master. You must be overwrought. I'm sorry."

Ewan nodded. Then his eyes narrowed. Slowly, he looked at the bundled corpse then back at Tristan. "Wait, lad. Let me think." He left the horse, walked a few paces, and then whirled.

"Can you wield a sword, Tristan?" His voice was suddenly serious, firm.

"I've had a wee bit of practice. But I'm not very good."

The squire's brow creased. "That might be a problem. Can you ride a horse?"

"Aye."

"Reading! Can you *read*, lad?"

"I can read Gaelic, aye. Also the Common Tongue."

"And write them both?"

"That, too. Aunt Brigid's brother was a former druid, and she insisted he teach me the magic of reading and writing. But much to my uncle's— and the druids'—great displeasure. We studied in secret, but the druids eventually found out."

"Did you also learn the blasphemy of druidry?"

"Nay. Only the writing. Aunt Brigid insisted only on the writing."

A slow smile spread across Ewan's face, lighting up even his eyes. "Bear with me a moment." He walked a few feet, staring at the bare ground as he went. He spun. "Do the names Faolukan or Elyon mean anything to you?"

"I heard them in the Roamers' camp yesterday. But I don't know much about them."

"Perfect. Absolutely perfect. With a bit of work, you'll do nicely."

Tristan shot him a quizzical look. "For what?"

"Why, my lad, I'm going to make you into Neil mac Connell, high prince of Ulster, with all the rights, privileges, and duties accorded him. And on my mother's grave"—he narrowed his eyes and stared at Tristan with all the seriousness he could muster—"you're going to save Ériu from the darkness."

CHAPTER 6

A STRATAGEM

You want me to do—what?" Now Tristan's jaw dropped.

Ewan grinned then slapped one leg with such force, the prince's black stallion whinnied and whipped its head around to look.

"You're going to save Ériu, lad. And you'll do it by taking the place of my dead lord here. Forgive me, Neil." He glanced at the body tied on the horse then back to Tristan. "You look and talk and even act, in most ways, like him. 'Tis so uncanny it makes my head spin. Sure, and we'll have to fill in a few gaps, probably more than a few, but 'tis as if this were meant to be."

"How am I going to do that—take your lord's place? They'll find me out. Then they'll kill me. Or throw me in the Ard Righ's dungeon."

"'Tis a risk, I grant you. But we've no choice in the matter. Neil was the only one, or so we thought. He was on his way to a high council for a great mission. And only he would do. He didna tell me why we came to this village." He raised a hand to his drooping mustache and caressed it, as though thinking. "But, lad, it must've had to do with you. There was something he didna tell me, some grand secret. Surely, it was about you. But right now, we must bury my lord Neil and begin to teach you a few things. For you are going to take his place." Then Ewan put both hands on his hips and smiled.

"You're daft." Tristan edged backward. "Touched in the head."

"'Tis all flying mad, no? But I think it'll work. It must work. First thing is to bury him before word gets out." He grabbed the horse's reins. "We need a shovel."

Tristan stared at him, his jaw open again.

"Are you going to stand there all day? Bring us a shovel and help me bury a dead prince."

Tristan cocked his head. "I suppose he must be buried. So I will help you. But no more than that." He ducked into the forge and returned with a shovel. Then he led Ewan down a trail to the east, avoiding the gardens where the women were working today. For half a league, they traipsed into the forest then veered off the path until they stopped at a grassy knoll.

They took turns digging until they had a deep enough hole. While the chaffinches in the branches at clearing's edge sang songs too happy and unsuitable for a funeral, they laid the body carefully at the bottom.

Sweating and breathing heavily, Ewan leaned on the shovel and looked down. "In life, Neil mac Connell, you were a heap of trouble." He wiped a tear from one eye. "But may Elyon welcome you to Neavh. May he greet you into his clan with open arms. And forgive me, my lord and old friend, for what we're about to do in your name. And Neavh help us if we're caught." He scooped a shovelful of dirt and threw it on top of the body.

When they'd turned the hole into a low mound of dirt, they began the trek back to the village, with Ewan leading the horse.

They walked in silence until the houses came into view. Then Ewan spoke. "So will you come with me, lad, and take my lord's place? I need your answer."

Lips pressed tight, Tristan scanned Hidden Pines' unmarked borders. "How can I leave my uncle and aunt? They depend on me."

Ewan scowled.

They crossed the field to the village, turned the corner, and found themselves in front of Cowan's house.

"Now that my lord's buried, I'll be in a heap of trouble if you do not join me."

"I can't. This is my home. 'Tis all I've ever known."

"You've no idea how important this is . . . what's at stake."

He gave the man a questioning look. "What exactly *is* at stake?"

Ewan shook his head. "Unless your answer is aye, I canna tell you." He put a hand on Tristan's shoulder, his expression serious. "But even I do not ken the whole story. I *can* tell you what will happen if you join me. It's the least I can do."

"All right, then. Tell me what you can."

"For a time, you'll become high flaith, one of the highest in the land. But if my guess is correct, we'll leave Ériu at once. I say we, because I assume they'll send me with you. Others will join us. Our journey will take us to strange lands few have ever seen. There we'll face danger and evil we canna even imagine. We may awaken creatures so ancient and foul even the memory of them has been lost. There are places and beings in this world, lad, that were meant to lie hidden, to sleep in darkness deep. But alas, I fear it will be our job to walk right into those places and bang on our shields with heads held high. Then we'll stand with sword and bow at the ready and take what comes. No matter what happens, we must press on to the end. But in the end, if we're not killed or imprisoned or ripped to shreds by monsters, well, then—we'll have saved every last man, woman, and child in Ériu from a terrible fate. That's what I have to offer."

"If you're trying to convince me, 'tis hardly the way to do it." A smile curved Tristian's mouth.

"Might have overdone it a wee bit, do you ken? But 'tis the truth. I'll not feed you lies."

"I'll have to think about it."

"Nay, I need a decision now. If you do not come with me this morning, I must return and dig my lord back up. And take his corpse to the palace. Dirty as it is."

"And then what?"

"Then wait for this land you love, even your little village here, to sink into darkness like so many others on the continent are doing even now."

"Darkness? What kind of darkness?"

"Even I do not ken the length and breadth of it. Join me, and others will tell us what they know."

Tristan faced the ground.

"Well, lad. What'll it be?"

"How can I leave my uncle and aunt? I'm sorry."

Ewan's face fell, and he breathed in deeply. "I canna convince you otherwise?"

Tristan shook his head, nay.

At that moment, Caitir appeared from around the corner of the roundhouse.

"Then I'll dig him back up." But Ewan just stood beside his horse, unmoving, with head down, as if all energy had been drained from him.

Caitir stopped in front of Tristan, her eyes gleaming. "They're here."

"Who?"

"The Roamers. Four of them, just now. Searching every hut at the far end of the village. Asking about anyone who recently visited their camp. And they've got fierce, curved swords."

He looked down the path between roundhouses then at Ewan, still standing beside his horse.

"Roamers?" Ewan lifted his head and caught Tristan's gaze. "Why would Roamers be looking for you?"

"Because I visited their camp two days ago. And I freed the siòg."

"You did *what*?"

"Released her chains, and she escaped. I hoped they wouldn't discover who did it."

Caitir put a hand on his arm. "You must hide in the forest. Tristan, if they find you . . ."

"Ewan?" Tristan arched a brow toward the squire.

"Aye?"

"I'll do it. I'll go with you."

Ewan's smile nearly broke his face. "Then we leave at once. I'll fetch my things from inside. Take very little. From now on, you'll be wearing Neil's clothing." He tied his mount to a nearby post. "You do not ken the importance of what you've just said." Then he sprinted into the house.

Tristan eyed Caitir. But her face showed no surprise. He followed Ewan inside, with Caitir close behind.

He went to the corner where he kept his belongings. But as he poked through what he owned, he found nothing he desired to take. Everything he valued was in his travel sack by the door. He crossed to Searlie's bed where Brigid was already giving her another dose of crimson oil. Caitir followed.

"Searlie, you're looking better. Very much so."

Her fingers gently closed about his. She sat up in bed and smiled. "Thanks to you, cousin."

"Aunt Brigid. Searlie." He glanced back at Caitir. "And you, too, Caitir. There's something I must tell you. I'm leaving the village."

Puzzlement creased Searlie's delicate face.

Frowning, Brigid thrust her hands to her hips. "What talk is this? Is it Cowan's beatings? Have they become too much?"

"Nay, aunt. This man, Ewan, wants me to come to Ewhain Macha with him on a mission of some importance. He can't tell me what it is, only that he needs me. And it involves great danger."

"I know all about it." Caitir sidled up beside Brigid. "I was hiding around the corner and heard most of it."

Tristan stared at her. That would be like her. Then he faced Brigid. "But there's another reason I must leave. When I was in the Roamers' camp, I freed the siòg from her captivity."

A gasp from Brigid. She put a hand to her mouth. A blank stare from Searlie.

"The Roamers are in the village now, looking for me. It seems I've little choice but to go with Ewan."

"You've been a good lad." Tears came to Brigid's eyes. "I'll miss you terribly. I'm sorry how Cowan treated you. You were like a son to me."

He leaned forward and hugged his aunt, trying to hold back his own tears.

Then Searlie reached both arms out to him. He bent down and hugged her. "I love you, Tristan, as if you were my brother," she whispered in his ear. "Always remember that."

From his traveling bag, Ewan gave Brigid a pouch clinking with coins. "Payment for taking your nephew from you. And for your husband losing his apprentice. If I'm right, your Tristan is destined for great things."

"How can that be? He's a bastard child, born to a harlot."

Tristan winced.

Ewan scowled. Then the squire shook his head as if he needed to focus on more immediate problems. "We must leave quickly. Now the three of you"—he studied Brigid, Searlie, and Caitir in turn—"you must not tell anyone what we're doing here. After I go, Tristan will follow me alone down the forest trail. Tell everyone your nephew just up and left. Tell nary a soul he followed me. And the man who died"—Ewan faced the wall for a moment—"tell them he was traveling through. A visiting noble from Connacht. And you"—he stared at Caitir, his dark eyebrows dipping together—"if you love this lad and your village, as appears to me you do, you'll not tell anyone what you heard this morning. You ken?"

Caitir swallowed and nodded.

"Tristan, I'll see you a league down the trail, waiting with the horses."

Tristan nodded.

Ewan took what little clothing and weapons he had brought inside for himself and his prince and hurried out the door.

Tristan said his final goodbyes to Aunt Brigid and Searlie.

Then he faced Caitir. "I don't know how long I'll be gone. Or if I'll ever be back. So I guess this is . . . goodbye."

Caitir's lips tightened. She glanced at the ground, the light fading from her green eyes. "You're my best friend, Tristan." Tears choked her voice. "What will I do without you?"

He pulled her close, and they hugged. "I'll miss you, Caitir."

As they parted, her eyes were moist. He slid a hand across her face. Then he leaned over and kissed her cheek.

A smile tried to form on her lips but failed.

Quickly, he stepped outside. Everything had happened so fast—he wasn't prepared for this.

He shot a glance down the path. No Roamers yet. He slipped behind the house, looked both ways, and ran until he was in the deep pines. He planned to skirt the village by way of the trees, bypassing the vegetable fields.

But he stopped, parted the pine boughs, and peered back across the yard at the roundhouse and the village of Hidden Pines. He'd spent all his life there. It was the only home he'd ever known. But there was no going back now, was there? Once he left today, he didn't know when, or if ever, he'd return.

As if to confirm his decision to leave, the weaver's dog began barking continuously, warning of intruders. Then four dark-haired, copper-skinned men appeared in the alley between houses, armed with curved swords, heading for his uncle's place.

Roamers!

They would watch his home, search the environs, and if they didn't find him, someday return. He'd heard of the Roamer vendetta oaths. Even after they moved on to Meath or Munster or Connacht, they'd come back next summer to Ewhain Macha. And they'd seek him out. Again and again. Until their revenge was complete.

One last time, he glanced into the village. His throat tightened.

Then he ran into the forest.

PART II

CHAPTER 7

METAMORPHOSIS

As planned, Tristan met Ewan far down the Ewhain Macha trail. There the squire put him on Neil's horse, a black stallion sided with leather armor. As Neil mounted, a soft whinny and a shake of its head escaped its muzzle.

They rode hard in silence until early evening. Then they veered off onto a scarcely visible side trail. When Ewan spied a bare hilltop through the trees, he left the path and led them to the top of a wide, grassy field. At one end rose a pile of boulders, and at its base, a dark opening leading to a cave.

"Neil, this spot will do nicely for your training tomorrow." The squire dismounted and began untying the cinch straps. A cool breeze blew through the oaks surrounding the hill, hinting of a cold night. They'd soon need a fire.

"You called me Neil." Tristan also dismounted.

"Aye. We must start calling you by the name you'll go by. You must forget you're Tristan. As of today, you've become Neil mac Connell, high prince of Ulster, son of the Ard Righ."

Tristan laughed. "You make it sound like this will work."

"It will, lad. Because it must." He threw his saddle on a level patch of ground and tied his dappled mare to a bush. Tristan followed his lead. As they collected firewood, they talked. "We'll start with your father, Connell."

"I've heard the king's ill."

Ewan threw him a glance. "'Twas the story spread to cover up the real problem. He's not the man he was. These last years, he canna seem to make a decision. And when he does, it bodes ill for all concerned. His brain is addled, Neil, torn with doubt. And worse, he listens to everything Corc tells him."

"Corc? He's the king's druid?"

"Aye. He's become Connell's main advisor, and the Ard Righ is all the worse for it. I do not understand the man. 'Tis as if he wants to destroy us, so bad does he advise the throne."

Tristan brought an armful of downed limbs to a spot near their saddles and dumped them. Ewan produced some dried moss and began striking a dagger hilt against flint. "What's worse, Neil"—Ewan bent closer to his work—"your father doesna seem to ken truth from falsehood. He lies now in all things, large and small. Someone asks why the treasury is so low, and he claims it's full. But everyone knows that's a lie. We tell him a lord has taken cattle from his neighbor in the dead of night. And the Ard Righ dismisses the accusation as if it were a trifle. Then that same thieving lord accuses one of his tenant farmers of questioning his integrity, and the king has the poor farmer tied to a stake to rot."

"Is there anything worse"—Tristan frowned and narrowed his eyes—"than a leader of men who knows neither honesty nor honor?"

Ewan stopped and caught Tristan's eye. He smiled. "Sure and certain, 'tis long since I've heard someone speak such sentiments with such force. I ken I'm going to like you, lad. Sorry—Neil." He raised his gaze to the sky as if asking apology from his dead lord.

Tristan also smiled. "What about me? This Neil I'm supposed to become?"

Ewan returned to striking his dagger, sharp and quick, on the flint. Sparks flew and the moss burst into tiny flame. He leaned over to blow lightly. As the blaze grew, he snapped twigs, added them, and then larger sticks.

"Neil, you say? Well, you drink too much, and there are few women that do not interest you. And you tell every one of them—without flinching, mind you—that they're the only one for you. You do not judge, because of course, then you might be judged. You are never serious, which I can see right now is going to be a problem. You wile folks with your wit and charm, and when that doesna work, you simply put your arm around them and tell them they're your best friend, even if you canna stand the sight of them. Works every time." Ewan reached into his pack, produced bread, cheese, and sausage, and passed some to Tristan. He also gave Tristan his own wineskin. "Ah, nothing like a fine meal and wine from the king's cellar to liven a campsite."

Tristan sat next to Ewan before the fire as they ate and drank. "But this is not the person I am. How am I going to fool anyone?"

Ewan shrugged and swallowed. "Think on my description of Neil's behavior. Try to live up to it. Or rather, down to it. I ken you're going to have to work at this. Another thing about him—he's never done a full day's work in his life."

"'Tis not me."

"I can see that. Working with you will be a refreshing change, lad. We may simply have to limit your interaction with Connell and Maeve. And especially Corc."

"Maeve?"

"Your sister. She's a beauty, all right. Her main goal seems to be to survive her brother, her father, and Corc. And she'll use whatever wit and charm she can to do it."

"How long must I perform this act?"

"Only a few days until, I hope, we'll be away. Then you'll have to keep it up onboard ship and on the trail. But those going with you will not know you as well as Connell, Maeve, and Corc. Some you've only met once or twice."

Tristan took a swig from his wineskin and finished eating. He pulled out his bone whistle and tried to blow a jig that was dancing in his head.

Today, the notes seemed to flow much better. He played for a time. The song sounded almost like he remembered it.

As Ewan listened, he cocked his head. When Tristan put the flute away, Ewan smiled. "You'll not be able to play that until we leave Ériu. Neil could never do such a thing. But I wouldna mind listening to such again, if the occasion arises."

Tristan's shoulders loosened. After a single practice, he'd already received a compliment. The siòg's gift was surely working.

"We need to spend the rest of the week in teaching and learning. 'Tis all the time we can spare. Then we must ride for Ewhain Macha. In five days' time, the council will gather."

"The council?"

"Aye. Concerned men from all over Ériu. Important flaith in high positions. We're hoping for the Ard Righ's blessing and attendance. But lately, Connell's stood against anything sensible. And then there's this—" Ewan leaned forward, bracing an elbow on his knee. "Besides convincing these lords you are Neil, there are tests you must meet. From the prophecy. If you do not pass these signs, well—then you can return home."

Ewan's glance turned toward the fire. "You simply *must* meet the signs." He laid down on the saddle. "We'll talk more tomorrow. And remind me to cut your hair so it looks like the prince's." Then he pulled his cape over him and lay still.

Tristan stared through the treetops at the reddening sky. The sun was nearly gone.

The odds against this working seemed great. How could he ever fool an entire palace and a gathering of high lords into thinking he was the prince of Ulster? And what were the signs Ewan was so concerned about? He rubbed the back of his neck. What had he gotten himself into?

After breakfast the next morning, Ewan led him to the center of the hilltop field.

"We'll start this morning with swordsmanship. Neil was one of the best in the land. This is probably the most difficult part of our deception. If anyone challenges you, my lord, we're in trouble."

"My lord?"

"Aye. You must get used to the title. I'll call you that from now on."

Ewan stood with sword in hand while Tristan held Neil's weapon. He examined it, tipping the smooth metal to catch the light. He'd rarely seen such a fine blade. When he banged it on his knee, it sang as if it were a musical instrument. Minute, interlocking swirls etched every space of the hilt. More designs followed the steel down its length. A deep blood gutter indented the tapered sword. "This is a well-crafted blade, Ewan."

"Neil was one of the best swordsmen in Ulster and had the weapon to match. Everyone knew it, and no one wanted to challenge him. That's our best hope. But you've got to be able at least to wield it like you know what you're doing. Let me see you thrust and parry."

Tristan leaped forward, thrusting the sword toward Ewan so he had to back up.

"Do it again."

Tristan struck out, but Ewan easily blocked it.

"Not bad. You say you've never fought a man with the sword?"

"Nay. I just make them. I do practice with Caitir, a friend. But neither of us is very good."

"The girl we said goodbye to?"

"Aye, the pretty lass with the sharp tongue."

Ewan smiled. "Practice is not like real combat. Now show me your parry." He raised his sword and struck down.

Tristan grabbed the end of his blade, tilted it sideways, and met the cutting edge with the flat.

Ewan struck again and again. Each time Tristan managed to block it. As Ewan and he exchanged blows, Tristan felt a growing assurance in his abilities.

"I do not understand. You say you are not very good. But—" Ewan tilted his head. "Let's practice some more."

For the next while they engaged in a mock battle until Ewan stopped them. "You're better than you said, better than I'd hoped." He wiped sweat from his brow with his sleeve. "But I can teach you a few things."

For nearly half the day, Ewan taught him how to improve his technique. As their practice progressed, Tristan felt more and more confident, several times getting the better of his teacher. Finally, after one particularly long exchange, Tristan made two quick thrusts, followed by a strong sideward blow that knocked Ewan's weapon from his hands.

Ewan stared at his blade lying on the ground then at Tristan. "Lad—I mean, my lord—you're almost as good as Neil himself. If I'm not imagining things, you've improved greatly even since we started practicing this morning." He shook his head, his eyes wide. "Where did you learn to fight like that?"

Tristan wiped his face then shrugged. Something told him to keep the siòg's gift a secret.

"I take back what I said. No one will ever question your swordsmanship. I'm truly amazed."

A fine drizzle began falling.

They sheathed their weapons, and Ewan announced, "Before we eat, we need to discuss palace etiquette."

"What's 'etiquette'?"

Ewan wiped the rain off his forehead and laughed. "'Tis learning when to bow and when to step aside. When to start eating and when to stop speaking. When to nod and when to offer the lady a hand. But 'tis also knowing how to say 'my lord' and 'my lady' and not sound like you're about to fall on your knees before the person you're talking to. I ken that'll be your problem. You're showing too much deference even to me, a vassal and a subordinate."

"I wasn't aware of it, my lord."

"Never call me 'my lord'. I'm simply Ewan."

Tristan tipped his face up. Suddenly, the drizzle became a roaring downpour.

Ewan grabbed his saddle and pack, motioned to Tristan who picked up his, and started leading him to—where? The cave?

Ewan rushed inside, but Tristan stopped at the entrance, staring in, holding his saddle.

"Come in, my lord. You're getting drenched."

Tristan breathed deeply. There had to be a cave, didn't there? He took two steps inside, just enough to escape the rain. At least he could stand up.

But this was a dark hole, and the light, already dimmed by clouds, began fading fast around him. The walls and the ceiling seemed to move closer on all sides, to darken and deepen. As he stared into the tunnel, its sides began to swirl. His heart beat faster. Though drenched, his face grew as hot as if he were standing in full sun. He tensed his jaw, fighting an uncontrollable urge to bolt.

He dropped the saddle. Then he backed into the downpour. Immediately, his heart slowed, and he breathed easier.

"What's wrong, my lord? Come inside out of the wet."

"I–I can't." Raindrops pummeled his forehead. He pulled the hood of his cape over his head and hovered just beyond the cave entrance.

Ewan raised a hand in a question. "I do not understand."

"'Tis a cave. I can't abide caves. Small places underground."

Ewan looked behind him. "But it only goes in about thirty feet and quits. Nothing to fear here."

"Still, it's a cave."

Ewan frowned. "This could be a problem."

Tristan hesitated, and then sprinted across the field to the nearest pine tree. There he slipped under its branches and waited for the rain to quit. Nearby, the horses had found a similar sheltered spot.

He'd rather face a raging bear than the dark, yawning mouth of a cave.

CHAPTER 8

THE DARKNESS OF CAVES

When the downpour stopped, Ewan brought their saddles back to the field and threw them on the ground with a thud. "What was that all about? Why such a fear of caves?"

Tristan shrugged. "I don't want to talk about it."

"Are we going to have dark secrets, you and I? We could be on the road together for many months. This fear—it could put everyone in danger."

Tristan stared at Ewan, walked a few paces, whirled, and came back. "All right. If you must hear it . . ."

"Good."

"About nine years ago when I was eleven, I was playing in the hills above Hidden Pines with Caitir and another lad—Bran was his name. That day we were playing hide and find on a hillside riddled with shallow caves. Again and again, we'd been told not to go there. Back then, I had no fear of caves.

"'Twas Bran's turn to find, and Caitir and I hid. I didn't know where she was, but I found a particularly deep tunnel leading straight into the hillside. When I could barely see light at the entrance, I sat down to wait.

"It was early evening, and unknown to us, Bran's father had called him home. It always took a while for someone to find me, so I lay down on a smooth rock, wrapped myself in my cloak, and waited. Before I knew it, I'd closed my eyes and fallen asleep.

"Sometime later, I woke. But by then it was totally dark. The sun had set long ago, and I knew I had to return to the village. But I was disoriented and no longer knew the way out. I touched the walls and crept along, feeling my way, thinking I was headed toward the opening. Suddenly, the floor dropped away, and I fell into a pit. My feet hit the wet rock at the bottom and slipped out from under me. Then I hit my head and blacked out.

"How long I lay there, unconscious, I don't know. When I woke, I was shivering, for my cloak had fallen to one side. I tried to climb out, but the walls were steep and smooth. I called for help, but only the echo of my voice came back to me, frantic and fearful. I began screaming, for I realized I was alone. Utterly alone." Tristan caught Ewan's gaze. Just thinking about that day made his heart race.

"My lord, do you realize you're shaking even now."

Tristan lifted his hands, both of which were trembling. He wrapped both arms around his middle and squeezed until he felt in control again. He looked back at Ewan. "Panic took hold of me. I didn't know if I'd ever see the sun again. It was so dark I began to hallucinate, to see tiny bursts of light. Then I smelled something foul near me. Shaking all over, like I was just now, I crept around the edge of the pit until my feet sank into something soft. It didn't move. Slowly, I reached down. My hand touched a pile of rotting fur. Some animal had fallen down there and died. It also had tried to get out. And it, too, had failed. Was that going to be my fate as well?

"I knew I'd been down there so long it must be day again. But the bottom of the pit held darkness so complete it closed in on me like a suffocating blanket. I sat and wrapped myself in my cloak and cried. And cried. Time seemed to stand still. I was as good as dead. I feared going to the Otherworld, to Manannán mac Lir. I feared the afterlife and the sea god's underworld realm.

"When I finally heard a voice and saw the light of a torch, they told me they'd searched for two days and nights. They pulled me, shaking and shattered, from the hole. It took me nearly a month to recover.

"And that, Ewan, is why I will not even go near a cave."

"Well, my lord. 'Tis quite a story." Ewan rubbed his chin. "Let's hope we do not have to go below ground, hey?"

Tristan nodded.

Ewan spent the afternoon and the next three days instructing him on etiquette, names, personalities, and the details of court life. He drew maps of the palace and Ewhain Macha in the dust. On the second afternoon, in the middle of a discussion on how Neil might walk into a room full of high flaith, a worried look crossed Ewan's face, and he slammed one fist into a palm.

"I forgot something. A very important detail. We should have done this days ago." He fished in his sack for a clay jar and a quill pen. "Take off your shirt and let me see your right arm. There's a tattoo you're going to need. I just hope it's not too late."

Puzzled, Tristan removed his cape, and then his shirt.

Ewan dipped his pen in what looked like blue ink. "If I paint this on now, let's hope it fades enough by the time we get there so nary a soul will notice 'tis a fake." But when he examined Tristan's upper arm, his mouth opened, and he stared. "H—how long have you had that?"

Tristan tipped the birthmark on his arm toward him. "As long as I can remember. Why?"

Ewan shook his head. "'Tis similar to a short, two-headed staff, methinks."

"Could be. So?"

"This doesna make sense." He stoppered his clay jar. "I canna tell if 'tis a tattoo or a birthmark. But at least we do not have to give you another. I fear my attempt would have been too obvious, anyway. Everyone would know it was recent."

"I don't understand."

"You'll see when the council meets." He shook his head again. "I heard, but didna believe until now, that many parents once gave their children such a mark. Somehow, word has gotten out."

"You speak in riddles, squire."

Ewan's face broke into a smile. "Good. Very good. You called me squire. Now let's continue our practice."

They spent the next two days going over detail after detail until Tristan's—Neil's—head spun. Slowly, he began to think of himself as the lord Neil, high prince of Ulster. Indeed, if this ruse were to be successful, he must start calling himself that from now on. In between these sessions, they practiced again with the sword until Neil was able to defeat Ewan in every bout.

How difficult it was to think of himself as Neil and not Tristan! But from here on, he must.

Finally, the last night came. While the last log crackled and fell into the coals, Neil laid his head on the saddle and pulled his cape over his head. Tomorrow, they would leave for Ewhain Macha. Surely, they'd prepared, but he was about to enter a world he didn't know and attempt to pass himself off as high flaith. If the ruse failed, both of them would probably be imprisoned, if not executed. Aye. The more he considered it, the more certain he became.

They were both flying mad.

CHAPTER 9

EWHAIN MACHA

The next day they took a route that skirted the Roamers' camp. When the forest path widened into a heavily traveled road, Neil knew they were close. Numerous clearings with roundhouses appeared on either side. Women called to their neighbors and put their laundry out to dry. Men chopped wood. And children squealed as they played hoops and sticks. Then the hilltop fortress of Ewhain Macha, regal and impressive, rose above the trees.

For as long as anyone could remember, Ewhain Macha had been the ancestral seat of the kings of Ulster and the high king of Ériu. The name itself held a mystical aura, always spoken with reverence and awe. Since time began, it had been the main city of Ériu. Once it was even the center of all that was good on Erde.

A warren of thatch-roofed roundhouses, large and small, clustered below the fortress. Half were stone, the rest wattle and mud. Too many now stood in disrepair. Some had even crumbled into moldering piles. Neil shook his head. Oh, how Ewhain Macha must have appeared in that age, so long ago, when it was the center of grandeur and light, when nobles and kings from all Erde came to pay homage to its king.

They climbed a road of crushed stone to the fortress. There they crossed a drawbridge over a deep moat lined with spikes and passed high earthen walls faced with timbers. Another moat encircled the inner wall, crossed periodically by movable log bridges—a second line of defense, in case an enemy broached the outer wall.

From the center of the hilltop's expansive plain rose a three-storied palace. Round, like most other buildings, it must be the biggest building in the world. At least three hundred feet across and fifty feet high, it dominated the plateau. Polished oak columns ringed each level. As they approached, its wide doors lay open, guarded by four men with spears.

To one side, the Tower of Dóchas rose above the town like something out of legend. Its name meant the Tower of Hope, though no one remembered why it had been so named. And certainly in these days, hope in the kingdom of Ulster and the isle of Ériu came in short supply.

"Are you ready, my lord Neil?" Ewan dismounted before the entrance and gave the reins to a servant.

Neil slipped off his stallion, grabbed his traveling bag, and swallowed hard. "Aye." But his voice quavered.

They didn't even have to announce their presence. The guards bowed and stepped aside, instantly acknowledging the prince's return.

Ewan led him down a long hallway over echoing flagstones. Neil tried to keep from gaping. As they went, he also tried to match Ewan's description of the palace with reality but found himself astonished by the building's size. Torches lined the hallways. Periodically, side-chambers led off into darkness. It didn't resemble anything like a cave. Fortunately, he had no fear on that account.

The hallway ended in a wide set of oak doors. Ewan pushed, hinges groaned, and Neil followed Ewan into a massive room, nearly a hundred feet by forty. Massive pillars lined both sides, hiding shadows beyond. A crowd gathered before King Connell, the Ard Rígh, ruler of Ulster and all Ériu, sitting on his throne.

Beside the king sat a man in a druid's white robe. He must be Corc. White hair to his shoulders. Clean-shaven face, long and thin, with stark cheekbones and gray eyebrows. Stern, pale eyes. Tall and lean, he seemed almost emaciated.

"You must sit beside the king." Ewan's voice was low, insistent.

"Will you be with me?"

"Nay. I'll be in front. From here on, my lord, you're on your own."

Neil gulped. Then he stepped through the crowd toward his new father, the Ard Righ. As he walked, all conversation in the room stopped. Neil tried—unsuccessfully he knew—not to stare at this king. Disheveled black hair trailed almost to his elbows. Thick, black beard and eyebrows, both untrimmed. Brown eyes shifted from the men before him to faintly acknowledge his son's approach. But the eyes held a sleepy, remote look and never seemed to focus.

"Ah, good." The king yawned without covering his mouth. "Neil is back." He slumped over a black velvet chair with one knee up on an arm, his robe falling open to reveal a dirty yellow tunic. He propped his chin on an elbow, which leaned against the throne's opposite arm. A shiny silver staff, crowned with bronze at both ends, rested beside him.

Neil was still walking to the king's side when he saw the large, wire-haired hunting dog curled up beside the throne. He could never resist a dog. Just before he took the lower seat, he stooped and patted the animal's head, scratched under its ears. The tongue reached up, licked his hand, and the eyes half-shut in appreciation.

A gasp slipped from someone in front. As Neil sat, he saw Corc's stare and the king's questioning glance. Ewan scowled and shook his head. Didn't anyone pet their dogs here?

He felt the court's full attention fixed on him, and him alone. His face grew suddenly warm. His chest pounded. He scanned the crowd of attendants and courtiers. Then he remembered what Ewan had repeated so many times: *You are their prince. Every noble and courtier who stands before you is your subject. With a word, you can have nearly anyone in irons.*

As instructed, he tried on a look of boredom and unconcern. It didn't fit. He shoved his hands beneath his thighs.

The king looked away and waved to Corc to proceed. Before the throne stood two men, obvious distress on their faces.

Corc's face and eyes remained emotionless. "My lord Neil, Angus mac Donaigh of Leinster and Cé mac Colla of Munster were about to present a complaint about the new harvest tax." The druid faced the two men. "Please begin."

Angus—a portly, middle-aged lord with flowing hair, wearing a shiny blue tunic, probably his best—stepped forward.

"My subjects canna pay such a heavy load, my lord. One cabbage for every three cabbages plucked? One bushel of grain for every three harvested? 'Tis all too much. Besides, not many can divide by three. The whole thing is simply impossible."

"What say you, Cé of Munster?" Corc nodded in the direction of a small man, with flaming red hair and a black tunic. Chain mail shone beneath. "You were about to give us your concerns."

"Me subjects will never pay this dratted tax. And I do not have the time or inclination to go 'round and harangue me tenants into paying what they do not have. And how am I supposed to extract one gold crown from each lehbrágan in Munster each year? They live among us in peace. Such a request would bring trouble. You mustna do this, my lords." Chin arched high in obvious defiance, he stared at Corc.

Corc raised an eyebrow in Neil's direction. "What does the prince say? The treasury is in need. Should we levy the tax?"

Neil opened his mouth then closed it. He swallowed. "Seems like a lot to take from the mouths of the poor."

Gasps resounded from the front row of colorfully dressed courtiers. One woman in delicate blue linen put a hand to her mouth and whispered to her coiffured male companion, dressed in striped yellow robes.

Corc frowned and bent his lips to the king's ear. The druid whispered something then stood. "The sprites are anything but poor. But I will throw the bones and let the spirits decide." From a large cloth bag, he produced a handful of polished white bones. He shook them inside his cupped hands then threw them on the floor with a clatter. He stood over the result, examining the skulls of chickens, the leg bones of foxes, the ribs of rabbits. He looked up. "My lords, Cé and Angus, you are right."

A sigh of relief escaped the crowd.

Corc cleared his throat. "In addition to the new harvest tax, the existing herd tax must increase. Each tuath will now pay ten cows or sheep from every hundred instead of five."

Whispers and mutterings swept the assembly. Angus's face began turning red. He shook his head, spun slowly around without saying a word. Then he stalked through the crowd toward the exit.

"You were not dismissed," Corc called to his back.

Angus merely raised one hand with the back of it to Corc, and then dropped it quickly, still walking away in silent protest.

But Cé stood his ground, put his hands on his hips, and glowered at the druid. "You'll not collect a shilling of it. A tax on cabbage, turnips, and wheat—man, this will cause rebellion. If I badgered me peasants for it, there would be death on me doorstep. And I, for one, will never give up more of me herds due to *your* mismanagement. 'Twill bankrupt me. Me and all the flaith in the land." With a deep breath, he faced the king, his jaw muscles twitching. "Connell, my lord, if you continue with such rule, Munster will be tearing up the Cairt Mhór charter and leaving the Alliance of Kingdoms." Then he whirled and stomped across the room.

Before Cé reached the door, Corc called out to the assembly at large. "His tuatha will never abandon the Alliance. And he'll pay the tax. Or the King's Riders will come and collect it for him."

At the end of the room, Cé whirled again. "Do that, and we'll meet them at the border with steel instead of shillings. Mark my words, druid!—they'll be collecting the business end of arrows and blades." He slammed the door shut behind him, the sound echoing like thunder.

Whispers and low mutterings filled the hall.

"He'll pay. You'll see." Corc wiped his brow and closed his eyes, perhaps betraying some doubt about the issue.

The king stared at the far end of the hall where Cé had gone, puzzlement twisting his face.

"Who's next?" Corc looked toward a sturdy, black-bearded man about fifty.

The man stepped forward and bowed low. "Dermid mac Duff, from Leinster."

"We know who you are, Dermid." Corc's face was still flushed from the confrontation with Cé and Angus. "And what further grievance do you bring us today?"

"No grievance, my lords." He bowed to Connell, who nodded in return. "Only a proposal. One that needs approving at the highest level. One that will save this country from the fate of others on the continent."

Corc's eyebrows rose, and even Connell slipped his dangling foot to the floor and sat up straight. "Don't leave us in suspense"—Corc's mouth curled into a sneer—"speak."

"I bring this request, not just from Leinster but also from other high flaith—princes, all—in Munster, Meath, Connacht, and even your own Ulster."

"What! Do you gather behind the back of the Ard Righ for secret action?" Corc's brows narrowed. "Do you bring rebellion before the court?"

"Were it rebellion, I wouldna be standing here, asking your approval and support, would I? Some of us did meet in secret, 'tis true, because we're concerned with the state of affairs on Ereb. An evil tide has cast a shadow over the Great Lands to the east. Messengers from Drijvendby, Romely, Etrusca, and Nordmark tell us a great fear has gripped the people there. Rumors say the Deamhan Lord, he whose very name I fear to speak, not only holds Sarkenos firmly in his power, but his spirit rises again in Drochtar, residing within the idol Crom Mord. And from there the darkness now threatens Conachtir, Gol Oras, and the plains tribes of Romely. 'Tis rumored their kings are now so cowed, they pay the Deamhan Lord tribute. Aye, my lords, the Great Lands are in a bad way."

"What does this have to do with us?" Corc frowned. "Our defense has always been the sea."

"Even here on Ériu something is happening no one has ever before seen. Anger, greed, and jealousy are increasing. Brother turns against brother. Sister against sister. Lords fight their subjects, and subjects rebel against their lords."

Corc held up a hand. "All conjecture. Havena men been in such a state since time began? You have much imagination, Lord Dermid."

"Nay, Corc. We've just witnessed some of it right here in this court. When was the last time you let your king leave this palace and walk the roads under the sun among his tuatha? When was the last time *you* did so? Then you'd see and hear for yourselves the state of things. Something's happening in Ériu the likes of which we've never experienced. And it all emanates from Drochtar."

"Bah! You've no proof of this. Only anecdotes, conjecture."

"We have proof of sorts." From the folds of his tunic, Dermid pulled out a scroll. "I have here Leinster's records of crops harvested and taxes collected for the last twenty years. There's been a steady decline, accelerating in the last decade. And this despite our efforts to plant more cabbage, leeks, barley, and wheat."

"Weather. It changes."

"Nay, my lord. The weather has not changed. And here, for the last fifteen years"—he produced another scroll—"are the records of men whose heads were removed for murder and rape. Also, those fined or banished for theft. In both, we see a steady upward climb. 'Tis proof. The crops are worsening, and the people are changing."

Corc shook his head. "This just shows the sorry state of Leinster's reign. Nay, you've built a case for your own bad management. And with such, you now dare to feed the people's fear?"

Dermid's face flushed red. "You insult me at your peril, Corc." He put a hand on his sword hilt.

Corc waved a hand. "Pardon, my lord. Perhaps I go too far." Fear momentarily twisted his face before he regained his composure. "Perhaps 'tis mere coincidence and next year things will improve."

"You would deny my evidence?"

"Right, then. Let us grant the scratchings on your scrolls give a hint of worsening conditions. I don't agree with your conclusion, but let's assume it for the sake of argument. What can anyone do about it?"

"We can bring back the Scepter."

At first, silence fell upon the assembly, as if a word that never should be spoken had been uttered. Then the room erupted into loud whispers as lords, ladies, and courtiers turned to their neighbors.

Now Connell slipped his feet to the floor and stood. As he did, the tip of some silver jewelry hanging around the king's neck swung out. Quickly, the king grabbed it, pulled it off his neck, and placed it in a pocket.

Then, as it became apparent Connell would speak, the room silenced. The king said, "I would hear more of this. What do you know of the Scepter?"

"That it once sat atop the Tower of Dóchas. That it brought hope to the people and wisdom to its rulers. And that it proclaimed the light and power of Elyon to the world."

"Where did you hear this nonsense?" Corc now stood beside the king, frowning.

"From a representative of the Capulum."

The room burst into pandemonium.

"The Leinsterman's half cut, and 'tis not yet evening," shouted a man in back. "There was never any Scepter."

"Aye, he must be stocious. For neither does the Capulum exist," spoke a woman somewhere. "Naught but old wives' tales."

"All rumor and legend," said another in front.

Corc snatched the king's bronze staff and pounded it three times on the floor. Slowly, order returned to the room. "The court is right, Dermid. The Scepter and Elyon are naught but campfire lore and legend. And no such group as the Capulum exists. Everyone knows this."

"The Capulum does exist, my lord. For thousands of years. In secret. And one of their number has stepped forward and told us the only way we can save this land of Ériu."

"Pray do go on." Corc sneered, and then stared at Dermid with cold eyes. "This tale you spin is quite entertaining."

"Long ago, in the golden age of men, the Scepter once sat in the Tower. 'Twas part of Elyon's plan for the race of men, as their sign of obedience and acknowledgment of him as the Lord above whom there is no other. But Faolukan, the Deamhan Lord's servant, stole and hid this great gift. For nearly twenty-three hundred years, the Capulum has searched for its location. Recently, they discovered its whereabouts."

"The location of the Scepter?" Connell's eyes widened.

"Aye, my lord. And they also know this: When the Scepter returns to the Tower of Dóchas, we will halt the darkness. There is also a prophecy about who must go and bring it back. But of that, I canna speak freely here."

He took a deep breath and went on. "All we ask, my lord Connell, is for you to give your approval and support to our mission. Then we will identify the man the prophecy says must lead it. So will you stand for your country, my lord, with your flaith? Will you honor us with your support in this great and perilous endeavor?"

Connell's mouth hung open, and he raised his eyebrows. He sent Corc a questioning glance. But Corc silently mouthed the word nay. Then Connell whispered in Corc's ear. Neil was close enough he could hear the king's words. "I ken we should approve this, Corc."

Corc placed a hand on Connell's shoulder and addressed the court. "While I confer with my lord, tell the servants to bring a lamb to the augury. This requires more than looking at bones. The rest of you, remain where you are." Then he led the king to an antechamber.

Immediately, all decorum in the room vanished into loud, boisterous conversation.

Ewan placed a hand on Neil's shoulder and leaned close. "This is why you are here, my lord." Amid the hubbub from the courtiers, Neil could barely hear him. "Although 'tis not certain, Prince Neil—the real prince—may have been the one of which the prophecy spoke."

Neil stared at his new friend and wagged his head back and forth. "But I . . . I am not . . . Neil."

"You're the closest thing we have. If they choose you, you must go. Too much is at stake to do otherwise."

Neil kept shaking his head while Ewan frowned.

At that moment, Corc led the king back in and gave orders for the assembly to move to the augury.

Neil followed the king into a small side room, with half the court crowding in behind.

Immediately, the odor of dried blood and rotten flesh assailed his nose. When the assembly quieted, a second druid led a lamb onto a large bronze platform nearly five feet square. While the creature bleated, Corc knelt and placed a dagger against its neck.

With a quick, practiced movement, Corc slit the animal's throat. Then both druids held the lamb as it fell, legs kicking in a death struggle. When it stilled, Corc made a deep incision on its underside to open the body cavity. Entrails and blood gushed onto the bronze bowl. For a time, Corc studied the mess. Then he stood and ordered everyone back inside.

When the court had adjourned to the main room and Corc had washed his hands, the druid whispered in Connell's ear. The Ard Righ scowled, appeared to study the floor. Then the king grabbed his bronze staff and struck it three times on the stone. After the room quieted, Connell addressed the petitioner from Leinster.

"Dermid mac Duff, my druid has read the entrails and heard from the spirits. I have heard his counsel and reached my decision."

"Aye, my lord?" A fleeting smile crossed Dermid's face.

"The request is denied." The king dropped heavily on his throne and threw one leg back over the throne's arm.

Corc stepped forward. "My lords, I brought the question before the gods. They tell me the Capulum doesna exist. They say the Scepter never sat in the Tower. And the name of Elyon belongs only to myth. Lugh and Danu and the spirits of forest, stream, and field gave me this truth. They are our gods, not some mythical creature named Elyon. Thus, any expedition to find the Scepter is foolishness. It will not be approved."

Dermid stood motionless before the throne. His jaw muscles twitched, tightened. He held both hands at his sides. They curled slowly into fists. Then he narrowed his eyes at the druid. "You will rue the day, Corc, when you set yourself up as advisor to the Ard Righ. Your words are poison, and your counsel is corrupt. I spit on this court and the decisions you force on the king." Dermid took one step forward and spat on the pointed black leather covering Corc's right foot.

He faced Connell. "My lord, you mustna listen any longer to this weasel. Corc's counsel leads the kingdom toward rebellion—in Leinster and, indeed, in all the lands of Ériu. No one will stand for this kind of rule. I beg you to change your mind."

Both of Connell's feet now touched the floor. His face contorted in fear, and his mouth again hung open. He looked to Corc and opened his hands in a question. Corc shook his head. Connell again faced Dermid. "I'm sorry, old friend. The decision is final."

Dermid stared at the king for some moments before he whirled on his heels and stomped toward the door.

When he'd gone, Corc wiped his brow and called an end to the day's proceedings. The assembly broke for the door.

Neil stood but was uncertain what to do next.

Ewan approached and whispered in his ear. "Go now to your room. Find your sister and acquaint yourself with her. If you can, ask her about the pendant she's started wearing. It troubles me. Tomorrow at noon, meet me at the stable. We were afraid of the kind of decision we heard today, and plans are already in motion."

"You're leaving me?"

"Aye. Before long, the guardhouse kitchen will be serving vittles. And I would fain not miss the evening meal. Remember, you are now Neil mac Connell, prince of Ulster. And after what I've seen today, may Elyon save the kingdom of Ériu. My lord, *you* may be our only hope."

CHAPTER 10

THE PALACE

When the room was almost empty, Neil found the spiral staircase and climbed, his footsteps reverberating off the flagstones. On the third floor, he'd been told, he'd find his private chambers. Ewan had drawn maps in the dust, but after exploring on his own, Neil made many wrong turns. One of these led him to a door he thought might be his, but to be certain, he knocked first.

A woman opened, gave him a half-smile, and bade him enter. From Ewan's description, she could only be Maeve. Neil tried not to stare. Her lush, black hair and eyelashes, her black, inviting eyes, and quick, flashing smile were spellbinding.

"Well, brother, I see you've returned from Tara upright, not carried in on the back of a horse."

"I have returned. And I'm sober."

"And did you have your fill of Tara's women? Were they as luscious and warm in bed as you remembered?" She crossed to her own bed, a bearskin suspended a foot off the floor by a wooden rod frame. She sat on the furs, and as she leaned back, her tunic opened to reveal long, shapely legs. He tried to remember she was supposed to be his sister.

"They were." He would try to play the part. "But I've grown tired of this constant pleasure-seeking, the drinking, and the women. As of right now, I'm starting life anew." He smiled as taught. If he started telling people he was reforming, maybe they wouldn't notice how different this new Neil had become?

Maeve's eyes widened. "You've said that only once before, but now, by Lugh's wings, I think you mean it."

Neil smiled like Neil was supposed to.

"Did you go to court today?"

"I did."

"What happened? As if I care anymore."

"Corc has convinced the Ard Righ—Father—to put a tax on the peasants' cabbages, beets, and wheat. And they've increased the tax on the lords' herds. The flaith are outraged. They say they won't collect it. That it will lead to rebellion."

"They're right, and 'tis pushing the flaith too far. Corc spends the treasury on foolishness. Such as making a solid gold throne for Father. How ridiculous."

Neil was aghast, but he tried not to show it. "Aye, how ridiculous."

"That's the first time you ever agreed with me on such a subject."

"Well, I . . . I've changed my mind."

Maeve squinted at him. "You hardly ever change your mind. What else happened today?"

"Father refused to let Dermid mac Duff lead an expedition to retrieve the Scepter."

"The Scepter? 'Tis but a myth." Her fingers reached for a pendant gleaming on the bed beside her. A silver crescent moon on a long chain. "Where was this expedition going?"

"Dermid didn't say. Somewhere on Ereb."

"Dermid? He probably has no idea." She stared down at the quarter moon, and her eyes seemed to glaze over. Her fingers traced an outline around the jewelry's edge, slowly, lovingly. "How would Dermid know anyway?"

"He says the Capulum told him."

"The Capulum?" She raised her glance as if from a trance. "Another myth." Eyes that only moments ago were bright and clear now glossed over, unfocused, as if drugged. "'Tis all myth and lies. And I do not care anymore."

"What's that pendant you're holding?"

"This old thing?" She looked down. Her gaze stopped on it, transfixed.

"Aye. Where'd you get it?"

"Something Corc gave me. It's become my favorite piece. He said it was to be our little secret. Between him and me. But I trust you."

"Can I see it?"

She raised her glance, and a frown crossed her features. "Why?"

"Just to touch it."

"Touch it?" She fixed her gaze on the pendant then on Neil. "Aye, you can touch it. But that's all." She lifted it toward him but left it attached to its chain.

Neil reached out and stroked the quarter moon. Even though she'd been fondling it for some time, the metal remained cold as ice. As his fingertips slid over it, a tiny shiver radiated through them, up into his hands, and then up his forearms. It was faintly—pleasant. Tingling but relaxing. Also cold. Suddenly, the reason for his leaving Hidden Pines didn't seem so important. Suddenly, he could see why she had such fondness for—

He jerked his hand away and stared at it. What *was* that thing? "I . . . I don't think you should be wearing it, Maeve. There's something wrong with it."

"Wrong?" She closed her fingers and covered it with her fist. "Not with my pendant. 'Tis my finest, best piece of jewelry."

"Put it away and never touch it again."

"Why would you say such a thing?" Her voice rose, and her knuckles whitened. "I like it. It comforts me."

"Jewelry isn't supposed to do that to people. Corc's done something to it."

She glanced across the room then back at Neil. "You're strangely different, Neil. You've never acted this way before. I think this new leather you're trying to wear is making you mean."

Uh-oh. Was he behaving too much like Tristan and not enough like Neil? "Have it your way, sister." He was supposed to call her that. He tried to give her a sly smile like Ewan had taught him to. "Wear it if you like.

But you don't need it. Your beauty outshines any piece of silver." Now *that* was something Neil might say.

She nodded. "Always flattering, aren't you? Well, go and chase yourself off."

He gave her another Neil smile. "I'm at your command. Anything for my favorite sister."

She smiled lazily and returned to caressing the quarter moon.

Leaving her room, he wandered the hallways until he found his chambers, and entered.

He dropped his worn travel sack beside a new bag of thick boar's hide with shoulder straps. Servants must have chewed the leather until it was supple. He transferred his things to the new sack.

His bed was like Maeve's, animal skins stretched taut over a wooden frame, piled high with furs and pillows. More comfortable than anything he'd ever slept on. So this was how the high flaith lived.

In the room's center, a log fire crackled inside a huge brazier. The servants must have just lit it. Smoke swirled about the ceiling and drifted toward the open window. By the far wall stood a low table with a flask of wine and two stools. He crawled up onto the pillows and closed his eyes.

Ewan was right. Something was wrong with Maeve's pendant. Had Corc put some kind of spell on it? It enthralled her so much, she couldn't think of anything else. He shuddered.

In a few hours, he was expected to show up for a dinner with the Ard Righ, Maeve, and maybe other nobility.

Only last year, he'd been told, his brother, Torradan—Neil's brother—had been killed while riding. Two years earlier, Neil's older sister, Aideen, had died of winter sickness. Surely, this palace had seen much recent tragedy.

The Roamers. Maeve's pendant. The Scepter. The spreading darkness. What if he just went home and returned to banging out plows and daggers in his uncle's forge?

None of it made for a restful nap.

Neil woke to someone tapping a fist on his door.

"My lord," came a servant's voice, "the others are downstairs, waiting."

He dismissed the man, as taught. Quickly, he found clothes in the prince's wardrobe on a corner bone rack—a plaid, knee-length kilt; a short, burgundy-and-yellow striped tunic; polished brown shoes, pointy and so soft, they were like fur. Everything fit perfectly. Yet wasn't he pretending to be something he wasn't? He'd once seen a high flaith riding through Hidden Pines, surrounded by servants, with nose held high. Would people think of him like that?

He dressed then followed the servant into the hallway and down a flight of stairs to a small dining room reserved for close family. High ceilings. Lush tapestries of green gardens populated with scantily clad maidens and handsome young men scampering behind with smiles and flagons of wine.

At the head of a low table sat Connell. On one side waited Maeve. On the other, Corc. Beside the druid, an empty chair. Neil swallowed and took his seat.

"Decided to finally grace us with your presence, young master?" Corc's head barely turned, as if his body were made of stone.

"Sorry. I was sleeping."

"And how was your trip to Tara?" Connell motioned, and servants brought in trays heaped with juicy beef, spiced pork, fermented cabbage, roasted apples, and buttered turnips. Trenchers of bread already lay before each of them.

"Wine, maids, and song. The usual." As Ewan had coached him to say.

"Of course"—Corc's voice dropped, low and serious—"but were you at all able to talk with Gregor about returning the cattle stolen from our fields?"

Momentary panic left Neil speechless. Who was Gregor and what cattle was he talking about? "Well, I . . . I was too busy. I never got around to that."

Now, Corc slowly turned his head and fixed his glance on Neil. "That was why you went, my *boy*. The insult must be amended. The cattle must be returned." His cold, lifeless eyes bored into Neil, and his voice carried a tone of disgust. "Is there nothing we can trust you with?"

"I . . . I'm sorry." Was he supposed to be sorry? He didn't know. He wondered if calling him a boy was supposed to be an insult.

"Never mind." Corc pulled meat and vegetables off the servant's platter onto his trencher. "I'll send someone else next week. We can't tolerate such theft across the border. We are supposed to be one kingdom. Though after today, I have my doubts."

"Too much rebellion, Corc." Connell chewed around his words. "Outright disrespect today."

"I agree. And you, young master," Corc addressed Neil, "do not ever again, in public, stand against your king or me. Even on matters as small as the harvest tax."

"But I agree with Neil." Maeve smiled at her brother. "I think we shouldn't tax the peasants more for harvesting their own produce."

Corc glowered at her. "Let the court's women tend to their poetry, music, and flirting."

She glowered back. "And let the court's druid mind his manners. Or the court's woman will not grace him anymore with her presence." Neil didn't see the chain of her quarter-moon pendant tonight. Maybe she only wore it some of the time? Her eyes seemed much more alive.

Corc sniffed and attended to his dinner.

"What about this Scepter?" Neil offered. "Is it myth? Or does it really exist?"

Corc gave a short laugh. "Myth, my lord. And today we've hopefully quashed any thought among the nobles of going after it. If we hear even a whisper of doing otherwise, I—we'll—send the King's Riders after them."

"The chopping block is stained red from all these executions." With too much force, Maeve stabbed a knife into a turnip. "And the dungeons can't hold any more prisoners. Have you been down there recently? Strange how we suddenly have so many rebels in our midst."

Corc shot her a frown. "You, my lady, should never go down to the dungeons. And what do you imply?"

"Only that a lot of folk, nobility and commoner alike, seem to be resisting your commands and decrees."

"We do what we must for the good of the kingdom."

"Even if the dungeons are bursting?" Now Neil dared to speak.

Corc set his two knives down and stared first at Neil then at Maeve. "Of all the flaith, the Ard Righ's children must stand behind their father."

Maeve scowled, pursed her lips, and took a wee bite of food.

It was time to throw in something Neil might say. "I'll go along with that. Just as long as there's plenty of wine, and you don't tax the women entering the palace after dinner."

Corc offered a thin smile and attended to his plate. "That, my lord, I would *never* do."

When the meal was over, Neil walked with the others upstairs. After the king and Maeve entered their rooms, Corc followed close behind Neil. Corc, it appeared, had a room on the same floor as the royal family. And he seemed to run nearly everything. Was this the way it had always been here in the king's palace?

As Neil creaked open the door to his room, Corc laid a hand on his shoulder. Neil raised his glance to the druid.

"There's something I want to give you, my lord."

Neil swallowed.

From a pocket of his white robe, Corc produced a quarter-moon pendant. "A piece of silver jewelry, very valuable, with special properties. Made especially for you." He bowed and passed the thing to Neil.

As Neil took it, even before it landed in his palm, he felt its cold tingling. This was far different from Maeve's. Stronger. More soothing. Much more intoxicating. A wave of nervous calm washed over him.

"'Tis our little secret. Tell no one about it." Then Corc smiled, walked down the hall, and entered his room.

Neil eyed the ice-cold crescent in his palm. Waves of pleasure shot up his arm to his shoulder and chest. Who now cared about the Scepter, the Roamers, or any other trouble?

But nay, this wasn't right. He jerked his hand away and let the thing clatter to the floor.

He stared at it. Was Corc trying to control him, just as Corc seemed to be controlling his new sister, Maeve? He reached down, picked the thing up by its chain, and without touching the quarter moon, carried it to his room. He must find a way to dispose of it.

Who else, he wondered, had received one of Corc's secret gifts? Then he thought of the silver jewelry hanging around the king's neck that he'd never gotten a good look at. Was it the same crescent moon as Neil and Maeve had received?

CHAPTER 11

THE COUNCIL

The next day as the sun approached its zenith, Neil told the palace guards he was going for a ride. Ewan was waiting in the courtyard, and together they mounted their horses. When he'd sat the stallion, it whinnied and threw its head from side to side, as if eager to go. Then the squire led him away from Ewhain Macha and onto a well-traveled dirt track.

Surprisingly, many were on the road that day, for they passed and were passed by several other parties. Neil couldn't help but stare as they overtook three red- and green-clad lehbrágan on ponies. When they'd ridden far from the city, they veered onto a smaller hunting trail. Their fellow travelers turned with them as though all had a common destination.

The forest opened onto a crowded clearing where wide slabs of rock sloped down to a flat staging area. Gathered on the hillside were nearly sixty men with more coming in from trails to the west and south.

"High flaith from all over?" questioned Neil. By their tunics, he identified the plaids and stripes from all five regions. He drew a deep breath then released it. How could he, a poor commoner, ever hope to pass himself off as a prince among such great and powerful nobles? How could Ewan ever expect *him* to save Ériu? Right then, he felt very small.

"Aye, and no high king." Ewan frowned. "'Tis a sad day when such an auspicious gathering must occur in secret."

They tied their horses to trees on the perimeter beside many others. On the flat below, Dermid mac Duff conversed with a group of men. About him hovered the aura of a leader. The two found seats in back, overlooking the gathering below. The low hum of conversation filled the arena.

He could have boiled a pot several times over before Dermid raised a battle horn and blew it. Talk stilled, and silence settled over the assembly.

Dermid pulled himself to his full height. "I call this first meeting of the Council of High Flaith to order." His voice boomed over the natural amphitheater.

"Let's get to it, Dermid," a loud voice bellowed from up front. "We ken why we're here. To oust Connell from the throne and put a lance through Corc's gut. And it canna happen soon enough."

Loud clapping, banging of swords on shields, and cheers erupted from all around.

Dermid held up his hands. "That, my lords, is what we must *not* do."

Boos and boisterous disagreements. Someone stood up and addressed the crowd. "We've all had enough of this Ard Righ. 'Tis either the heads of Connell and Corc on pikes, or the Alliance must end and the clans go their separate ways. What other choice is there?"

Cheers rose from the assembly.

"Aye," said another. "Before I'll be reducing me herds by a tenth and stealing cabbages and carrots out of me peasants' mouths, I'll go to war with Connell and his brood."

"And the lehbrágan willna part with our gold for his sake," shouted the high voice of a sprite somewhere. Seated, he couldn't be seen above his larger companions.

Now many stood and began beating their swords on shields. The assembly rose as one. Some shouted threats against Connell and his druid.

Dermid let this go on for some time. Then he blew the horn again, and the group quieted. "I, too, have lost patience with Connell." He planted hands on hips and drew his gaze over the crowd. "Just yesterday, I told him to his face he was bringing the Alliance to ruin. I would like nothing better than to skewer the druid Corc with the point of my blade."

Again, the crowd erupted in applause.

"But nay, my lords. Calmer, wiser heads have counseled what would then happen. They've convinced me it would lead to the opposite of what we desire—to disaster." He paused to let his words sink in.

"And so we convene today to hear a better way, perhaps the only way, to save this land we all love. 'Tis why we reached out to each and every one of you. We've kept our eyes and ears open. We ken your sympathies and where each stands on these matters."

Many now looked to their brothers, perhaps wondering if this were true.

Dermid raised a hand for their attention. "Now I must introduce one whose counsel I ken you'll want to hear. He's spent his life studying the old texts, or what remains of them. He's discovered things no man has hitherto known. Ancient things. Secret things. And this afternoon, he'll tell us the only way this situation can and must end. Some of you will be skeptical, for he is well known to you. You will be surprised by his true role. I'm speaking, of course, of Cairbre the Wise."

Heads nodded and voices murmured. "Cairbre. Aye."

"What you haven't known until now, and what must remain a secret when we leave here, is Cairbre is more than just Ériu's greatest historian and scholar." Dermid looked at the faces of the men in front. "My lords, Cairbre is head of the Capulum."

Silence swept through the group like a moonbeam. Men began whispering to their brothers.

"They say that as a young man he dabbled in white magic," came a voice to Neil's right.

He turned in time to see an older man whisper back, "Who has not heard that rumor? But who of us hasna done things in our youth we've since regretted and abandoned?"

Now Dermid walked to the side and helped an old man in a pale blue robe to the center position. His gray beard flowed to the middle of his chest. Wrinkled hands rested on a gnarled walking stick. A wizened face with bushy eyebrows addressed them.

"My lords, 'tis true," began the old man, and everyone quieted to hear, as his voice had not the timbre of Dermid's. "The Capulum *does* exist. As head of the organization, I hold the dubious title of Capulum Righ. But should this fact become known beyond this gathering, my life would soon be forfeit. I trust, my lords, you will keep it in confidence."

Cries of "We will!" and "Aye!" met this confession.

Cairbre smiled, but then his face became somber. "The Lost Ages lasted over two thousand years, ending only three hundred years ago. During that time, the ancient knowledge was swept away. Burned. Plundered. And simply forgotten. But long ago, farseeing men saw what was happening and banded together to create what we call the Capulum. Their purpose? To assemble, preserve, and make sense of what little knowledge was left. During those difficult years, our small band of scholars, priests, and warriors dedicated itself to preserving the teachings of Elyon."

More murmurs in the assembly.

"Aye, Elyon does exist. As does the Pneuma. I will speak more of Elyon later.

"In the early days, we met in the open. But the kings of Ériu, their hearts turning always to evil, would discover our gatherings, destroy our texts, and kill many of our order. Thus did we go into hiding. As still today we must hide. For though the mood of the age has changed, the hearts of kings have not.

"And so for the last twenty-three hundred years we have worked in secret, meeting in caves; forest clearings; shuttered, candlelit rooms. We studied and we prayed. And we found clever ways of preserving the old knowledge, sometimes hiding it in the most obvious of places. But we kept our secrets well, waiting for the time they were needed most.

"And that time is now." He leaned forward over his walking stick, catching the glances of those in front. "My lords, a darkness is spreading over Erde. For some time, Faolan the Traitor, otherwise known as the Deamhan Lord, has been woken from his tomb, plotting even now to make the lands of Ériu his own."

Murmurs and whispers swept through the crowd. As men turned to their brothers, Neil saw fear in many eyes.

"What's just as bad, his ancient confederate, Faolukan the Grim, has been raised from what should have been an eternal sleep. News from the east travels slowly. Much of it we cannot trust. But aye, the rumors are true. Not more than thirty years ago, while some of you were still being weaned from your mothers' breasts, both the Deamhan Lord and Faolukan escaped from Heyerrah Bosch, the prison tower in the sands of Sarkenos. Faolukan then remade Crom Mord, the dread idol into which the Deamhan Lord has entered. He has resided there ever since. At the Deamhan Lord's orders, Faolukan raised an army and captured the desert fortress of Samotun. For some time, the Sarkenians have bowed before the dark one's evil.

"Only five years ago, Faolukan marched his Wolf Guard through the Conachtir hills and the southern plains of Ferachtir. He carried Crom Mord over the Pass of Mam Giorag into the barren lands of Drochtar. Once again, the Deamhan Lord has made Cathair Duvh—that foul city on the slopes of Drochcarn—his own. Aye, its people again sacrifice their children and youth to the Crom Mord idol. Children and youth, my lords! And each death increases the Deamhan Lord's growing evil.

"Soon, the darkness will burst forth, sweep the plains, hills, and forests, and find its way into the heart of every soul on the Great Lands of Ereb. My lords, take no comfort in Ériu's island isolation. Even now we hear rumors that the Deamhan Lord's spies walk our paths and befoul our forests, turning good to evil, right to wrong."

"Are we doomed, Cairbre?" A young flaith's voice piped up front. "Can we do anything to stop this?"

"We can, my friend, and I'm coming to that. Many here have heard the old tales about the Scepter—that it existed, that it once brought us hope and gave wisdom to our king, perhaps now our greatest need.

Everyone assumed the stories were myth. But sometimes, myth is based in ancient reality.

"As the Capulum's titular head, I vowed to investigate. Thus did I send a young acolyte to climb the Tower of Dóchas and examine more closely what, exactly, was up there. You've all climbed it, of course. In my youth, I often trudged up its winding staircase. Alas, no longer.

"From our investigations, we have ascertained the tower is the tallest and oldest structure in all Ériu. Parts of it are cracking, aye, but it has withstood the millennia remarkably well.

"When my student studied the high platform floor, he found in the center a large round stone. He pried it loose. Underneath he discovered a hole filled with gravel. Many might have stopped there. But my acolyte was curious. He dug out the rocks until he unearthed the tip of an ancient, metal rod. When he pulled, this rod, constructed from the finest, hardest steel, rose to a height of five feet. When twisted, it locked in position. On its crown, seven metal leaves reached up. They seemed especially designed to hold some kind of device."

"The Scepter," more than one voice called out at once. "'Twas for the Scepter."

"Exactly. But as my bright, young student was replacing the rod, he discovered words inscribed on it in a language he'd never before seen. He copied them down. And I will soon reveal what they said.

"Then he returned everything to its place and started down the steps. But as he descended, he happened to notice something else. Every few feet on the inside wall was a single design. Etched in rock in such an ornamental way, each appeared as merely decoration, part of the tower's artistic purpose. Now this was very odd. One design here. Another there. All the way down.

"As I say, my young acolyte was very bright. So he copied them all down. For he realized they were the characters of a long-forgotten language, not the Common Tongue we all speak today. It took us many years to find the ancient book holding the meaning of this message. 'Tis a prophecy, actually. One that unfolds around us even now."

Again, he paused as Dermid brought him a scroll. Cairbre passed his walking stick to Dermid and unrolled the scroll.

"We estimate this message was carved in stone a millennium after the tower was built—nearly twenty-three hundred years ago. I begin with the first part."

The silence in the forest amphitheater was now total. Even the wind died and the birds stopped singing.

I, Airril mac Duvh, Ard Righ of all Ériu, do record these words for all who come after: Weep and mourn, my beloved people, for we have lost the Battle of Two Rivers. The Deamhan Lord's servant, Faolukan the Grim, has stolen the great gifts of Elyon. Alas, the light from the Scepter has gone out. So, too, has the—

Here, Cairbre stopped and raised his head. "My lords, these most important of words were lost, inexplicably damaged in one small section of the tower's wall. I continue,

—been lost. Hear now the vision that possesses me with force, that nightly breaks the sweat on my brow and disturbs my sleep:

Ages will pass, and the people will lose all knowledge of the truth. You, my progeny, will forget Elyon, his wisdom, his light, and his truth. And no longer will you anticipate the coming of the Savior.

Once again, the Deamhan Lord will rise in the east. Then will you turn from all that is good. Anarchy and rebellion, famine and murder will bedevil you. Foolishness will become wisdom. Dishonor will seem like honor. And cruelty will replace mercy.

But when the shadow of evil touches Ériu, some among you will cry out for deliverance.

Listen now, my progeny, to the end of my vision. Elyon, in his mercy, will hear your cries. Then will he raised up one among you. Beware then and know the Ard Rígh is corrupted. So gather the flaith without him and seek the five signs. The one who bears them is the Toghaí, for he will precede the Savior. Send the chosen one to redeem yourselves from the evil that all of us, together, have wrought.

Oh, Elyon! Forgive us what we have done!

Cairbre cleared his throat again and glanced around the clearing. "The next section declares the signs. Dermid will read them later. They will help us choose between the two candidates."

"What candidates?" came a loud voice from the back. "What are you saying, old man?"

"Aye," said another. "You speak of Elyon and ancient scrolls. Are you saying he's real? That such a Being exists?"

"That's exactly what I'm saying, Boodan of Munster. And you've suspected it all along. Most of you have. That's why we chose you and brought you here."

The murmurs began again. They increased in volume until the entire assembly was engaged in discussion with his neighbor.

Neil faced Ewan. "This great warrior who's going to save Ériu—he cannot be me."

"Do not judge too hastily, my lord. Look. Dermid is again picking up the horn."

When Dermid blew "The Call To Assemble", Neil and those beside him quieted.

Cairbre rose to his full height and faced the crowd. "I can now tell you what was inscribed on the ancient rod atop the Tower of Dóchas. At first, we made no sense of it, for the language was different from the one on the tower's spiral walls, in another long-forgotten script. After many years, a single book was found in a treasure cache buried in Connacht. So many books were lost. This one, alone, returned to us. Was it chance?

Or the hand of Elyon? Who can say? But it provided enough so we could translate it."

He unrolled the scroll, and after clearing his throat again, he read.

> Herein in ages past sat the Great Scepter, bearing the wisdom and hope of Elyon. On a terrible day of infamy, Faolukan stole it from its cradle and secreted it in the Kingdom of Dark Trees.

Cairbre raised his glance. "We now call that place the Waldreich. I will go on."

> Prize what is now revealed, for many have died to learn it. In Schwarzburg Fortress, in the grand hall, have men seen it. A saber-toothed beast, ageless and undefeated, does guard it. Go now, brave warrior, you who are true of heart and worthy of spirit, the Toghaí chosen from the many. Give your life so others may live. Traverse the swamps and dark forests. Find the stolen hope and salvation of Ériu. Bring back wisdom to your leaders and hope to your people. Others have tried and failed. Only the Toghaí can return Elyon's great gift to the Tower. Only to you is given success.
>
> Let the light of truth reign again over Erde.
>
> And know, brave warrior, that when you retrieve the first, the second will also be revealed.

Swamps? Dark forests? Saber-toothed beasts? A chill rippled down Neil's back. Surely, they would choose one of the great nobles from this auspicious gathering, an accomplished fighter, not him?

Now Dermid stepped forward. "The purpose of today's convocation, my lords, is this: Our plan is first to select faithful companions to accompany the Toghaí. Then Cairbre will read the signs from the tower's walls. At that point, we will let the Company choose between the two candidates as to which of them meets the prophecy.

"Know that the Company's quest is perilous, a mission into danger like few have ever seen. We don't know if those we send out will ever come back. But the Capulum will pray for them. The fate of us all rides on the outcome. So I ask you, great leaders of Ériu, should we select the Company and the Toghaí, retrieve the Scepter, and return it to the Tower?"

At first, there was silence. Then came a single cry of, "Aye!" Followed by a dozen more. Then several flaith began to clap. Then all the assembly broke into riotous applause, clapping, cheering, banging their swords on shields. A few birds who had settled on nearby trees took flight. It was as if the men, having been silent too long, now gave voice to a growing excitement.

As the enthusiasm continued, Dermid led the old man to a seat. After a time, Dermid again blew his horn for quiet. "We will now select those who will accompany the Toghaí. You have all been seated by kingdom. So let each kingdom decide on the one man you will send.

"And today, as befitting a race that has stood beside men for the last three hundred years, the lehbrágan will choose one of their own. Because our two candidates come from Ulster, as they must, you from Ulster have no choice to make. Cairbre will have the final say over the fitness of your selections, so choose well. We await the names."

As the nobility of each kingdom bent heads and began heated arguments, Neil addressed Ewan in tones so low, only the squire could hear. "You brought me here with a plan to replace Neil mac Connell. You said I'd save Ériu from the darkness. But who am I to lead the likes of these high flaith?"

Ewan frowned. "Remember what I told you. You *are* Neil mac Connell. This will work."

"'Tis *that* which troubles me. I am *not* Neil mac Connell. We are deceiving them."

"Do not think of it that way, my lord. Let the signs decide."

"And the signs will show I'm not the one. This has all been a grand mistake. How can I go on with this?"

"You can and you must. You and I have done all we can. Let us now wait for the signs' verdict. If you are not chosen, you may return home."

Neil breathed easier. Surely, that's what would happen.

One group after another sent a messenger down to Cairbre with a name. Finally, Dermid blew the horn for quiet.

"You have chosen, and Cairbre says you've chosen well. The first name on the list is my own, representing Leinster."

"Aye, Dermid," shouted a heavy man wrapped in thick fur. "And who better to lead the Company?" Murmurs of agreement coursed along the gathering.

Dermid tipped his head in acknowledgment and went on. "The second is Camran mac Blàr, a prince of Munster. As you are called, will you please step down to the front."

A stocky, black-haired man rose, smiled broadly, and began threading his way through the seated nobility toward Dermid.

"The third is Finnean mac Friseal, a prince of Meath."

A red-haired lad of no more than twenty jumped up and bounced between bodies toward the front. As he neared Dermid, he flipped off the hat from the head of a man in the first row. It fell down onto his lap.

"On this journey, Finnean, your jests will land you in the Otherworld," said the man, frowning, as he retrieved his hat.

"Better a jest than a knife in your chest." A few chuckles arose as Finnean shot him a backward smile.

"The fourth is Machar mac Maon, a prince of Connacht."

A few hands clapped, but the more common response was a general whispering. A tall man, perhaps fifteen years older than Neil, now stood. Above a neatly trimmed brown beard and strong cheekbones, a faraway look haunted his eyes. As he strode confidently to the front, his chain mail crinkled and squeaked on top of a leather vest.

Beside Neil, someone whispered, "The Cloaked Rider. There's one to fear."

The man to his right nodded.

"The fifth will represent the lehbrágan." Murmurs swept the crowd until Dermid raised his hand for silence. "The little people are part of us now. Long ago, they pledged to help us in war and in peace. They mend our shoes, our clothes, create useful tools, and pay taxes. And so today, we make them a part of this great undertaking. Luag mac Laise, will you join us? We welcome your war-axe."

A sprite dressed in reds and greens capered to the front, bowed, and stood with the others. Next to the tall warrior, Machar, he appeared most diminutive.

"Now you've heard the names of the five. The sixth must come from Ulster, the only kingdom not yet represented. As I call the candidates, please step forward.

"The first is Ros mac Doughall of the Ballymena clan."

Clapping from those around him. Neil tensed, fearing what Dermid would say next.

"The second is Neil mac Connell, prince of . . ."

But he didn't hear the rest. He was suddenly lightheaded, feeling faint.

Ewan shoved an elbow into his ribs. Neil stood and walked, dazed, toward the front.

"A drunkard and a womanizer?" called someone. "Sure, and he'll borrow and cheat his way to the Scepter, and then forget it and come back with the country's wives."

Laughter from several quarters.

Dermid raised his hand for silence once more. "The inquisition of the signs will now commence."

Chapter 12

The Inquisition of Signs

Neil stepped to where Dermid pointed as he and Ros faced the crowd. Then Dermid stood before them holding the scroll and spoke. "Only the Toghaí can meet all five signs. Cairbre, along with those chosen for the Company, will judge the first two." He glanced at each of the Company. "Men, listen carefully to their answers."

The chosen five nodded judiciously.

"I will start the first question with Ros."

Ros smiled, lifted his face to the crowd, and winked.

"Ros, what were the circumstances of your birth?"

His smile vanished, and his face fell. Then he inspected the ground.

"Your birth? Can you tell us about it?"

Ros looked up. "When my mother was pregnant and almost ready to deliver, she ran away from my father. They told me she hated him, that the two quarreled bitterly." Obvious embarrassment reddened his face. "Two days into her flight, she birthed me on a forest path. A day later, she died. Some travelers heard me crying. They found me lying in her cold arms. I almost died."

"This was in Ulster, aye?"

Ros's face showed pain as he examined his feet. "I . . . I'm sorry." His face was downcast, as if he feared his revelation would put him out of the running.

"No need to be sorry, Ros. We kenned the tale. It was one of the reasons we chose you."

Eyebrows arching, Ros lifted his glance. Clear puzzlement etched his features as Dermid faced Neil.

"Now for you, Neil. I ken your story is well known. Would you like me to tell it?"

"Aye, do tell it." He breathed a sigh of relief. Ewan should have told him more about this.

"As most here already know, on the day of the prince's birth, Connell was out hunting. But Neil's mother, the queen, died in childbirth. Then for some reason, Fionna, the midwife, abandoned the new-born prince and vanished. She hasn't been seen since.

"But Neil's aunt, Mordag, was waiting outside the birthing room. She saw what happened, and when the midwife left, Mordag stole the babe from her sister-in-law's deathbed.

"Mordag's plan was to kill the child and point the deed at Fionna, the midwife. But Connell returned sooner than expected. When servants informed him of Mordag's flight, he pursued her into the forest. They argued, and Mordag admitted to the king she did her deed because she wanted her own son to inherit the throne. In a fit of anger, the king slew his own sister there under the trees and retrieved the baby Neil. Later, he found and slew Mordag's son. Is there anything you want to add, Neil?"

He shook his head. He'd only heard pieces of that story, and it puzzled him.

"Why did you have them tell this, Dermid?" shouted a man in front. "These are dishonorable births, both."

"Exactly. Now I will read the first sign as recorded in Airril mac Duvh's vision so long ago:"

The first is the sign of humble birth, for though he be flaith and a child of Ulster, the Toghaí will be born in ignominy and shame.

Dermid now addressed only Cairbre and the Company, who stood behind Neil and Ros. "What say you, men? Do our candidates meet the first sign?"

They gathered in a cluster. When every head nodded, Cairbre stepped in front. "They do, indeed, meet the first sign."

Neil looked down. What he and Ewan were doing was wrong. How could he ever have agreed to this?—fooling everyone into thinking he was someone else. All these men thought he met the first sign, but he wasn't flaith. Above all, he must be honorable, and with this sign, he was clearly lying. How could he let this continue?

But then, he didn't have to say anything, did he? Soon, he would fail the other tests. Then this ruse would end.

"For the next sign, the Company will again judge, for this knowledge is well known to all." Dermid lifted the scroll and read.

> The second is the sign of steel, for he will wield a sword of
> truth and power against all that is false.

He lifted his glance toward the Company. "You know well the swordsmanship abilities of both men. What say you?"

Now the group convened in a circle. From where he stood, Neil could hear most of the heated discussion. Everyone agreed that he, Neil—rather, the real Neil—was better than Ros, but Ros could hold his own in a fight. Then Cairbre suggested the words might mean something other than "swordsmanship". The discussion went on and on.

Finally, Cairbre left the others and shuffled to the front. "Though there are other possibilities, we agree the words most likely mean 'swordsmanship'. Granting that, even though Neil is the better, we deem both men meet the second criteria."

"Very well." Dermid addressed the larger crowd. "Because of Cairbre's wisdom and study in these matters, he alone will judge the last three."

Again, Dermid lifted the scroll.

The third is the sign of the Scepter, not of metal or clay or any man-made thing, but singed in flesh, marked from birth, on the right, not on the left.

"Cairbre, we look to you to decipher the meaning of these cryptic words and judge."

The old man approached Ros. "Ros, do you have an unusual birthmark anywhere on your body? If so, please show it to me."

Ros's face flushed. Eyes narrowed, he shook his head.

"We know you do. May we please see it?" Cairbre raised his eyebrows.

Ros stared at the old man. Slowly, he turned his back to the crowd, removed his tunic, lowered his loincloth, and revealed his buttocks.

Boisterous laughter filled the clearing.

"And a mighty fine bum it is, Ros," came a voice from the front.

Ros shot a scowl behind him toward the heckler.

Cairbre bent to look. A mark discolored Ros's right buttock in the form of a two-headed oval. The old man bent closer. Finally, he said, "Ros, you may clothe yourself. Now for Neil. Same question."

Neil pulled his tunic to his shoulder and presented his right arm to Cairbre.

The old man examined it for some time before nodding. Then he spoke to the crowd. "Ros has a mark faintly resembling a two-headed scepter on his right buttock. The sign is vague, but not unduly so. Neil has carried a mark on his right forearm since birth. It is remarkably like a short, two-headed staff and certainly meets the criteria. I deem both meet the sign."

Cairbre cleared his throat and again lifted the scroll. "Now we come to last two, perhaps the most important of all."

But at that moment, a thin-faced man rode into the clearing and down to the rock platform where Dermid stood.

"What is it?" Dermid's face tightened with concern.

"The King's Riders"—the man jerked his head toward the south—"on the trail from Ewhain Macha. Headed this way."

"How many?"

"About thirty. Heavily armed."

"Let's take them here and now." A tall man stood and raised his sword. "We'll show them that the flaith of this land willna be bullied by druids and a king who's lost his sense."

"Aye," came a shout from another. "I can take five with me bow before they cross the clearing."

Nods and cries of agreement swept the assembly.

"Nay, my lords." Dermid frowned. "'Twould be the undoing of everything we planned here. We must hide until they pass. These woods are deep. We can go uphill beyond the ridge where they willna see us. I will watch and send someone to get you when they're gone. Leave nothing here for them to find. Let us hide our trail well."

With much grumbling, the men rose as one, gathered their things, and began leading their horses up the slope in single file, leaving but one trail to cover.

As they climbed, Neil followed Ewan. Dermid was leading his horse before them when he stopped the squire. "Will you take my mount, so I can watch for the Riders?"

Ewan nodded and took the reins.

Then Dermid put a hand on Neil's shoulder. "My lord, will you wait with me? I would have a few words."

Neil shot a desperate glance to Ewan, who simply shrugged and continued with all three animals.

As the rest of the group ascended the hill, Neil huddled with Dermid behind a large boulder. The last man to leave swished a piece of brush and sprinkled a few leaves and twigs over the path.

Neil found himself alone with the high lord who'd apparently convened this mighty gathering. Sweat beaded up on his forehead.

"My prince, what think you of these proceedings?"

"I . . . I am surprised. I thought the Scepter was just a myth."

"But perhaps you heard the rumors?"

"Aye, but until today I never believed them."

Dermid nodded. "Sadly, 'tis what most of us thought. I admit, I'd hoped to speak with you privately before this. Then this opportunity arose. I warn you, I plan to speak plainly in the brief time afforded to us."

Neil gulped. If only Ewan were here. "Plain speech is always welcome, my lord. But about what?"

"We do not ken how this will turn out today. Both you and Ros seem to meet the signs. We knew that already. Only the Company can judge which of you is the Toghaí. But now I must ask you some personal questions."

Neil shifted his position. "But you will soon judge between Ros mac Doughall and me. So I ask you, my lord, is such a discussion as you suggest—is it not unseemly?" His fingers dug into the moss behind the rock. Should he be talking with such boldness to such a man? But then he was the prince, wasn't he? Or so he must believe. And something about the request seemed wrong.

For a moment, Dermid gawked at him as if taken aback. "'Tis not, my lord. And aye, we must have this conversation. Ken that I promise not to let our talk influence my decision. But forgive me if I speak freely. At this point, either of you could be chosen, but if 'tis you—well, I'm sore troubled by the life you've led."

Neil was silent. What could he say? From what he knew of Neil mac Connell, the prince's lifestyle also troubled him.

Dermid scowled. "You sleep with every woman who winks sideways at you. You never turn down a mug of ale, and you drink more than anyone I know. And, my lord, I've a stable boy who cares more for the affairs of state than you."

Neil pretended to examine the moss. Should he feign remorse? "Not an exemplary life, is it?"

Dermid squinted at him. "Nay, 'tis not. But what if we decide you *are* the chosen one? Within days, you will become a leader of the most important mission we've ever undertaken. But leadership is a trait I've yet to see in you. My lord, the fate of Ériu—aye, perhaps even of

Erde itself—may soon rest upon you. Forgive me again, but if you are chosen, are you ready to take on this task, to lead with responsibility and honor? Or will you continue on your path of debauchery, lechery, and drunkenness?"

Neil raised his glance to Dermid's and held it. He *knew* he wouldn't be chosen. In fact, he'd just about made up his mind that tonight, after the others had gone to bed, he must end this farce and return to Hidden Pines. But he must say something now, something the real Neil would say—or *should* say, if he'd been an honorable man. "You are right about my life. For lately, I . . . I have begun to realize that such behavior is not . . . becoming . . . to a high prince of the realm. And if I am chosen—though I doubt this will happen—then I promise to change, to carry out my task with all honor. And to the best of my abilities."

Dermid's mouth opened, closed, and then he smiled. "I admit, I hadna expected such a serious reply, such contrition. 'Tis not like you. But I am well satisfied with your answer, my lord. Well satisfied. With Elyon's help, I believe we will bring back the Scepter. And again, forgive my being so bold." He bowed.

"You are forgiven, my lord Dermid." Neil's gut twisted. He'd just lied to the man, deceived him. But what else could he do? Aye, tonight he would leave—*must leave*—for home.

The lord nodded. "But listen. The Riders. They're coming."

Dozens of hooves thundered over the hard ground. Chain mail, swords, and spears clinked and clattered together, scraped against leather. Dermid poked his head around the corner of the rock, but Neil stayed hidden.

After some moments, the Riders' horses seemed to pass. Neil shifted position, ready to stand.

Roughly, Dermid's hand pushed him back down.

Then came a voice from the clearing. "Do you ken, Eacharn, that something has gone on here recently? Many tracks leading here simply stop."

The whinny of a horse preceded a gruff second voice. "Aye. Someone's met here, possibly this morning. Maybe yesterday. I ken 'twas a large group. But they're gone now."

"We'll catch them, Eacharn."

"If Corc has his way, we will. Now we must hasten to the Dunnford Road with all dispatch."

"Aye, we've seen nary a one of the rebels 'twixt here and Ewhain Macha."

Horses' hooves clattered over rock and, more distantly, onto hard-packed dirt. Then silence.

"That was close." Dermid shook his head. "If you would, my prince, go back up the hill and send down two men to be our lookouts. And tell the others they may return."

Neil nodded and climbed the hill. But as he walked, he wondered how he would tell Ewan of his decision to leave tonight.

CHAPTER 13

THE TOCHAI

It took time for the murmurs of conversation, the clopping of horses' hooves on stone, and the swish of buskins over packed ground to die down. Finally, everyone returned to their seats, and the Company, Dermid, Cairbre, and the two candidates were back in position up front.

"I hope we'll not be interrupted again." Dermid wiped his brow. "As I was saying, Cairbre will now judge the last two signs."

The aged scholar walked again to the center, his steps slow and halting. As he spoke, his voice barely carried over the crowd. "Ros, what do you know of Elyon and—pardon me for darkening the day by speaking their names—of the Deamhan Lord and his servant, Faolukan?"

The entire assembly fell into silence. When Ros spoke, his words were hesitant. "I've heard . . . their names. Mostly I ken what I've heard here tonight. Not much more than that."

"And you, Prince Neil? How much do you know of these?"

"Very little. I've heard the names before. I know they say Elyon created the world. And I know what was said here tonight."

"Very well. As we suspected, you are both mostly ignorant of them. 'Tis sad how the flaith of this land know so little of such matters. Yet the prophecy predicted exactly this state of affairs. I will now tell you a story and gauge how you react. I warn you, 'tis a long tale."

Neil nodded soberly, but Ros grinned.

"Before anything existed, there was nothing. Neither Erde nor sun nor moon. Only emptiness. There were just the persons of Elyon and the Pneuma, and they were One Being, though how this can be is beyond our ken. Beyond these two, some texts hint of a third person, but of him, we know little. Together, these two—or three—made the worlds. They created a world called earth and a moon that shines at night. Then they created a reflection of earth—our world, this world called Erde. The moon, 'tis said, is common to both. How this can be is a great mystery, yet we believe it to be true."

"Cairbre," shouted a stout warrior from the back. "Who hasn't heard the old tale about the moon and another world? You're saying 'tis true?"

"I am. Erde is like a reflection of the trees when you look in a quiet, forest pool. It's like the echo that comes back when you shout into a well. 'Tis not your original shout, and always a wee bit different. What comprises the echo is not only the world's lands, but also its stories, and perhaps even some of the people who live there. Some of us also believe, based on a single cryptic passage, that there exists a second echo, distant, fainter, in a world called Middle Earth. But 'tis only conjecture, based on a single difficult sentence.

"In any event, Elyon created Erde and then men to fill it. 'Twas from Ériu that men spread out to the Great Lands of Ereb. And when those men worshiped Elyon, Erde began in prosperity and glory.

"But to serve as a test of men's love for him, Elyon gave them a great gift. As long as the Ériu cherished it and kept it safe, the lands of Ériu and Ereb, indeed all Erde, would know peace and prosperity. The gift, of course, was the Scepter. Later, Elyon gave us a second gift. Unfortunately, as I've said, its name and the nature of it have been lost to us.

"So the land flourished. The people were happy. It appeared Neavh had come to Erde."

"'Tis as I thought," said a thin, mustachioed man, jumping up. "Ériu was always meant to be at the center of things."

Dermid spoke from his seat in front. "Before pride carries you away, Donnan, you need to hear the rest of the story."

Cairbre cleared his throat and went on. "Early in Erde's history, besides the races of men and the lehbrágan, Elyon created the siòg, the fairies. He also created other beings, of which we know little. The siòg lived in Neavh with Elyon, but on occasion, they walked the roads and forests with men. One of the siòg—Faolan was his original name—became their leader. He was Elyon's most trusted servant and was granted more power than the others. For a time, he even ruled as high king of Ériu from Tara in Leinster.

"But the power Elyon granted him was not enough, and Faolan lusted for more. Finally, about five hundred years after mankind appeared on Erde, Faolan rebelled against his maker, taking many of the siòg with him.

"His patience exhausted, Elyon forever banished the rebels from Neavh. He even forbade them to be called siòg. They would now be called deamhans. Then he cursed them so they could never again take the physical bodies of men or lehbrágan. They would henceforth become incorporeal spirits. But they soon learned to inhabit the bodies of crows, wolves, or foul beasts, or to live inside cold stone or metal idols.

"Thus did Faolan the Traitor, in his spirit state, wander abroad, seething with anger and hate. Taking the form of a crow, he flew to distant Sarkenos. There he haunted the desert nights, the tombs of fallen kings, and high mountain caves. And that is where he happened upon Boiteag mac Clodach, a disgraced priest of Elyon. Boiteag had traveled to the desert lands to escape the scorn he'd engendered in Ériu for crimes unbecoming to his holy order. Sensing a weak faith, Faolan appeared to him in a dark, hovering cloud. And then he turned the man from all that was good to all that was evil. And in that evil, Boiteag found his calling—one might even say greatness.

"At Faolan's urging, Boiteag discovered the dark arts of magic. Thus did he become the first of the druids—the arch druid. Boiteag then fashioned the Stone of Crom Mord. And into that dread stone idol did Faolan enter and live.

"Crom Mord soon became the center of a new and terrible cult. The idol itself was a fearsome beast, and upon the stone altar beside it,

Faolan's growing sect of druids sacrificed both adults and children. With each death, his power deepened and grew. That was when folk stopped calling him Faolan and began calling him the Deamhan Lord. And that was when a terrible darkness of the soul seeped across the desert sands of Sarkenos.

"To reward his arch druid, the Deamhan Lord granted Boiteag a portion of his power, giving him immortality on Erde. He also gave Boiteag a new name; henceforth Boiteag would be called Faolukan the Grim.

"Meanwhile, word of Elyon, shining out with the Scepter's light, was spreading ever stronger across northern Ereb. To escape the light, the Deamhan Lord ordered his arch druid to take the Crom Mord idol that was his home and flee through the pass of Mam Giorag over the Sfarsit Mountains. In eastern Drochtar did the two settle, far from the Scepter's light. And there, darkness descended over that nation of barren wastes, windswept plains, and rumbling mountains."

"As still it remains, Cairbre." A heavy-bearded man rose from the throng's center, his leather vest crinkling. "Who doesna fear the name of Drochtar and Cathair Duvh?"

"'Tis so," said Ros. "But, Cairbre, what does this have to do with the signs?"

"That, precisely, is where my tale now leads. When Elyon saw how easily the southern and eastern peoples of Sarkenos, Ferachtir, and Drochtar abandoned him for Crom Mord's dark allure, anger filled him. He wanted men to acknowledge him. More than that, he wanted men to love him.

"But oh, how they did abandon him! How those three countries sacrificed their own children to a stone possessed by a deamhan! We are stubborn, evil creatures, are we not? We know what is right, what is wrong, but we follow our own desires. And all too often those desires lead to evil."

"Aye, Cairbre." Dermid spoke up. "Look at Connell and Corc."

Murmurs of agreement drifted from all sides. Some hands even slapped knees.

"But what about the second great gift?" said a wiry-haired young prince in front. "Where does that fit in?"

"Thank you for asking, for I'm coming to that." Cairbre motioned to Dermid, who brought him another draught of water. "Elyon had every right to pour out his wrath on the people for rejecting him. Instead, he did just the opposite. He sent them a second great gift.

"We believe it was housed in the Tower's base in a special alcove." Cairbre's forehead creased in lines of puzzlement. "But 'tis odd, my lords, that we know so little of it. Many ancient documents seemed about to refer to it, only to be damaged or scratched out in exactly the wrong places. We've even found blank spots where one might have expected its mention. 'Tis as if men within the Capulum itself, against our founding principles, tried to purge its existence from our collective memory."

Frowning faces peppered the crowd. Puzzled looks. Shaking heads.

"Aye, 'tis puzzling, indeed. Our spoken history hints that once a year Elyon's second gift would speak to the people a few words that filled them with hope and life and joy. It spoke only in the presence of a single, chosen individual. But the words were Elyon's words, and they were repeated far and wide across Erde. The second gift augmented the first. And after it appeared, many who had given their children to Crom Mord in Sarkenos and Ferachtir turned away from the Deamhan Lord's idol and returned to Elyon. Only foul Drochtar was left to wallow in wickedness.

"Over the next centuries, with both gifts secure, the Deamhan Lord's power gradually withered. Again and again, Faolukan's armies would surge over Mam Giorag to the plains of Ferachtir, only to be defeated by forces many times smaller and less well trained.

"Thus did Erde's Golden Age continue, extending it through the first thousand years of man's existence. With the two gifts in place, Elyon's name was ever on the lips of men. And his love filled many hearts."

"Is that how it will be again?" A young, handsome flaith spoke up from the center. "Will these gifts, if we find them, bring Neavh to Erde?"

"Aye, my lord. That is what we hope. But the people's hearts were ever evil. Once again, all over Erde, the people drifted away from Elyon, even worse than before. The Deamhan Lord felt this weakness of faith and pounced. On Samhain eve, on the twenty-sixth day of October, in the year 1008, Faolukan and five riders rode through Ériu on a mission. That night, they stole both the Scepter and the second of Elyon's great gifts. Then the Deamhan Lord's servants fled with them across the sea.

"And at the very moment the Scepter left the Tower of Dóchas, the world changed. Instantly, every heart on Erde felt the loss. The hope and joy that seemed to float on the air one moment was replaced the next with a sense of great foreboding, a feeling that just around the corner, grim darkness itself was coming."

"We had great treasure in our hands, did we not?" His leather crinkling, the heavy-bearded man spoke again. "Elyon trusted us, and we let him down. Where were the guards? Where were the swordsmen to cut down the thieves? Where was duty and honor?"

"Good questions all." Cairbre nodded. "Where indeed? Because for the next seventy-five years, Faolukan visited a terror upon Erde such as the world had never seen. Purges, executions, invasions, oppressions. The carnage only halted when Patrick of Ulster—he who was filled with Elyon's spirit—alone tried to hold back the darkness. He lured Faolukan to Sarkenos, bringing Crom Mord with him. There did he trap them both in the Tower of Heyerrah Bosch.

"But it was too late. The Scepter and the second great gift were lost to the world. The Deamhan Lord's evil had already ravaged the lands. 'Twas the combination of the two, we suspect, that began the Lost Era. For almost two thousand years, civilization itself went into a long decline. The depth of man's depravity grew, bringing famine, disease, decay, and abandonment.

"Only slowly, during the last three hundred or so years, have we begun to climb out of this dark period. But then, about forty years ago, The Deamhan Lord and Faolukan escaped from the tower at Heyerrah Bosch. They are rising again, and without the Scepter sitting in the Tower, who can stop them?

"And that, my lords, is the history of our world, the story of Elyon, and of the Deamhan Lord and Faolukan."

"But what of the Savior?" the heavy-bearded man spoke again. "He who was referenced in the Scepter's cradle. We've all heard rumors of him."

"Aye. Oral history says that someday a great Savior, righteous and bold, will come to Erde and free us from oppression. He will destroy evil and lead us to a new Golden Age.

"But that's about all we know. As you say, we've only a few words about him etched in metal atop the Tower. I regret how so much of our history was burned, buried, or forgotten. 'Tis as if agents of the Deamhan Lord himself, during the Great Purge, wormed their way into our midst and erased it."

Silence descended on the crowd.

Cairbre addressed both Ros and Neil. "Have either of you heard this history of Elyon and Erde?"

Both Ros and Neil shook their heads.

"As expected. What you've heard today was only known to a handful of souls. So, Ros, what do you think of it?"

Ros scratched the back of his head. "'Tis an interesting tale, my lord, if a bit fanciful. I've always heard Elyon was only a myth. I do not ken how such a Being can have done all you say he has." He frowned. "My lord, can I mull it over and think on it before I give you an answer?"

Cairbre nodded and faced Neil. "And you, my lord? What is your reaction?"

Neil's head was spinning. Many things now started to make sense. Elyon had made the world, and the Deamhan Lord was destroying the good in it. His heart raced, and sweat broke out on his forehead.

He fell to his knees. "My lord Cairbre, 'tis all true. I sense it. I know it. Elyon is the source of all that is good and right, is he not? And by returning the Scepter to the Tower, Ériu will again show him its obedience and love. If we do not . . . I mean, if *you* do not, then the Deamhan Lord and his evil will prevail."

Cairbre smiled, walked toward Neil, and laid a hand on his shoulder. Neil's face grew warm.

With his hand still gripping Neil's shoulder, Cairbre faced Dermid. "'Tis clear to me who is the chosen one. It is Neil. He is the Toghaí. I will now read the last two signs, and you'll see why I believe this to be so." Lifting the scroll with both hands, Cairbre read.

> The fourth is the sign of ignorance, for through no fault of
> his, he will know little of Elyon, Faolukan, or the Deamhan Lord.
> The fifth is the sign of speech, for when he hears the truth
> of the Creator of all things, he will utter words of nobility, honor,
> and a pure heart.
> Let the people send forth the Toghaí and pray.

He raised his glance to the crowd. "What we've heard from Neil is exactly what the signs require. He *is* the chosen one. Of this I'm certain." Cairbre spread both hands toward the group.

The men assembled began clapping and banging swords on shields.

Neil gulped. It was all a mistake. He wasn't flaith. Why had he ever opened his mouth? His stomach twisted in knots, and he feared he might be sick. Without a doubt, he must leave tonight and return home.

As the applause died down, Cairbre raised his staff and continued. "But, my lords, we could not send Neil on such a journey without his faithful squire, Ewan mac Ninian. We discussed this beforehand and decided that if Neil was chosen, then Ewan must go with him—that is, if he doesn't mind the lack of culinary arts on the trail." He smiled toward the back of the crowd. "Ewan, please come to the front."

Grinning ear to ear, Ewan sprinted through the crowd to stand with the others. All those chosen for the mission now stood in a line before the assembly.

"That makes seven. A much better number than six." Cairbre motioned for Ros to depart. Scowling, the prince left the front.

"Men of Ériu!" Cairbre pulled himself to his full height, and his voice gained strength. "Today we begin the path away from darkness. We must ask Elyon for his favor on these men—and for Luag—as they walk into danger, evil, and death. Not all may return. But if—nay, when—they bring back the Scepter, the light of hope will once again shine over our fair lands. Men of Ériu, I give you the Company of the Scepter."

Clapping and cheers. Everyone rose. Some beat swords on shields. The din went on and on. Neil worried the noise might carry past the clearing. Indeed, Dermid glanced nervously down each end of the trail.

While the crowd's roars died out, a man approached Dermid and spoke in his ear. Dermid scowled. Abandoning his horn, he lifted his hands for quiet. Finally, order was restored. "A final warning before we part. Has anyone received a medallion like this?" Dermid held up a quarter-moon pendant.

Sweat rose again on Neil's forehead. He dared not raise his hand now, not after they'd chosen him for such an important task. He scanned the assembly. No one else acknowledged the request.

"Beware of these devices." Dermid shook its chain. "They are evil. Several of our number have reported receiving them from their druids. They will sap your will and resolve. We do not know if they have a connection to Faolukan's business or not. But with Cairbre's help, found in the old texts, we've discovered a way to neutralize their magic. If you melt them down and recast them into the same shape, they become just an ordinary piece of jewelry. And that particular spell will never work on that person ever again.

"Let us now depart in groups of two or three, no more. Take side trails to avoid the King's Riders. Above all, this meeting must remain secret. May Elyon go with you all."

As the rest of the assembly began filing out of the clearing, Dermid called the Company together under a large oak.

"Men, the fate of Ériu rests with what we do in the weeks and months to come. With your approval, I will lead this expedition. Agreed?" He looked around.

No one raised an objection.

"Good. But let's get something clear, Luag." He faced the sprite. "Will you agree if we call you by the term *man* from here on? I canna keep making a distinction between men and lehbrágan."

Luag nodded gravely. "If 'tis easier for the tongues of men, I can be called by the word *man* and not take offense."

Dermid smiled and laid a hand on the sprite's shoulder. Then his glance swept over each of them. "Men, even now a ship is being readied on the docks at Áth Cliath. Neil and Ewan, you must sleep tonight in the palace as if nothing happened. Be careful to arouse no suspicion. Tomorrow, take what you need but pack lightly. Perhaps say you're going for a ride then take the Áth Cliath road. The rest of us will make camp on Artair's Ridge and await your arrival."

He smiled, gripped each shoulder one at a time, and then stood before them with hands on his hips. "Now 'tis a pact we must make between us." He put his right hand out, palm down.

Then, one at a time, they laid their right hands on top of his until they formed a single mass.

"No matter what happens, we must trust in Elyon and press on to the end. Are you with me, lads?"

Though his heart wasn't in it, Neil joined them as they raised their voices in unison, saying, "Aye!" and at the same time raising their hands to the sky.

"Then tomorrow"—Machar was grinning—"we ride for Elyon and the return of his glory."

CHAPTER 14

hIGh pLAces

To anyone on the Ewhain Macha trail that day, it would have seemed especially busy. Neil and Ewan rode together. A hundred yards ahead and another hundred behind, more flaith from the gathering followed on the same road. Far in the rear came more men and two sprites.

The sun shone, chaffinches sang their warbling songs, and a light breeze rustled the leaves above their heads. A fine afternoon for a ride. But the brightness of the day could not diminish Neil's distress.

"They chose me, Ewan. And I am greatly troubled." He looked to the squire.

"Have courage, my lord. The gathering of flaith has decided. You *are* the chosen one."

"Am I? Isn't this all just a fraud? Haven't you and I just fooled every flaith in the land with a terrible subterfuge? And this just as I learned the truth about Elyon, he who created the world."

Neil's black stallion whinnied and shook its head, as if to emphasize the point.

Ewan glanced at him. "I'd always thought Neil was the one. But after today, I was nearly convinced otherwise. You've surprised me, Tristan."

Neil faced his new friend. Ewan hadn't used his real name for days. "In what way?"

"I was sore puzzled why Neil insisted on going to Hidden Pines. You, of course, were the reason. Somehow, he knew there was another in the land who was his exact double. I've heard of such things, but this . . . you"—he waved a hand—"'tis uncanny. More than uncanny. He never told me, but 'tis clear he planned to meet with you before the council."

"But we cannot be related. My mother was a woman of the night. She'd had so many men, she could never tell me the name of my real father."

"I ken that. But 'tis powerful strange how the two of you look and act and talk so alike in every way. As if your taking his place was meant to be. Only you—you are more . . . responsible."

"A strange thing that. Still, I'm not the Toghaí. I'm not flaith."

Ewan frowned and shook his head. "If only you were. You met every other sign, even the birthmark. Yet, somehow, word must have leaked out. Years ago, it was rumored, some parents had begun to give their children that mark as babes. So that might explain it. I do not ken."

"But when you heard the story of Elyon, you fell to your knees and believed—you really *believed*. That was what nearly convinced me. But now you remind me you are not flaith. So, aye, you canna be the prophesied one. Still, we must continue in our deception."

"I don't know, Ewan. Nay—I *do* know." He glanced at the trail ahead. How would Ewan take what he was going to say next? "Tomorrow, I must return to Hidden Pines."

The squire pulled his mount to a stop and stared at him.

"I can't continue in this deception . . . any longer. It's . . . it's dishonorable."

Ewan's face showed pain. He half closed his eyes and scowled at the ground. "Nay, lad. Nay." His voice was soft, defeated. "If you give this up . . . we're . . . finished. You. Me. All of us."

"But my pretending to be the Toghaí—it's a lie!"

"So what if it is? The council of flaith has chosen. Cairbre has chosen. Sure and certain, if you do this terrible thing, the Company will abandon the quest. Perhaps the council, too. Then the Deamhan Lord will win."

His face warmed, and he grew lightheaded. Nay, Ewan was wrong. This was wrong. "They can send Ros. Maybe he'll come around and believe in Elyon. Somewhere out there is the right person who *is* the Toghaí. But that person isn't me. Nay, how can I continue in a lie? I've made up my mind. Tomorrow—nay, this very night!—I'm going home."

"I'll not accept that. I ken you'll change your mind. So tomorrow, I'll be waiting for you in the courtyard. No matter what you say now, I'll be there. Waiting. You will come. You'll see."

"Wait if you want. Tonight, after everyone's gone to bed, I'm taking the road for Hidden Pines."

Ewan watched him for a time in silence then glanced at the road ahead. Neil didn't sense anger from him, only—deep disappointment? Or disbelief? For the rest of the ride, neither of them said a word.

Back in Ewhain Macha, Neil tried to avoid everyone for as long as possible. Alone, he left the palace and wandered the nearby lanes. A woman carrying two pies called out her wares, but no one stopped to buy. As passersby watched in amusement, a husband and wife took their shouting match into the street. Neil stepped aside as a hay wagon rolled past, its wheels clattering over cobblestones.

He felt relieved by his decision but also uneasy. Relieved that soon this ruse would be over. But uneasy at the consequences that would follow. Back home, he'd have to keep watch for the Roamers. If ever they even came near the village, for a time he'd have to live in the woods.

But after he'd gone, what would they think in Ewhain Macha? That someone murdered the prince and hid the body? Or that Neil had been overwhelmed by the responsibility and vanished? He didn't care. Let the council pick someone more qualified. All he had to do was play out his role until tonight.

Then he would end this sham.

His wandering brought him to the Tower, fifty yards from the palace walls. Atop the fortress hill, it dominated the sky. Intrigued by Cairbre's speech, he climbed the spiral steps, noticing on the way the strange characters and their exquisite design. At the top, he found himself alone with a whispering breeze. He walked to the edge and surveyed the sprawling fortress town of Ewhain Macha and the squalor beyond. He'd heard that, in eons past, even the huts below the hilltop bespoke of grandeur and prosperity. Now all seemed poised on the verge of ruin.

Behind him, a scuffling of feet on stone. He whirled.

Maeve emerged from the stairwell. "Brother, where've you been all day? I looked for you all morning."

"I went for a ride with Ewan."

"At supper last night you barely drank your wine. And you just seem . . . different. Does something trouble you?"

He leaned back against the stonework balcony and caught her glance. Should he give her reasons for behaving like Tristan and not Neil? Or should he tell her his real thoughts? Did it really matter anymore? "The decisions the king is making with Corc's advice—they are not good."

She stood beside him. "I ken you're right. I, too, have been concerned about this. But again, 'tis not like you to worry over affairs of state. I do believe you've put on a new set of furs." She smiled, took the pendant out of her pocket, and began to stroke it. "But it matters not."

"Maeve?"

Her gaze fixed on the crescent moon, she didn't answer. Her eyes became distant.

"You like the pendant very much, don't you?"

She nodded without looking up.

"I fear for you."

She raised her glance to him.

"Let it go for a moment. For just a moment."

She looked at it. Then at him. She slid it back into her pocket.

"Can you hear me now?"

"I can. Always could."

"'Tis not good, this pendant. It bewitches you."

"I canna help it. The thing calls to me." Her gaze was drawn to her pocket. "I have trouble . . . resisting . . . its calling."

Neil leaned against the balcony. He glanced again at the jumble of thatched rooftops across Ewhain Macha. "Why are we so weak, Maeve? Why do we lie—to ourselves and everyone around us? And why can't we turn our backs on something that so obviously leads to our undoing?"

"I do not ken. You are so thoughtful, Neil. So serious. Something's happened to you recently, and I do not ken who you are anymore."

"You're right. I'm not the same person I was. People have shown me the future, and I don't like what I see. There's a darkness spreading over the land, sister—if I may call you that. And they want me to stop it. But *I* can't do the thing they want me to do. It won't be me." He turned from the ledge to face her. "Maeve, I'll be leaving soon. Then you must be strong. You must not succumb to Corc's wiles, to any device he gives you, or to your father's poor judgment. *Someone* must be strong. *You* must be strong."

She smiled. "I'm always strong. You've gone through some kind of fire, brother. And I like this new person you're making of yourself. But you worry me. What do you mean you're leaving?"

"Leaving. Just . . . leaving. Tell no one for now. I sense I can trust you. Except for that blasted pendant."

"Nay. There's nothing wrong with it." She glanced toward her pocket, started to reach for it, halted, then slipped her hand inside and brought it out again. "You're always leaving, aren't you? Always heading off for some woman somewhere."

She began to stroke it. "Nothing wrong with it, nothing at all." Her eyes glazed over.

"Maeve?"

No answer. She was staring at it, absently rubbing its shiny, metallic surface.

After a time, he gave up on her and started down the stairs, alone. He found his way back to the palace. He had an afternoon to idle away, but the day's events had drained him of all energy, so he returned to his room. He lay on the bed, convinced that after supper when everyone had gone to bed, he would leave.

He slept a few hours then walked onto his room's wide balcony overlooking Ewhain Macha's external wall. He sat in one of the carved wooden
chairs beside a small marble table and poured himself a glass of wine
from the decanter the servants had left. For these last few hours before
his departure, he might as well live the life of Neil mac Connell, high
prince of Ulster.

Far below, the sounds of a busy afternoon rose to his overlook—cart
wheels creaking, hammers pounding on anvils, women arguing over the
price of barley, vendors hawking their wares. The smells of baking bread,
iron forged on hot coals, manure spread over hay—all drifted up on the
breeze. He took a sip of the wine.

Above, a red hawk soared while pigeons flew low and ducked for
cover below the balcony. The hawk dove, but its prey eluded it. Its talons
empty, the hawk veered off and climbed.

They said birds were omens, didn't they? The pigeon escaped death.
So what did that mean for him? He shook his head, took another sip of
wine, and set the clay cup on the table.

Then it appeared, as surprising as a flash of lightning out of a clear
blue sky—

A bright circle of light.

Glowing.

Filling the opposite side of his balcony.

His mouth opened, and he stared.

The light pulsed and expanded into a ball crowded with every color
of the rainbow—waves of brilliant light so intense the rays seemed to
shoot through him into his inner being. But buried within that blaze of
phosphor and gold, amber and red, blue and green, he felt the presence
of a powerful Being. As its rays washed over him in wave after wave, Neil
sensed power, truth, wisdom, judgment, and—aye, even love—filling
his soul.

Then a voice spoke, but the words formed inside his head, seeming to write themselves in pure light inside his mind. Strong words, clear and commanding words. Words laden with power.

"Do not fear, Tristan mac Torn, for I am with you."

He pushed back from the table and dropped his head in his hands. Whatever, whoever, this Being was, it held all the power of the world, all the wisdom and truth that ever was. He feared for his life. He feared for his unworthiness in the presence of such a pure Being. "W–*who* are you?"

"I am He who was, who is, and who will always be."

"Oh, this can't be happening. What have I done?"

"Fear not and listen. You will not *return to your home. You will do the deed they've chosen you to do. You will be what they want you to be."*

He tried to open his mouth but stumbled on the words. "B–but I'm not who they think I—"

"You are enough. You will go."

"B–but—"

Then it was gone. In an eyeblink, the light vanished. He lifted his gaze and stared across the balcony's empty floor. He sensed its passing as though some powerful wind had rushed past, tearing off the tops of trees, knocking over houses, but leaving him, alone, standing, gaping in awe.

All he could do was lower his head to his hands and shake. He shook because of the power he'd felt, because he'd glimpsed a love so deep, a power so great, and a goodness so pure, there could never be another like it. In its presence, he felt less than a worm, and all he wanted to do was hide.

After a time he stood and wrapped his arms around himself.

Elyon! It was him, wasn't it?

A sense of relief, but also of fear, washed over him. What could he do now but obey? How could his life ever be the same again?

He staggered to his bed, lay down, and wept. He wept because he was a blade of grass that greens in the spring and dries to dust in the fall. He wept because the stars in the night sky—each one created and named by Elyon, and this he somehow knew—shone bright, clear, and beyond number. He wept because Tristan was born, would live his life, and die, and he could never attain the tiniest speck of the knowledge, power, or purity of the Being he'd just witnessed. He wept because he'd glimpsed the depths of infinity, the timelessness of eternity, and he was but a mote of dust swirling on the breeze, barely a flicker of a candle's flame, a tiny spark in the shadow before a great and blazing sun.

When he recovered somewhat, he stood from the bed. He smoothed his tunic. Then he wiped his eyes and returned to the balcony's edge. Beyond the city stretched a horizon of green treetops. Above, a cloud raced across the sky. Even further to the west hovered the burning blaze of the sun. And all of it belonged to Elyon, all created by him, all the result of a few words spoken at the beginning of time resulting in this world, the moon, the stars, and all the worlds beyond.

He raised his eyes to the sky. "I am yours, Elyon. Whatever you require of me, I will do it." Then he bowed his head and stood motionless before the memory of the Creator of worlds, the presence that had just visited him.

After a time, he left the palace for the nearby shops. There he found a smithy. His voice shaking, he told the blacksmith he would be returning that night and require the use of his furnace and tools.

One final act must he perform this night, before he left in the morning with Ewan. He must purge the evil Corc had given both him and Maeve.

"My lord." The man bent over almost horizontally. "I can fashion or fix whatever you require."

"Thank you, but nay. I'll have someone with me who knows what to do." The necessary lie soured his tongue. The real Prince Neil would know nothing of forge work.

The blacksmith bowed in acquiescence, and Neil returned to the palace, still affected by a presence that lit his inner being like a fire.

Neil arrived late at supper. He was soon startled by an exchange between the druid and Maeve, who'd obviously again left her pendant behind.

"Corc"—Maeve clanked her wine glass too hard on the table—"this evening you look as if you've seen a ghost. Are you well?"

"This afternoon, I . . . I felt something odd. Disturbing, actually. Something I've never felt before. And it's sapped my strength, made me a bit ill."

"Maybe you've been breathing too much incense, looking at too many entrails."

He waved a hand in dismissal. "The feeling has passed. I'll be all right. Yet . . . it was . . . *disturbing.*" During the rest of the dinner, Corc was morose and said little.

This suited Neil just fine as he tried to avoid all serious conversation. He tried to drink more wine to live up to Neil's reputation but quit after three glasses. The wine seemed to have no effect on him tonight, so filled was he with his memory of Elyon's presence. Then he returned to his room, glad to keep the façade alive for this last evening in the palace.

Long into the wee hours, he lay in bed, waiting, not sleeping, still marveling at the power of the afternoon visitation.

When only silence reigned in the halls, he rose and approached the table on the balcony where he'd left Corc's crescent-moon pendant. He grabbed it. Immediately, the warm, inviting tingling spread up his arm. He scowled at the thing. Tonight, he must recast it. Aye, it must be done. He would put it in his pocket, take it to the smithy's, and melt it down. But a moment later, he found himself still holding it, still feeling its seductive power and the beginnings of . . . cold . . . inviting . . . ecstasy. Shaking his head, he left the balcony, and stepped out the door.

In the hallway, only silence reigned. He trod slowly, trying to muffle the echo of his steps over stone.

Outside Maeve's room, he listened but heard nothing. He tried to open the door, but it was locked. Where were the tools to unlock it? Drat! He'd left them in his room.

He started back the way he'd come but heard footsteps. He backed into an alcove behind the bust of some ancient ancestor. A guard was patrolling the hallways. Too risky. He'd have to skip Maeve's pendant and recast just his own.

Striding across the hallway and down the staircase, he gained the main door, and slipped outside. He crossed the courtyard and came to the palace gate. It stood open. Almost outside now.

"My lord?" a man's voice queried from behind.

He whirled. One of the palace guards stood to attention, holding a lance.

"Can't sleep. Going for a walk."

The man nodded, and Neil continued to the forge.

Once inside the smithy, he found the furnace fire still blazing. The blacksmith must have stoked it for him before going to bed. He added more wood, fired it hot with the bellows, and sought what he needed.

But his pocket was empty.

He searched every fold but couldn't find it. How odd! He was sure he'd pocketed it. Hadn't he? Now he'd have to go back to his room and return here to recast it.

He retraced his steps, nodded to the guard, and mounted the staircase to the top. But as he turned the corner, he nearly knocked over another soldier coming down the hallway. Tonight, the palace guards seemed to be out in full force.

"Went for a walk," he muttered then slipped into his room.

There on the balcony table was the quarter moon. He was sure he'd taken it. Yet there it lay. Shaking his head, he picked it up by its chain, careful not to touch it. He thought about going down again then stopped.

Could he really pass the guard patrolling the hall and the guard at the palace entrance, telling them both, once again, he was going for yet another walk? Nay, it would appear odd. He yawned. Suddenly, he was tired. He'd have to recast it in another place, at another time.

He gave the pendant one more glance and secured it inside his pack. Then he went to Prince Neil's bed and fell fast asleep.

Chapter 15

The Trail to Ath Cliath

Neil arrived early in the courtyard. Ewan was already there, holding the reins of two mounts. When he saw Neil approach, a wide grin nearly split his face. "I knew you'd come." He slapped his knee. "I knew it."

Always ready for a ride, Neil's stallion pawed the cobbles with a hoof and whinnied.

"Ewan, I realized yesterday I *am* committed to Elyon's cause. He *is* the one true Being who created the world, before whom there is no other. And, Ewan—we *will* find the Scepter. We *must*. Or die trying."

"Aye, my lord. You've had a rethinking, sure and certain. I knew you would. Aye."

"Sure, and a rethinking is what I've had." He returned Ewan's grin with a smile.

Ewan's joy carried them through the torch-lit palace gates into the morning's semidarkness. Under his cape, Neil wore the tunic decorated with red circles. At his belt was Neil's sword and dagger. Tied to his saddle was the new traveling bag. He'd packed the heavy chain mail inside the bag. Beneath his vest, carefully hidden, lay the pendant.

They passed the huts and stables covering the fortress hilltop and crossed the drawbridge. Descending the hill, they entered a warren of streets, shops, and crumbling roundhouses. From somewhere came a dog's muffled bark.

Soon, they left behind all signs of Ulster's capital and entered a foggy forest trail. Leafy branches walled them in, reached through the mist, and wove a ceiling.

For some time they traveled in silence. The road to Áth Cliath sometimes followed the banks of the River Liffey. The trail took them through a field bordering the river then veered off into deep forest. Fog clung to the path and drifted through the trees on all sides. Their horses' hooves made only muffled clops.

Ewan smiled. "Do you ken I've never been anywhere but Ériu? Never been to sea. Nor to Armorica or Esperandula."

"Nor I."

"Methinks 'tis a grand adventure we've begun today. And I'm sore glad you're here, my lord. Sore glad. But we may not return for months. Maybe years. You've no idea how long they've been planning this."

"*They*? You mean the Capulum? Are you privy to their plans?"

"Ah, I've said too much. They only let me in on some of their secrets. I—"

"Wait!" Neil pulled back on the reins. A shiver rippled down his shoulders.

"What?" Ewan also halted. A worried look crossed his face.

"Someone's following."

Ewan frowned, shifted in the saddle, and peered into the mist behind them. "This trail's the only way to Áth Cliath. Many come this way."

The fog thickened, seeped in from all sides. Only the trunks of the trees—silent, lonely witnesses to their passage—were visible. Like some ethereal tide, fog even slid over the horses' hooves.

Neil's horse whinnied and shook its head. It, too, sensed something was wrong.

Ewan peered into the mist. "How can you hear anything in this soup?"

"Quick, we must hide!"

Ewan looked behind him. "Perhaps 'tis only jitters about—"

But Neil had already slipped from his mount and was leading it into the fog-shrouded trees.

"My lord," Ewan whispered, following, hurrying to catch up, "I do not see—"

"Ssshhh." Neil stopped when the mist swallowed the trees on the trail's far side. An icy breeze seemed to slip under his tunic and caress his skin. Yet the air was still.

The stallion's eyes were now wide with fear. Neil gripped its muzzle and petted it.

Ewan grabbed the muzzle of his own mount, also uneasy, and tried to calm it. From the look in Ewan's eyes he, too, now felt whatever was coming—something unnatural? From the Otherworld?

Muffled hooves padded down the trail. Neil stared through the soup. Two figures atop black horses appeared as shadows in the fog. But they had stopped too close to the path. Were he and Ewan still visible? The first figure halted his mount, lifted a nose to the air, and pivoted in Neil's direction.

The body held the shape of a man. But the face! It was that of a beast. With a long, furred muzzle and black nose. The same kind of creature Neil had seen on the trail out of Hidden Pines. Then it sniffed.

"Púcas," Ewan whispered. "Shapeshifters!"

"Get along, now!" came a sharp voice from behind the creatures. "Our quarry lies ahead." Riding into view was a tall man on a horse. A gray cape covered his body. A hood hid his face. The timbre of his speech was cold, powerful, slightly tinged with an accent Neil had never before heard. And it bore disdain for the servants he commanded. Neil shivered again.

Facing the trail, the creatures spurred their horses. All three moved on.

For some moments, Neil and Ewan waited in silence. Ewan's eyes were wide as he turned to Neil. "I thought I'd never see another of those things. I thought they preferred the dark, would never come out during the day? Maybe the fog—"

But he fell silent as another figure appeared on the trail behind the first three. A tall man riding a black gelding. Dark cape. Heavy brown beard.

"Machar," said Ewan. He started leading his mount toward the trail. Neil followed.

At the sound of Ewan brushing aside leafy saplings, Machar's sword sprang from its sheath with blinding speed. He whirled his mount to face them. But when the tall lord saw who approached, he sheathed his blade. "Glad I am that you two got out of their way."

"How did you ken they were following us?" Ewan nodded toward the trail.

"I heard rumors of strange folk about. So I waited and followed you at a distance. Neil, we can't let you face danger alone. You're too important."

Neil nodded, for a moment not really believing it. But then, he realized Machar was right.

Ewan patted his horse's neck to calm it then mounted.

Machar shook his head. "Somehow the enemy has learned of the council's plans. This is not good."

"What about the rest of the Company?" Neil mounted his horse. "They're right in the path of those things."

"We must warn them." Machar was already kicking his mount. "We can't let them be surprised. Sure, and 'tis a most inauspicious start to our expedition."

As Machar led, Neil and Ewan rode behind. But all the way, Neil rested his hand on his sword's pommel. For the next league, he scanned the fog, expecting at any moment to repel an attack.

Soon the trail climbed a hill. As they ascended from the valley, the mist began to dissipate and the sun to shine between gaps in the clouds. Then all the path to the hilltop became visible. Above them, atop Artair's Ridge, waited the rest of the Company.

The púcas and their leader were nowhere to be seen.

"Where did they go?" Neil surveyed the trees on either side. The only open space was the trail. Deep forest claimed the slopes on either side.

Machar shrugged.

Behind them came a new sound—the thundering of many hooves.

"What's that?" Neil shifted in the saddle and glanced back. There, fog still shrouded the trail, but he saw nothing.

"The King's Riders! We must climb." Machar kicked his horse and began climbing in earnest. "Perhaps 'tis why the púcas hid. Their hearing is more acute than ours."

"Now we're in for it." Ewan spurred his mount. "First changelings. Then the King's Riders. Can anything else go wrong?"

Neil followed, wondering the same thing.

On the hilltop, they dismounted and met the others. Leather creaked, scabbards clanged against leggings, and chainmail crinkled as the two groups joined.

"'Tis some beginning, Dermid." Machar tied his horse to a bush up the slope, as did the others. "I suppose you've heard the riders?"

"Aye. And here they come now."

Everyone peered at the trail below. When the king's men emerged from the valley fog, Neil counted thirty soldiers. Eacharn, the captain of the guards, led them.

"My lords, here's the situation." Dermid stepped out in front. "If we travel on, they'll be catching us well before we reach Áth Cliath. And on their terms. But here on this hilltop? 'Tis a good position. I say we stand and fight."

"Seven against thirty, my lord?" Ewan fingered his bow. "Can we do it?"

"We have the high ground. Just before the summit, the trail narrows. Up here, they can only send two at a time against us."

"Then let them come." Machar drew his sword. "We've little need for secrecy now. And if 'tis blood they want, then 'tis blood they'll get."

"Aye." Finnean nocked an arrow to his bow. "I can drop three or four before the first one strikes a blow."

Luag, the sprite, rammed the butt of his axe on the ground. "Bring them on. Me blade awaits."

"If it comes to it"—Neil drew his sword—"my blade is also in the fight." But the blood was pounding in his ears. He'd never been in a real battle, and the King's Riders looked like veterans, all.

Dermid watched the advancing soldiers. "Good. But it may not come to that. Let me talk with Eacharn first."

"Talk?" Camran slammed down the head of his axe, sending rock chips flying. He leaned against the handle and spat a good three feet away. "What use is talk? Let me sever a few heads first. Then we'll talk."

Dermid shook his head and raised his hand. He told Ewan and Finnean not to shoot until he gave the word. When the King's Riders were within a hundred feet, Dermid rode down the hill and met them halfway.

Eacharn halted his men. The large man filled his chain mail to bursting. His brown mustache hung down below his chin, and his bushy eyebrows rose halfway up his forehead.

"Nice morning for a ride, no?" Dermid leaned forward in his saddle, then back.

"You ken why we're here, Dermid. I've orders to bring you back to Ewhain Macha. Or—"

"Or what, Eacharn? You'd spill the blood of your second cousin because *Corc* said to?"

"'Twas my lord, the Ard Righ, who gave the order." Eacharn's eyebrows dipped in a frown.

"And 'twas Corc, that weasel, who whispered in the king's ear to make him do it. The druid's poisoned his reason and sense. If this continues, he'll bring all the flaith down upon the throne in blood and anger."

"I'm not here to discuss the druid or his advice." Eacharn looked up the trail toward the Company, paused, and then frowned. "'Tis not me affair."

"Do you not ken what we're doing here, man? We're trying to save the kingdom."

"I ken nothing of that. I've me orders."

"And if you carry them out, we'll have to cut you down. We've two archers, a fierce axman, an eager sprite with a broad axe, and three swordsmen, including Neil mac Connell, the best in the land. Perhaps half of you will live to walk away today. Perhaps some of us. And for what?"

Eacharn's forehead creased so his eyebrows nearly touched. "For duty."

"We're on an important mission, Eacharn. I suppose it matters not who knows about it now. We've been sent by the highest flaith in Ériu, by a gathering of leaders from every kingdom, and we're to bring back the Scepter and save this land. 'Tis our only hope."

Eacharn's eyes widened. "The Scepter? But 'tis only . . . myth."

"Nay, 'tis real, and we ken where it is. But the chances of finding it, of defeating the evil protecting it, and returning alive . . ." Dermid spread his hands in appeal.

"The Scepter . . ." Eacharn stared at the ground and scratched his head. "I didna ken."

"Aye, and we presented the affair to the king and his chief druid in court, but they wouldna bless our mission. Corc seems bent on destroying us. Do you really want to spill blood over this? Do you want to fight the prince, the king's very son, over this? Let us go in peace."

"What would I tell Corc?"

"That you lost our trail. That we took the southern route to Menapia, not to Áth Cliath."

"A good story, that. I ken I could convince me men of it."

"I hear The Merry Bull now brews some of the best beer in Ulster. 'Tis only a short ride south on the Menapia road."

A smile raised Eacharn's lips and mustache. "A plan more to me liking this fine sunny morn than spilling the blood of kin and the king's own son." He stretched out his hand. "Aye, there's much sense in it. May the gods go with you, Dermid. Both with you and your company."

"'Tis for Elyon we ride, Eacharn, not for the gods of the druids. Aye, he exists. And 'tis *his* Scepter we seek." Dermid reached across, and the two shook hands.

Eacharn returned to his men and conversed with them for a time. Then the captain led the group back down the hill. As they left, smiles brightened many of their faces. Probably at thought of an afternoon at The Merry Bull.

"My mouth hangs agape, and I stand in awe." Finnean smiled. "My lord could fain talk the teeth from a saw."

"Well done." Machar sheathed his sword. "But we need to ride. Just before the King's Riders showed up, two púcas and their leader were following Neil. They must have heard the sound of the hooves and vanished into the forest. But certain it is, they'll soon be back on our trail."

"Trouble and more." Camran frowned.

"And we havena even left Ulster." Dermid mounted as did the others. "But, lads, we've a ship waiting for us at Áth Cliath. So let us ride."

CHAPTER 16

THE INN

All that day they rode fast, pausing only to rest the horses and eat. Neil's constant companion was the clopping of horses' hooves, the rustling of leather, the crinkling of chainmail. They traveled through hamlets big and small, plunging deep through forests of oak, ash, and birch, then emerging on the western banks of the River Liffey.

They rode hard until, by late afternoon, a wide, grassy plain spread out before them. Another trail led west. Beyond, the wide expanse of a second river blocked their way.

Ewan waved a hand to the plain, to the River Liffey in the east, and to the Blackwater River in the south. "'Twas here, my lord Neil, that The Battle of Two Rivers was fought."

Neil nodded. Many times before he'd traveled here, for the western trail led to Hidden Pines, only half a day's hike distant. And whenever he'd passed this way, a shivering unease had always touched him, as if some dark secret hovered about the place. Until today, he'd never understood why.

Now, with Cairbre's explanation, he knew the reason for his disquiet. Now, the sense of history, of the great events of the past, whelmed up before him like an Otherworld spirit on Samhain eve. For here, long, long ago, is where the army of Ériu fell to the forces of the Deamhan Lord. On this very spot, darkness had overcome the light. Evil had defeated the good. And the Dark Eras had begun.

This time of year, no one could ford the Blackwater, so Dermid paid the ferryman the going price for passage. Then they floated across on the barge, the broad waters swirling and crashing against the logs. For many more coins, the boatman agreed to park his craft on their side and not cross again until the next midmorning, thus giving them a good head start.

Their camp overlooked the river, and all night Neil smelled the muddy banks. Even though the river should have kept them safe, he wondered if púcas could swim, if somehow he would waken with wolf-fangs at his throat. But the night was uneventful.

They woke early and rode hard again through the next day.

The sun was low as they trotted into the busy port town of Áth Cliath in the kingdom of Leinster. Dermid left them, saying he must go to the docks and check on the readiness of the curragh that would take them to the Netherwelt. Neil followed the rest as they ambled along the dockside row of tall houses and inns, stepping around sailors filling holds with bales of wool, bundled leather goods, crates of iron tools, and barrels of ale bound for Armorica, Esperandula, Rijkshavn, even far northern Hrímland where the snow didn't melt until late summer. Nearly two dozen oceangoing vessels hugged the dock and piers reaching out into the harbor. Permeating the air was the smell of the salt sea, tarred timbers, fish piled in crates on the docks. And from the open doors of the dockside inns, pipe smoke, fish chowder, and ale.

As instructed, they took two rooms at The Pipe And Mug, only two streets from the water. Much later when Dermid returned, they convened downstairs for supper.

After three days' ride, Neil welcomed the cozy warmth of the room's central fire, the sound of mugs clinking, men laughing and talking, the smells of baking bread and frying fish. He sat with the other six at a large table by the wall. Serving girls brought them each a tall mug of beer with a foamy head, a hunk of fresh bread with a slab of butter, and a wooden bowl brimming with fish, clams, onions, and cream. They attacked the food with gusto.

A man in the far corner produced a small harp and plucked a rapid dancing song. Another beside him played a violin with such quick changes of notes, the entire room seemed to come alive. A bodhrán joined in, and Neil's foot began tapping in time to the music.

"Our ship is *The Fair Winds*," Dermid said between mouthfuls above the music. "She's a fine, two-masted curragh. Seventy feet of Celtic craftsmanship. We leave on the early-morning tide."

"How long a journey?" Ewan lowered his mug.

"About ten days with a fair wind." A rare smile broke Dermid's features. "That was a pun."

Ewan smiled. "What about the horses?"

"Canna take them. There's little room on board. She's only got two holds, both filled with cargo."

For a time, they ate in silence until Dermid set his mug down. "But an uncommon vessel on our jetty troubles me. A ship of no origin I can determine. Wooden-hulled. Black-sailed. 'Tis docked near ours."

"Why be troubled, my lord?" Camran lifted one eyebrow. "Áth Cliath harbors many a vessel from distant parts."

"I didna like the look of her crew. Or the interest they took in my conversation with Captain Blàthan."

"You see trouble on every corner, Dermid." Camran waved a hand in dismissal and swilled another draught of beer.

Machar scowled at the tabletop and scratched his beard.

At that moment, a woman's voice called from across the room. "*Tristan*. Hey, Tristan!"

Neil looked up, the blood rushing to his face. Caitir! What was *she* doing here? He shot out of his seat and shook his head for her to be silent. But either she didn't understand, or she was ignoring him.

The others gave him questioning looks.

Finnean smirked and remarked to the others. "I guess a false name lays a false trail for an angry husband, no?"

Laughter and smirks.

"She's a comely wench, I do say." Camran tapped his mug on the table, spilling some over the top. "Leave it to our Neil to pick the fairest.

And perhaps she's quick under the furs, hey my lord?" He gave Neil a wink.

More snickers from around the table. But no humor touched Machar's face.

Caitir crossed the room and stood beside the group, smiling. "What a surprise, Tristan. And look at you and the company you're keeping."

Neil quickly put his lips to her ear and whispered. "I'm *Neil*, Caitir. Call me *Neil*. Remember, I'm now a prince of Ulster."

Caitir smiled and said loud enough for all to hear, "Silly me. I forgot the lad wants me to call him Neil. Can I join you men for supper?"

Neil motioned to a seat beside him, and she sat. "This is Caitir, a serving wench I met in Hidden Pines."

Caitir kicked him under the table. Neil shot her a frowning glance and kicked her back.

A real serving girl passed, and he ordered another bowl of chowder and bread for Caitir. "Where's Cathal?"

"Father went to bed early. Said the trip had worn him out. We've sold one wagon full and might have a buyer for the second." To the others, she added, "Father's a cooper. I'm helping him bring his barrels to market."

Caitir's glance went round the table. But when she saw the sprite, her eyes widened. "You're a . . . a lehbrágan?"

"Aye, lassie." Luag grinned and tipped his head, but so little of him showed above the tabletop, his beard landed in his chowder. "That's what we call ourselves." He wiped his beard with a piece of bread.

"Will someone introduce me, or are your names a secret?"

"She's forward, she is." Finnean winked at Neil.

Dermid nodded, and with this permission, one by one they gave their names and titles.

"High flaith all and me just a peasant girl. What kind of gathering draws my Neil so far away, if I may ask?" She scanned the circle, smiling.

Dermid frowned. "'Tis not for young maidens to know. I *can* tell you we've a ship waiting to take us tomorrow to Ereb. So tonight, you can tell your Neil goodbye."

Ewan was sitting beside Neil, and now he whispered in Neil's ear. Neil nodded.

"So 'tis a secret mission you'll be—"

Quickly, Neil leaned over and planted his lips on hers. To his great surprise, she returned the kiss. It lingered.

When they parted, Neil whispered in her ear, "That's quite enough. Remember, you're just a serving wench who's made hanky-panky with a prince."

He pulled apart, and she stared at him. But her eyes narrowed.

Luag grinned.

Finnean winked. "And does Caitir of the village so piney serve one husband or many?"

"I'm unwed, my lord, if that's what your rhyme implies. I just serve the men when they come through." She glanced at Neil, and a sly smile crossed her face. "In whatever way they want."

Neil looked to Finnean while Neil's left foot kicked her leg again. "She's just serves tables. She exaggerates."

"Would the lassie's fair father be happy or madder"—Finnean's grin was wide—"to see you together, like birds of a feather?"

She faced Dermid, one eyebrow raised. "Does he always speak thus?"

Dermid raised an eyebrow at Finnean. "I fear 'tis our curse, lass."

She again faced Finnean. "My father doesna care for our courtship but says nothing. Well does he ken Tri—I mean Neil. We've known each other forever. Isn't that right—Neil?"

"'Tis true. I've been stopping in Hidden Pines ever since that first time." Neil scratched his chin. "Has it been six years, Caitir?"

"Aye, it has." She put a hand on his. "And in that time we've grown quite fond of each other."

"Why, you were barely a man then." Dermid smiled. "And you've been seeing this young lass all that time? This is indeed a surprise. But how would the Ard Righ feel about marriage between flaith and commoner."

Neil shook his head. How *would* the king feel? Somehow, he needed to silence her. This conversation was heading into dangerous territory. "No one's talking marriage. We're just . . . casual friends."

Again, she narrowed her eyes at him and nodded. "Aye. Only casual."

Then silence gripped the room. The musicians stopped playing. The men by the fire, the patrons at the tables beside them, even the serving girls—all stopped what they were doing and gazed toward the entrance. In the open doorway stood a tall man in a gray cape.

A coldness, like an icy wind off the moors in winter, swept past him, chilling Neil's back and legs.

The Company shifted in their seats to behold what manner of person could cause such a stir.

The man's beard dropped, long and thin, to his chest. A cowl hid much of his face. As he strolled along the room's edge, the black of night seemed to follow him. At a small corner table, he stopped before two old men sipping beers. Without a word, they grabbed their mugs and hurried to another spot. The man sat, pulled out a pipe, and slowly—as if nothing else in the world mattered—stuffed it. Then he lit it.

"Strange character, that one." Dermid waved a hand toward him.

Machar frowned. "He's looking in our direction. If I'm not mistaken, that's a robe of the druids of Sarkenos. See the red quarter moon on the sleeve?"

Quarter moon? Neil's gaze fixed on the man. Was he imagining it or was the stranger staring at him?

"Ignore him." Camran took another swig from his mug. "Many are the strange characters who pass through Áth Cliath."

"Could that be the same man we saw with the púcas on the trail?" whispered Neil to Machar.

Machar squinted at the man then lowered his glance to his mug. "If so, then we're in for a heap of trouble."

Gradually, the ambient conversations began again. The musicians returned to their instruments, filling the air with sound—but now muted, hesitant, without their previous zeal.

Neil's glance remained fixed on the druid. A sudden urge to touch the pendant gripped him. His right hand reached into his pocket. His fingers worked the chain, drawing the crescent moon up toward his palm, then—

What was he doing? The compulsion to touch it wasn't his own. He jerked his hand out of the pocket as if bitten.

"Is something wrong?" Caitir touched his arm.

"Nay. Nothing." He dug his fingers into his palms. He wouldn't hold the thing. Nay, he wouldn't, mustn't. Somewhere, he must find a forge and remold it. And soon.

The gray-caped druid laid a hand on a passing serving girl who carried a tray of mugs. She started, almost dropped the tray. She looked down. Then cautiously, she lifted a mug from her platter and laid it before him. The druid took it and his pipe. Then he stood and began walking toward them.

"Nay, nay. He's coming here." Caitir's gaze fell to the table. "Now what do we do?"

Machar whispered, almost to himself, "Nothing good can come of this."

As he approached, the others turned in their seats. Now Neil had a good look at the man's face. Long and thin like his beard, it held no emotion. Cold as stone. A thin white scar ran along his right cheek and under the beard. Before anyone could object, he sat in the empty place between Camran and Neil.

Neil shuddered. It was as if icy fingers were sliding down his back. This was the same feeling he'd had on the trail. Only far stronger. Who *was* this man?

"Far from home we travel, Machar mac Maon and Dermid mac Duff." Cold as his face, the man's voice sent tremors over Neil's skin. "What brings such high flaith together so far from keep and hearth?"

"And how does a stranger ken our names?" Dermid's face tensed, appeared hard as stone.

"Who doesn't know the names of such illustrious nobility? And of their comings and goings in secret forest gatherings."

Everyone stared at him in silence. No one moved. Neil's arm muscles tensed.

"'Tis not for strangers to remark on the private affairs of others." Machar fixed an unflinching gaze on the man.

"And how do you ken our comings and goings?" Dermid's hands gripped his mug as if he were about to strangle it.

"Ah, but let me introduce myself. Then no stranger will I be. My name is Faolukan." He paused and searched each of their eyes.

Machar, usually unflappable, seemed stunned. His mouth opened, but no words came out.

Dermid, too, appeared dumbstruck. White knuckles clenched his mug. His face lost its color.

A coldness swept over Neil, even though his heart was beating fast. Too fast.

At the council, Cairbre said this man had been "awakened" with The Deamhan Lord, that he was the Deamhan Lord's ally. And that he'd lived in eras long past. Again, the icy fingers played havoc with Neil's back and shoulders. He wanted to flee from the table and run.

A smile flitted across the man's lips, and he went on. "Some call me 'Faolukan the Grim', but that is their appellation, not mine. My enemies make too much of my past. Did you know, my lords, that I'm fond of dogs? So how can any man who likes dogs be called grim?" Again, his glance searched each of theirs.

Finally, Machar spoke. "What do you want, druid?" His jaw was set, and his hands had formed fists on the tabletop.

"Why, I want you to turn back. To give up your foolish undertaking. Return to your homes in peace. For if you cross the Sea of Albion and set foot in the Netherwelt, they will be the last steps you ever take."

Strangely, his words wormed their way into Neil's mind, to find a place where they seemed reasonable, right, and wise. He *wanted* to believe what the man said. Didn't the man like dogs? Maybe he wasn't as evil as the stories said? Aye, they *should* turn back. But another part of him said, nay, such thinking was wrong. He shook his head.

Again, the desire to hold the pendant washed over him. He dug his fingernails into his palm and fought it.

"No one"—Machar's fists clenched and unclenched—"no one tells the flaith of Ériu whither or when their feet will trod."

"Nay, for surely you are a proud and stubborn race." The corners of Faolukan's mouth dipped in a frown. "I know because once I was one of you. Long ago, your race treated me unjustly, for something so trivial, I—" He stopped in mid-sentence, his jaws tensing. Moments later, he went on. "But I do not ask my favor without offering something in return. Instead of the foolish trinket you seek"—he opened his free hand, palm upward—"I can give each of you more than you ever dreamed.

"You, Camran mac Blàr, haven't you always wanted to replace your father and become rí cóicid over all Munster? Well, this I can grant you. And you, Finnean mac Friseal, I can make you king of Meath."

He puffed on the pipe, sent a few smoke rings across the table. "Dermid and Machar, you wish to depose Connell and replace him. I can give you each your own kingdom and put Neil here on the throne of Ulster as Ard Righ. Would that not also please you, Neil? You tire of your father's rule, do you not? With my help, an endless stream of women, wine, and merrymaking will come your way."

Then he faced the sprite. "Luag mac Laise, join me, and for the first time ever, your people will receive their own lands and houses. Indeed, I will give you the castles of all who reject my offer, with new lands in a new kingdom and slaves over which to rule."

Even as he spoke, Faolukan's words appeared to Neil reasonable, generous, and worth considering. He looked to the others, and they, too, with the exception of Dermid and Machar, were smiling dumbly, nodding their heads. But something gnawed at the back of his mind, warning him to beware.

"And with everything I grant comes this promise—you will never die. None of you. Through the power of my master, I can give you life on Erde without end." He paused, sent more smoke rings toward the ceiling. "And what, you ask, must you do to receive all this?

"The answer is simple. Take the easy path. The sane path. Turn back now. Turn back and pledge to serve my master. The world will be better when all are ruled under one kingdom, one master. This I believe with all my heart. Finally, there will be peace on Erde. An everlasting peace. Know that I make this offer to no others. Only to those here assembled. Do not refuse it lightly."

Silence swept the table. Neil felt his heart pounding. He'd heard the words, and at first, they sounded reasonable, but now all he wanted to do was run for the door.

"Rí cóicid over Munster?" As Camran spoke, a glint lit his eyes. "And you would depose Connell and his druid?"

"The druid Corc would remain in Neil's service, but as to the rest—aye."

Camran nodded and peered into his mug, a hint of a smile turning his lips.

"My people would have their own lands?" Luag's eyes, just visible over the tabletop, brightened.

"That is my offer."

Machar slammed his mug down hard. Beer spilled over his side of the table. "Your words are poison. And your promises cheap." Neil woke from the spell the man's speech had cast. Machar gazed at each of his companions in turn. "Have you all forgotten our mission? Are you so easily swayed by this druid's cheap word spell? We turn aside for no man—if that's what he is anymore—or for his treacherous promises."

"Listen, Machar of Connacht." Faolukan's eyes narrowed to dark slits, and his voice, so pleasant and soothing a moment before, suddenly grated harsh, cold, and terrible. The icy fingers on Neil's skin dug deeper. "You—all of you—are infants in this world. You know nothing of what lies across the sea or the terrors that await beyond, terrors that answer to me and my master. I hold the powers of an arch druid. The wind, the rain, the forests, and the swamps answer to my command. Even the trees bow to my spells. I give you fair warning—go home now, while you can. Turn back and serve my master."

Machar stared at him, his face set. "You keep speaking of your master. Name him!"

"When Erde was born, my lord was there. He answers to no one and refuses to bow to the Enemy. For this, we were both imprisoned. For a time he slept under the sands of Sarkenos, and I with him. But never again will we let another servant of the Enemy entomb us.

"My master's power never died, but it reached out from his tomb until he drew to himself the one who finally freed us.

"Thus does Crom Mord live again, called the Deamhan Lord by some. As was foretold, he now rules Cathair Duvh in Drochtar. He is my master, and I serve him with my life. If you resist and reject my offer, our armies will lay waste your towns, destroy your castles and your fortresses. We won't stop until your lifeless bodies lie crushed and bleeding beneath our boots. And all you hold dear will lie smoking in a ruin of ashes."

The muscles on Machar's face tightened. He pushed back from the table, nearly knocking Finnean and the others off the bench. His sword left its sheath.

Dermid, too, drew his sword, and he rose, as did the entire Company.

With deliberation, pressing his left hand against the tabletop, Faolukan stood. The room grew cold. The musicians stopped playing. The men by the wall stopped talking and sipping their beer. Everyone in the room now gazed toward the eight and Faolukan. Even the fire, so warm and bright only moments ago, cooled and dimmed. The dark of night gathered about the druid, spread out in a chilling, grim circle. "You don't want to start anything here. Look toward the door."

Neil turned his head. Two men had entered the inn and now stood silently by the entrance. But their faces were odd. Wide, bony foreheads. Thick noses. Jutting cheekbones.

Púcas!

Machar saw the men, but his hand never left his swordhilt. "All right, then. We've heard your threats. We see your abominations. Now away with you! Go chase yourselves off!"

Still holding his pipe, Faolukan took a few puffs, then leaned over and knocked the still-glowing ashes onto the wood of the tabletop. He gave Machar a lazy glance. "I confess, it makes no difference to me what you decide. To bestow lands, titles, even immortality—this I would have done, but grudgingly, I admit. Now I suppose I can look forward to the terrors and dangers I can bring upon you when you enter the lands under my control. Alas, it would have been easier the other way." He stuffed the pipe in a pocket. "But you've made your choice, haven't you?"

He flashed them another cold smile that vanished as soon as it curled his lips. Giving them his back, he strode across the room, through the door, and out into the night. The púcas followed.

The fire's warmth returned. Slowly, the music began again. The old men shook their heads, faced away from the door, and again sipped their beers. And the seven, along with Caitir, again took their seats. But now in a stunned silence.

Ewan poured beer on the glowing ashes left behind by Faolukan's pipe.

Machar lifted his gaze to the ceiling, opened his hands, and spoke. "O Elyon, we haven't even left Ériu, and the greatest enemy of all time now stands against us. Help us, for Faolukan himself has risen from his tomb."

PART III

CHAPTER 17

AT SEA

After Machar prayed, he dismissed the silent group to their rooms upstairs, saying they must leave well before dawn. Once the others had gone, Neil lingered with Caitir while mustachioed men talked in low tones, mugs clinked at nearby tables, and worried glances swept their way.

"Tristan, what kind of trouble have you gotten yourself into?"

"I fear the worst kind. But the mission we're on is more important than anything I've ever done. They're all depending on me, and I can't let them down."

Still sitting beside him, she smiled, laid a hand on his. "You're nothing if not honorable. Regardless of what they say in Hidden Pines. I ken you'll do well. But that man Faolukan—" She shuddered, unable to finish.

"'Tis troubling, nay?"

"Still, you're going on an adventure. And I'd like to go with you."

"'Tis not possible. The men would never have it. And I'd be worrying about your safety all the time."

Caitir stared long into his eyes. Without warning, she leaned toward him. He didn't move, let her come close, and then her lips were pressing onto his. The kiss was even longer than the one he'd used to quiet her earlier.

"Before today, Tristan, we've never kissed." She breathed heavily as they parted. "I rather like it."

"I know." He felt his face getting hot, his heart beating faster. "So did I."

"We've always been just friends, you and I. I suppose that's the way it will always be."

Neil dropped his glance to the table. "I . . . I don't know. I'll be gone for a long time. Let's figure it out when I return."

She peered into his eyes without smiling. "I wish I were going with you."

He shook his head.

"What a grand adventure you'll be having. And you men keep it all for yourselves."

Neil smiled. "Wish me luck, Caitir. And a safe journey. We've made a terrible enemy tonight."

"I ken he was your enemy even before you left Hidden Pines." She stood, crossed the floor, gave him one, final parting smile, and then climbed the stairs to her father's room.

He sat for a few moments at the table, nursing his beer. Caitir was right. Faolukan was the worst enemy anyone could imagine. He even knew their mission and their names.

Neil shuddered, took a last sip, and then headed to his room.

In a moonless night as black as tar, Neil joined the others at the end of a pier. There a ship squeaked and groaned against its pilings while a cluster of hanging lanterns creaked side to side and lit the deck. He crossed the gangway, descended to the deck of *The Fair Winds*, and sat on plank benches with the other six.

He stopped a passing sailor and pointed at the empty mooring beside their curragh. "What ship was docked there, lad?"

"My lord, 'twas a black-sailed vessel. No name did they give her. She left at midnight, and sore glad was I to see her gone. Gave everyone the willies, that vessel."

Neil nodded. Surely, it was Faolukan's. And it had sailed ahead of them.

A deep voice boomed across the deck. "Heave to, lads. Let's get her away 'fore we lose the tide." Neil shifted in his seat to look upon a heavy, red-bearded man who must be Captain Blàthan. The captain stood with arms folded on the raised afterdeck. Its platform sheltered the aft hold beneath. Neil looked toward the bow. The foredeck, too, was raised about five feet, under which lay another hold. The holds carried barrels of ale, salt, bundled leather goods, even timber.

Men let go the ties and, using long oars, pushed *The Fair Winds* from the dock. Already the outgoing tide helped carry the vessel from the pier. A clatter arose as the oars were stowed.

"Half sail on the main," bellowed the captain. Four sailors clambered up shrouds to let down flapping canvas. The breeze caught and—snap, it was full. Faster now, they pulled away from the wharf. The ropes vibrated, the masts creaked, and the sea slapped and swished against the hull. Behind them, the few lights from the harbor disappeared. The wind picked up. On their left, they passed a warning fire from the Howth Peninsula. Leaving the harbor's protection, the curragh now rose and dropped on light swells. The captain called for full sail on the main and mizzen. Soon, they were racing over the waves.

A dark sea crashed by on either side. The further from shore they went, the stronger became the wind, the larger the swells. Slowly, up and down, moved the deck. Ewan rushed to the railing and became ill over the side. Dermid followed. Suddenly, Neil felt his stomach churning. He, too, ran to the rail and lost most of the night's meal.

Beside him, Ewan hung his head over the railing. "No one told me about this part of the adventure."

Neil's answer was to join him at the rail with his head also over the side.

Soon all the travelers but Machar were ill. "It'll pass," Machar called from his seat with an amused expression. "You'll soon be seafaring lads, all."

Neil hoped it was true. He heaved again.

Not long after, the day dawned gray and windy. Whitecaps filled the sea to the horizon, and Neil felt no better. To greet the morning, sailors brought them food and ale, but a single glance sent him groaning and rushing again to the railing.

Dermid was already there. "'Tis my third sea journey and no better this time."

Neil lifted his glance to a dark rise on the horizon. "The Wicklow Mountains?"

"Aye, 'tis the last we'll see of Ériu for a while. The captain said we'll be heading east before noon."

He gripped the rail and stared at a distant bare peak, glinting from a sun poking momentarily through the clouds. "Will we ever return, Dermid? Will we ever see our homes again?"

The older man put a hand on his shoulder. "Aye, my lord. We will because we must. Sure, and when we find the Scepter, we'll be bringing it back to its rightful place. And if what Cairbre says is true, it will return your father to the man he once was. And Ériu will return to a time long before we were born, when it was the hope of all Erde."

Neil hoped it was true. Staring at the distant mountains seemed to calm his stomach. He returned to the bench, curled up in a ball, and slept.

All the rest of that day, they sailed before a strong west wind and made good time. As predicted, their course led them east, leaving behind all sight of land. Neil slept most of the time.

At first light on the second morning, Neil woke feeling much better. He stood on deck, swayed with the swells, heard the creaking hull, watched the horizon, and realized his nausea was gone. Did he now have what they called his *sea legs*? When they brought the morning meal, he devoured it like a starving man. Better yet, he kept it down.

"The wind's changing, lads." The captain leaned over the rail, squinting to the southwest where clouds gathered. "Let out sail for a broad reach and a southwest wind."

Sailors on either side answered by loosening the sheets, giving more canvas to the wind.

As the day progressed, the seas became heavier. The hull crashed through the waves, shooting spray to either side. Sitting in center deck, the Company was protected from its wash. But Neil seemed always wet from a constant mist borne on the wind. All day they made good progress to the southeast. All but Camran had recovered from the seasickness.

On the morning of the third day as Neil was eating bacon and hardtack—the fresh bread was already gone—a commotion arose behind him.

"Here now, come out of there." The voice belonged to one of the sailors.

"A stowaway," shouted another. "A dratted woman!"

"Bad luck, that," cried someone ahead of Neil. "Never did a woman come aboard but trouble follows."

Neil stood and faced the shouting.

"And sure," came a familiar voice, "you'll be taking your hands off me if you do not want my knife to remove them for you."

Caitir! It was Caitir, and one of the sailors held both her arms as if she was going to escape. Caitir kicked him in the shins. He cried out, stepped back, and swore.

Neil walked quickly back just as Captain Blàthan arrived. "And who is it who's stowed away on me ship without passage or permission?"

"My name's Caitir nic Cathal." She looked up to see Neil. She waved a hand toward him. "And I'm with him."

The captain eyed Neil then Caitir. "Is this true, my lord? Is she with your party?"

"I fear 'tis true, captain. She was asked to stay on shore, but as you can see . . ."

Blàthan frowned and put his hands on his hips. "Well, we've no choice, do we? Until we reach the Netherwelt, lass, you'll sit with the others. On shore, they can decide what to do with you. Sure, and now I'm owed for another passenger." He turned away, muttering. "And now bad tidings will surely follow."

Caitir leaned down to pick up her traveling bag, bow, and quiver. She answered Neil's frown with a broad smile.

"What are you doing here, Caitir?"

"I'm going with you on your journey."

Neil shook his head.

"You say nay, but am I not already on it?"

Dermid and Machar came up beside them.

Finnean smiled and said, "Women's light charm can bring men to great harm."

Dermid glared first at Finnean then at Caitir. "Lass, I do not ken what you think you're doing. But at Drijvendby, you'll be returning to Ériu on the first available curragh."

Caitir smiled and stood where she was with arms akimbo.

"Do you ken, lass?"

She nodded ever so briefly, the smile only faltering a wee bit.

Dermid faced Neil. "She's here because of you. When we reach port, you'll make sure she returns. This is not a journey for women!"

Neil nodded.

Dermid headed toward his seat. Machar stifled a smile, gave Neil a wink, and followed.

Just then, Camran said, loud enough so everyone could hear, "How is it a drunk and a womanizer is the Toghaí who meets the signs. I do not ken such a thing. He brings along his wench, and now, mark my words, bad luck will be upon us all."

"Don't mind him." Neil stared at her. "But you shouldn't have come."

She looked down at her feet then up into his eyes, still smiling.

Now the corners of his mouth slowly rose in an answering smile. He put a hand on her shoulder. "You're quite the lass, you know that, Caitir? But what did you tell your father? He'll be worried to death."

"I left him a note. He was sleeping so soundly, he wouldna notice a thing until daylight. By then, I figured, we'd already be far out to sea."

"Well, your grand adventure will be to Drijvendby and back. But weren't you seasick in that hold? On deck I certainly was."

"A wee bit, but I just slept. Last night I ate the last of my food. Today it was time to come out."

"Then let's get you breakfast." And thus saying, he led her to a seat beside him.

When Ewan saw her, he shook his head. "Lass, you've some pluck, following us here. But you ken you canna go where we're going?"

"So they tell me."

When they brought hardtack biscuits, salt pork, and beer, she ate and drank her fill.

The next day a wall of black mist arose from the sea in the east. As far as Neil could see did it stretch—one long black wall rising at least a hundred feet from the waves in all directions. He stood at the rail, staring, while the hull creaked and whitecaps rolled on, crashing against it, sending spray high into the air.

"Beyond the mist lies the country of Albion." Dermid waved a hand over the railing. "From before anyone can remember, the black mist has guarded its borders. 'Tis said nary a ship can cross that misty veil and survive. In a time long gone, the black haze arose suddenly, blocking all travel in or out. No one kens what lies beyond. But we assume 'tis a great evil, possibly as great as the Deamhan Lord himself." Dermid wiped a hand across his brow.

"My friends, this world holds many mysteries. Some of them we'd just as soon not delve into. We've enough trouble as it is." Dermid shuddered. "As for us, we'll be sailing due east. Far to the south sits Armorica and the lands of Ereb."

"How long a trip do we have?" Caitir came up beside Neil.

"Eight or nine days left, if the wind holds." Dermid looked to the aft deck. "The captain says we've two weeks' provisions. More than enough, even in bad weather."

All that day they sailed steadily eastward in a choppy sea. When the wind turned and came from the west, they ran full sail before it.

Then in early afternoon, the lookout in the mainmast crow's nest gave a startled cry. "On the port bow. What comes? O Danu, save us!"

Neil rushed with half the men to the rail and looked at the sea ahead. Not two hundred yards distant, a black, curved neck carrying the head of some large creature streamed through the water in their direction. Behind, it left a wake of churning water. It was coming on fast.

"What is it?" Beside him, Dermid squinted at the thing.

Suddenly, it dove, and a massive body slid under the waves, trailing a long, black tail. From this distance, Neil couldn't guess its length, only that it was big. Very big. Then it was gone.

They stood at the rail, watching, waiting.

Then its head burst out of the sea, followed by an enormous black mass, two huge flippers on either side. In the few moments it swam under water, it had traveled far. Neil got a better look at it.

Its massive body was nearly seventy feet long, and the waves slid over serrated fins down its back. A tall, curved neck reached twenty feet in the air, supporting a head as wide as the largest barrel. On each side, two huge paddle fins dug into the waves and propelled it forward.

"Oh, Neavh and Ifreann, what's to become of us?" said a sailor at the rail.

"'Twas the woman, mark my words," said another. "Women are a jinx at sea. Always are."

"Keep calm, lads." The captain stood beside them. "I've met their kind before. As soon as it sees us, it'll be over the horizon quicker than you can shave a baby."

"But, captain," said a sailor beside Neil. "It seems to be heading straight for us."

Captain Blàthan leaned over the rail and stared at the oncoming beast.

"What in Erde!" He raised his voice for all to hear. "Trim sheets and give the tiller a turn to the south. We'll see if it follows."

Men adjusted the lines, the tillerman responded, and the ship turned. Everyone watched to see if the monster would change direction.

Then it raised its head, opened its jaws, and gave an earsplitting call, like someone blowing a massive battle horn echoing down a mountain valley. "Aaaahhhhh-Ooooooooohh. Aaaaahhh-Oooooooh."

The eerie sound was like nothing Neil had ever heard. A shiver ran down his back.

"It follows!" the red-haired man in the crow's nest cried out. "The blasted beast is following."

Indeed, the sea monster was heading southwest toward them.

The captain watched for some time as the distance between creature and ship narrowed. When it was only fifty yards away, he gave new orders to head due east with the wind. "I've never seen one of these beasts harm a man or vessel. Ever. Yet it follows us."

Machar now stood at the rail, watching the monster approach. "Captain, I'm thinking there's something wrong with it."

"Hey? What do you say?"

"You said 'tis not in the nature of these creatures to go near ships. Yet it heads toward ours with dispatch and apparently with an ill will. It may be under a spell."

Blàthan gawked at Machar, his mouth open. "A spell, you say?"

"Aye. From someone on the black-sailed ship that left before us."

Luag gripped his axe and eyed the creature, shivering. "I should never have left the forest."

The captain returned his gaze to the oncoming monster. "Perhaps we can outrun it."

Only a hundred feet distant, the monster was swimming due south when the ship turned east. Then the vessel began pulling away, leaving it off the stern. But the creature now swam just behind and to port. Steadily, it was gaining on them.

Raising its head to the sky, it gave another trumpeting, earsplitting call.

Machar's voice rumbled low as he said to the captain, "I believe it's going to attack."

Chapter 18

CREATURE

The captain stood before Dermid and Machar, fear written plainly on his face. "My lords, this is beyond my ken." His voice lost the force of his earlier command. "Any suggestions would be welcome, indeed."

Dermid looked to the captain, then to Machar, his jaw tense. "We fight it."

Machar nodded then shouted, "To arms, men! Finnean and Ewan, string your bows. The rest, get your blades ready, and Luag and Camran, your axes."

Neil followed the others and scrambled for his sword. But the sailors had no weapons and just watched with terror-stricken faces as the creature closed on their wake.

"'Twas the woman," muttered a sailor. "Brought evil tidings on us all."

"Aye," said another, "the woman."

Soon, its towering neck stretched even with them, only a dozen feet off the port beam. The monster's bulk slithered back beyond the after-deck. Neil shuddered to see it so close. Long thrusts of its paddle fins would send it rushing forward. Then flippers reached ahead and thrust, gliding it forward again. Now its neck, as tall as their mainmast, turned toward them. Light blue orbs floated inside black, slitted eyes, gazing down at them from a great height. Neil trembled at the coldness, the strangeness, of those eyes.

"It sees me," came a cry from the crow's nest. "Oh, Neavh and Ifreann!"

No, you fool. Keep quiet!

The neck snaked toward the sailor. Its cavernous mouth opened to reveal rows of razor-sharp teeth. The head tilted, like a lizard's, as its eyes seemed to widen and examine the man. But he was trapped, and the jaws clamped, crunching bone and flesh. The red-haired man screamed, writhed, and twisted. The creature pulled away from the mast, opened its jaws to get a better grip. But the sailor slipped free and fell. He hit the deck with a horrible crunch. Quickly, the creature's neck snapped down. Jaws closed again and lifted the victim. Then it flung the lifeless body over the rail where it plopped into the sea.

The neck swung back to the deck, its mouth again open. The jaws struck at a second sailor running from the railing. The monster's teeth closed. It lifted the man high into the air.

Two arrows sprouted from its neck. Then two more. The sailor squirmed inside the beast's jaws. He screamed. Dermid and Machar rushed forward with swords drawn. Neil followed. But the beast retreated so fast, their blades swung only upon empty air. "Help me," the man screamed. "Help me!"

As it swam away with its catch, Ewan and Finnean fired again, but their shots missed.

With quick thrusts of its flippers, the beast glided a hundred feet to port, still keeping pace with the ship. Then it threw its head from side to side until the man's cries stopped and his body went limp. The jaws opened, its neck swung up, and the body slid down its throat.

Neil's heart pounded, and the blood pumped through his head so fast, he felt dizzy. What kind of spell could direct such a mammoth creature from so great a distance? What other great powers did Faolukan possess? He shook his head.

"Can we make space in one of these holds?" Dermid asked the captain. "And hide your men in there?"

"Aye, at once." The captain gave orders, and sailors began rolling enough barrels onto the deck to make room for the crew.

"Everyone without a weapon—into the hold before it returns." The captain tied the wheel then led his sailors past the barrels into the aft hold and started tugging shut the door.

Caitir still stood behind Neil. "You should go into the hold." He motioned toward it. "There's nothing you can do here."

"I can stay and fight." She strung her bow. A quiver of arrows lay across her back.

"Nay, Caitir. 'Tis too dangerous."

She shook her head and stood her ground. Neil frowned and returned his glance to port. He had no time to argue with her.

"How can we ever fight such a creature?" Camran waved his sword. "It reaches down so fast, and its neck is so high, we've nothing to hit."

That gave Neil an idea. He spoke quickly. "When it comes again to port, what if a few of us stand on the starboard rail as bait? It will have to reach all the way across the deck to get us. Then the rest of us can hide under the port waling and strike up from beneath."

Machar gripped Neil's shoulders and smiled. "Ewan and Finnean, we need your archery, so you'll shoot from the starboard rail. You, too, young lass, since we can't seem to rid ourselves of your help. But whose sword will stand with the archers and protect them?"

Neil swallowed. "Mine will."

Machar nodded. "Dermid, Camran, and Luag—we'll hide beneath the rail. Now!" The four rushed to the port waling and ducked beneath it.

Neil stood with the two archers and Caitir. The four backed up as far as they could against the starboard rail and waited.

Again, the monster swam in from the port side. The first volley of arrows hit the beast along its neck. More projectiles struck its back. One after another, as fast as they could shoot, arrows sprouted from its hide. Blood ran from the shafts until its neck glistened red.

When it was only a dozen feet away, the creature wagged its head, raised its mouth to the sky, and released a deafening roar, "Aaaahhhhh-Oooooooohh. Aaaaahhh-Ooooooooh." With lightning speed, it lowered its head far across the railing and reached for the three exposed men and Caitir.

Two more arrows struck. Its neck snaked across, jaws open. Neil backed all the way against the far rail until he could go no farther. The monster's neck was fully extended now. Its teeth clamped down and clicked together—on nothing. Neil stepped forward, swung down hard, felt the blade hack into thick flesh.

He jumped to the side. He'd made a deep gash on its head above an eye. Blood now ran into that glassy orb and drenched the deck. Its jaws opened and snapped again on empty space with a loud clicking. It pulled back and up, its head hitting a spar above. A crack resounded. As it did so, Machar, Dermid, Camran, and Luag bent low beneath the far railing, under the monster's extended neck. Then their swords stabbed and cut. Axes swung into flesh as if they were felling a tree.

The creature bellowed once, backed away from the deck, gave three thrusts with its flippers, and shot fifty feet away from the ship. Another arrow landed on its side. Then its head plunged under the waves, and it dove, its massive black hide sliding under the water, leaving a trail of red. A plume of pink water shot high, carried away by the wind.

Where it had been was now only foam and a swirling whirlpool.

The men rushed to port. For some time they examined the foaming water. Yet no sign of it emerged.

"Look there!" Finnean pointed to a spot nearly a hundred yards distant. A head burst from the deep, brought with it a fountain of water and a rising black mass, glistening wet. The creature rose, then crashed atop the waves, pushing aside mountains of water. Then it just seemed to float, bobbing in the foam, its head drooping. The ship, meanwhile, kept running before the wind, pulling away to the east.

The monster drifted, unmoving, its neck arched, glistening red, its head hanging low. It fell farther and farther behind until it was only a speck on the northwestern horizon.

Dermid knocked on the aft hold. "'Tis safe to come out now."

When the sailors and captain emerged, they looked around in amazement.

"This is a tale me grandchildren will be telling their grandchildren." The captain slapped Dermid on the back. "I saw the whole thing through a crack."

"'Twas Neil's idea that bested the beast." Dermid walked to Neil, reached out his hand, and they shook. "But if ever we need bait again, I think we shouldna risk you, my lord."

Neil smiled. "That's fine with me."

Dermid stood before Caitir with hands on hips. "You're a brave lass—I'll say as much. How many shots did you get in?"

"Eight, at least."

Dermid gave her an appreciative nod. "I'm glad you were there. But you'll still be leaving us at Drijvendby."

"Can I not change your mind, my lord? Can you not use another archer?"

Dermid held her gaze. For a moment, Neil wondered if he *might* change his mind. But he shook his head and returned to his seat. Yet as he did so, Neil glimpsed a rare smile.

As sailors began to clean up the mess on deck, Neil stood at the rail, watching the waves, breathing deeply of the salt air, trying to calm his racing heart. Faolukan had said he would bring them terrors and dangers they could never imagine. How could there be anything worse than that sea monster?

After supper as the sun neared the horizon, Caitir and Neil sought an isolated spot at the farthest tip of the foredeck. There the prow parted the sea with a continuous slapping and swishing.

"The one called Machar"—Caitir's voice came soft, worried—"said the creature was bewitched. What kind of business have you got yourself into, Tristan?"

"You must no longer call me Tristan while on ship, even when we're alone. From now on, I'm Neil."

"All right . . . Neil. But what about my question?"

Neil watched the waves for a time. "If I tell you all, it's only to convince you this trip is too dangerous, and you must turn back. Above all, you must keep everything I tell you a secret. Will you promise?"

"I promise."

Then he told her about his vision of Elyon on the balcony at the palace and their plans to go to the far country of Waldreich and find the Scepter. He told her about the prophecy, how everyone thought he met all the signs, and about the six chosen to go with him. When he finished, she fixed him with widened eyes.

"This is fantastic, Tri—Neil. And this Elyon—he is real?"

"Aye, he is most definitely real."

"And he spoke to you?"

"That he did."

She gawked at him in obvious wonder. "But what if they find out you aren't who they think you are?"

He frowned. "Ewan fears that the Company, as we call ourselves, will abandon the quest, and the Deamhan Lord's darkness will win."

Caitir shuddered. "Then you must continue in the deception."

Neil gazed across the darkening waters, calming even now. "I've lived my whole life under a cloud of shame. I was born into dishonor. My mother sold her reputation for a few coins. My father was a fool, squandered everything he ever owned, and went deep into debt. All anyone's ever called me is a *bothach*, the lowest of the low. Even when I worked at my uncle's smithy. All my life the villagers of Hidden Pines have snickered and laughed at me behind my back. Now I'm forced into deceiving these *flaith* in the greatest quest of our lifetimes." He hung his head. "Will I never flee shame and dishonor?"

"Someday, Tristan, you'll be recognized for the person you are, not by the names others call you. If you are successful in this, surely they'll forgive the deception."

He arched his gaze her way. "Maybe."

She laid a hand on his. "I ken you're the most honorable person I've ever met."

He smiled. "Thank you, Caitir. But if the truth be told, you're the only one who thinks so."

CHAPTER 19

AN ILL WIND

On the ninth day, they sighted the peaks of the Blue Mountains on a peninsula of Armorica to the south. Dermid said the mountain chain once reached all the way to Etrusca and the Golden Sea, some three hundred fifty leagues to the southeast. In the Great Upheaval, part of it shook to the ground and crumbled into the Fell Bogs. All that day, they hugged the coast, driven by a strong west wind.

On the morning of the tenth day, a massive wall rose from the southern horizon. It began at a lonely point at the foot of the Blue Mountains, marched into the sea, and led on, seemingly without end, toward the east.

"The Great Seawall of the Netherwelt," announced the captain to the Company who all hugged the starboard rail. He slapped his thigh and smiled. "Lads, that means we'll be in port by evening."

"How far does it go?" Finnean gaped, his mouth open.

"Nigh on for twenty leagues until it joins the swamps of Nordmark. 'Tis fifty feet high and took a hundred years to build. Keeps the worst of the waves from knocking the Nether folks' houses about."

"Why should they have to worry about that?"

Captain Blàthan just winked. "You'll see. I'll not spoil the first sight of it with me paltry words."

Their course led them a league off the seawall until, by late afternoon, a massive dark opening came into view. "The sea gate." Blàthan pointed. "There we'll be rowed through the channel."

When the ship was just north of the gate, the captain gave orders to take in sail.

Machar and Dermid stood beside Neil as they drew close to the massive stone structure. He could just make out the figures of giant octopi, squid, and whales carved into its surface.

A sudden, strong wind rose from the south. For a moment, the sails luffed and flapped.

"Odd. She's been blowing steadily east for days." The captain raised his voice. "Close haul her, lads. We'll have to tack the last wee stretch."

They took in sail and began to zigzag. But the wind blew stronger. Soon the seas around them rose in angry swells. The ship lurched one way then another as it fought the wind, but they made no progress.

"I've never seen such weather so close to the wall. But look east. There she's calm."

"The same to the west." Dermid inclined his head. "This wind blows only a few hundred yards around us."

"Look to the wall." Machar's voice rumbled low, troubled. "To the figure on top of the gate."

Neil peered through the spray and the wind. He could barely make out the silhouette of a caped man standing on the high berm. Both hands were raised. Off to the side, two shadowy figures waited.

"Could it be—?" Dermid shielded his eyes with his hands.

"Aye." Machar frowned. "It is. And he's casting a spell on the wind."

"Monsters and spells," muttered Blàthan. "Well, there're few winds, barring a storm, that'll keep *The Fair Winds* from port. I reckon we'll make progress against it."

But try as he might, the captain's persistent tacking brought the vessel no closer to the gate. Then the wind roared, and the swells grew worse, rising to a height of twenty feet. As the ship climbed to the top of one swell, Neil looked east to calmer waters. The same in the west.

All evening they sailed, yet never seemed to gain a single yard on their goal.

Gradually, a strange compulsion came over him. He desired greatly to touch the crescent-moon pendant. He balled his hands into fists, fighting it. He looked through the darkening light at the lone figure atop the wall, tried to focus on him, but—suddenly, the familiar feel of the cold metal was in his palm. A tingling started in his fingers, ran up his arms. It soothed and calmed, but in a strange, nervous way.

Surprised by the strength of its intoxication, he caressed it, let its prickling cold radiate up through his shoulders, settle in his chest. Aye, that was fine, indeed. The tingling changed to warmth, tinged at the edges with icy cold. His eyes half closed as he gripped the pendant tighter. He'd never experienced such pure ecstasy. How could he ever give this up? Thoughts of the Scepter, the mission, reaching the Netherwelt—all receded into mere foolishness. All he needed was the pendant. He stayed at the rail, fondling it, giving himself over to it.

Someone touched his shoulder, and he started.

"'Tis dark, my lord." It was Ewan. "You're wet, and 'tis near midnight. You should rest."

Neil shook his head as if waking from a dream. He released the pendant. Instantly, pain cramped his fingers and wrist. Had he been here half the evening? He shuddered. What had happened to him? "Thank you, Ewan. I guess I was dreaming on my feet."

By dim lantern light, Neil saw concern on Ewan's face. "Are you all right, my lord? You look—ill."

"I'm fine." Then he left the center deck and went to the bench where he curled up and fell instantly asleep. The last thought he had was that he needed to melt the thing down at the first forge he came to.

By morning's light, the ship was in the same position as the afternoon before. The wind roared and threw salt spray across the deck.

"Faolukan must be getting tired. Look." Machar pointed again to the top of the seawall, where the men accompanying him now held both his arms aloft.

"But still the wind comes." Dermid stared at the man on the wall.

The figure raised his hands higher. In an eyeblink, the wind grew to gale level. Now even their zigzagging couldn't hold them in position. The winds blasted the ship farther and farther out to sea. Soon the wall disappeared entirely from view.

All the rest of that day, through the night, and into the next, the fierce wind came on, and though the ship tacked against it, they lost more and more distance. They were now far from the shores of Ereb.

But the farther they were driven, the lesser came Neil's desire to fondle the pendant, though it never quit. To keep himself from absently touching it again, he wrapped it tightly in a strip of leather.

The next morning the southern wind died, replaced by a gentle westerly breeze.

Dermid looked to the captain. "How far do you ken we've been driven?"

"I've no way of knowing. 'Twas a powerful gale brought us here."

For half a day they sailed south until, once again, the Netherwelt Sea Gate appeared as a dark opening on the horizon. This time, they sailed to within a quarter league when, once again, a lone figure rose from the wall, lifted his arms, and the fierce wind roared against them.

"Nay, not again." The captain slammed one fist into another. "'Tis back to tacking, lads."

The ship close-hauled, zigzagged, and again fought the wind. But even as the sailors fitted the rigging for the change, the winds strengthened and the swells rose to a terrible height.

"We're losing distance fast." Dermid's voice was low. "And Faolukan seems to have recovered."

Indeed, the druid now stood on his own, without support. But to Neil's eye, he thought the man seemed a bit unsteady on his feet.

"We canna go on like this," the captain muttered. "We should have docked three days ago. Tomorrow we must go on half-rations."

A loud groan escaped a man nearby. Shifting in his seat, Neil saw Ewan's fallen face.

"This is the bad luck I predicted." Camran frowned. "'Tis the woman who's brought this upon us."

"Nay, Camran." Dermid scowled. "This is the work of Faolukan."

Other ships off the port and starboard beam struggled, also kept from entering the Nether country.

Then Machar prayed, loud enough for all to hear, asking Elyon to allow them to pass through the sea gate.

Neil looked to the receding wall, wondering if the gale would stop right then, but nothing happened. As he watched the dark figure with raised hands, the desire to touch the pendant came again with overwhelming power.

Nay, he must not give in. The device came from Corc, did it not? From another druid. It was evil, and he must fight it.

Yet his hand was already fumbling with the leather ties, and—aye, it was undone. A sudden wash of tingling cold raced through his fingers, up his arm and brought again the icy-warm bliss. Such ecstasy, shooting up into his inner being! He gave himself up to it. Time seemed to stop as the icy warmth embraced him, carried him away. His eyes half closed. He never wanted it to stop.

"Neil!" A shout from behind. Dermid's voice. "Step away from the rail. Or the seas will wash you overboard."

Neil jerked his hand out of his pocket. But his fingers still gripped the quarter moon. He stared at the giant waves on which the ship now rode, up and down, bearing them farther and farther from the seawall. How long had he stood there in a pendant-induced trance for the seas to have grown so wild, so terrible? The deck swayed violently.

He stepped away from the rail but tripped as he lost his footing.

The pendant fell from his hands, slid across the deck.

Dermid's foot slammed down upon it.

Neil regained his feet, feeling the pendant's loss as keenly as if he were a clay beaker someone had just shattered. He trembled, knelt for the silver jewelry, but was too late.

"What's this?" Dermid reached down, grabbed the pendant by its chain, and held it aloft. His glance narrowed and bored into Neil's. "You were given one of these? By whom?"

Neil began to shake. Both from the absence of the pendant and from the harshness of Dermid's glare. "From . . . from Corc. I was going to remold it, but—"

"But what?" Camran came up beside them. "You had this evil thing all along and didna tell us? What's wrong with you?"

Now Machar joined them, as did the entire Company. Everyone fought to keep their footing as the wind whipped their capes and blew salt spray in their eyes. "Camran's point is well made. Why didn't you tell someone?"

"I . . . I don't know. I wasn't going to touch it. I was going to keep it until I found a forge to break the spell. But we left too quickly."

"Did you touch it?" Machar's frown matched Dermid's in intensity.

"Aye, my lord." Neil cast his gaze to the deck. "I didn't want to. I tried to keep from doing so, but it had a power over me I didn't expect."

"How often have you touched it?" Machar's voice was grim.

Then Neil told them everything, even how he tried to get the princess's pendant to remake it but couldn't risk going into her room unnoticed. Then he described how he arrived at the blacksmith's forge, only to discover he'd left his own pendant back in his room.

"'Twas surely the magic of the spell made you leave it. And you say the princess has one too? That she, also, has fallen under its spell?" Machar shook his head. "This device is evil, Neil. I'm only just beginning to understand how evil."

"If 'twas Corc's work"—Dermid slammed one fist into another—"then Corc's in league with Faolukan."

"Aye, it appears so," said Machar. "We knew his counsel was bad, but not with so terrible a purpose. This only confirms the urgency of our mission."

"What are we to do with him?" Camran shot a glance at Neil. "How can we ever trust him now?"

"Let's not be hasty with our judgments." Machar's stare was glassy. "Neil *is* the Toghaí. We should expect that the Deamhan Lord's servants would single him out for attack. More so than against any of us. And who of us could say we'd have resisted better?" He surveyed the others. All except Dermid lowered their glances. "I also remind you—he tried to break the spell of both his and his sister's pendant. Surely, 'twas the thing's magic that prevented it."

"I do not like this." Camran's jaw tensed.

"Dermid, you must give him back the pendant." Machar motioned with one hand.

"What?" Dermid raised it by its chain and lifted one eyebrow. "Shouldn't we destroy it?"

"Nay. To break the spell, it must be melted and remade, and we've no kiln aboard. We must wait until we land."

"But why should *he* hold onto it?" Camran scowled. "Has he not proven himself untrustworthy?"

"No one else must carry the thing. Neil himself must bear it until he destroys it. Only that will ensure its power over him completely departs."

"And how do you ken so much about it?" Camran spread his feet and put his hands on his hips. "Who made *you* the expert?"

Machar glared at Camran, and his nostrils flared. "You won't challenge me, Camran. Or you'll get the worst of the conflict."

Camran didn't budge but held Machar's stare. "I thought Dermid was in charge here?"

Dermid stepped closer. "I am. But let us understand something. All of you." He glanced around the circle of the Company, now swaying on the shifting deck, but his glance stopped at Camran. "I trust Machar's judgment and advice more than any other. I do lead this mission, but I will defer to Machar in nearly every case. His knowledge of these affairs, his experience, and his judgment are far beyond my ken. Let's just say there are things I canna tell you yet."

"All right, then." Camran's face was flushed. "But I do not like the way this is going."

"Like it or not, Neil must carry the device until we reach a forge. He is the one predicted by the prophecy. If we canna trust him, then our mission is over. And if we fail . . ."

For a time no one spoke. The deck swayed. The wind tore at the rigging and whipped Neil's cape about him.

Then Dermid held the pendant out to Neil.

Neil took it by its chain. In front of everyone, he wrapped the thing again in leather, being careful not to touch its surface. Then he tied it up with leather straps and slid it back inside a pocket.

"Good. You've secured it." Machar laid a hand on his shoulder. "Now you must resist its power with all your might. 'Tis a powerful spell someone's fashioned for it, so powerful it troubles me. But I have confidence you'll fight it." Machar smiled.

Neil tried an answering smile, but it vanished. He dropped his glance to the deck and closed his eyes. He'd let everyone down. This entire mission depended on *him*, and already he'd harbored an evil device, had given in to its wiles, and now brought dissension and doubt to the Company. He shook his head.

"I do not like any of this. How can we trust him . . ." Camran's voice trailed off as he walked away.

The wind temporarily abated. In its silence, the others' footsteps drifted away.

"Do not listen to him." It was Caitir's voice, low in his ear. He opened his eyes. The others had taken their seats on the plank benches. "You did what you could. I believe in you."

Neil caught her gaze and wiped a tear from one eye. Was it the wind or his shame? "This is starting badly. Now the men don't respect me."

"That's foolishness. They'll come to know you like I do."

Neil nodded, not sure he believed her. Above all, the one thing he needed to be was honorable. But now, that was the one thing about him the Company would surely doubt.

Yet he was charged to bring back the Scepter. That was now his most important goal. Perhaps even more important than honor.

For two more days, a gale raged and blew the ship far out to sea. Then, as before, the south wind abruptly died, replaced by a gentle breeze from the west. They started south once more, but the previous evening they'd eaten the last of the hardtack and salted bacon. Now Neil's belly was empty and growling. Only of beer did they have plenty, but without food, it did not satisfy and brought only a headache.

They sailed a day, a night, and a morning, and again approached the seawall. By late afternoon, they were within seventy yards.

"I see no sign of him." Dermid scanned the top of the wall. "Perhaps he's exhausted?"

The ship sailed even closer than before. They were almost fifty yards from the yawning channel leading to the bay beyond. Neil could see again the sculpted forms of giant sea monsters on each side of the gap.

Slowly, a gray-caped figure rose from the escarpment, helped by three others.

"We're closer than we've ever been. And look, three men now hold him up."

"Púcas?" Neil asked.

"Possibly. They can be púcas by night and men by day. But he must have no strength left in him, or he wouldna need such help."

As if to bely the thought, the druid shook off his supporters, stood to his full height, and raised his arms. The wind shrieked and the seas bulged. The next blast threw the ship sideways, tipping its masts far to the lee before they righted. Gusts tore at the rigging, vibrated the ropes nearby, and nearly knocked Neil off his feet. Walls of water topped by foaming waves grew out of the sea right before his eyes. The ship climbed to the top of a giant wave then rode the churning, swirling waters to the bottom.

At its height, Neil felt again the powerful urge to pull out the pendant, hold it, let its icy warmth wash over him. He bit his lip and told himself that whatever happened, he would not give in. Then, at the top of the next massive swell, the wind stopped. So did the urge to touch the pendant.

He spun quickly toward the wall, now some two hundred yards away. Faolukan had collapsed onto the berm. Figures stood around him, tried to lift him, but he could no longer even stand.

Within moments, the swells lost their strength, settled, and the waters calmed.

"Fit her for a beam reach, laddies." The captain was smiling ear to ear. "By dark, we'll be eating stew, drinking ale, and smoking our pipes."

Neil looked up but saw no sign of the men or their master.

As the ship approached the channel, the captain ordered the men to furl all sail. Soon, three longboats manned with oarsmen rowed out to meet them.

"Been days since we've hauled in a single vessel," said a sailor below as he caught a line from *The Fair Winds*. Then the smaller craft towed them into the channel. Sheer stone rose fifty feet on either side, taller than their masts. As soon as they entered, the boats tugged them to the right for two hundred feet, straight for three ship's lengths, and then guided them left for another two hundred feet. Cut into the stone on both sides were the figures of giant sharks, whales, and sea monsters with long necks. They emerged from the stone walls into a bay dotted with little islands.

The captain raised half canvas, and they began to sail past the largest island, dominated by a stone and timber palace. Thickly clustered on all sides were two- and three-story houses, each painted a different color.

Blàthan slowed the ship as a merchant barge laden with sheep rang its bell and passed in front.

Machar came up beside Neil at the rail. "In the distance is Drijvendby Palace, but Blàthan is heading for Koopman's Winkel on Handelport Eiland. That's where he'll deliver his goods and we'll buy supplies."

"You've been here many times, haven't you?"

"Aye. For all my thirty-five years, it seems I've lived most of them away from home. How I long, sometimes, just to spend a winter at home by the fire in my father's castle, stroking a dog's fur. Cruachain is a wonder to behold, Neil. But you've been there, haven't you?"

Neil nodded, hoping Machar wouldn't press him for details.

"In summer I like to hunt the forests of Connacht and fish its cold streams." Machar sighed. "But sometimes lately, it seems I've grown a stranger to my own country."

"I know the feeling." Neil smiled inwardly.

"I must tell you something, Neil." Machar laid a gentle hand on his shoulder. "Before this trip, we never really spent any time together. Whenever your house would visit mine, or mine yours, I always seemed to be on the road. All I knew about you came from rumor and gossip. So when they told me you could be the one we were looking for, I was originally aghast. I thought, how could a womanizer and a drunk be the Toghaí?"

Neil shuffled his feet. "I understand. I've been trying to change."

"I know." Machar nodded. "So in these last two weeks, after Dermid told me about your conversation, and after seeing you in person, my mind is now set on a different path. You're not the person your reputation would indicate. So now, I'm proud to call you . . . my friend." He gave Neil a broad smile and stuck out his hand.

Neil gripped his hand, returned the smile, and they shook. "Thank you, Machar. That means a lot to me."

Machar slapped Neil on the back and leaned against the rail again. He pointed to a small island now filling their view. "There. Drijvendby Palace is coming up. I hope we don't have to stop."

"So you know the king?"

"Aye. And when I arrive, he always wants me to stay at his palace. But I hope we can enter the city quietly, find discrete quarters, and leave as soon as we're outfitted."

"Why?"

"Because Joost is always eager for news. Too eager, I think. Always prying into business that's not his. And now I don't know which way he leans. When I left here a year ago, an emissary from Drochtar was just arriving. Who knows what wiles or bribes he's placed on the king. If Joost now leans toward Faolukan and his brood—well, let's just say we don't want to stay long in Drijvendby."

Neil nodded, and they watched as the island grew close.

From nowhere, a twenty-foot sailboat appeared beside *The Fair Winds*. On its stern flew a huge, tricolored flag.

"Blast!" Machar hit a fist into a palm.

"What's wrong?"

A page dressed in a brightly colored, striped tunic was already calling up from below, "Master of the ship! I've an urgent message from the king of Drijvendby."

Captain Blàthan hurried down from the upper deck to where Machar and Neil stood. Dermid came right behind him. Blàthan leaned over the side. "What is it, lad?"

"That the passengers from Ériu, most noble and worthy—and you, too, Captain—are invited to dine tonight in the great hall of the king's palace. I await your answer. And, Captain?"

"Aye?"

He lowered his voice. "If I were you and I wanted to keep King Joost well pleased, I'd be answering in the affirmative."

Captain Blàthan looked to Dermid and Machar with raised eyebrows.

"Dermid." Machar frowned and spoke in a low voice. "You must tell him, aye, that we'll attend his dratted feast. What other choice do we have?"

"None, unless we want trouble."

"Apparently, we've already got it. How did he find out we were here?"

"How, indeed?"

Chapter 20

King Joost

When Neil stepped off the boat onto Joost's palace island and had his first close look, he was astonished. A hundred feet down the dock was an enormous handle of wood, nearly three feet thick and bound with iron. It began fifty feet inland and stretched out beside the island, down into a much larger wooden plane just visible beneath the sea. It creaked inside its mounting, sending its complaint even to where he stood. For what purpose it was made, he had no idea.

The palace itself was the biggest building he'd ever seen. Wide stone stairs led up to an arched, columned entryway. Carved marble banisters on each side resembled curling waves. From the top of the building sprang dozens of masts with furled sails, but that made no sense. What would a spit of land crammed with buildings need with masts and spars? Between the palace and the nearest island was a short causeway. Other islands dotted the near horizon. And each isle ended in a point.

A page clothed in a brightly striped, blue, yellow, and green tunic emerged from a nearby booth. "This way to your quarters, my lords." He bowed, smiled, and spread one hand toward the palace steps.

The Company, plus Caitir, followed. Dermid held in his hands a note from Captain Blàthan, who sent his deepest regrets, saying he had goods to deliver, new cargo to take on, and sailors to watch over. Before they parted, Dermid had advised the captain in sharp detail where and when to meet him on the morrow to take Caitir back with him. But now he crumpled the note, mightily displeased that the captain had backed out of the dinner.

They followed the boy's echoing steps up the grand entrance into a columned foyer four stories high. The tiled images of fish, sea cucumbers, and waves inlaid the floor. When asked, the page explained the creatures. Then the boy led them to a third-floor riser and down a marble hallway with eight doors, each with the symbol of a different fish or sea creature. "Supper is served at dusk. Take any room—they're all ready. Baths have been drawn, and garments laid out for you. Leave your clothes in the box outside the door, and they'll be cleaned and returned tonight." He bowed. "The lady may use this room." He pointed to a door sporting the image of a clownfish. He bowed again and departed.

Finnean raised his head to the others. "The king sees to our health with baths and a supper. Before so much wealth, I feel like a pauper."

Neil gave a short laugh. "He's abundantly rich, is he not?"

Machar nodded. "Joost's kingdom sits at the coastal center of northern Ereb. And the people pay a heavy tax. But nearly all his trade is with the seaports and river cities of Armorica, Noregr, and Nordmark. Travel inland is far too difficult."

"Is that not where we go?" asked Neil.

"Aye, my lord. But tomorrow. Tonight, let us enjoy the luxury Joost lavishes on his guests. It'll be the last we'll see for many moons. Enjoy your baths." Machar winked and entered his own quarters.

Neil entered the room and gaped. A bed with pillows piled atop quilts over a wool-filled mattress. A marble table held a decanter of wine, two glasses, a small round of cheese, and two apples. He ate an apple in four bites, and then began munching on the cheese—the first real food he'd had in days. With a glass of wine in his hand, he gazed out the window over the bay. Bells ringing to warn of their approach, ships sailed to and fro between mast-bedecked islands. It created the busiest watercourse he'd ever seen.

In one corner of the room stood a tub—marble, again—already filled with water. He dunked a hand inside. *Heated.* Towels and soap and clothes befitting a prince lay nearby on a polished black bench.

He plopped his traveling bag down, undressed, piled his clothes into the box in the hallway, and lowered himself into the tub.

He opened the door to the knocking of a page and the rest of the Company waiting in the hall. Dressed in a striped blue blouse, a thin plaid tunic, and billowing pants of the finest cloth, he felt pretentious, elegant, perhaps a mite foolish. This was far from the smoke and charcoal-stained leather tunic he'd worn for most of his days.

The page led them down flights of stairs into a marble-floored foyer, past rows of granite columns, into an enormous hall lined with tapestries. The king sat at the far end—a small figure in the distance. As they walked the ballroom-gallery, each step an echo, Neil studied the giant tapestries.

Holding scenes from Ereb's distant past, they were, in effect, a history of Erde. Battles with great leaders on prancing, armored horses. Mail-clad infantry trying in vain to fend off a cavalry charge. The horses' nostrils flared. Chariots flew banners, dropped soldiers at the front, and returned empty. The dead and dying littered the fields. Swords, lances, and arrows protruded from the fallen. Tapestry after tapestry. Battle after battle.

"We've lost the context for most of these." Machar came up beside him, his voice low and reverent. "Few have ever seen what your eyes behold today."

"I've never seen the like." Ewan's mouth hung agape.

Neil's glance fixed on a scene of hooded men in black hauling frightened women and children from a hut. Behind them, a village burned while men's bodies lay crushed and bleeding on the ground. Smoke blackened the sky.

"That one's particularly disturbing." Machar shook his head. "We've little left of our history, but men still shudder when they tell of the Great Purge. 'Twas a time when the Deamhan Lord's soldiers terrorized every land on Erde. Only because of Elyon's protection was Ard Cúl Dín, the high mountain refuge, hidden from attack. Rumors have also circulated of a race of secretive forest people who survived."

Neil stopped before a scene of men crossing a river on small boats, but many were wounded and bloodied. Dejection and defeat marred every face. Behind came hooded riders on black horses. When he saw their banners carrying the silver crescent moon, he shivered.

"The Battle of Two Rivers," Machar whispered. "Where Faolukan's armies defeated the combined forces of Ériu, Armorica, Esperandula, and Noregr on the plains of Ulster. After that fight, Airril mac Duvh gave up his crown and fled to the Wicklow Mountains where he lived in hiding till his death.

"Many years later, after numerous failed expeditions to bring back Elyon's gifts, he sent his son, Breandan—alone—to the empty, abandoned tower. In that day, all entrances to the Tower of Dóchas had been sealed. But somehow, Breandan climbed to the top, made his way down the steps in the dark, and there, over a month-long period, he inscribed in stone the message Cairbre deciphered for us at the council. Every few days, Breandan would haul food and water to the summit—also oil for his torches so he could continue the work."

"How did you discover this?"

"A rotting scroll we found with the same trove that told us about the Scepter. This was only a few years ago."

A voice reverberated from down the hall. "Come, come, Machar. You can gawk at my tapestries later. Supper awaits your presence."

He whispered to Neil. "'Tis the king. We must tarry no longer."

Machar led them down the corridor, their footsteps echoing all the way, until they stopped before a long table. At the back of each seat rose an enormous, fluted half-shell, streaked diagonally with brilliant yellows and reds. At the table's head sat a small man wrapped in folds of colored robe. His blond mustache curled up at both ends, accentuating the blond point of his dainty beard. The half-shell ensconced behind him was the biggest Neil had ever seen, leaving a wide berth on either side. What creature had once lived in such a house at the sea's bottom? The shell was so large, that, if the other half closed upon it, the animal could have easily swallowed three men whole.

"Welcome, again, Machar mac Maon." When the king smiled, his eyes narrowed. "'Tis not often we receive such illustrious company. So few visitors are worthy of my table. Too many merchants, guild members. Always a paucity of nobility."

Machar bowed low. Neil and the others followed his lead. "We are honored, my lord, that you receive us so."

At King Joost's urging, Machar introduced the Company, one at a time. Joost nodded at the mention of Dermid's name. "I remember your last visit." Then he spread his hands wide. "I regret that another of my guests is unable to join us tonight. He's in his room, quite ill, attended to by his servants."

Machar's forehead creased in lines of concern. "Ill, my lord?"

"Exhausted from overwork, I should say. But all of you, sit and eat." He waved his hands, and the group sat on cushioned chairs, far more comfortable than the hard wooden benches Neil was used to in Ériu. "I find the best conversation proceeds on full bellies."

The king raised a lazy hand, and three musicians began playing melodies with a shell-shaped lute, a tambourine, and a flute—melodies that bespoke of rolling ocean waves, sunlight on a calm sea, and gulls circling overhead.

Servants brought trays of smoked halibut, boiled clams, mussels, and squid.

Neil examined the tableware. Instead of the usual two knives, there was one knife and a second instrument much like the serrated bill of some large fish.

"Swordfish beaks," said their host. "Good for getting to the heart of the matter." He stabbed a tiny octopus in the center and held it high, its cooked tentacles dangling.

This course was followed by beef cooked with turnips, onions, and carrots. When the servants brought bread with butter and pastries made with honey, the king said, "All ingredients imported from Ériu. And the wine is from Burgundia."

After they'd eaten and drunk their fill, Joost waved a hand, and the music quieted. "My lord Machar, what errand brings you with so many companions back to our fair city?"

Machar held his glass to his eyes, examining the wine's clarity, and then set it back down. "Trade, my liege. We come on an important mission of commerce."

Joost raised an eyebrow. "I complain of too many merchants, and now, you've become one yourself? And what can Ériu offer us that we do not already trade for in abundance?"

"'Tis not with the Netherwelt that our mission attends, my lord."

Joost tilted back his head and, for a moment, said nothing. "Then with whom?"

"With the forest people of the Waldreich."

Joost stared at him, his eyes narrowing, and then threw his head back and laughed. "You're joking, of course?"

"I'm serious, my lord. We plan to leave tomorrow, with haste, and enter the Fell Bogs."

Joost resumed his stare. "That course is unwise, my friend. We trade with the forest people but infrequently. They do not welcome foreigners like here in the Nether. Even for guides, the country between here and there is treacherous. Always shifting, sinking, changing. And then there are the swamp spirits." He seemed to shudder. "Many die on the trek. Commerce is simply . . . impossible. But you know this, so let me ask: What is so valuable in the Waldreich that you risk your lives for it?"

"Gold, my liege."

Joost raised an eyebrow again. "Gold? Certainly, you don't believe the old rumors? That somewhere in the deep forest, beyond the murderous forest folk, the savage wolves, the magical, treacherous streams, lies a treasure trove?"

Machar gave him a half-smile. "We do."

"Then I drink to the health you still have tonight. For on the morrow"—he smiled and hoisted a full glass—"who knows?"

They all drank to his toast.

"But, my lords, a far different story of your coming has reached these kingly ears." Joost poked his swordfish beak at the hunk of beef on the serving tray before him. "They say you seek not trade, but—how shall I say it?—the Scepter." His utensil lifted the meat and pointed it at Machar. "Is that not so?"

Machar held the king's gaze, his jaw tensing. "My lord. Do you question . . . what I have said?"

King Joost returned Machar's stare. His hand tilted the beak to the side. "Should I?"

"I say we go to the Waldreich for gold. Does the hospitality of the Netherwelt palace now include the questioning of its guests' motives and truthfulness?"

For a time Joost's stare focused on Machar. Then it moved to Dermid. The others were in various states of examining the table, their hands, the room's far corners. The cry of a gull shrieked through the open second-story window.

Joost ate the meat and dropped the beak onto his trencher. "If that's what you say you seek"—he pushed back from the table—"who am I to question?"

Dermid, too, pushed his chair back. "Tomorrow, we have a long journey. We thank you for this unexpected feast. But, my lord, if you'll excuse us?"

Joost waved a hand. "We've finished the meal. And, it seems, the conversation as well. Aye, you may leave. All of you." He stood and strode from the room.

They left the hall in silence. Then the page led them back to their third-floor quarters. When the Company was alone in the hall, Dermid whispered to Machar, "That was troubling. And who might the ill guest be?"

"Who do you think? Sure, and now we must leave at first light without delay." Machar fixed Caitir with an intent stare. "Tomorrow, young miss, the first order of business is to hand you over to Captain Blàthan."

She nodded.

Dermid shook his head. "I do not like this. Joost knew of the Scepter and our mission. And if Faolukan is here in the palace . . . ?"

"Why canna we leave right now?" asked Finnean.

"We can go nowhere after dark. The causeways will be lifted soon."

"Lifted?"

"Aye. So we'll leave a few hours before dawn, just after they're reconnected." Machar scanned the Company. "Lock your rooms tonight, my lords. Even while Joost lulls us with luxury, he advances our enemy's plans."

"I'll be knocking early." Dermid opened the door to his room then glanced back with a frown. "We canna leave here soon enough."

Chapter 21

Drivenoby

It seemed Neil had barely fallen asleep when he heard the knock. Darkness and the stillness of a harbor asleep still lingered beyond the window. His eyes half-shut, he opened the door.

"'Tis time, my lord." Ewan smiled. "We leave at once."

Still in his loincloth, Neil found half the Company already standing in the hall with their gear. When Caitir saw him in a state of undress, she put a hand to her mouth and smiled.

"One moment." He shut the door. Quickly, he dressed in his—Prince Neil's, that is—tunic and pants, which servants had washed and returned. He reappeared with his traveling bag.

After waiting for Finnean, they followed Machar down the steps to the grand foyer.

Two guards—one old, one young—stood on either side of the door holding long spears tipped with the barbed beaks of sharks. As the Company approached, the elder of them spoke, "The king requests that you not depart without his leave." The guard bowed low and then stood at attention, snapping the butt of his spear hard on the stone.

Dermid moved forward. "We already took our leave last night. Please step aside."

But the guards now left their positions and stepped to the archway's center. They crossed their spears. "We have our orders. No one is to leave without King Joost's permission."

The Company halted. Dermid looked behind him to Ewan, Finnean, and Caitir. He nodded then faced the guard again. "Let's be reasonable. We've said our goodbyes to your king. You've no reason to keep us here. We'll be on our way, and you'll be moving aside." Then he sidestepped to reveal three archers behind him, arrows taut in their bows. "Won't you?"

Neil rested his hand on the hilt of his sword. Leather rustled as the others also readied their weapons.

The younger guard's glance swept from his companion to the archers to Dermid. Fear widened his eyes. The older one scanned the Company. Then he took two steps back to the wall, hesitantly moved his spear into an upright position, and stood at attention. "If you have taken your leave of the king then . . . I guess you may pass."

Dermid bowed and led the Company through the gap. They descended the palace steps at a run.

"We must make haste," breathed Machar. "They'll now alert the palace. Faolukan's men or his púcas will surely follow."

The island was so small, they soon reached the wharf where Captain Blàthan had deposited them yesterday. Faint light spilled over the eastern horizon. Now Neil glimpsed his first look at the bay since last evening.

Everything had changed.

Where yesterday there had been only one island linked by a long causeway, today at least a dozen clustered on all sides. Short causeways connected them all.

"Wh–what?" Ewan spoke for all. They stood in the half-light, gaping at the change.

"Aye." Machar jerked his head toward the new scene. "These are *floating* islands. Today is market day, and they've all sailed close to each other. All the better for us."

"They *float?*" Luag asked. "And . . . sail?"

"Aye. 'Tis why they call it Drijvendby—the Floating City. And notice, each island has a bow, with rudders on the port and starboard. We stand now at the stern. But we must hurry to Koopman's Winkel—if we can find it among these blasted, shifting causeways. Blàthan should be there, waiting for us."

He led them at a brisk pace over the first causeway. Halfway across, it rose to a high arch, leaving enough clearance beneath for a small ship to pass. Their feet clapped down the stone into the streets of another island bearing three-story, multicolored homes, the windows all dark. Many bore signs with pictures advertising the merchandise for sale within—aged cheeses and salted meats; breads and sweet pastries; parchment and scrolls; imported wool, cotton, and silk; leather goods; brass pots and cauldrons; pine barrels; pipes and pipeweed.

At the island's far end, they exited to the right onto another isle much like the first, only with smaller, poorer huts. On the next isle, the buildings held signs for inns, with pictures of foamy mugs, fish, loaves of bread, roasting pigs, and smoking pipes. They crossed island after island, causeway after causeway until Neil was thoroughly lost.

Dim light filled the eastern sky, and lanterns began appearing in upstairs windows.

Machar stopped at the top of an arch and looked up and down the canals. "That way," he said.

On the next island, a scantily clad woman—gaunt, pale, and holding a baby—stepped toward the men. Rags wrapped the child. "Three shillings and I'm yours. What say you, men, to an early-morning romp?"

Dermid spat in her direction. "Go back to the hole you crawled out of. And take your bastard brat with you."

"I do it to feed him!" Neil sensed tears in her voice. "But you lords— you'd know nothing of that, would you? You've always had everything." Then she fled down an alley, clutching the babe to her chest.

"Offal like that"—Dermid spat again—"do not have the right to walk the streets with decent men and woman."

Machar grunted approval.

Neil felt lightheaded as the blood rushed to his face. Long ago, that could have been him in his mother's arms as she accosted strangers in the street. Was that what her life was like? If Torn hadn't taken her in, would Neil be living on the street today, in some similar unworthy state?

Like a living thing, the shame and the dishonor whelmed up inside him. He staggered onward behind the two powerful leaders. When they learned the truth, was this how Dermid and Machar would view him?

He glanced at Ewan and Caitir, both now staring at him. Caitir flashed a weak smile, as if to reassure him. Ewan just pursed his lips and looked away.

They passed two more floating islands and arrived at Koopman's Winkel. Here, almost every sign advertised wares or services. Machar went straight to the "stern" or wide part of the island holding long wharfs for at least three dozen ships. He led them to the center of a middle pier, where the creaking of wooden hulls against the wharf never stopped.

But *The Fair Winds* was nowhere to be seen.

"Where is he?" Lips pressed tight, Dermid scanned the wharfs again.

A dim light now filtered from the gray clouds above. The sky appeared laden with rain. Sailors were just beginning their morning chores.

Machar walked back down the pier and conversed with a man in better dress than his fellows. Moments later he returned, a frown etched on his face. "*The Fair Winds* dropped its cargo last night, picked up a new load, and set sail early this morning."

Dermid slammed a fist into a palm. "He was supposed to wait for Caitir."

"Aye, and now what are we to do with her?"

"I'll not go on a dangerous mission with a woman." Camran raised his voice for all to hear.

"A woman along brings a man to song, turns his mind to her frills and glamor," said Finnean. "Her wiles and smiles bring a man to woe, and his trouble is measured in miles."

"Not true, Finnean." Machar's frown deepened. "And do you have to say everything in your blasted rhyme?"

"Nay, my lord. But the rhyme pleases me." He was quiet a moment, and then added, "And it eases me."

Machar scowled. "I'm beginning to regret *your* coming, Finnean. But we're talking about the woman. The choice we face is to leave her here, alone. Or take her with us."

Caitir looked to Neil and Dermid, a worried expression lining her forehead. "You willna leave me here by myself, will you?"

Dermid shifted his feet. "Nay, lass. We canna do that. Slavers, and worse, stop at these docks."

"We cannot leave her behind." Neil's tone was firm.

"Neil's right." Machar faced Dermid. "I don't believe I'm saying this. But, aye, now she must join us. At least she can shoot a bow."

Dermid shifted his feet uncomfortably. "It appears we've no choice in the matter."

Caitir clapped her hands and threw her arms around Machar.

He gently pushed her away. A smile briefly broke his features.

"You're all daft." Camran raised his voice. "Finnean's right. If the woman comes along, we'll be cursed. I say she stays."

Machar faced him with hands on his hips. "And I say she's coming. This is the second time you've set yourself against me. Perhaps you should be the one to stay here and wait for the next ship back? We don't need a rebel in our midst."

Camran's stare seemed to melt. He lowered his head then said, "Forgive me, Machar. The woman can come."

Machar nodded, his jaw muscles tensing. Then he faced the others. "Now I must haggle for two swamp boats. The rest of you follow Dermid to Koopman's Winkel."

Neil followed the lord as he headed to the far pier and the outfitter.

◆•◦❉◦•◆

The newly bought supplies were stacked on the dock beside the two flat-bottomed boats Machar had obtained. Neil and the men began tucking everything into the bow, stern, and center where no one would sit. An occasional small wave scraped and rubbed the boats against the wooden pilings.

"These were the last swamp boats available until this afternoon," said Machar with a smile. "All the better to avoid pursuit."

"Aye, and as we left the Winkel," said Dermid, "Caitir saw six men in black capes running across a far causeway."

"Did they see you?" Machar stopped stuffing packs under a seat.

"I do not think so. They were headed off onto a side street."

"'Tis only a matter of time before they learn we've been here. But no matter. They can't follow until they've outfitted and found boats."

Dermid nodded.

With all the gear securely stowed, they shoved away from the dock. Machar, Luag, Neil, and Finnean manned the lead boat. Dermid, Camran, Caitir, and Ewan lowered themselves into the second. Each scow was long, narrow, and fitted with five plank seats. Under the seats and baggage, a set of oars and poles were nestled against the hull.

When their oars rowed them out into the channel, it began to pour. Neil snugged his hood over his head as the raindrops plopped around him. He was surprised how fast the boats could go, and soon they'd left the cluster of islands for the open bay. The choppy water pitched and slammed into the flat boats. Several times a wave broke over the bow.

"'Tis clear these vessels were not meant for the open water." Luag's hands gripped the waling so hard his knuckles whitened.

"'Twas a rough and stormy dark harbor as the men pulled out and rowed harder." Finnean's face blanched nearly as white as Luag's. "In a gray and rainy wet autumn, they struggled and went to the bottom."

"Enough, Finnean. Too soon do your rhymes take a dark tone. And it's not even autumn yet. But, lads, we're almost over the worst stretch. Drijvendby Bay is not big. We'll pull in—over there." Machar pointed to a cluster of islands just ahead.

Moments later, the two boats were safely docked inside a calm channel. "Before we go on, Neil and I have some business to attend to. This should take no longer than a morning's stroll through the meadow. My second errand will likely take longer." Then Machar led Neil up the dock and down a side street.

"How did you know this isle has what you're looking for?" Neil cast a sidelong glance at the tall, thin warrior. "And what *are* we looking for?"

"Each island flies different flags. This one flies the 'anvil and hammer' and the 'boat and paddle' flags." He gestured to the pennants flying from the tallest mast. "Ah, this establishment will do nicely." He stopped before a shop with an open front. Just inside, a small idol of bronze sat atop a pedestal—the god Goivhniu, the same one Cowan worshiped.

Neil breathed in the familiar smell of burning coals, heated iron, and fired clay. As they entered the forge, a lad not much younger than him stopped pumping a bellows and looked up. In the corner, an older man, his face scarred by years of sparks, beat a hammer on a white-hot dagger. He stopped and faced them.

A sense of unreality washed over him. Here, he was, a peasant masquerading as a noble and a high prince of Ulster. Now he was facing a younger version of himself. A few months ago, this could have been him. It was like walking into his own past.

"We've urgent need of your skills, smithy." Machar raised a bag of coins. "And we'll pay double for fast work."

The elder man stuck the blade in the squelching pan. Steam hissed and rose in a cloud. "At your service, my lord." He set the dagger aside and bowed low. The apprentice's eyes widened. Nervously, he, too, bowed.

Machar inclined his head, and Neil pulled the package containing the pendant out of his pocket. But as he unwrapped it, the quarter moon fell into his palm. Instantly, the familiar tingling, the hot-cold sensation, shot up his arm. Had it grown stronger in hibernation? His eyes half-shut. His palm closed about the pendant. He felt a wave of ecstasy rising, threatening to overwhelm him.

But nay, he mustn't let it. He opened his fingers and jerked his hand away. The thing clattered to the floor. He looked to Machar at his side. But the tall lord said nothing, just watched him. Neil reached down, picked up the thing by its chain. Then he walked across the room toward the blacksmith. "This piece . . . it must be . . . recast. Remake it into exactly the same shape." He gazed again at the pendant. He battled a sudden urge to take it and run out the door. He bit his lip and passed it to the smith. "Do not touch it unnecessarily."

The blacksmith took the device by its chain and held it up. "It looks perfect. Why do you want to recast it, my lord? I canna do better than this."

"'Tis bewitched, proprietor." Machar put a hand on Neil's shoulder. "Only by remaking it can we remove the foul druid's spell cast upon it."

The man's eyes widened, and he examined it with more caution. "Then we shall remake it with all dispatch. I care little for druids or their spells."

Instantly, Neil felt a moment of panic. He wanted to cry out, to stop this. Was the thing so bad they had to *kill* it? Even after being dormant for so long, it now felt as if it were a part of him. The smith was already preparing the form and the clay. It wouldn't take long now. The apprentice was pumping the bellows, getting the fire hot.

He whirled and bolted for the street. Once out in the bustle of vendors hawking wares, women clutching parcels, and men wheeling barrows, he breathed deeply.

"'Tis a powerful hold the device had on you, my prince." Machar came up beside him. "But you fought it well. I can see as much."

Neil nodded. They stood there for some time, waiting, watching people come and go, when an unexpected sense of relief washed over him. *It was done.* He strode back inside.

The smith had just poured the molten silver into its new form. Neil fixed Machar with a smile. "The curse is gone."

Machar held out his hand, they shook, and he clasped fingers on his shoulder.

"Well done, my lord."

They waited for the silver to cool.

After they left the smithy, Neil dropped the pendant into the first canal they passed

Machar led Neil back to the boats. Then he and Dermid entered the streets on a second errand. A long while later they returned with a tall, lanky, blond-haired man about forty, with thin, sunken cheekbones, a sun-seared face, and a faraway look in his eyes. In one hand, he carried a large pack.

"This is Sem DeVliet," said Dermid. "He will guide us through the swamps." Dermid introduced Sem to everyone, but the guide merely nodded and stepped into Neil's boat without saying a word.

They rowed back into the bay, which soon divided into smaller channels. Tiny sunken islands appeared on all sides, bearing cypress and black ash, and once, a cawing, squawking crow. Reeds and bulrushes now grew in clustered, tiny forests. Then the water turned stagnant. Finally, the reeds forced the channel into narrower and narrower passages filled with the deafening songs of crickets. Sem called the rowers to a halt.

He spoke loud enough for all to hear. "My lords, ahead lies the Fell Bogs. My advice is to turn back now."

Machar faced him, frowning. "We hired you to lead us there, DeVliet. So guide us."

"Aye, 'twas your wish. And you've given me a heap of silver to do it. But this warning's my duty, so I warns you again. Many times have I entered this foul place. Too many goes in and doesn't come out again. Something's happening in there, my lords. Changing for the worse, it is. And before we goes on, 'tis my duty to warn you again. Will you still go in?"

"We will go in."

Sem stared at the tall warrior and exhaled. "Then I enters the bogs with a clear conscience. If all doesn't make it out again—well, you were warned."

CHAPTER 22

THE FELL BOGS

Not long after Sem gave his warning, the rushes crowded so thickly against the hulls they could no longer row but had to stow the oars and bring out the poles. Two men now stood on opposite sides of the boat. First one man stuck his long, slender pole into the muck, pushed it forward, its wood scraping against the rail until he pulled it out. Then the man on the opposite side did the same. In this way, they pushed the boats through vegetation seemingly clinging to the keels with a will of its own. Occasionally, they entered scant stretches of open water where they could row. But then the reeds would thicken and out again came the poles. Everywhere roared the sound of crickets.

Occasionally large, moldy mounds stuck up from the water, some bearing ruined columns or jumbled piles of stone. A few held entire rooms, but with shattered walls, gaping holes. All were roofless. Near these the crickets were silent.

"Some are tombs, my lords." Sem spat in the water. "Never does we go near these ruins. Bad things happens to those as camp on them. Stay away from them."

They stared at the stones, discolored with moss, some crowded with vines.

"You pays me to travel, not to gawk, my lords." Sem rubbed his face and grinned.

Thus chastised, they returned to poling. After a time they were able to row again, but then had to go back to punting. But the farther in they went, the fewer places they found to row.

In this way did they travel until sunset. Then Sem drew them up on a sunken island, barely ten yards across, with two downed ash trunks rising just above ankle-deep water. Dermid handed out bread, cheese, and salted beef. Machar poured wine from a copious skin into wooden mugs.

Already, dark shadows from nearby ash and cypress fell across the island. The buzzing of insect wings, the chirping of crickets, filled the air. Wisps of vapor rose like wraiths, slowly twisted, and vanished above them. Neil barely started eating when a cloud of gnats enveloped him. He tried eating with one hand and swatting with the other. By the time he'd finished, the air was thick with bugs.

"How can anyone sleep with these dratted insects?" Camran struck viciously at the cloud around him, but to no effect.

Sem slid one of several round containers out of his pack and pried off its lid. He stuck his finger into its yellow grease, lifted it to his nose, breathed deeply, and smiled. "Stink grease keeps them away. Everyone, smear it on your face and hands. Only thing that helps. You get used to the smell."

Neil stuck his finger into the goo he'd been passed and brought it up to his nose. Immediately, he jerked his hand away and gagged. How could anyone bear such foul stuff on their cheeks? He held the finger at arm's length. Instantly, the gnats swarmed his eyes, nose, and ears and started biting. But around his extended finger—a wide empty space. The stink grease won. He brought the outcast appendage back and spread the foul substance over his cheeks, chin, ears, and forehead. The smell was like something from the latrine combined with the fumes of a sulfur pit he'd once come across a few leagues from Hidden Pines. After trying and failing to hold his breath, he resumed normal breathing. But at least the bugs were gone.

"How does one sleep on a log?" Camran eyed the fallen trunks.

"Logs is fine for me. For you?" A flicker of a smile passed Sem's lips, and he shrugged. "Maybe a few of you in the boats. You drapes yourself over the trunk like so." He laid facedown onto a sack he'd placed on the log, with both hands falling to either side. "Or on your back like this." He flipped himself over and laid with his hands crossed. The log was wide enough so both of his feet lay flat. "But don't fall off. Snakes in the water."

"Snakes?" Caitir's eyes were wide. "I've heard of them. I do not ken I will care for snakes."

"But, my lords, and my lady, pay close and careful heed to my next warning." Sem sat on the log and waved for them to approach.

The Company moved closer.

"If you sees any lights in the fog, do not go to them. Ignore them. 'Tis very important what I say now. No matter how they calls you, ignore them. We're not near their lair yet, but sometimes, they travels this far north. Now I'll say it again. If you sees any lights or bright, swirling colors, under no conditions will you look at them or go to them. Understand?"

Neil could barely see heads nodding in the gathering dark. "Who are they?"

"They goes by many names. The lantern folk. Marsh spirits. The Aeshitha."

"The Aeshitha? That's what they're called?" Machar's tone was so intense, the others looked his way. "Are you certain?"

"I am, my lord. So you know of them?"

"The ancient texts speak of them. Long before the Great Upheaval, before the mountains plunged and the three rivers changed course, back in the First and Second Eras, this was a dry, fertile land called Saxia."

"Aye, my lord. I've heard the name whispered once or twice."

Machar nodded. "The Saxians prospered and built a great country and city called Überhort. Their lands covered all this swamp. Back then it was much higher. Then came the Third Era, the Age of Darkness, and the Deamhan Lord's reign of terror. During the Great Purge, as Faolukan's army approached his castle, King Lange pledged himself to the Deamhan Lord. He gave over all his armies, wealth, and power to Faolukan. He saved his kingdom, but at—well, at a grand price, indeed.

"When Faolukan's soldiers dragged women and children from their beds and burned their huts, 'twas often Saxian warriors who helped him do the deed. But what angered Elyon, even more, was *how* they served—with eager hearts and especial cruelty. Whole communities were slaughtered on a whim; entire villages were wiped out when one man resisted. Such terror we wish never to see again."

"You speak names few dare to utter in these parts." Sem wagged his head. "Elyon. The Deamhan Lord. Faolukan."

"Names that soon will be known again throughout Ereb. When the Deamhan Lord's reign ended, then did Elyon's wrath fall upon this wayward country. An earthquake greater than any before—it shook the land. It shook even distant Ériu. The once-great city of Űberhort and its surrounding towns tumbled into rubble. Then the land sank. The rivers flowed in. And Saxia became what you see today."

"But what about the Aeshitha?" asked Caitir.

"For the evil they did in Faolukan's purge, Elyon judged the Saxians. Sure, the rubble and the surging waters killed their mortal bodies, but the Saxians didn't die. Elyon cursed not only their land, but also their souls, for evil must be judged. He made them into the race of spirits called the Aeshitha." Machar narrowed his eyes at Sem. "When you spoke their name just now, I made the connection. Sure, and for over twenty-three hundred years, they've wandered bodiless, frustrated, hungry for revenge, stripped of life, but denied the peace of death. Cursed as wraiths, they live now only to lure others to their deaths. Out of revenge. Hatred. And spite."

Neil shuddered. What worse terror could await them than this?

"And a fine tale this is. But how is it"—Camran's voice was defiant—"that you ken so much about things no one should ken?"

"And who are you"—Dermid's voice shot back from the darkness—"to question one so wise and knowledgeable as Machar? Keep your tongue, Camran, or you might just lose it."

It was too dark now to see the expressions on their faces. But Neil expected the veins on Dermid's face would be bulging. Perhaps Camran's as well.

Neil heard a grunt and then sloshing footsteps leading off toward the boats. Camran had gone.

"Time to sleep, my lords." Sem broke the tense atmosphere. "We've a long slog ahead of us tomorrow."

A few followed Camran to the boats. The rest walked toward the tree trunks.

After Sem's warning, Neil went to his pack and took out the small brass case containing the tallow the Roamer woman had given him. If spirits were about, perhaps he'd have need of it. He dropped it into the deep pocket of his tunic holding his bone whistle and tied the flap shut.

Then he followed the others to a trunk. Thanks to the reek of the grease, the bugs stayed away, but laying across the log was uncomfortable. He closed his eyes and tried to get used to the smell. Yet sleep eluded him.

From over the horizon, some unknown creature uttered a desolate cry—a low, lonely, howl from something big. This was answered by a similar, longer cry from the opposite horizon. Then distant, ferocious growling, accompanied by the high-pitched squeals of some doomed prey. Then silence.

Sitting up, he opened his eyes and stared into darkness broken only by the intermittent flashing of glow bugs. What kind of beast could live in such a watery wasteland?

He listened to the plops of tiny amphibians from nearby pools. Then began the sawing of crickets. They started slow and grew louder until the chorus reached a deafening crescendo. Something big plopped and splashed in the nearby water. Then the crickets fell silent. But soon, they began again, the noise building until it again drowned out everything else.

What a strange country they'd entered. Once a dry, prosperous land, now only a wet grave, cursed by Elyon, owned by wraiths. How had he ended up here, in a dread swamp where even guides feared to tread? Last night he'd taken a hot bath, laid on soft pillows, and eaten a feast, greater luxury than he'd ever experienced. Tonight he lay on a bumpy log, his nose puckered from stink grease and the smell of mud, his ears filled with the sounds of strange creatures.

He laid back on the trunk and listened to the swamp's night sounds. It was late when he finally slept.

The next morning the gnats had gone, but they woke to a fog so dense Neil could barely see the end of his tree trunk. The crickets had quieted, and they ate a quick breakfast in silence. Much to his surprise, Sem hurried them into the boats.

"How can you see anything in this mist?" Dermid asked.

"If we keeps close to the trees on the islands, the mossy side tells me which way to go."

And indeed Sem drove them on, hugging the faint shoreline near the largest submerged island. When the sun finally burned the fog away, leaving behind a thick, muggy air, they learned it was past midday. They poled all afternoon until evening.

Again, they found a submerged island with downed trunks.

"Half the trees seem to have died, Sem," said Dermid, as he examined their new resting place.

"Aye, my lord. Death is finding a home everywhere in the Fell Bogs. Even among the trees."

Sem warned them again about the lights, if they came, which he didn't think likely as they were not yet in the deepest swamp. To the strains of another cricket chorus, they spent another miserable night on logs coated with soft moss. At first, this seemed a comfortable choice, but later, they discovered it bore nests of tiny crawling insects. They didn't bite, just crawled. When morning dawned, muggy and hot, Neil shook his tunic free of bugs. He felt he'd hardly slept at all.

For most of the next two days, they had to pole constantly through channels choked with reeds, grasses, stunted scrub trees. They passed more and more ruins, spending more miserable nights perched atop wet logs. But they never saw the lights Sem kept warning them about.

On the fourth day, the poling became more and more difficult, until, by afternoon, the water was only inches deep and the hulls grabbed the vegetation beneath. Cattails and cordgrass slid and scraped constantly along the hulls. Now every foot gained took an effort.

"We're making wee progress, Sem DeVliet." Machar stared at the mass of tangled kelp and slimy grass rising almost to the black water's surface.

"Aye. But we must keep on till we gain the road. It gets better after that."

"Ah, the road. I do remember what comes next, though I wish I didn't. How far is it?"

Sem just shrugged and rammed his pole in again. Soon the water became even shallower, blacker, and Sem raised and stowed his pole. "Now we gets in and pulls. But tie your shoes or you'll lose them. Who comes with me?" He produced lengths of cord, threaded the leather through holes in the top of his shoes, and tied them tight to his ankles. Then with one swift motion, he jumped into water, reeds, and mud up to his knees.

After securing his boots, Machar joined him. Dermid jumped out of the other boat. But when Finnean leaped, he nearly tipped the craft over. Only Dermid's quick hand saved them.

"Oh, for a forest and heather, horse and dry leather." Finnean scowled. "But a foul swamp of slime, muck, and weather? Never!"

Sem arched an eyebrow in Machar's direction. "Is your friend touched in the head?"

Machar rolled his eyeballs. "Sometimes, we think he is."

The men in the water grabbed lines and began hauling the boats toward the horizon, fighting muck, slime, and thin grasses with every step. Despite tying his shoes, Finnean lost one and had to stick arm, shoulder, and face into the slimy water to retrieve it. His shoe came back filled with mud and weeds. At all times, at least one man stood in each boat and poled.

Too short to jump in, Luag insisted on poling while the others were in the water. "I'll not sit here like a helpless babe," he said, "while others do me work for me."

When the first group returned to the boats and gave the effort over to a second shift, Finnean cried out from the opposite boat. "Bloodsuckers! Dratted, blasted bloodsuckers. All over me."

And indeed, black, slimy leeches had found their way under his leggings. One by one, he picked them off. The others found that their legs, too, were covered with them. When Neil returned to the boat after his shift and pried the first leech from a bloody calf, he shuddered.

All afternoon, they took turns punting the boats through heavy cordgrass and muck. Then in early evening, Sem called out for all to hear, "My lords, behold—the bog road."

Neil lifted his gaze to a dark line on the horizon.

"'Tis about blasted time." Camran scowled as he sat dripping in the boat, unraveling a trail of grass and reeds wrapped around his knees, plucking leeches from a bloody leg.

"But," Sem added, "we'll not make it before dark."

They trudged on. The gnats returned, accompanied by mosquitoes, and, of course, the roar of the crickets. They stopped to smear stink grease on their faces and bare arms. When the sun's red disc touched the western horizon, Sem called a halt to the day's efforts. "We stops here for the night."

Ewan stared at him. "Aye, laddie. We're sore knackered. All of us."

"Looks as if you all needs rest." One side of Sem's mouth lifted up in a half-grin. "Tonight we sleeps in the boats. Remember what I said about the lights. Especially here. We could be seeing them tonight. But there's usually only one or two."

Neil nodded with the others. Dermid passed out more bread, cheese, and hardtack. The wine, especially, was welcome. He pulled off his wet shoes and tried to rinse off the mud.

"Look behind us, my lords." Ewan's tone was worried.

Neil jerked his head around to gaze back where they'd come from. Far across the swamp, barely visible on the horizon, a boat carried at least four men.

"Who are they?" Dermid squinted and peered at the distant vessel.

"I don't know." Machar stood to get a better look. "Whoever they are, they're also stuck in the weeds. I'd guess at least half a day's punting from us." He turned to Sem DeVliet. "How often do others travel this route?"

"A few does trade with the forest folk. A fool's business that. Done it myself out of desperation. Foolish and dangerous, but gainful. But 'tis not likely those are traders. Too many in one boat. Traders go alone, leave space for their goods."

"Look." Machar pointed. "A man stands and raises both arms. And can you hear that?"

Though impossibly distant, a sound was now traveling over the swamp, a voice carrying dark words in a guttural, grating tongue. The sound of crickets, the frogs, the cawing of crows—all stopped, as words of evil passed like a fell wind above them toward some unknown destination.

"Faolukan!" Machar shouted.

Sem's eyes widened. "Faolukan the Grim? Behind us?"

Machar nodded.

"'Tis a name not often spoke. And when spoke, men shakes their heads and remembers a great mourning. Tales told of grand tragedy. Of terrors dim remembered from their grandfather's grandfather's time. If I's to have known this." He shook his head. "There's not enough geld in Drijvendby to have made me come here."

"Would you turn back now and face him?" Machar frowned. "Get us onto dry land, guide, and we'll double your fee."

Sem rubbed his neck and glowered at the water. "You've not been forthright, my lords. I'll take your geld because you're right. We can't turn back with him behind us. And I'll take it because I never turn down extra geld. If he's who you says he is, we must go on. But I don't like this. Nay, not one bit."

Machar gazed across the dimming swamp at the lone boat. The sun had almost set. "You don't understand the importance of this mission, Sem DeVliet. If we fail, if Faolukan wins—then the evils of this swamp will be as nothing compared with the reign of terror Erde will see next."

Sem slowly raised his glance to Machar's. "What's to come is to come, and certain, the future may be grim. 'Tis today and tonight I worries about. But—" His face froze. He squinted off in the direction Faolukan's words had gone, and his jaw dropped. "My lords. Look!" He waved a trembling hand to the south. "The specters, the lantern folk—even now, they comes."

Neil stared toward the distant road. Lights seemed to float above the swamp, gliding up and down, winking and bobbing and swirling.

The Aeshitha. Hundreds of them. Heading straight for the Company.

CHAPTER 23

THE AESHITHA

Onward they came, the dancing, phosphorescent lights, too many to count, floating and gliding and lighting up the bulrushes and cattails below. All the Company stared at their approach. Blue and green, red with hints of yellow, they winked and glowed and drifted ever closer.

Around the Company now settled the silence of the tomb. The crickets, the frogs, the crows—all fell silent.

"Remember, my lords. Don't stare at them. Don't look at them." A note of fear had entered Sem's voice. It trembled as he added, "But never have I seen so many. Never so many."

Still, Neil stared. They were beautiful, dazzling, enchanting. Even Machar, Finnean, and Luag stared. How could they not help but do so? He'd never seen anything like them. In all his years, he'd beheld nothing as beautiful as these luminous creatures.

"Don't look, my lords. Mark my words. Don't look. Or they'll bewitch you."

Neil tore his gaze from the oncoming lights. Every so often, he chanced a quick glance to assess their progress, but always returned to stare at the shadows in the bottom of the boat.

"Be aware of . . . the man beside you." Sem's voice quavered. "If someone goes over the side, pull them back." Barely under his breath, but loud enough so Neil could hear, Sem muttered, "So many. Never seen so many."

Suddenly, the landscape around the boat glowed with a dim, fluttering blue light. He felt their presence now as a vague and growing desire gnawing at his soul. Neil fixed his gaze on his feet, but—out of curiosity so intense he nearly shook—he kept his eyes open. Dull swirls of red and green, blue streaked with yellow, dark shadow flames flickering with shimmering color—they danced around the bottom of the boat and filled his eyes with wonder. He struggled but didn't look up.

"Come to me, Tristan. . . ." In his ears, a woman's voice, pleasant, seductive, enticing. "Look at me, Tristan."

A desire similar to the pendant's pull washed over him. Maybe because of his experience with that device, he was able to resist. Still, the urge to look was strong.

Lights capered and whirled all about him. Glimmering shadows alive with color capered at his feet. Still, he focused his glance at the boat's bottom.

"You want to look, Tristan. . . ." She'd used his real name. How did she know? "Come to me. I won't harm you. Come. . . ."

He heard a splash and spun in its direction.

"Caitir!" Dermid called out.

She was in the water, walking toward a cloud of twisting, writhing lights. Within them appeared the form of a man, handsome, black-haired, beckoning.

Still shoeless, Neil jumped overboard and sank to his knees. He began trudging toward her, pulling one bare foot out of the sucking mud, planting the next in the slime, trudging on. He must reach her.

He heard another splash, loud behind him, and Machar called out, "Finnean, stop!" Neil glanced back. Finnean was headed in the opposite direction. Then came a second splash as Machar jumped in after him.

A multicolored vapor hovered directly before Neil. It coalesced into the shape of a woman. A robe of pale white light floated around her, the garment folding on wisps of air. The cape opened at the neck almost to her breasts, revealing a white nape, skin as smooth as pale velvet. Golden hair, luscious and flowing, shimmered with a dim light. Wide doe-eyes gazed into his own. Beautiful eyes, filled with every color he could imagine, swirled and lured him. A white face, expressionless, glowed with pale radiance. A slender white hand stretched out and caressed his face. Warm, yet icy, her fingers sent a delicious tingling across his cheeks, much like the ecstasy of the pendant.

Gazing into her eyes, he wanted to follow her.

"Aye, Tristan. Come with me." The voice calmed, enticed. Yet it was also cold. "You want to join me. You know you do. Come with me."

He felt the urge to follow, to be with her. She was the most beautiful creature he'd ever seen. And she wanted him to be with her. He took one step aside from his path.

"Neil!" A shout from behind. Dermid's voice.

"Don't listen, Tristan," said the cold, mesmerizing voice. It seemed to come from inside his head. "Follow me." He stared into her eyes. He felt as if he were falling into a well, yet enjoying the sensation of exhilarating flight, believing he'd never hit bottom. Pale fingers reached out and grasped one of his hands. The icy cold shot up through him and—

What was he doing?

He wrenched his hand away, tore his gaze from the specter's. Instantly, the desire to follow her diminished. As if blown by a sudden gust of wind, the Aeshitha woman jerked back, her human form disintegrated, and she became just a mass of churning light.

Where was Caitir? There. Trudging into a darkness lit only by swirling red and blue-green lights. He tromped toward her. The woman specter followed beside him, hovering just out of reach, but didn't resume its human form.

"Look at me," it whispered, but his gaze was only on Caitir now. As he gained on her, shouting erupted from the boat behind him. Far, too far behind him. How would he ever find it again in the dark? Someone cried Camran's name. More splashing as someone went to rescue him. Would they all succumb to these spirits?

Caitir followed the lights farther away from the boats into the night.

"Caitir!" he called. But she didn't turn or slow. He trudged closer. The form in front of her still held the shape of a young man, handsome, beguiling, beckoning her forward. Long black hair fell to his shoulders, swam on currents of air. His chest bore a coat of chain mail, dimly lit, glinting and sparkling. Always the man floated backward, drawing her onward.

Lit by dozens of swirling Aeshitha, a large mound appeared out of the night. Four stone columns of different heights, cracked and jagged, their crowns broken off, rose into the dark. This mound was wider, taller than the others they'd passed.

Caitir climbed steps to the top and disappeared over the edge.

Neil slogged faster, the muck sucking at his feet. Now the specter hovered before him, lighting the way, not slowing him down. Almost as if . . . as if it *wanted* him to follow where Caitir had gone.

When he gained the mound, the spirit withdrew. The stench of dank mold soured his nostrils, that and the foul odor of something long dead. He stepped onto the stone stairs. Solid ground at last. All around him dozens of Aeshitha hovered, some with pale faces, others with hands grasping, reaching out, then receding. Their swirling lights illumined the ruins.

Now on firm ground, he ascended quickly to the top, and then halted.

Steps led down into a dark, circular hole in the ground. Beside it rested a massive round stone that once sealed the opening. The hole's darkness yawned, swirled, seemed to grow before his eyes. From below echoed the sounds of dripping water.

A dark hole in the ground. That's where she went.

His heart raced so fast he thought it would burst. Staring down into the blackness, he staggered back. The hole, still seemingly growing in size before him, filled his vision.

Whispers surrounded him. Dozens of whispering voices, cold and pleading. "Come with us."

"Come down, Tristan."

"She's down here, waiting for you."

"Come down, Tristan."

He was still staring into the hole. When he breathed in, he realized the air rising from below was as cold as ice.

Already, he was chilled. His wet legs, damp tunic, slogging through the mud in bare feet, and now breathing the icy air of the hole—all combined to chill him as if he had lain naked in deep snow. A shiver started in his shoulders, shook his upper body, then traveled to his hands. It wouldn't stop.

They'd taken her underground, beneath the swamp. Into darkness. He knew what he had to do. Yet every fiber of his being told him that nay, he couldn't do it. How could he ever go down into that black hole?

Yet he placed one foot on the first step. The second foot dropped to the step below that. Shivering, he descended two more steps, his bare feet hitting cold, wet stone. His heart thudded, about to burst in his chest, but it didn't warm him. The icy air rose about him, hugged him, and he saw his own breath. He wanted to turn and run, go back outside, away from this dank pit, anywhere, just not—below. But Caitir was down there. His lifelong friend.

Caitir, why did you go down there?

And then he realized she was much more than a friend, wasn't she?

Three more steps, and the darkness grew thicker, deeper, closer. He reached to his right, felt for the wall, and touched wet, dripping rock. He closed his eyes—it didn't matter now; the dark had engulfed him—and took a half-dozen slow steps down, feeling along the rock. Each tread on stone was like an icy hammer hitting the balls of his bare feet. Another dozen steps, quicker than the last ones. His hand slid across a slimy, gooey section, then back onto wet rock.

From somewhere ahead, water dripped, echoing, into a pool. He descended ten more steps then opened his eyes. Nothing. Total darkness. His heart raced. He was breathing too fast. Tiny spots of light burst before his eyes. But he knew they weren't real. The same thing happened the last time he was trapped in a dark cave. Then fear itself had captured him, and he'd waited to die, hoping death would come soon. That must not happen again.

"Caitir?" he called, and the word echoed back to him. Who knew how deep this went? He wanted to scream and run back out.

He felt along the wall to the right, inching one foot forward, remembering the cave of his youth where he'd fallen into the pit—the pit where he'd spent days in the dark, believing he'd never see the light again. The hole where, for a time, something in him had died.

Slowly, he advanced into the darkness. From somewhere ahead came breathing.

"Caitir?"

"Tristan!"

"Caitir, I'm coming. Are you all right?"

"A–aye." Her trembling voice echoed from far to the left. "I'm cold."

Fearing a pit, he dropped to all fours and groped his way forward with his hands. Inches at a time, he slid his fingers over muddy wet stone and crawled toward her breathing. He called her name again. When she answered from the right, he changed direction.

His fingers touched a leg. Caitir's warm leg. He came up beside her, and she threw her arms around him. She was shivering. They embraced, held each other, savoring the warmth of their bodies pressed together.

From far above came the sound of laughter and a heavy stone grinding over rock. Then came a loud, deep thud, as of a boulder falling into place. Only the dripping water now broke the silence.

"The door?" His voice shook as it echoed off the ceiling. "Are we trapped?"

"I . . . I do not ken."

He helped her stand. Knowing there were no pits between him and the steps, he started leading her across the room.

But suddenly, he could see. The floor beneath him appeared under a faint light. The ceiling was made of cut stone, and once was flat. Now it grew long, dripping spikes of rock.

"Who—?" a low voice, filled with malice and authority, boomed, "who wakes me from slumber?"

He jumped at the sound and whirled. In a far corner, surrounded by gray light, sat an imposing figure on a throne. Draped in kingly robes of darkest, deepest red light. Large hands bore a sword, glinting in pale white light. A thick beard covered his chin and seemed to whirl with colors of darkest brown. The specter's glance fixed on him and bored into his.

Neil's heart thumped so hard, spots bounced before his eyes. He staggered, took a step back. His hand reached for his sword, but—oh, no!

He'd left all his weapons in the boat. All he had was the small case given him by the Roamer woman. A lot of good that would do him now.

Beside the spirit lay piles of molding goods. Towers of rotting books covered in mold. Piles of coins, their shapes barely visible beneath layers of moss.

And there—a stack of swords, lances, axes, and armor, so tarnished that none gleamed.

With a shudder, he realized the nature of this place. It was a tomb. And those were the grave goods of the deceased.

The apparition advanced, one slow step at a time. A dim light—not colored like the Aeshitha outside, but pale, gray, cold as death—filled the room.

"Answer me, stranger." Its voice was deep, low, and thunderous. "Who are you? Why are you here?"

"I am Neil mac Connell." He continued the deception, even down here. "And the Aeshitha led my friend Caitir down here. We only want to return to the surface."

"The Aeshitha?" Its eyes widened. Then it laughed, but its mirth hinted of distant, echoing thunder, and it chilled him. "Ah, yes. We are Saxians no longer. He took that from us, didn't he? Long ago, we lost who we were. Now they call us the Aeshitha." It looked at its own arm as if seeing it for the first time. The spirit grasped an elbow and laughed again.

"Who am I, Neil mac Connell? A spirit or a king? Is it possible to be both?"

"I don't know, my lord. But you bear the trappings of a king. Are you King Lange?"

"Lange? Aye, that is my name." Stiff, it stood from its throne and spread a hand toward the pile of molding rubble. "And these are my royal trappings." He laughed again, louder. But its mirth, like continuous thunder before a storm, carried only threat.

Then it frowned and raised the sword so its left hand could grasp the blade. "He sent you to destroy me, didn't he? Don't lie to me. 'Tis not enough to have imprisoned me here, never being allowed to roam my lands, see my castle, the greatness of Überhort, my fields, or my orchards, so beautiful and bountiful. Instead, he traps me in a tomb and sends you to kill me."

"Nay, my lord Lange. I came not to harm you. But nothing of the past remains. All your lands—they're underwater. All is now swamp, muck, and mire. And your castle—'tis in ruins."

The spirit cocked its head. "Ruins and swamp, you say? Muck and mire? Nay, you lie!" Anger widened its eyes, and, its blade singing, it slashed the air. Obviously, that was the wrong thing to say. Then it began striding toward Neil with narrowed eyes.

As the specter approached, Neil pushed Caitir off into a corner. The apparition didn't seem concerned with her. Not yet.

When it was within a yard of him, it swung the blade. Was the weapon real? Neil leaped to the side, toward the steps. If the blade came from the pile of weapons, then aye—it was real. The spirit struck again, and he ducked and moved to his right, away from Caitir, toward the weapons pile. If only he could get to a sword.

The specter moved closer and slashed sideways. Neil backed up, barely averting being hit. It lumbered slowly but relentlessly toward him. It seemed unable to move with speed.

Neil circled ever to the right. A few more steps, and he'd be within reach of a weapon.

Without warning, it thrust its blade at Neil's left side. He backed up, but too late, not fast enough. The blade cut into his left arm. At first, he felt no pain, only a jab into flesh. He slid his right hand over the wound. It wasn't deep. But his hand came back red.

He whirled and there, at his feet—the pile of weapons. He reached down and grabbed the first sword on top. It was wet, slimy, and pitted, but it was something. He ran his fingers over the blade to remove some slime.

"Hah! The assassin now reveals his true purpose. But think, Neil. To you, I am only a spirit. I remember that now. Your blade cannot harm me." It threw back its head and laughed.

Blood ran down to Neil's fingers. A stab of pain shot through him. A fit of shivering ran up from his wounded arm, along his shoulders, and then stopped.

But he had a blade. He took three steps forward and brought it down hard at the spirit's head.

It just stood there, unmoving, and let the edge slice through itself, as though it were composed of nothing but air. The sword finished its swing without effect. Then the spirit put a hand on top of its head where the sword had passed through. It examined the hand and laughed again. "I haven't had a good sword fight in ages. Let's begin."

It struck down at Neil's head. He stepped aside and knocked away the blow with a clash of steel. The spirit's weapon, at least, was solid.

It swung to Neil's left, but he grasped the other end of his blade with his left hand, ignored the shooting pain, and parried.

Then it thrust straight for Neil's gut, and he answered with a blow that knocked the weapon aside.

"Ah, very good. Only a true swordsman could do that."

A wave of dizziness washed over him. An unnatural coldness was seeping up from the wound.

The specter struck again. Neil parried.

It sliced sideways. Neil blocked and backed away.

Then he remembered. The brass can with the tallow. From the Roamer woman.

He pulled it out and, still holding the sword, fumbled with the top. But he couldn't open it.

The specter's sword sliced straight down at his skull. He brought his own weapon up to meet the blow, but his grip on the sword was too loose. The weapon flew from his hands. He backed up, tripped, and went down onto the pile of weapons. Still holding the brass can, he finally popped open the top, stuck a finger deep into the tallow.

He reached for his fallen weapon.

The spirit's sword came down again, Neil rolled, but the blade's edge sliced across his chest. He winced, felt a warm wetness forming there. The blade had cut a long, but shallow, swath through his tunic.

He launched himself to his feet. With one quick swipe of his finger, he drew the tallow over the blade.

In a blinding flash, the slime and pits and age vanished from the steel. The weapon began to glow. Then it became so bright he had to squint.

The specter halted, its eyes wide. Then it backed up. "What magic is this? What have you done?"

Neil held the blade before him and took a swipe at the specter's side. It parried.

Then it lunged, thrusting its weapon straight at Neil's stomach. He knocked it aside with such force, the spirit's sword clattered to the ground. Seizing his chance, Neil thrust the blade straight into the king's chest, halfway to the hilt.

The specter looked down at the glowing steel sticking out of its gut. Neil pulled, felt the tug of its body gripping metal until he freed the weapon.

The king staggered back a step. It tottered forward a step. With unbelieving eyes, it stared at its wound, now bleeding heavily. "O Saxia!" it cried. "I am undone." Then it collapsed to the floor and lay still.

"You've killed it." Caitir rushed to him. "Oh Tristan! You're wounded."

Dropping the weapon, he staggered. "Aye."

He fell to his knees. A coldness, a strange numbness, gathered around his wounded arm and seeped in from his chest where the blade had nicked him. He felt the life draining from him. "Caitir . . ."

She blinked at him with frightened eyes. "Aye, Tristan?"

Her words came as from across an empty, echoing hall.

"I . . . I'm afraid. The wounds are . . . unnatural. Cold. My sight . . . going dark."

Her fingers grazed his cheeks. Warm fingers. Almost hot against his flesh, now cold and growing colder. "Don't die, Tristan. Please, don't die."

A hot tear fell against his icy cheeks.

Then he slipped away into darkness.

PART IV

CHAPTER 24

AFTERMATH

For days, Neil lived in his dreams. There'd been brief moments of semiconsciousness. Then Caitir was beside him, speaking his name, wiping his forehead with a cool cloth. At those times, he remembered the fight with King Lange's specter. He heard other voices—Machar's, Ewan's, Luag's—discussing him, and the chopping of wood, the crackling of a fire. But then the cold blackness returned, radiating up from his throbbing arm, seeping in from his chest. The black, deadening poison of a spirit wound.

Again and again, his dreams took him down a forest path to the entrance of a mound tomb, yawning black and deep before him. Currents of air whisked him off his feet, down the steps into a subterranean tunnel, lined with unnaturally bright trees of green, blue, and black—pulsing and wavering. A wide path opened in the trail, leading down into darkness. Red and yellow flames flickered ominously over the sides, calling him, inviting him down, and he had trouble resisting their allure. Was that the Underworld below? Just beyond, another path led up to a tunnel of bright, ethereal light, beckoning him rise to a place of refuge and happiness. But spirit guardians with flaming swords blocked the way.

The current drifted, taking him to first one, then the other path. But always, fragile life drew him out of the supernatural tunnel, back to where he lay on a bed in the swamp. How long this went on, going to and returning from the paths between worlds, he couldn't remember.

Today, for the first time, the dream receded, fading to a distant, unreal memory. The smell of moss, mud, and mold filled his nostrils.

He opened his eyes. He was lying on the ground in a dank forest, water dripping off the trees. Beside him, Caitir was kneeling, and they were alone.

"Tristan?" She put a hand on his cheek.

He smiled. "Aye. 'Tis me. Always has been."

Tears ran down her cheeks. "You've come out of it. You're going to live." Then she knelt, buried her face in his chest, and sobbed.

"If this is what happens when I live, what would you have done if I'd died?"

She raised her head, wiped her tears, and smiled. "It's been four days now. Machar's been giving you oil of crimson, and yesterday, it ran out. It should have revived you long before now. We thought you were going to die."

He felt for the spot on his left arm where the specter's sword had struck. And for the cut on his chest. The flesh in both places was tender but healed. "It still feels a bit numb."

Machar appeared beside Caitir and smiled. "Well, my lord, you seem better."

Neil smiled.

Machar called out to the others, visible now at the end of the clearing, "He's awake."

Neil tried to sit up, but Caitir put a hand on his chest. "Not yet. You should rest."

He sat up anyway. Black ash trees surrounded them, but he could barely see their trunks through a heavy fog. Half the trees were dead. "Where are we?"

"On one of the few dry islands in the swamp." Machar waved toward the shadowy trunks. "To mislead Faolukan, Sem led us here after we left our boats at the log road. It's been days since our pursuer went down the road."

"What happened to Finnean and Camran? I saw them follow the swamp spirits out of the boat. Where are—?"

Machar closed his eyes. "Both dead. And the Company, Neil, is in disarray. Dermid and Sem have gone back to Drijvendby."

Dead? Gone back? "Wh–what happened?"

Ewan appeared and knelt by his other side. He laid a hand on Neil's shoulder. "I'm glad you're back, my lord. We were powerful worried about you."

Luag stood behind them, and he, too, nodded.

"Why did Dermid go back? 'Tis not like him."

"My lord"—Machar frowned at the ground—"soon after we set up camp, a bog adder bit him. Sem told us he had only days to get Dermid back to Drijvendby where he had some root of argyle that might cure him. But the cure—'twas not certain. Mind you, he had only days, or Dermid would die. So he took one of the boats and returned. When they left, Dermid's face was already deathly pale."

"B–but Finnean? Camran? How did they die?"

Caitir stood between the men and waved her hands. "Sure, and that's enough. You'll be leaving him alone till he's got some food in him and is better rested. Then you can do your talking." She scowled and hurried toward a spit of meat roasting over the fire.

"The lass is right." Machar stood as did Ewan. Luag backed away. "He's barely back from the grave. We've time later to tell what happened."

"Aye," said Ewan, and he walked to the far side of the camp.

Caitir brought him a spit of meat, some bread and cheese, and he ate like a starving man. Even when she told him it was snake meat, he didn't care. It tasted like chicken.

After the meal and some wine, he was so sleepy he laid back and fell instantly asleep.

When next he woke, the fog was gone and the dim light of early morning threw the shadow of an ash tree across his bed. Ewan was cooking something over the fire. Machar was chopping wood. Neil stood in the chill air, wobbled a bit, but crossed the camp without falling.

"Well, well." Machar whistled low and dropped his axe. "You're looking much better today. My lord, you've slept another entire day."

"I feel almost myself. But now you must tell me what happened." He sat on one of the fallen trunks they were using as benches.

"Aye, you need to know," said Machar.

Caitir joined the group and also found a seat.

Machar threw another log on the fire and stretched his feet toward the flame. "When you killed King Lange—and, Neil, that was some powerful feat!—the Aeshitha seemed to know instantly he was dead. They stopped their attack, and every one of them flew to his tomb. They just clustered around it, moaning and swirling. Hundreds of them. And they've been there ever since. But how did you kill him? He was a specter, and no sword of mortal man should ever have pierced him."

As Luag arrived and plopped into another seat, Neil explained how he'd used the magic tallow. He made up a story about buying it from a wandering Roamer he encountered in Tara. How could he ever explain the gifts the siòg bestowed on Tristan mac Torn?

Machar shot him a grin, but it quickly vanished. "How many more surprises do you have in you, my prince? In any event, it saved us. But not Finnean. Nor Camran."

Silence fell upon the group. Neil closed his eyes for a moment, remembering Finnean's annoying jests and Camran's opposition. Now he wished for their return. Then he whispered, "How did they die?"

"Shortly after you went for Caitir, Finnean followed one of those things out of the boat. I went to bring him back. They tried to entice me as well, but I knew their tricks. I wouldn't look at them, just closed my eyes, kept walking, and waved them aside. But Finnean was mesmerized. They led him on and on—into a trap.

"By the time I reached him, he was neck deep in quick mud. Nothing I could do. No trees, no rope, nothing to throw him. I just stood there, helpless . . ." Machar closed his eyes. "Helpless as the mud rose to his mouth. Then it covered his nose. He struggled for a time, his eyes pleading with me. But there was nothing—nothing, I tell you—that I could do. Then he went under."

"How horrible."

"Aye. Horrible, indeed."

"What about Camran?"

"Dermid followed him far out into the swamp. The spirits lured Camran toward a tomb like the one you went into, only much smaller— must be hundreds of them out there. Dermid saw Camran disappear down some steps. But before he could reach the tomb's island, the spirits slammed a stone across the opening. It was too heavy, so he returned to us.

"And that was the moment," continued Machar, "when the spirits all stopped hovering around us. Instead, they started a great wailing, and they began gliding toward the spot where you, Neil, had gone in.

"We followed Dermid back to where Camran had disappeared. We were able to move the stone. By now, we'd lit torches, and when we descended, we found Camran's body at the bottom, sword cuts in a dozen places. But the spirit that attacked him had fled. Like all the others."

Around the clearing—somber faces, shaking heads. From somewhere off in the swamp, a bird cawed. Even more distant came an answering caw.

Machar went on, "Then we wondered if they'd set a similar trap for you. So we followed the direction you went and discovered King Lange's crypt. Hundreds, nay, thousands, of mourning Aeshitha surrounded it, sending a terrible, unworldly keening into the night. I tell you, my lord, when we heard Caitir's muffled cry, it took all the courage we had to walk through those spirits. But they were no longer interested in us, only in their mourning.

"When we rolled aside the stone, Caitir, here, was waiting for us at the top."

"After you killed the king," said Caitir, "his light slowly died." She laid a hand on his knee. "You were unconscious, and I was desperate to take you outside and get help. So I dragged you up the steps. I discovered the spirits had blocked the way out, just as we'd feared. Then I just held you and waited, not knowing what else to do. You were so cold. I knew the life was draining from you. I wished I knew more about your Elyon. Maybe I would have prayed to him. But I'd never laid out food or beer or gifts for him in secret forest places, so I didn't think praying to him would do any good. Instead, I kept calling out, hoping someone would hear me. It seemed like forever until the others rolled the stone away."

"Lass, when things calm down, we must tell you about Elyon." Machar smiled. "My prince, you saved us. Killing their king has sent them all into deep mourning. But if you're better, we should leave this place. This morning, if you're able."

Neil nodded. "I'm well enough."

"We've lost three of our number." Luag scanned the group. "Should we go on?"

Machar looked to Neil, and his voice lowered. "Should we?"

"We must." Neil stood. "If their deaths are to mean anything, we must go on."

"Aye." Ewan also stood. "I'm for going on."

"Me, too." Now Caitir stood.

"Then I'm in as well." Luag also stood, smiling.

"Good." Machar slapped his knee. "Then 'tis decided. We'll continue the quest. But there's something I should tell you that I've kept secret until now."

Now everyone was watching him.

"I am a member of the Capulum. As is Ewan, here."

Neil stared at Ewan. He'd already guessed Machar was in some way involved with the group. And Ewan had blurted to Neil he'd obtained secret knowledge from somebody. Neil had suspected some connection with the Capulum. But to learn that his own squire was, indeed, one of them? "You never told me," he whispered.

"Forgive me, my lord. We've all taken an oath not to reveal our affiliation."

Luag's eyes widened as he regarded both men. "A surprising revelation, this. So why do you tell us now?"

"Because"—Machar glanced at each of them—"I sense 'tis the right thing to do. Two of our number have fallen. Dermid's been bitten by a poisonous adder, and his life hangs in the balance. So from this moment on, we must have no more secrets. Agreed?"

Everyone but Neil nodded. Then Neil raised his head and said, "Aye." But in saying it, a wave of lightheadedness swept over him.

"My lord, you look ill," said Ewan.

"'Tis nothing." Nothing but deception and lies. Machar had been honest with them, and here he was, continuing the lie that he was flaith, that he was the Toghaí. Neil waved a hand. "I'll be all right."

"My lords," said Machar, "We face the greatest villain evil has ever produced. But with courage, fortitude, and the Toghaí among us, I ken we will prevail."

Neil winced. What if he told them—right now—who he really was? Would they go on? He opened his mouth to speak.

But nay, he must do what Elyon commanded him to do. He must be what they wanted him to be. Even if he had to continue in this deception that he was someone else.

CHAPTER 25

THE FOREST

For a brief time that morning, as crows cawed and crickets chirped, the party of five slogged through swamp until they found the narrow east-west bog road. The bog roads were constructed of logs nailed onto pilings sunk deep into the mire. In half a league, they came to a wider road leading south. They had stepped only a few paces onto this new route when Machar stopped them and broke the silence. "Our Company is much reduced, but in one way, we're much stronger."

"How's that, my lord?" said Neil. After eating some breakfast and breaking camp, he felt much better. Perhaps his lightheadedness was only the aftereffect of the spirit wound.

"We're now of one mind. And one will. My lads and, of course, my lassie—we *will* find the Scepter. Nothing can stop us now."

"I believe we will, Machar," said Neil, his tone serious. Elyon had told him to be what they wanted him to be. So the Toghaí he must be.

"Aye, my lord." Ewan grinned.

"We'll find it, sure as gold." Luag smashed his axe onto the boards.

"Sure, and I have faith we'll find it." Caitir put a hand on Neil's shoulder.

"If we put our faith in Elyon, lassie, we will. And now, before we enter the last and easiest section of the bog, let us kneel and ask for Elyon's favor."

"Pray?" Caitir whipped her head to the side, throwing locks of blonde hair over her eyes. She raised her eyebrows in puzzlement.

"That's right. I fear we've done too little of that lately." He motioned, and all five knelt on the logs. "Lord Elyon, Giver of Light, Enemy of Darkness, we ask your blessing upon us. Go before us this day and part all evil from our path. Give us a quick journey between here and the Waldreich. To each of us give strength, courage, and wisdom. And most of all, confound and confuse Faolukan and his master, the enemy of everything you have planned. In your holy name do we ask this."

When Machar was finished, Neil felt light of heart, filled with warmth and joy. "Thank you, Machar."

"You're welcome, my lord. And now 'tis time for walking." Machar rose. "Too long have we been sitting. I think today we'll make good time today."

Even with one out of four logs missing or rotten, walking here was far easier than trudging through the muck. Their new route was wide enough for two or more to walk side-by-side, with occasional spots where two chariots could pass abreast. With the fog gone and the sun bright, the swamp's gloom temporarily receded.

"What we're lacking is a tune." Machar seemed almost joyful. "Does anyone know 'The Road'?"

"My lord, Neil is a wonder on the bone whistle." Ewan nudged Neil. "Can you play it, my lord?"

Caitir groaned and shot him a sideward glance.

"Aye?" Machar's eyebrows rose. "When did you learn the flute?"

Neil just smiled then untied his bone whistle from the pocket inside his tunic. He put the instrument to his lips and began to play from memory. But as the notes sprang out, keeping time with their walking pace, Caitir's expression changed from painful anticipation to surprise and wonder. Luag grinned. Machar looked back with an approving nod and began to sing. Ewan clapped and joined in.

"To traveling, we sing our song.
To places lost in times long gone.

We take the road that winds beyond,
That leads ahead, goes on and on,
Through rain or sun, though fast or slow,
O'er hills and swamp, the high, the low.
Where e'er it ends, we do not know.
Forever on, the road it goes."

Caitir joined in, and they sang as many verses as they could remember before starting over and singing it again.

After a time, Luag set foot on a log that collapsed beneath him, sending him up to his neck in swamp water. He laughed as the others pulled him out. "That'll teach me to mind me steps whilst trying to carry a tune."

Machar nodded. "I guess we can't sing and walk these logs at the same time. But 'twas a powerful fine tune we carried, nay?"

"'Twas that, my lord." Ewan smiled.

"Neil, that was some fetching flute music."

Caitir's eyes were wide as she fixed her gaze on him. "How did you learn to play that thing so well so quickly?"

"My secret." Then he put his instrument away and concentrated on walking.

As Machar predicted, they made good time, crossing many leagues before sunset. They did so even though they had to stop often and rest for Neil's sake—he'd only just recovered from his illness. Luag, too, had trouble keeping up with his short lehbrágan legs. All day they passed the crumbling, fallen ruins of ancient palaces and country towns. Broken columns and tumbled stone blocks lay half-submerged in muck, covered with vines and moss, remnants of a proud, ancient Saxia lost to earthquake, flood, and the passage of time.

Several times that day snakes slithered across the logs. When a poisonous swamp viper curled up in the middle of the way, showing no inclination to move, Machar sliced off its head with his sword and flipped the remains into the water.

Early that night, as heavy fog closed in, they camped on the road itself. With the fog, the ruins, and the cries of strange creatures in the distance, the bog's ever-present gloom once again enveloped them.

They had barely started supper when a strange luminescent bird swooped out of the night. Its wingspan exceeded that of three vultures laid side-by-side. It circled above, shedding a pale, violet light, emitting an eerie, vibrating sound, as of sticks beating rapidly together. Shiny black orbs examined each of them with slow, menacing care, as if to determine whether they were worth a meal. Hooked claws as long as a man's forearm trailed beneath like a wasp's stingers. Its red, illuminated beak appeared able to rip a man in two with one bite.

Machar drew his sword, as did Neil. Ewan and Caitir readied their bows. Luag's axe was raised high. The creature circled twice more, hovered a while, then flew away.

"What *was* that thing?" Caitir returned her arrow to its quiver.

"I don't know." Machar watched its pale luminescence fade into the night. "There are creatures in this world far older than man, creatures we'd do well not to disturb."

Neil shuddered and returned to his meal.

All the next day, they trudged through a heavy mist that left their skin damp and their feet slipping over the logs. Here, the road lay in worse repair. Many times, one or another of them fell through rotten timbers into the black water. Two more nights did they spend in the bog, ever seeking but never finding, a comfortable position atop the hard, bumpy logs.

Then one morning, they woke to a slow, steady rain.

"I do not ken if I'll ever feel dry or clean again." Ewan wiped his brow and pulled his hood further over his head.

In front of Neil, Caitir mumbled agreement as she stepped over a gap between logs.

By noon, the rain quit, and the road often led over tiny islands of soggy ground. Then the path abruptly stopped at the edge of a dank, dripping forest.

Machar smiled. "We've reached the end of the Fell Bogs. By tonight, we'll be in the Waldreich. Keep a sharp eye out for deer. Roasted venison would be a welcome change from hardtack."

Ewan beamed. "Glad will I be to leave this mire. Gladder still to have the taste of venison between my teeth."

Soon, they were walking under tall white cedars and green firs. Then the land rose, and they ascended a low hill through elms, maples, and birch. The breeze carried the smell of lush leaf and fresh growing things. Chaffinches sang complex songs, and squirrels chattered. From the top of a rise, Machar led them into a low valley verdant with saplings, crossed by bubbling brooks. All day they traversed hill and valley, one after another.

True to Machar's prediction, by early afternoon, they came upon a deer herd. Ewan and Caitir quickly fitted arrows to strings and brought down a large buck. They dressed the carcass, tied it by its legs under a pole, and carried it.

In midafternoon, they climbed out of a valley to a low pass between bare peaks. Far below, all the way to the south, stretched a vast expanse of thick, dark green.

"The Waldreich." Machar breathed the name with reverence. He spread one hand toward the forest. "For a hundred and fifty leagues, it stretches thick and unbroken to the Kracken Mountains in the south. Few from the west have ever gone where we are about to go. 'Tis a country of wild clans, ravenous wolves, treacherous magic, and danger."

"And a powerful deep forest it appears, Machar." Ewan stared at it and frowned. "When do we eat?"

Caitir laughed. "If you were tied to a tree and surrounded by wolves, I ken you'd still be asking what was for supper."

"A man needs his priorities."

"I second those sentiments." Luag winked.

Machar grinned. "And sure, let's find a place to cook and eat our venison before hunger withers Ewan to a bag of bones, and starvation steals a few inches from Luag's height. We should also make some jerky. It'll be a welcome addition to our provisions."

He led them halfway down the slope to a glade where a rushing stream splashed into a pool of clear water. At the forest's edge, Caitir gathered herbs. Meanwhile, the men made a fire and rigged a spit. They cut thin strips of meat, rubbed them with the salt that each carried, and dried them on a wooden grill Ewan had fashioned, being careful to dry, and not cook it. In this way, they preserved enough meat to last for weeks.

Finally, they cut huge slabs of venison for each of them and Ewan began roasting them over the fire. While these sizzled and dripped fat into the flames, Machar and Ty hauled the unused carcass far off into the trees, in case some predator caught its scent. They returned in the dark in time eat their fill.

The butchering was bloody work. The moon was up, and Caitir now went alone to the pool's farthest end to bathe. The men, and Luag, found the nearest rock beach where Neil doffed his clothes and ducked under the frigid water. By a half moon, he could barely see the end of the tarn and the outline of Caitir's naked form slipping into the pool. He smiled, remembering how they and the other children of Hidden Pines used to discard their tunics and swim in the forest brooks back home.

But they were no longer children, were they? And Caitir was now a beautiful young woman. Funny how he hadn't thought of her that way until after they'd kissed at the inn. And since she was on the quest, he'd come to realize how much she meant to him. No longer was she just a childhood friend. Now she was a woman. And his relationship with her was growing deeper and in a different direction.

When they had dried and slipped under their furs, Machar spoke softly, "Just west of here, perhaps less than a day's journey, is a fortress city hidden high in the mountains. 'Tis a refuge of the Capulum."

"A Capulum refuge?" Neil's heart leaped. He shifted and braced himself on an elbow to face the older man. He didn't remember Machar ever having spoken of this before. "Will we stop there?"

"Nay, the monks of Ard Cúl Dín have a tendency to . . . interfere. Too often have they clashed with Cairbre and the Ériu Capulum. We must bypass them. We can't risk further delay. I only mention it in case . . ."

"In case what?"

"In case something happens to me and you need help on the return journey. But know this, the fortress lies hidden from the enemy's eyes. Only those who belong to Elyon can see it."

Neil nodded. Machar's words were yet another reminder of the danger they faced.

"Now sleep well, for tomorrow we enter lands upon which few have ever set foot."

Even as he heard the words, Neil's eyes were closing and sleep was calling. On a bed of soft pine needles, he slept better than the night on the lofty bed at Joost's palace.

Wasn't that a lifetime ago?

The next morning they descended into the deepest forest Neil had ever seen. The oaks grew so tall and the overhead canopy of leaves so thick, little of the sky shone through. From the dark leafy ceiling fell an unnatural silence, broken only by the falling of their feet upon hard ground. The scent of damp moss, the decay of fallen trunks and last fall's rotting leaves hung heavy on the air. Of underbrush there was little. An occasional bird song dropped down from the leafy canopy. The topside world seemed distant, unnaturally separated from the gloom below.

Under the Waldreich's semidarkness, even the squirrels scattered silently and disappeared as the Company approached, as if fearing to make a sound.

The farther they traveled in the dark wood, the heavier became the air, the deeper the gloom.

"Is it like this all the way?" The moment he spoke, unease washed over Neil at the way his voice broke the stillness.

"I fear 'tis so, my lord." Machar stared at the dim path ahead. "Or so I've heard."

Caitir came up beside Neil, her eyes wide. "I do not like this place. It feels like the inside of a tomb made of trees."

"Aye." His glance searched the murk on either side, expecting at any moment to see—what? Ghosts? Stalking predators? He shook his head and continued on. He was imagining things.

They could only guess if noon had arrived when they broke for a midday meal, as the semidarkness blocked any view of the sun.

"I must tell you I'm uncertain of the way." Machar chewed on venison jerky. "We're following this deer trail, but—I hope it's the right one."

Caitir looked to Neil, her brow creasing. Ewan met their gazes with raised eyebrows.

"Do we have another choice?" Neil shrugged.

"I'm thinking it leads south into the heart of the Naz. We may meet them along the way, but few know much about them anymore. Only the tales a rare traveler brings back. Not many dare trade with them. Traders always meet them far back at the forest's edge at predetermined sites. Never this far in. Indeed, those who've ventured this far into these woods, well—they never return."

No one spoke. The forest's silence seemed to drop around them like a heavy mist.

"Will the Naz know the way to Schwarzburg Castle?" asked Neil.

"They should. But they may not tell us."

"Why would they not welcome us, Machar?" Caitir's face was barely visible under the dark, leafy ceiling. "We're not without our social graces. And we've even bathed."

Machar gave a short laugh. "Ah, lass. From what we know, the Naz allow few strangers through their lands. They've become an isolated, suspicious folk. The real question is not whether they'll welcome us. 'Tis whether they'll shoot us full of arrows before we even see them?"

Caitir's eyes widened again.

"But let's move on." Machar stood. "We must travel as far as we can before evening. Nights in the Waldreich are full of danger."

As they followed Machar deeper into the wood, Neil thought he heard a distant howl. Or was it only the wind through the treetops far above?

CHAPTER 26

THE DEAMHAN IDOL

For the next two days, they trekked along deer paths leading farther into a deepening wood. The only sounds were their feet treading over the soft loam. On the third night, they camped in almost total darkness and built a crackling fire to push back the gloom. Huddling before the flame, they ate a few berries they'd gathered and some jerky, washing it down with wine from their skins. No one felt like talking.

They'd barely laid down in a circle around the flames, smoldering too much of wet, fungal wood, when came the beating of distant drums. Neil sat up straight. How far away was it? A quarter league? With the pounding came the sound of many voices chanting to the beat. Ewan and Caitir also sat up. Luag's eyes opened wide and stared straight up into the treetops. The firelit shadows deepened the furrows on his brow.

Then a distant howling rose into the night, a sound as of deamhans escaping from the Underworld. After a time, the howling ceased, and they heard only the drums.

Machar rose and stirred the fire until the logs separated and the flames went out. "Best we don't invite any visitors tonight. Whoever they are."

By the ember's dying light, Neil saw Caitir's expression, frozen with fear and expectation. "I do not ever want to meet them."

"Aye, lass." Ewan turned his face toward the distant sound. "No good can come of any business conducted in the wee times to drumming such as that."

"We need to rest." Machar laid down on his cape. "We'll need all our strength for the trek tomorrow."

Luag pulled the furs over his head so nothing of him could be seen.

Neil laid down but could not sleep. The drumming and chanting started again, continued long into the night. A scream—a woman's scream?—sliced the air, raw and piercing. Then came the growling and snarling of many beasts. The drumbeats rose and fell, rose and fell, before fading into the distance. Then all was quiet.

He lay motionless, straining to hear more. But all that came to him was the memory of the scream, the growling beasts, the drums, and the dead stillness surrounding him now. He couldn't exorcise the scream from his head.

"Oh, Elyon," he whispered to himself. "Protect us from what lies ahead."

It was late when he finally slept.

When Neil heard the others rising, he woke and joined them for a breakfast of salted venison. But as they started along the deer track, a nameless unease weighed upon him. Again, the dark and oppressive trees closed in, and no one spoke. The drums of yester eve still hammered in his memory.

Machar led them on a path from one twisted mammoth trunk to another. When a large acorn dropped onto the dead leaves beside him, Neil jerked his head toward the sound with his sword nearly out of its sheath. But he saw nothing.

A dim light shone through the trunks ahead. Was it a clearing? Caitir shot him a faint, sideways smile as the others picked up the pace. Any hint of sun after so long under these baleful trees should have been welcome.

But the others had barely started for the light, when an even greater apprehension gripped him, sending shivers along his arms and shoulders. Ahead, he was certain, lay something unnamable, dark, and evil.

"Wait!" he called. "Let's go around."

But the others had forged ahead and didn't hear. He hurried to catch up.

Machar was leading them at a fast pace toward a lightening circle of trees. Other paths now joined theirs, and the way grew wider. They had stumbled onto some kind of main thoroughfare.

The forest ended in a wide field. From the clearing's center, a dozen vultures burst into flight.

Here, the sun's light filtered down through a gray cloud ceiling onto a grassy glebe, punctuated by tree stumps. Dominating the circle in the middle, a stone statue rose ten feet high. It carried the image of a bearded man, grim and solemn, peering down, a crown of bronze twigs encircling his head. Eyes of jade seemed to bore into Neil's with malice. Here, he realized, was the center of his nameless fear.

Below the statue lay a rock slab and the object of the vultures' attention. As he approached and smelled the rot and corruption, his heart pounded in his chest.

Chains held a skeleton to the slab. Small bits of flesh, still red, clung to the bones. By the tufts of long golden hair the carrion eaters had left behind, Neil knew that last night's screams had come from this woman.

"There was quite a crowd here. See the footprints." Machar pointed at the ground beside the slab. "And—what's this?" He knelt beside more markings in the dirt.

Ewan knelt as well.

"Wolves?" said Machar. "But the prints—they're too big."

"Aye, my lord." Ewan whispered his words. "Dozens upon dozens of them. And methinks they're the largest their breed ever produced."

Machar looked up at the statue. "That abomination—'tis Wodan's likeness. I've heard tell of sacrifices to him by the forest people but didn't believe it. This is worse than I'd feared."

Neil's glance caught a jumbled pile of white at the clearing's far end. Leaving the others, he strode across trampled grass and bluebells. When he came upon it, he froze. "Come," he shouted back. "Come quick!"

Caitir ran up beside him and stopped, her lips parted wide. Then she averted her gaze and braced a trembling hand on his shoulder. Soon Machar and Ewan were standing beside him, also staring.

"Bones." Ewan's voice rose. "Hundreds—nay, thousands—of bones. This has been going on for a long, long time."

"Aye, and 'tis clear to me now what happens here." Machar wiped his brow and sent a quick glance around the clearing. "The Naz bring their sacrifices to the statue. Then the idol calls the wolves to feast on live . . . human . . . flesh. While the Naz—ah! They watch!" Machar glanced again toward the trees. "This can only be work of Faolukan and the Deamhan Lord. Surely, a minor deamhan is trapped within that stone. One of the Deamhan Lord's spirit followers, meant to enslave the Naz to his will."

Neil shuddered again.

"We must leave here at once."

They followed as Machar led them across the clearing toward the main path at the field's far end.

At the entrance to the dark forest tunnel, something told Neil to look back. He spun. There, moving in shadows through the trees on the other side—

The silhouettes of wolves. Dozens of them.

But they were the largest wolves he'd ever seen. Misshapen, with hunched backs, huge forepaws, bulging eyes, and a row of bony spikes down their backs.

"They're here," Neil whispered as loud as he dared. "Run!"

CHAPTER 27

WOLVES

The others looked back, saw what Neil saw, and they ran.

Neil and Luag were last. As he ran, his feet slapping hard and loud on the path, he shot another glance behind him. The pack was racing across the clearing toward them. But their paws barely touched the ground. His glance whirled back to the trail ahead. Now he sprinted in a race for his life.

He gained another twenty yards. Again, he looked back. The beasts had crossed the field and gained the trail. Behind him, dead yellow eyes shone through the forest darkness. And Luag was falling farther behind. The fear in the sprite's eyes contorted his face.

"That tree." Machar pointed fifty yards away to a huge, spreading oak with wide, horizontal limbs. "Climb it!"

Ewan and Caitir ran flat out toward it. Machar slowed and let them pass. Neil's feet slammed onto the hard-trodden dirt trail. He tried to make each stride longer than the last. He was breathing heavily. His pack slammed up and down against his back. Already, sweat drenched his shoulders, back, and forehead.

Ewan arrived first at the tree. He clambered to the first wide limb, some ten feet above the ground. Caitir raced right behind him.

"Faster, Neil and Luag." Machar stopped at the trunk's base and spread his feet apart. His sword left its sheath. "Luag, *run!*"

Behind him, Neil could hear the footpads of many wolves.

"Faster, Luag." Worry rippled Machar's voice. "*Luag.*"

Neil shot a quick glance back. Luag was far behind. He'd never make it. Neil stopped and stared. Could he help the sprite?

Nay, it was too late. The wolves had surrounded him. Then from the midst of the circle of snarling beasts came Luag's battle cry. Neil saw the sprite's axe swing high, heard the yelp of a wolf as the blade hit home, again and again. But it was too late for the sprite.

"Run, Neil!" Machar yelled. "Save yourself."

Other wolves were swarming past the battle with Luag, heading straight for Neil. Turning, he ran. The trunk was only ten yards ahead. His feet slammed over the dirt track. His heart hammered against his ribs. He felt their breath on his neck—but that was impossible. They must be farther behind than that. Must be.

Five yards to go. Then two.

He sprinted past Machar, nearly leaping off the ground onto the tree. From behind came growling, snarling. Off to his right, a black shadow leaped into the air toward them. Planting a foot in a crevice of gnarled bark, he launched himself upward.

Then came the yelping of an animal, followed by the sound of Machar's sword slamming into its sheath. Machar's feet scratched, scuffled over the bark below him.

When Neil gained the first limb, he finally dared look down. Machar was just beneath him. One creature leaped, its jaws open. How could anything so big jump so high? Its teeth clamped onto Machar's tunic.

Neil lay flat on the limb and reached down. He slapped a hand onto Machar's wrist. His friend struggled to keep his balance. Machar's tunic ripped. Gripping only cloth between its teeth, the wolf hit the ground with a thud. Another wolf leaped. Its jaws clicked shut on air before it, too, fell back.

With his free hand, Machar stretched for a better handhold and regained his balance. Then he joined the other three on the limb.

Neil settled on his stomach against the bark, his heart beating wildly, sweat pouring off his forehead. He squinted into the shadows where Luag had gone down. In the darkness, it was too dim to see anything. The forest filled with the sounds of snarling, teeth ripping flesh from the sprite's body.

Luag was gone.

Machar leaned back heavily against the main trunk, breathing fast. He shut his eyes and shook his head. But one of his feet dangled over the limb.

Below, another wolf, its shoulders as tall as a man's, leaped.

"Look out!" Neil yelled.

Machar pulled his leg up just before the monster's jaws would have clamped on a shoe.

"We'd better climb to the next limb." Neil looked up. "They'll never get us up there. And it's even wider."

"Aye, my lord." Machar glanced down. "I count over twenty of them. With more hiding under the trees."

The next higher limb held ample space for two. Neil and Caitir stepped from that branch to a second one growing at right angles to Machar and Ewan's. This, too, was wide, nearly horizontal.

Neil tied his and Caitir's backpacks to a branch.

"Poor Luag," breathed Caitir. "I canna believe . . . he's gone."

"Aye, lass," said Ewan from the next limb. "With those short sprite legs, he couldna run fast enough. I've never seen beasts so large. And they're all—twisted."

"They are . . . that," said Machar through gulps of air. "'Tis Faolukan's doing—these creatures. They are bespelled, all of them. And now we are only four. Luag died well, fighting them to the last."

"I should have gone back to help," whispered Neil.

"Nay, my lord," said Machar. "There was nothing anyone could do. They came upon us too fast."

No one said anything. Neil stared at the spot where the sprite had made his last stand.

After a time, Ewan's voice broke the silence. "How long do you ken they'll wait?"

"I don't know," said Machar. "I'm thinking these are wily creatures, with tricks aplenty."

"If we put a few arrows in their hides," said Ewan, "perhaps they'll give us some distance?"

"Let's do it." Caitir grabbed her bow and quiver. As Neil held her, she leaned over and shot. A yelp screeched from below. "That one's for Luag!" she cried.

Another yelp as Ewan's arrow also found its mark. After Caitir had shot a third time, the pack moved away from the oak's base, with one of their number limping.

Caitir shot again but missed.

"We can't keep this up." Ewan's voice came again. "Or I'll use up all my arrows."

"I'm also running low." Caitir wrapped her remaining arrows tightly to her quiver and hung it and her bow over a branch.

"Perhaps they'll give up and move on." Weariness laced Machar's voice.

Neil lay against the trunk. Then Caitir stretched back against his chest. "You make a comfortable pillow," she said in a low voice. "But you're wet."

"I've been running."

"Look," she said. "The fiends are just sitting there, watching us."

The wolves had separated into two groups. One group sat on their haunches, about twenty yards distant, staring up at their prey. Neil saw only dark shadows and yellow eyes. The second group sat on the opposite side, also waiting, watching. Their eyes seemed to glow in the dark.

Thus did they wait all morning until Ewan declared it time to eat. They ate more bread, venison jerky, and the last of the cheese. With his wineskin empty, Neil took a pull from his waterskin. "My water's running low."

"Mine, too," said Ewan.

"Then we must ration what's left." Machar's voice rose again. "Appears they're waiting us out."

All the rest of that day, they waited. Evening fell, and in the darkness, Neil could no longer see the wolves. Soon after nightfall, an eerie howling arose from the forest around them, reminding them they were not alone. On and on it went, until late, when the beasts quit.

As he finally relaxed against the main trunk, he feared falling from the tree. But with Caitir nestled up against his chest, he never once slipped. In this way did he spend the night, sleeping poorly but resting nonetheless.

In the morning, the wolves had moved to another spot. Only their yellow, glowing eyes were visible. Still, they waited and watched.

Neil heard Caitir's whisper, "Are you awake?"

"I am."

"The others are still sleeping." She spoke so quietly only he could hear. "Can I ask you something?"

"Aye." She had lain against him all night, and now he shifted his legs.

"What will happen if you find the Scepter and bring it back it to Ewhain Macha?"

"What do you mean? The prophecies say Elyon's light will return to the Tower. And we'll hold back the darkness."

"Nay, not that. What will happen to us? To you and me?"

He was glad she couldn't see him now, as he was frowning. What *would* happen to them? He couldn't go on pretending to be Prince Neil, could he? But how could he go back to his old life, beating red-hot metal on the anvil in his uncle's shop? Could he ever again be his uncle's errand boy, only an assistant? Maybe he could leave Hidden Pines and start his own shop somewhere?

Or did she imply more by her question? Ever since they'd begun this adventure together, he'd felt an increasing closeness to her. She was the only anchor from his past life now, aye, but there was more to it, wasn't there? He could almost envision the two of them as—what? Man and wife? But until this journey, he'd never thought of her that way.

A shiver of excitement ran down his back. Was it possible? Or was his imagination running away with him?

"Neil?"

"I'm thinking."

"Well, you're doing it too slowly."

He was sure she was smiling now. She shifted her body, turned her head so he could see her. And she *was* smiling. "You do not ken, do you?"

"Nay, lass. I do not ken what will become of us."

"Look!" interrupted Ewan's breathless voice from the other side of the tree, "in the branches above."

Neil scanned the limbs higher up. Then he saw it.

A bird of such beauty—he gasped. A forearm's length from claws to beak, its feathers shone like satin gold cloth. Its head carried a wide plume bursting with reds, violets, and greens. The colors were so bright, they seemed to blaze with their own inner light, even here in the depths of dark Waldreich. Its beak glinted shiny black, a beak meant for cracking seeds, not tearing flesh.

Then it sang.

A warbling song echoed through the wood, banishing in an instant the forest gloom. The complex melody was happy, lilting, uplifting, almost laughing, and like nothing he'd ever heard.

To Neil, the music spoke of joy and peace. Its melody carried him high into the topmost reaches of the wood where he imagined the sun shone, the wind blew fresh, and treetop vines laden with flowers clung to the highest verdant twigs bursting with fragrance. He saw himself with the bird, flying above the trees, floating on cool currents, free from the forest world below.

The song went on and on.

Suddenly, the bird quit and cocked its head. It eyed the humans clinging to the nearby branches and flew back to the treetop world from which it had come.

"Amazing." Machar eyed him from around the corner. "Never have I seen such a beautiful creature."

"Nor I," said Neil.

"Despite everything"— Caitir's voice was soft—"there is good in this world, isn't there?"

"Aye," said Ewan, joining in. "I canna ever remember a song so beautiful it made me forget how much meat the creature had on it."

"And sure, Ewan"—Caitir's voice vibrated with mirth—"you'd be putting us on. Never would you eat a thing of such beauty."

"Ah, lass, you do not ken what a hungry man would do to see that colorful chicken roasting on the spit."

Laughter filled the treetops, and for the first time since they entered the Waldreich, Neil forgot about their plight.

Another day passed. Then another night. By now, they'd drunk all their water.

On the morning of the third day, the wolves were gone.

"I do not see them." From around the corner, Ewan's voice carried hope. "Do you ken, can we get down from this blasted oak?"

"Let's wait a bit more," said Machar. "They're clever, these wolves, and I fear the stone deamhan directs them."

They waited half the morning. But with no sign of the beasts' return and with thirst driving them, Machar finally gave the word to descend.

When he found himself again on the ground, Neil stretched his legs.

"Quickly, now." Machar waved them on. "Let's leave this accursed place."

"What about Luag's body?" Neil waved in the direction he'd fallen.

"No time. We can't risk their return."

Neil nodded and ran behind Machar as he trotted down the trail. The others followed. Unable to keep such a pace, a hundred yards later Machar slowed to a fast walk.

Again, Neil brought up the rear. Every so often, he stopped, turned his gaze to the forest behind, and watched and listened. The Waldreich's trees were so wide and tall and carried such heavy foliage above, barely anything but mushrooms and pale ferns grew in the semidarkness.

After a league, the trees yielded grudgingly to a rock outcropping where a circle of sunlight poked through. Here, lean grasses clung to rock crevices, mice hurried into cracks, and a rabbit fled into a hole. A herd of roe deer bounded away into the shadows. But the trail passed by this oasis of light and grass and dropped again under gargantuan oaks, the land's unrivaled conquerors.

Back in the forest dark, an occasional squirrel would scurry up a branch. A rabbit might dart off into the shadows. And each time he heard such a creature, Neil's hand went to his sword, and his heart thumped harder.

Then the trail dipped into a rocky vale where a narrow stream bubbled over mossy stones. Here, among the rocks, the trees grew slimmer and the day shone brighter. Everyone knelt to drink deeply from the cold water. They began filling their skins. But as Neil unstoppered his leather container and began filling it, a shadow crossed through the trees to his right.

He froze and stared at the spot. Another shadow, large, passed beside the first. He scanned the trees on all sides.

Dead yellow eyes gleamed in the darkness from the trail beyond.

"They're back." Ramming the stopper back into his skin, he searched for a tree to climb.

He saw none. Down in the vale, the trees were too small. The bigger trunks clustered up on the high bank.

"Quickly." Machar rose and pointed. "We must gain that ridge."

They started running up the slope toward the taller trees. But they hadn't gone ten yards when a dozen wolves appeared on the trail in front.

Neil whirled. Wolves were closing in behind them.

Ewan's whisper was hoarse. "We're trapped!"

CHAPTER 28

THE NAZ

Neil drew his sword from its sheath, as did Machar. Ewan and Caitir nocked arrows to strings, ready to strike. They formed a tight circle, facing out. The wolves began to close, their teeth bared. All around them now came the sound of snarling, growling beasts. Too tall for normal wolves, their backs were hunched and spiked. Their forelegs bulged. Their eyes glowed yellow. And their fangs curved long.

"We'll make a fight of it, lads—and of course, my lass." Machar waved his sword. He raced two steps toward the pack, swung his blade in a wide arc, nicking a foreleg, taking one by surprise. The wolf backed up. "Before we die"—resolution thickened Machar's voice—"we'll take as many of them as courage allows."

"Aye," said Neil, reaching deep within himself for courage. "Let them come." But even as the words left his mouth, sweat beaded up on his forehead.

His gaze swept from side to side as he tried to find the one who'd come on first. Two wolves rushed in from opposite sides. Arrows flew from Ewan's and Caitir's bows and hit their marks. Neil heard the yelps, saw the beasts pause, but they kept coming. Two more wolves joined those two. Caitir and Ewan shot again. Arrows sprouted from their flanks.

One beast ran straight for him. Its jaws opened then it lunged. He slashed down with his blade, opening a red crevice in its head. The creature shuddered, pulled back. Neil brought the weapon high and sliced across its throat with all his strength. Blood gushed out. The monster staggered, backed up, and dropped to the ground.

Another wolf thudded down beside that one, bleeding heavily from a second, then a third arrow from Caitir's quiver.

He glanced behind him. Ewan, too, had brought down a beast. Machar was just finishing off his second.

The flute.

What was that? Why had those words popped into his mind? Strong, haunting words in the middle of a battle?

Another huge lupine form closed in on Caitir. Only two yards distant, it opened its jaws and lunged. Caitir let fly an arrow into its open mouth. Neil stepped forward and chopped with his blade, cutting off a forepaw. The creature backed up, licked its wound, and limped away, a second arrow sticking from its side.

The flute. Use the flute.

Again, the words formed in his mind, unbidden. Ethereal, forceful, otherworldly words. Was he imagining it?

He shook his head and met another creature's snapping jaws with two quick slashes of the blade. It, too, backed away. The pack seemed to withdraw and regroup.

"I've only got one arrow left." Tension thickened Caitir's voice.

"And I'm out." Ewan reached for his sword.

Now the wolves began to charge, all at once.

The flute, Tristan!

He couldn't ignore the words any longer. He sheathed his sword, fumbled inside his pocket, and yanked out his bone whistle.

"Neil, fight!" Machar's words cut sharp. "What are you doing?" No sooner had he spoken than a wolf attacked. Machar and Ewan barely met it with their blades before its jaws would have closed on Neil.

Neil put the instrument to his lips and blew.

The tune came from nowhere. He'd never heard it before, but the notes seemed to form in his mind and just fly from his lips. Soothing, calming notes. Long, fluttering notes that rose to a soaring crescendo, then fell back, sweet and slow, to a quiet, soothing melody. Notes that brought light and joy to the depths of the vale.

The wolves paused and ceased snarling. They stopped wherever they were, forming a ten-foot-wide circle around the four. Their heads cocked and listening, the animals sat on their haunches.

"Whatever it is you're doing, my lord, keep it up." Surprise and hope had entered Machar's voice.

While he played, Neil began to walk, slowly, toward the two wolves who blocked the way up the hill. The animals watched him and listened but didn't move. He kept walking, approaching jaws that only moments ago would have ripped off half his leg. One beast in front padded off to the trail's side, sitting again on its haunches, staring at him with cold, yellow eyes. Then the second one moved aside.

The path was free. But the beasts were close. Oh, so close.

He started climbing the hill, his three companions close at his heels.

The beasts followed, only yards behind. Ewan brought up the rear.

He played and he played. He made music he never thought possible. He sent sounds of joy and light and hope into the darkness. And the wolves listened, followed closely in a hypnotized silence, but didn't attack.

Breathless now, Neil found it difficult to both walk and play the flute, but he kept on. If only he'd been able to drink some more of the water from that stream. For another mile, they traveled. Then half a mile more. Neil played his instrument, the wolves following beside them— close, silent, listening, ever present.

After they left the vale, the forest deepened. They walked again in stuffy semidarkness. But playing without rest, without water, made Neil lightheaded, dizzy.

He stopped for a moment to catch his breath. Instantly, the wolves' snarling resumed.

"They're attacking again." Machar's voice rose. "Keep playing, Neil."

So Neil blew again on the flute, and the creatures stopped their advance. But he was tiring—how much longer could he keep this up? Spots began to dance before his eyes. He needed to stop for a breath, and drink.

For a single moment, he stopped long enough to say, "I need to stop. Let's climb a tree."

But as the words left his mouth, the wolves raced forward. Caitir loosed her last arrow.

Machar rushed at the lead wolf, hacking down with his blade. Ewan stabbed it in the neck, and it fell. But as Ewan contended with that beast, a second rushed Machar from the side.

Jaws snapped shut around Machar's right leg.

Ewan's and Machar's blades sliced down upon it. They hacked and stabbed until it shuddered and died.

But Machar fell back, bleeding badly. The wound was deep.

Neil thrust the flute to his lips and played again. His lungs would soon fail. He was so lightheaded, he feared he would pass out. But if he quit, the wolves would injure someone else. The creatures came on so fast, he didn't think he'd have enough time to climb a tree. No matter what, he had to keep playing.

Caitir bent to Machar's wound and bound it with a piece of spare tunic. It bled quickly through the cloth.

Machar stood, ground his teeth, and grunted. Neil played, and they continued walking.

Only a dozen yards farther on, the spots came again before his eyes. He staggered forward, then back. Then he regained his balance. As if someone else was playing, he heard the notes fly from his bone whistle.

A few feet further. A few more notes. But the music began to fall apart. The melody faltered. He was so dizzy, he couldn't walk straight.

Just a few gulps of air. Just a few moments to breathe deeply and clear this lightheadedness. That's all he needed.

Then from above, rope ladders were dropping all around them. Caitir and the others grabbed one, rose as the ladders rose, and were pulled toward the treetops.

He forced out a few more notes. At any moment, he would pass out. Then a ladder was dangling in front of him. Even as he continued playing, he looped an arm through the rungs.

The ladder rose, lifting him off the ground, and he stopped playing.

Snarling wolves rushed in from all corners.

He breathed deeply, sucked in huge gulps of sweet air.

Below, a wolf leaped, caught its teeth on the last rung of his ladder. It hung on for a few feet then released its grip, its body slamming onto the dirt below.

The ground fell away. Rising higher beside a great trunk, he passed the lower branches and was lifted into the treetops. He emerged through a narrow hole in a wooden deck.

Rough hands pulled him flat onto his back, pinned him down. The trapdoor slammed shut beside him. A tall, thin man with a blond beard stood over him. The man pointed a knife at his throat. Caitir, Machar, and Ewan already stood on the platform floor a few yards away, bound and guarded.

"Who comes to the Waldreich unbidden, trailing wolves with magic?"

"I . . . I am Neil mac Connell."

"From whence do you come?" The man's wiry blond beard bristled with his speech. His short, tightfitting tunic of green and brown hugged his form, then loosened and swirled over his bare knobby knees.

"From Ulster in Ériu."

Now other hands lifted him upright and bound his wrists with rope. At least ten men, all bearded, dressed in browns, grays, and greens, surrounded the four. Each held a heavy, bulbous club. They examined the travelers' packs, squished their water and empty wineskins. Then they gathered all the travelers' knives, swords, and bows into a pile.

"Ériu, is it? Long it is since that name's been spoken here. And you three"—he fixed his glance on the others—"do you come from the same?"

"Aye." Machar stood beside the hole where he'd been pulled through. Already his makeshift bandage glistened bright red. "We all hail from Ériu."

The one in charge glanced at Machar's wound and spoke quietly to a second man, who immediately left on some errand. The leader now addressed Neil. "What business have you in the Waldreich, magic weaver?"

"We seek the Scepter."

All activity on the deck ceased. The gang of green- and brown-clad men stared at him. The man before Neil, obviously the leader, frowned.

Neil faced him. "Are you the Naz?"

"The Naz we are."

"My friend here is wounded. He needs help."

"I've already sent for someone to attend him."

"I've given you my name. Now, what's yours?"

The man cocked his head, as if considering the request. "Egon. Now be quiet." He whispered something to the others, and the group began leading the four along squeaking wooden walkways.

They followed narrow, rickety paths strung between the trees with only a single, thick rope looping alongside for a railing. Some boards had long since crumbled away, rotten or missing. With his hands tied, Neil feared to fall from such a great height. Far below, night cloaked the forest floor. Ahead, Machar limped slowly. Neil feared he was losing too much blood.

But they were above the gloom, and sunlight now trickled down through glistening green leaves. They passed hundreds of houses built around the massive trunks of ancient oaks. Wooden houses with open windows and timbered roofs, chinked with mud, lime, and twigs, fronted by wide porches with railings. As far as he could see, the treetop city stretched into the forest on all sides.

Once, it was clear, this place had seen greatness. But now, too many structures were abandoned, their porches collapsing, roofs punctured by fallen limbs, eaten away by decades of moss and rain. Vines choked dead-end pathways to the right and left. Everywhere hovered an air of decay and abandonment, a sense of ancient glory lost.

The Naz stopped before a long, swinging plankway leading up to the largest structure yet.

Above, a towering building wrapped a massive, hoary trunk. Moss draped its roof. Vines hung in ragged tails beside its walls. Rope cables from nearby trees supported a series of three wide decks climbing from the building, cascading up toward a second massive trunk. On the first of these high platforms, the backs of brightly dressed men and women clustered around the edge, facing inward.

From the group's center, someone screamed. Then came a moan, as of someone in great pain.

But Egon led them away, down a lower plankwalk that dead-ended. There a man met them with a handful of wide leaves and ointment. He cleaned Machar's injury, salved it, and tightly wrapped the wound.

"You are lucky, stranger," said the man, "that we treat your wound instead of giving you a matching gash on the other leg."

When the man had finished, Egon pointed Neil and Machar toward two log seats hung on ropes from pulleys above their heads. "Sit and hang on."

Neil sat, and immediately the floor dropped away. He held on tightly and descended, swinging and twirling all the way. But where was he going? Alarm churned his stomach as the rope seat fell. Then he looked down. Below was a wide, circular room woven of intertwined branches, lined with dead leaves. The seat deposited him on the floor. Machar toppled beside him. The seats rose, and soon, Ewan and Caitir joined them.

Then the seats disappeared into the deck above, and the trapdoors slammed shut.

Neil peered over the edge. Their giant basket hung suspended by four thick, squeaking ropes attached to neighboring trunks. A huge baffle guarded the exits along each rope, making escape impossible. The ground, wrapped in night, lurked at least seventy feet below. No roof spread above them.

Moments later, a trapdoor in the walkway above opened, and a rope let down a small bundle containing their skins, now filled with water. They grabbed the waterskins and drank deeply.

"How's your leg?" Neil nodded to the leaves wrapping Machar's wound.

"In time, it will heal. But the beast's teeth cut deep."

Neil winced. Even if they escaped from here, Machar would be unable to travel for many days, perhaps weeks.

"Do you think they'll feed us?" Ewan poked through his pack and meager store of rations.

Machar grinned. "We are lucky to be alive."

"Where are we?" Caitir tipped her gaze to the plank walks above.

"This can only be the ancient city of Hochnest." Machar waved a hand toward the houses beyond.

"And this treetop basket?" She bent over the edge. "'Tis a prison?"

"Aye, lass. 'Tis a Naz prison."

CHAPTER 29

KING VEIT

Long moments later, the trapdoor opened and a small basket of nuts and berries was lowered to them. All the rest of that day and into the night, they waited, listening to the ropes squeaking in the breeze, but no one came or even brought news about what was going to happen to them. They slept huddled on the mat of crushed leaves lining their prison floor.

They woke to the sound of Egon's voice from above, as the log seats dropped again.

"Sit and rise," he called. "Your judgment awaits."

They did as commanded and were pulled up. At the top, the Naz again bound their hands.

But as Machar stood, sweat drenched his pale brow.

"Are you feverish?" asked Egon.

"That I am. I fear the bite has poisoned me."

Egon frowned. "We will apply more salve. But there's only so much we can do for a wolf bite."

Then their jailers marched the four along the plankway, taking a turn leading them up a flight of steps to the large platform they had glimpsed yesterday from below. Machar limped badly, adding one more confirmation that he wouldn't be making any long journeys anytime soon.

A crowd of Naz awaited. They wore tunics dyed green, brown, and yellow. Some had stuck feathers in their hair. From a few necks dangled strings of white bones. Neil looked closer. Were those the fingers and toes of men? He shuddered.

"Bring the interlopers." A voice boomed across the platform. "And the magician." Those assembled stepped aside to let the prisoners pass. A tall man leaned back against a massive throne of black, shiny wood. He scratched a blond beard, tinged with red. His cloak, also red, filled the seat to either side of him, beside carved wolf heads at the ends of each armrest. Behind him, three pikes rose from the platform's edge, carrying the severed, dried heads of three unfortunates.

Egon pushed Neil toward the throne with his club then slammed it hard onto the floor. Others prodded Ewan, Machar, and Caitir up beside and behind him. Three more clubs rammed the platform.

"Kneel before King Veit, monarch of the Naz, ruler of Hochnest and the forests of the Waldreich." Egon laid a heavy hand on Neil's shoulder and pushed him to his knees. He shot a glance back to see the others behind him also kneeling.

"Are you he who mesmerizes the beasts with music?" King Veit addressed Neil.

"I am." He raised his glance.

"What is your name?"

Neil gave it.

"Do you possess more magic than this? Can you cure a spider bite? Or make yourself invisible?"

Neil shook his head, nay.

A few in the crowd behind him snickered.

"Would you be a druid, then?"

"I am not, my lord. Merely a traveler on his way through your lands."

"No one ever travels through the Waldreich. Unless they are desperate. Or lost."

Neil shrugged.

"I would hear the music you played that so bewitched Wodan's wolves that they did not tear you limb from limb. Play for me now what you played for them."

A man dressed all in white, sitting off to the side, waved his hands and stood. "I advise against it, my lord. He could bewitch us all."

Veit held up a hand and fixed Neil with a stare. "Does my druid speak the truth? Will you bewitch us?"

"Nay, my lord. I will not."

"Detlef disagrees, yet I would hear this magic fife. Know that Egon stands ready and alert behind you. If he even remotely suspects such a thing is happening, he will knock you senseless. Now play for me."

Neil glanced behind to Egon, who nervously fingered his weapon. Neil faced the king and nodded. Pulling out his bone whistle, he fitted it to his lips.

Then he played. But the song that came to him was different from the one the wolves heard. It soothed, yet energized; calmed, yet uplifted. The notes just seemed to form in his mind, move through his fingers, and spill out from his lips. It was a tune of comfort and peace. How long he played, he didn't know. Long enough that he knew he'd spun melody and music into a pleasant, enticing story. Also long enough that he thought he should end it. When he was done, he slipped the flute back in his pocket.

Silence filled the court. Men and women gazed at him with faraway expressions, a few faint smiles. Then they began to beat their chests. Soon the entire assembly was pounding their fists on their chests.

"Well done, Neil mac Connell. I would hear more of this music. Now I see why the wolves did not attack. Magical, indeed, are the notes flowing from your fife. Not bewitching, but . . . speaking to us of a country beyond our imagining. Comforting. Peaceful. I bow before your excellent skill." The king bowed.

Neil also bowed.

"Now tell me the truth, young man, why are you here?"

"We came to seek the Scepter."

Veit eyed him, silent for a time. "I believe you speak the truth. No one would be foolish enough to use that in a lie." Then he sat up straight and stared at Neil. "But surely, such a quest will lead to your deaths." He fixed his glance on the other three. "For all of you."

"Nevertheless, my lord," said Machar, "we—"

A club struck from behind with an audible thunk. Neil spun back in time to see Machar dropping to the deck. For a moment, he just lay there. His hands still tied, slowly he pushed up to a kneeling position.

"Speak not unless you are given leave to speak." Egon prodded Machar with his club.

The king grunted and again faced Neil. "Why seek you this treasure?"

"Because long ago, when it sat in the Tower of Dóchas in Ewhain Macha, it pleased Elyon, he who created the world. It showed him our obedience and loyalty. Then peace and prosperity filled Ériu. Indeed, all of Ereb. And when it returns to the Tower, it will do so once again."

Murmurs swept the crowd. Men and women whispered among themselves.

"Silence!"

The court fell quiet.

Veit eyed Neil, and his fingers twisted his beard.

"Do you know where this Scepter is, my lord?" asked Neil. "Can you help us find it?"

Veit's eyes opened wide. "From anyone else I would consider such a request, unbidden, as brazen insolence." He pulled on his beard and eyed Neil. "But you are a magic weaver. So I will tell you this—it's in a place I know. But one you'd never live to see."

"Nevertheless, we must go there."

"If you are compelled to die, I would rather your deaths serve a more meaningful purpose." He looked to the druid. "Detlef, can you suggest something?"

Detlef frowned, stared off into the trees for a moment, and then whispered long in the king's ear.

The king glanced at the floor. Then a smile lifted the corners of his mouth. "Very well. You, my magician friend, I will save from your foolish quest. You will become my slave. I would hear more of your flute. I'm certain you're hiding more magic than what you've shown. That is my command."

"Nay," cried Caitir. "You canna."

Egon's club poked her back. "Be silent, woman."

Caitir shot him a look to freeze a river.

"As for you three"—Veit waved a hand at them—"you will become offerings to Wodan. Your deaths will soothe his anger, grant us a good harvest of nuts, mushrooms, and venison, and mollify his servants, the wolves."

"Nay!" Neil stood. When Egon's club scuffled the floor behind him, Neil stepped forward.

Veit shook his head, and Egon backed off. "And why should Master Wodan not be given the flesh and souls of your companions? More and more does he demand of us. As you see, the Naz are few and getting fewer. You are interlopers, who came here uninvited."

"Nay, great king. I'll do what you want." Neil closed his eyes then opened them. "I'll use my . . . my magic for . . . anything you want. Any task. Just don't feed my friends to the wolves."

"Anything?" Veit cocked an eyebrow.

"Aye. Anything."

Veit narrowed his eyes at Neil. "No matter how dangerous the feat?"

Neil nodded.

Veit again summoned the one called Detlef to his side, and together they conferred. Neil couldn't hear what they were whispering, but the conference went on so long, he began to fear what he'd just done. Finally, Detlef withdrew. Veit again gazed at Neil.

"Here is my proposition, Neil mac Connell. If you do the deed I ask—impossible though it is—I will free you and your friends."

"Whatever it is, my lord, I will do it."

"Good. You will go to Beilzig City, where my enemy, Queen Hedwig, reigns over her accursed land. There you will steal from her the ancient Horn of the Reich that rightfully belongs to the Naz.

"In my father's time, she convinced the traitor Volkard, a mere chamberlain he was, to steal it from *us*. She accepted it as a bribe—*accepted* it, mind you—and admitted him into her service with high status. I will have it back, this Horn, for it was made by King Reinhard himself, he who in ancient times founded the Naz and this city of Hochnest.

"It carries magic, Neil mac Connell. Magic that once brought victory in battle and kept the wolves from our trees. It brought prosperity, just as you say the Scepter brought to your people. To Hedwig, the Horn is useless. But to us—well, it is beyond price. My magic flutist, will you bring me this treasure?"

Neil bowed. "I will try, my lord. But only if you free my friends."

Veit smiled. "Very well. Egon, my chief ranger, will accompany you on your journey."

"I beg your forgiveness, but I would rather take Ewan, my squire."

"Nay. Your friends will stay here as security."

Neil frowned. He looked at the deck then at his three companions. "I will not go unless one of my friends goes with me."

Veit nearly jumped off the throne, his eyes widening, hands gripping the carved wolf heads until his knuckles whitened. Detlef again approached the king and whispered long in his ear. At length, Veit nodded.

"My druid makes this suggestion. The woman will be of little use to you and only trouble for us. If you insist on taking someone, take her. But I warn you, foreigner. Make no more demands. Or I'll give all of you to Wodan, magic weaver or no."

Neil bowed. "Thank you, my lord. I will go with Egon and Caitir and do what you ask."

"Good. A willing magician works better than one under threat of force. You will leave tomorrow."

Neil bowed. Then Egon led them back to their high prison.

When they were alone again inside the treetop basket, Neil said to the others, "I fear this new quest takes me far from our goal of finding the Scepter. But what choice did I have? At least Caitir will be freed."

Machar shifted position and winced. His face was pale and sweaty. "Neil, you spoke and acted well today. They think you are a magician, and you kept up the ruse. That's using your head. I admit, this side trip is unwelcome. But I see no other way for us to find the Scepter unless you do what Veit wants. He knows where it is. Perhaps if you retrieve the Horn, he'll tell us."

"Maybe so." Neil brushed dry leaves from his legs. "No offense, Caitir, but I could have used Ewan's help."

"I ken." She put a hand on Neil's knee. "He's better skilled and a far better squire than I could ever be."

"I would gladly have gone with you, my lord." Ewan smiled. "But what rotten luck, for Machar and me to be trapped here like this."

"Some in the Capulum, including Cairbre"—Machar's glazed eyes focused on Ewan—"hold to the view that there's no such thing as luck. They say everything that happens—good *and* bad—occurs because the hand of Elyon has directed it. Or allowed it. If such be the case, then we must make the best of this situation and trust Elyon will guide Neil to do what is needed."

"I hope you're right." Neil felt very small right then. "Because I don't like the idea of leaving you two here. In this place. With these folk."

"I'd put more trust in a nest of vipers than in Veit and his druid." Caitir's eyes showed fire. "They planned to sacrifice us!"

Machar nodded. "In eons past, we would never have been treated such. The Waldreich of old was a place of wonder, where the trees let in light, and the forest floor burst with life and plenty. The ancient tales speak of a far different Hochnest, where travelers were met with savory food, sweet drink, dancing, merriment, and treetop rest for as long as they wanted. Life and energy once flowed through these woods as the Naz carried on a brisk trade with their neighbors. That vision is but a memory lost, words inscribed on some aging parchments found in a cache of scrolls under a Capulum hideout.

"Now Veit rules a people enslaved to a deamhan. They've sacrificed their own for so long, their hearts have grown hard and cruel while their city rots and falls into ruin. Yet greatly do they desire the return of their ancient horn. Veit seems to think it will restore what they once had. It may not be so simple. Yet if Neil can retrieve it, perhaps Veit will keep his word."

"I'll bring it back, Machar."

"I think you will. With Elyon's help, you will."

PART V

CHAPTER 30

A PARTING

Early the next morning, two trapdoors opened with a squeak of hinges, and two rope seats dropped down for Neil and Caitir.

"Give us a moment, Egon," Machar called up. He gripped Neil's shoulder. "Put your trust in Elyon, my lord. Pray to him. Ask him to guide you, and you will succeed."

Neil grabbed his hand and squeezed. It felt hot. "Thank you, Machar. I don't know much about praying, but I'll try."

Now Machar addressed Caitir. "Help him where you can. It may be wise if you don't go inside Hedwig's palace but wait instead at the gates and learn what you can of events. You may be of more use outside. Especially if Neil finds himself in trouble. Do you understand?"

She nodded.

He squeezed one of her hands, and then fell back to a sitting position, his face pale. How ill was he really?

"One more thing, Neil. Something I haven't yet mentioned."

"What's that?"

"We haven't seen or heard from Faolukan since we entered the Waldreich. I don't know why. But should you encounter him when you leave here, I must tell you something I've kept secret from all of you." He sat back, his face wet with sweat. His words came in labored spurts. "'Tis rumored Faolukan . . . may have captured Thrag . . . the barghest. And harnessed him for his will."

A cold shiver ran down Neil's back. "A barghest?"

"Aye. When Elyon cursed the siòg, some of them he made not into deamhans but into foul creatures of darkness. They have not the reasoning power of men, but only of beasts. The Deamhan Lord conjured up special powers for a handful of them, such as Thrag. Know that wherever this creature goes, the light soon fails. Some say it's a large black dog or a bear with fangs and claws, but don't trust such claims. No one has ever seen it. Only what it leaves behind, after its talons have struck out from the night and left a man disemboweled. Or missing an arm or a leg."

Caitir's face was horror-stricken. "What can anyone do against such a monster?"

Machar closed his eyes and shook his head. Then he rummaged in the folds of his tunic, undid some ties, and brought out a small leather satchel. "This gemstone carries a blessing of light from Elyon. The Capulum has borne it through many generations. We think it's the same device the great prophet Treasach gave to one of his followers to defeat a similar creature. But it was never used." He passed it to Neil.

But as Neil's hand brushed Machar's feverish fingers, he became alarmed. Would the Naz medicine cure such a fever?

Neil opened the tiny sack to reveal a brilliant yellow gem as big as a horse's eye, wrapped securely by a silver chain. "How does it work?"

"If you chance to meet this dweller of the dark, bring it out and hold it high. It will light your way. It may even repel him. But it will only work for the length of one day. At least so the texts imply."

"Thank you, Machar." Neil tied it to a spot inside his inner pocket.

"Good. Wrap it tightly and keep it always on your person."

"I will."

"But alas, there is more to its use." Machar sighed. "It only works under one condition."

Neil looked to him, his eyes questioning.

"Its light shines only if the bearer holds no fear. He must put his trust in Elyon. Otherwise, when he needs it most, its light will darken and go out."

The blood ran from Neil's face, making him lightheaded. Just hearing about the barghest sent cold shivers down his spine. How was he never going to show fear? The thing lived in—nay, it created—its own darkness. And now Machar was telling him that if he let himself fear the one thing he feared more than any other—great darkness—then that would disable the very light he needed to turn aside that fear? He wanted to scream.

"Not a smidgen of fear, Neil." Machar squinted at him as if he could understand his thoughts.

Neil swallowed then nodded.

"One more thing. From everything we've read, most believe this gemstone was Treasach's. But, my lord, some disagree. We could be wrong."

"You're telling me it may not work at all?"

"Right. But in Beilzig City, you'll probably never need it. My lord Neil . . ." He laid back, breathing heavily. "I'm proud to call you my friend. We're all counting on you. And remember: No matter what, you must press on to the end. Now go in peace." Then Machar closed his eyes.

Ewan embraced Neil. "Sure and certain, my lord, you *will* do well. Find their blasted Horn and come back to us."

"I will."

Then Ewan hugged Caitir. "I ken you'll be as good a squire as me."

Caitir gave him a half-smile. "I'll never be able to replace you. But I'll do my best."

Neil and Caitir took their packs, sat on the log seats, and Egon lifted them through the trapdoors. At the top, the Naz beckoned toward a pile of their confiscated weapons. Neil found his sword and knife and grabbed Machar's bag of coins. Caitir took her bow and quiver.

Then Egon led them on a series of creaking walkways high above the forest floor. They passed one abandoned and rundown house after another. Some abodes were mere skeletons, poles stripped of logs and planks. Finally, they left the city behind, and the high walkway ended.

Descending a ladder into the silent semidarkness, they met two men on the forest floor. The men held the reins of three enormous deer-like creatures, but with long, blunted muzzles and humps on their backs. Each beast stood at least seven feet tall at the shoulder, and they bore sharp, spreading antlers nearly ten feet wide. They were saddled and ready to mount.

"Wh–what are these creatures?" Neil pointed.

"Elch. Now we ride." Those were Egon's first words since they started. "You two *can* ride, can't you?"

"Horses," whispered Neil. The animals before him were twice, maybe three times, larger than anything he'd ever ridden.

Caitir swallowed. "Aye, only horses."

"You'll find elch ride much the same. But they're often cantankerous and strong-willed. You must show them who's in charge."

Neil grabbed his animal's reins, reached high with his foot so he could reach the stirrup, and mounted. He sat far taller than on a horse. His beast's wide antlers appeared capable of throwing or gouging even the biggest wolf.

Caitir mounted the elch beside him. Within moments, she had it turning right then left. "This is not so bad," she said. "He's a bit balky, but this is not so bad."

Egon kicked his mount, and they took a trail heading east. But Neil's elch wanted to go its own way. Suddenly, it charged off into the forest at right angles to the others.

"Behave, you poor excuse for a horse."

As if it had heard, the animal came to an abrupt stop, throwing Neil over its head and onto the ground. He rolled to the side. Unhurt but bruised, he brushed himself off and stared up at the beast.

"Are we going to be friends, elch? Or enemies?"

It eyed him stupidly.

He approached, but it backed off. "Easy now." Circling around from the side, he mounted again and shortened the reins. He guided its head to the right. This time when he kicked, it went where he directed. Finally, he rejoined the others who were waiting.

"He's a bit balky," was all Neil could say.

Caitir stifled a giggle. Egon simply frowned.

All that day they rode a main path, once taking a left fork when the trail split. According to Egon, they were heading east. They saw no wolves, and the elch made good time. Throughout, their Naz guide was silent, almost brooding.

That night, Egon let the three elch run free while they climbed a tree to sleep. "Never sleep on the ground in the Waldreich," he warned.

The next morning, the Naz blew a whistle, and they waited for some time until their mounts reappeared. Again, they started out through the now-familiar semidarkness, oppressive under hoary oaks grown too large and close together. Ever since they'd entered this forest, all life seemed to have fled to the treetops.

By midafternoon, the trees thinned, and more light filtered to the ground. Soon they emerged at the bank of a wide, swift-flowing river where Egon dismounted. The river's current flowed so wild over the rocks, even the banks where Neil stood seemed to shake and rumble.

"This is the Grauwin." The Naz spread his hands wide. "It runs from the Kracken Mountains in the south, all the way to the Fell Bogs in the north. Remember that landmark." He pointed to the middle of the river and a small island composed of two hulking boulders, topped with stunted trees lush with leaf. The waters churned and tumbled, white and angry, around the rocks. "Two leagues to the northwest is Beilzig City. Now you must continue alone and on foot."

"You're not going to wait for us?" Neil's mouth gaped.

"Nay. The risk of my being discovered is too great. And now I'm to tell you this: You have only until the next full moon to finish your task. If you haven't returned by then"—he shook a warning finger—"we'll assume you failed. Then we'll give your friends to Wodan."

Neil shuddered. "How will we ever get back to Hochnest again?"

"I will leave these two elch." He produced a diminutive bone whistle with no holes. "They might stay here. Or they might wander off. When you return—if you return—call them with the whistle every once in a while." He walked down the trail to a massive oak, pulled out his knife, and cut three hash marks on the trunk. Then he shoved the whistle into a loop of leather on one saddle. He unsaddled the two beasts and hid all their gear high up on the marked trunk. "When you recover your mounts, take the trail heading west from this landmark. After that, there's only the one main fork; bear right. Ignore all the secondary paths. Your greatest worry is wolves, but they don't much care for this particular kind of elch.

"One more piece of advice: Hide your weapons outside the castle. The Pruss will simply steal them from you."

Then, before Neil could thank him, Egon mounted and returned down the path without even saying goodbye.

"They do not let him out much, do they?" Caitir gave him a wry smile.

Neil returned her smile and shouldered his pack. Then they walked downstream toward Beilzig City.

❖

After several leagues, the river banks gave way to high stone fences enclosing pastures of domesticated, grazing deer. Archers with dogs guarded the side nearest the forest where the trail passed. Neil waved, but the men didn't wave back, just stared with open suspicion at the two travelers while the dogs barked. One spat on the ground and gave them his back.

He saw no houses, only a few ruined structures beside a trail that now widened into a road.

When the city came into view, it was not where Neil expected it to be.

Nearly all its buildings clustered in the center of a vast island, around which raging waters sped at a furious pace. From where he stood, he heard in the distance a low rumble, like continuous thunder. The very ground beneath him seemed to shake. A quarter league downstream mist rose and gathered in a roiling cloud.

"Is that some great falls I hear?" Caitir squinted downriver.

"It must be."

From a junction of three roads, a wooden bridge extended to a small rock island near the middle of the Grauwin. But when he saw the sculpture of iron guarding the entrance, the blood rushed to his head, and his stomach lurched. He stopped. Perched high atop a rod was a large, quarter-moon crescent, red with rust. The wind twisted the thing on its squeaky, rusted swivel.

He pulled Caitir to the side. "This is bad. That symbol—'tis the same as the pendant that almost bewitched me."

Caitir stared at it. "What does this mean?"

"Faolukan has influence here."

He shuddered and tore his gaze away. Already, he sensed a wave of evil coming from the place. How had the Deamhan Lord's dark presence reached so far? Was every kingdom on Ereb coming under his control?

His stomach tightened. Suddenly, he feared for Caitir. Aye, how could he leave her within the walls of a city where Faolukan held sway? Again, he realized how much he cared for her, how much he feared to lose her.

What he did next was more out of instinct and emotion than from anything else. He yanked her away from the bridge, then across a nearby field, to the shade of a wild apple tree.

"What are we doing here?" Caitir arched a puzzled brow.

"Caitir, I . . . I need to tell you something." He looked away, not knowing how to begin.

A half-smile curled one side of her mouth. "What is it? This is not like you, Tristan mac Torn."

"Neil. Even here, you should call me Neil." He grabbed both of her hands. "Do you know, lass, how much you mean to me?"

"Of course. And you mean a lot to me."

"That's not what I mean. I sense we're about to face great danger. Not that we haven't already. But I've been thinking about it. About you and me."

"You're acting strange, Neil. What are you trying to say?"

"That I . . . I . . . love you."

Her jaw dropped, and her eyes opened wide.

"That's what I wanted to say." He searched her eyes. "And I've said it."

"You canna mean *me*? There must be some mistake."

He nodded and smiled.

For no apparent reason, she was crying. Tears streamed down her face.

"What's wrong? What did I say?"

She shook her head, wiped the tears with one hand, and then hugged him.

He drew her tight to his chest and wrapped his arms around her. "I didn't mean to upset you."

"You didna upset me, silly lad. You've made me very happy."

Then he gazed into her eyes and kissed her on the lips. She reached her arms around him in a hug. When they parted, his breathing came hard, and his heart hammered inside his chest.

She smiled then said, "Very happy, indeed, Tristan mac Torn."

He smiled back. After a time he said, "Come. 'Tis time we entered the city." But as they crossed the field, he didn't understand why making her happy would lead to tears.

They crossed the bridge to where it ended at the small rock island. Between that way station and the island city yawned a gap of some thirty feet. A drawbridge on the island cast a shadow over the Grauwin's black waters, churning and tumbling against the rocks on this side. Beside them, a toll-keeper lounged against a post.

Neil approached. "How much to cross?"

"You're not from around here, are you?" The toll-man stood up straight and cocked his head.

"Nay, I'm a traveling musician from Ériu. The woman is my wife."

Caitir shot him a wry smile.

"What business have you in Beilzig Stadt?"

"I want to see the queen."

"The queen, is it? Well, it's two marks to cross. But I doubt she'll see you. Touched with an evil melancholy, she is. And we're all suffering for it."

Neil nodded and gave him two of Egon's coins.

The man waved toward the island, and the drawbridge lowered. Then they crossed into Beilzig City, the realm of Hedwig, queen of the Pruss.

CHAPTER 31

UTA

Even from the bridge, the sound of tumbling water was deafening. But they had a good view of Beilzig Castle sitting atop a gentle rise and dominating the island's northern end. Tall towers at three corners guarded a street running parallel to a wall ringed by battlements. A square keep commanded the center. Fronting the river, the keep's wall of white rock rose sheer and high.

One particular feature struck Neil more than any other, and, seeing it, his stomach tightened. A long platform hugged the keep's high, outside wall. From the wall, six booms dangled iron cages over the raging torrent below. All but one cage was empty. That one contained a desiccated corpse, clothed in shredded rags, a white skull looking down at them from black eye sockets, a white leg bone sticking out through the cage.

They stared at the grisly sight.

"I do not like this, Neil."

"Aye, this place portends ill. But we must carry on."

They left the bridge and entered one crooked street after another, all of which seemed to lead away from the palace. Pictures painted on wood announced taverns, coopers, fishmongers, cheese mongers, tanners, and butchers. But the people appeared cowed, wary, and avoided eye contact with him. When he approached a boy carrying firewood to ask directions, the boy ran away without speaking. When he said hello to an old, wiry-haired woman hauling a single fish, she only frowned and looked at the cobblestones. Many shops were boarded up or dark. Of those that were open, many displayed empty baskets, bare floors and shelves. Like Hochnest, an air of decay and abandonment hovered over all.

They jumped aside as a two-wheeled carriage, clattering over the cobbles, nearly ran them down.

After many twists and turns, they rounded a corner and beheld a lane snaking beside the castle's fortress wall. They walked the street, avoiding the refuse thrown down from windows above. The rains would carry off the garbage and cleanse the cobblestones. Eventually, they came to a latticework gate of iron bars, wide enough to admit a horse and carriage into the palace yard. Was this the main gate? Just inside, four guards lounged against spears. Neil led Caitir into an alley across the street.

"You must wait here."

She looked at the street then at the guards. "What will I do until you return?"

He held both her hands. "Remember those flaky pastry rolls you used to make? The ones with honey and nuts inside? I'll wager they've never tasted the like here. Use these coins"—he gave her Machar's bag of golden coins—"and buy what you need, no matter how dear. Become a street vendor and sell your rolls to the guards, cheap." He unbuckled his baldric and also passed her his sword and knife.

"Ah, so it's a pastry lady I'm now to become? While you save the kingdom of the Naz, retrieve their magic horn, and rescue our friends, I'm to sell sweet rolls?" A forced edge sharpened her banter, as if she was trying too hard. She tried unsuccessfully to smile.

"Aye, lass. And while you're selling to the guards, learn what you can. I may be inside for days."

Caitir nodded. But was that a hint of fear he saw in her eyes?

He pulled her close, hugged her, and then parted. "Like Machar said, if I get into some kind of trouble, it's best if you're not also caught up in it. I may need someone on the outside to come to *my* rescue." As he took both her hands, her eyes gleamed moist.

"I'll do what I can. Take care . . . Tristan."

"I will."

Then she surprised him by pulling him toward her. She pressed her lips against his and wrapped both her hands around his head. Energy, like some ethereal, intoxicating wine, shot through him. When they parted again, he smiled briefly. He didn't want to leave her here, beautiful and alone, in this strange city, especially with this feeling of foreboding heavy upon him. "Will you be all right?"

She straightened. "Of course. I ken how to take care of myself. First off, I have my dagger. If anyone tries anything untoward—"

"I'd hate to be the one who underestimates you."

She smiled.

He flashed her one last smile, gripped her hands tightly in his, and kissed her once more.

Then he left her in the alley and walked toward the iron gate and the four guards.

"I'm a traveling musician," he announced to a burly man standing behind the bars. "And I'm here to perform for the queen." It was as good a ruse as any he could think of to gain entry.

The man stared at him then at his companions. He laughed. "Ja, and this afternoon, I myself will be drinking tea and eating strudel with her majesty and kicking my bare feet up on her divan."

His companions slapped their thighs and laughed. Then the burly man stuck his spear through the bars at him. "Now get along. The queen's got no time for the likes of you. 'Specially in her current state."

Neil backed to a safe distance then put both hands on his hips. "I think she'll want to hear me play."

The guard scowled. "If you don't move along, we'll come out there and play a game of skewer-the-pig with your ribs."

The other guards laughed again.

Neil frowned and eyed them for a time. Then he drew his flute from his tunic pocket and put it to his lips. He began to play.

A woman and young child passing on the street stopped to listen.

Neil smiled inwardly as Caitir ambled out from the alley to stand beside the two.

A vendor wheeling a creaky cart with a dozen leeks slowed and joined the gathering.

The notes spilled out of his instrument and filled the street. Two more passersby joined the others as a crowd formed.

The burly guard's eyes widened. The other soldiers crowded close to the bars and listened. Neil lost track of how long he played.

"Open the gate," commanded a woman's voice from inside. "Let him in."

Neil continued to play while the guards creaked the gate inward. A young woman, not much older than he, stood within. Pale, blonde hair hung straight to her shoulders. A hint of dark circles surrounded wide, doe-like eyes. Blue and gold stripes interlaced her royal red tunic.

He stopped playing. The woman beckoned, and he entered the courtyard. Then the gate clanged shut behind him.

At a wave from her hand, the guards bowed and backed away. "What kind of music was that?" she asked. "I've never heard such playing."

"'Twas only a bit of the flutist's skill, my lady."

"Nay, if I'm any judge, it was infused with magic. Are you a magician?"

"Some have called me that. But I will only use what skill I have to do good, not evil."

Her eyes widened even further. She stepped back, regarded him for some moments. Then she led him across the cobbled yard to a bench on a patch of grass under a tree. He sat where she pointed, beside her.

"Magician, will you play for my mother, the queen? That's what I heard you telling the guards as the reason you came here."

"Certainly, my lady."

She smiled and extended a hand. "I am Princess Uta."

Neil took her hand and brushed his lips against her fingers, just as Ewan had taught him to do in such a situation. He thought about using his real name. Instead, he took Machar's advice. "Neil mac Connell."

"Your name, your accent—from where do you hail?"

"Ériu."

"Ériu! Far, indeed, have you come, Neil mac Connell. I can't remember ever seeing a traveler from Ériu. How did you survive the journey through the Waldreich?"

"My flute. The wolves don't attack when they hear my music."

"Indeed! A magician you must be!" Then she said nothing for a time while she gazed across the yard. "My mother is unwell, Neil of Ériu. I believe she's dying. Slowly. Could you use your magic to cure her, bring her back to the way she used to be?"

"What ails her?"

"She's been bewitched. Four years ago a man from the east came to us. And nothing's been the same here ever since. But they say our present darkness started long before then, even before I was born. I'm told once our trade extended even to ancient Saxia, to Gol Oras on the Plains of Romely, and further down to the great city of Remus in Etrusca, where glorious buildings once stood, supported by columns of stone reaching to the sky. Alas, I'm told this is no longer.

"The ancient legends also tell of Prussio homes—our homes—bursting with joy and a people whose hearts were filled with song. Such a description seems impossible when applied to us now." She gazed into his eyes. "When you came into the city, Neil, did you see such joy in the peoples' faces?"

He shook his head.

"Nay. We are in a decline that each day grows. And with every word she utters, each command she gives, my mother hastens the fall. I tell you this because I sense something good in you. And because you're a magician. If you could cure her, I . . . I'd give you anything. Ja, anything at all."

"I can't promise I can cure her."

"Can you try, Neil mac Connell? I know of no other magicians. And you've shown me you have skill."

"Aye, my lady, I will try."

"Good. Now think of something worthy to ask for. If you cure the queen, nothing is too great."

"There is something. But nay. 'Tis too much to ask."

"Speak. What do you want?"

"I've heard of a great treasure the Pruss possess. Were you to offer me this treasure . . ."

She frowned. "Speak its name."

"The Horn of the Reich."

"What!" Then she stared at him so long, he thought he'd just made a blunder. "I promised you anything, true. But *that?*"

"I'm sorry. 'Tis too much. I take back my words."

"I did promise it, did I not? But you're too late."

"Too late? Why?"

"Because my mother has sold it. It was our greatest treasure, and she bartered it away for a few weights of gold. To bolster a treasury made scant by her poor decisions."

Neil's heart sank, a leaden weight pressing against his stomach. "Where is it now?"

She looked sideways at him with sudden intensity. "Was it *this* that brought you here? Did you come here under false pretenses?"

A moment of panic shot through him, and he squirmed. "I . . . I'm sorry. But . . . aye."

"If I did not sense something in you . . . under different circumstances . . . I might have you hung in a gibbet over the river."

He swallowed. "Is that what's to become of me now?"

"I think not."

"Thank you, my lady." He bowed.

"I am desperate, Neil. And I see yours are not ordinary requests. Perhaps because yours are not ordinary skills. I'm sorry I cannot offer you the Great Horn, or—I don't know—I might possibly have given it to you. My mother valued it greatly. But it did nothing for our people."

Neil bowed low again. "What about my question? Where is the Horn now?"

She gazed across the courtyard. "'Tis in the kingdom of Schwarzburg."

Neil stared at her, feeling suddenly lightheaded. "Then there is something else you can give me—if 'tis in your ability to do so."

"What is that?" she said with a raised eyebrow.

"A map leading me to Schwarzburg."

She smiled. "And what would you do with such knowledge?"

"I would go and recover the Horn. And another item I seek."

"And for this, you would cure my mother?"

"If 'tis in my power to do so."

She caught his gaze and her brows narrowed. "In Father's time, my people became concerned when all trade and communication with Schwarzburg simply ceased. So he sent a delegation to reestablish commerce. But when they returned, they brought word of a land desecrated, a people in decline, and a great evil spreading out from its castle. Schwarzburg had nothing to offer us then, and we little to give them. That was our last contact—many years ago now—that we had with them. But some of the home guard who accompanied that delegation are still living today and know the route. So I will commission a drawing from them, painted on leather to withstand the elements."

Eyes aglow, she took both of his hands. "Aye, if you do what I've asked, I think I can give you your map."

Neil squeezed her hands. "Thank you, my lady. But I have one more question."

"Speak it."

"Who bought the Horn from your mother? Who took it to Schwarzburg?"

She bit her lower lip. "I dread even to let the name pass my lips."

"What was the name, my lady?"

"The very one who came from the east and bewitched my mother—Faolukan the Grim."

CHAPTER 32

QUEEN HEDWIG

Princess Uta stowed Neil's pack in a safe place in the servant's quarters on the first floor. Then she led him up an echoing, circular stairwell to the keep's top floor. They walked down a long hallway to a room with a single guard outside.

"Lately, she's only been seeing a few trusted advisors," said Uta. "Sometimes, she won't even see me." She ignored the guard and knocked on the door.

From within came only silence.

"Mother?" Uta knocked again.

"Come in, child." The queen's voice quavered.

Uta pushed open the door and led Neil inside.

Queen Hedwig sprawled over a divan in semidarkness. Her unwashed nightdress crumpled around her in disarray. The dying fire at the far wall flickered and cast dim shadows across a pale face, the visage of one who hadn't seen the sun in years. Her matted hair hung in thin white locks. When Uta entered, the queen looked up, her eyes widening like a deer surprised in the forest.

Beside her on a stool sat a druid in a flowing white tunic. His thick, black beard and sunburned face contrasted starkly with the queen's deathly pallor.

At the foot of the bed slept a small white poodle, its hair a dirty gray. Neil had a powerful urge to pet it but held off.

"Who's that with you?" Hedwig's fingers barely motioned.

"This is Neil mac Connell, a musician of extraordinary talent. And he's here to bring some cheer into this dismal room." Uta fixed the druid with a steady gaze. "Lutz, you will please leave us, now."

The druid frowned but didn't move. "And where, musician, do you call home?"

Neil stared into the man's dead eyes. "Ériu."

Lutz's glance shifted to the queen. "My lady, I think it unwise to let a foreigner into your chambers with you in such a state. Especially one from Ériu. Who knows how he got here? Or if he's even telling the truth?"

Hedwig's glassy eyes tried to focus then examined Neil. "Who do you say this is?"

"A musician." Uta stood her ground. "And I will not have your druid interfering with my attempt to bring light into these dark chambers. Tell him to be gone."

Her head trembling constantly, the queen's gaze wandered to Lutz. She lifted her hand as if it might fall off her arm then waved him away. "Do as my daughter asks."

Lutz rose, bowed, and headed to the door. But as he passed Neil, he narrowed his eyes, slowed his pace, and glared.

The instant the druid was gone, Neil knelt to the poodle and caressed its fluffy head. At first, the dog emitted a low growl. But as Neil's hand scratched under its ears, the growl vanished, and the dog gave him a quick upward glance of appreciation. He stood under Uta's disapproving glare.

"Why was Lutz here again, mother?"

"To approve some requests from Drochtar."

"What kind of requests?"

"They want to station a small camp on our eastern border. Just a few scouts. I said it was permissible."

"You should never have agreed to that."

Hedwig reached inside a pocket of her gown, her fingers searching. She brought back a fist closed tightly around some object. But her eyes unfocused and sleep pulled on her lids. "I know," she whispered. "But it doesn't matter. Not really."

Neil strained to see what was in her grasp.

"Mother, put that thing down and listen while Neil plays."

The queen's head turned gradually, as if with effort. Her pupils rolled around in their sockets until they found Uta. "What?"

"Put it away and listen."

Hedwig looked down at her palm, and her fingers opened. Revealed now was a silver, crescent-moon pendant.

Neil shuddered. So, after many years, this was what happened to someone under its spell? Suddenly, he feared for Maeve back in Ewhain Macha. How many more of these things were in the hands of other kings and queens across Ereb?

"Will you put it away, mother? Please?"

Hedwig eyed the pendant then dropped it on the divan beside her. "Ja, child. I've put it away." But her gaze remained fixed on it.

"Now play for her, Neil."

Neil brought out his bone flute and held it for a moment. He knew instinctively what kind of tune was called for—something soothing, yet awakening. Healing, yet also a call to action. He didn't know how he knew this, just that he did. Putting the instrument to his lips, he blew.

He started softly, weaving and shaping the music into one long series of wavering, rising notes. For a time the notes undulated like a slow-moving river, calming and relaxing. Then came a storm, bringing wind and wave, and the waters and the music rose. The notes climbed higher and higher with the rising gale, while his heart raced in time. He went on and on. Finally, he brought it to a close.

He raised his glance to the queen. She watched him with open mouth and wide, alert eyes. Ever so slowly, her hands began to clap. "Excellent, my boy. Excellent."

Uta beamed. "You see, mother. Joy *can* enter this room. Joy without that thing in your hands. You don't need it now."

Hedwig glanced at the pendant. "Nay, child. Never say such a thing." Then her fingers closed about it, and she caressed the silver jewelry again. Her pupils narrowed, rolled up in their white sockets, and her head lolled.

"Mother!"

The queen ignored her and continued stroking the pendant. Her head now rocked back and forth.

Several times Uta repeated her request. Finally, she waved both hands in the air in disgust. "Come." Then she led Neil from the chamber.

In the hall, the druid paced. At the sound of their footsteps, he spun to face them.

Uta accosted him. "You conspire against us at your peril, Lutz. A foreign army on our very borders? What brazenness!"

The druid raised one side of his mouth in a half-smile. "It's only a few watchers."

"How many? A hundred? A thousand?"

Lutz grinned.

"Ten thousand?"

"It's no concern of yours, my lady. They're heading west. And little miss"—he narrowed his eyes—"you are not queen here. Not yet."

"But someday, I will be. Then you'll rue the day you brought my mother to such a state with your vile, bewitching gifts."

The druid smiled, bowed, and like an eel between wet rocks, slipped back inside the queen's chambers.

"He's a worm. Four years ago, Faolukan left him here as our advisor. Now I can do little to blunt his influence."

"I know what ails the queen." Neil's words were slow, serious. "I can save her."

Uta stopped, grabbed both his hands, whirled him around to face her. "What?"

"'Tis the—"

Uta put a finger to his lips to silence him. She searched his eyes. Then she pulled him close and kissed him on the cheek.

When they parted, his eyes were wide with surprise. "Wh–what?"

"I don't know why I did that. Maybe because I've known so few men here like you. Someone Lutz doesn't control. Maybe because I trust you like I've never trusted anyone. But we shouldn't be talking here. Often, the walls have ears." Then she led him down the spiral stairs through the close marble foyer and into the courtyard. On a seat under a tree, she whispered, "Go on."

"'Tis the pendant she wears. It carries a druid's spell. Now I've seen what happens when the bearer holds one for too long." He clenched and loosened his jaw. "And I fear for another back home who carries the same device."

"I'm not surprised. I was hoping you'd know what to do. Whatever you need, I'll do it."

"We need to get the pendant away from her for a couple of hours. Then I need sole access to a smithy's shop. I know how to recast it, and that will break the spell."

Uta's smile nearly split her face. "You've more skills, I see, than a mere magician's. But getting into her quarters—ah, 'twill be difficult. There's always a guard. The druid hovers about her like a vulture around a carcass. And lately, his spies also watch me. Let me think." She paced away from him then quickly returned.

"When she's awake, the thing is nearly always in her hands. So the deed must be done at night. Then Lutz will also be in his bed, or, if the past is any guide, in someone else's. Aye, tonight—a potion for the guard! I myself will take it to him to make him sleep. When it's done its work, you may enter her room and steal the pendant."

"Why can't you get it from her room instead of me? You won't be noticed."

She shook her head. "I cannot be long from my room or my chambermaid, who has become Lutz's personal spy, will become suspicious."

Neil nodded, uncomfortable with all the chances this plan involved.

"There"—she pointed across the square to a hut with a sign for a bellows—"is the castle smithy's hut. He should have all the metalworker's tools you need. I'll let him know I have need of his establishment. Tonight, the shop will be yours."

She brought him to a halt in front.

He peered through the open door at a man pounding on a white-hot sword then back across the courtyard. "'Tis a long way across this yard. What if someone sees me?"

She shrugged. "Tell them you're on an errand for me."

"Then tonight it is." He looked across the cobbles. "Who is that woman lurking in the shadows."

"That's my maid, Lutz's spy. We need to leave at once. Follow me."

She led him back to the tower keep and a room on the ground floor where servants slept. "Stay here until this evening. When I've got the potion, I'll come for you. I do believe the gods themselves have sent you here."

Neil caught her glance. "Not the gods, Uta, but Elyon. He is the one true God of the world."

She started. "Long has it been since that name has been spoken in these halls, and then only in whispers."

"In the future, may it be shouted from the rooftops."

"But only if you free my mother from the spell."

He nodded, and she left, leaving him alone in an empty room.

But as time passed, the shadows from the flickering torches, the occasional echoes of a guard's footsteps in the hallway, and his pounding heart seemed to scream at him.

He was taking too many risks.

CHAPTER 33

IN THE PALACE DARK

It was still early when Uta poked her head into the room he shared with two other servants. One was asleep, snoring loudly. The other attended to duties elsewhere.

"I know it's earlier than planned," Uta whispered, "but I have to bring the guard his mug now. My maid has already become suspicious."

Wordless, Neil followed as she led him up three flights. At the top, they passed a soldier heading down. He nodded to them as they passed.

"Usually, there's no one about at this time."

Neil frowned as they entered the long hallway leading to the queen's room. Before they'd gone ten paces, the princess pulled him into an empty side chamber. "Wait here until I come for you."

Her footsteps echoed down the hallway, and he waited alone. He found a bench against a wall and sat in semidarkness lit by flickering torches from the hall. The silence deepened. Time seemed to slow. Then feet treaded down the stone passage. They stopped outside the open door where he hid.

A shadow blocked the entryway. The form of a woman. He released the breath he'd been holding.

"He's not asleep yet." Uta's voice came from the shadows, breaking the silence.

"I thought you were another guard."

"Sorry. I was checking to make sure no one was coming."

"What's the problem?"

"He only drank half the mug, and then asked for some water. The potion may still work. But now it will take more time, and he'll probably not sleep soundly. I've never done this before. We talked about his wife as I made some excuse about wanting to know all the guards better. But I don't think he believed me."

"Then we can only wait."

"Nay. *I* must return to my room. From here on, it's up to you. Only you. But the longer you wait, the greater the danger that you'll be discovered so far from your quarters. Servants—even musicians—are not allowed to wander the halls unless called for."

Neil bowed, and she left.

He waited. In the distance, the patter of rain hit the palace walls. Good. It would deaden the echo of his feet on stone. He stuck his head into the hallway. Empty now.

He walked slowly, glad for the falling rain outside. But when the downpour suddenly ceased, his next steps sounded like thunder. Cringing at every footfall, he trod the length of the hall.

Ahead lay the door to the queen's chambers. The guard sat slumped in his chair. The potion must have finally worked.

Outside Hedwig's room, he listened but heard nothing. Easing open the door, he entered a receiving room. He crept past carved, wooden chairs and a divan into the next chamber. Two paintings lined the walls. Like large, dark eyes, their colors faded to black in the room's semidarkness. The queen lay curled up on a high bed over pillows and furs. He checked the dainty table closest the door. No pendant.

At the foot of the bed, the poodle rose its head and gave a low growl. Neil knelt, let it sniff his hand, and then stroked its back. The dog lay down again.

She slept on her side with furs up to her waist, facing away from him. He walked to the bed's other side then crept forward, looking for the piece. Neither was it on a chain around her neck.

There! Lying on the furs just beyond her fingers. Her palm lay on the chain.

Gently, without touching the quarter moon itself, he pinched the chain between two fingers and drew.

She began to turn over.

He gave it a yank, and it came free. He waited to see if she would react. But she remained asleep.

He realized he was holding his breath. Now he let it out. Walking on the balls of his feet, he gained the door. Then he slipped outside and eased it shut. The mechanism hooked with a loud click. With a loud yawn, the guard shifted in his chair. Then his arms rose in the air.

Neil froze.

The man stretched his arms, folded them across his chest. Neil's breathing sounded in his ears like a tempest wind. He tried to breathe more softly. He stood only a foot behind the man's back. If the guard shifted his head even a few inches or reached behind him, he'd discover Neil was there. Neil closed his eyes.

Again, the guard yawned then slumped back against his seat. For long moments, Neil remained motionless. He could have boiled a pot twice over before he dared move. When he thought it was safe, he took a step. No reaction from the man. He crept forward. Farther away now. Ten feet. Now twenty. He increased the pace. Outside, the rain began again, covering the sound of his footfalls. Hurrying down the hall, he turned the corner and took a deep breath.

At the spiral staircase, he looked up, then down. No one was about. Quickly, he made his way to the ground floor and crossed the marble foyer. Straight ahead was the entrance. He stepped out into the yard into a light rain and breathed a sigh of—

"You there!" a man's voice hailed from behind. "Turn and identify yourself."

Neil's heart leaped in his chest. He spun to face a soldier stationed just outside the keep, holding a lance.

"What business have you in the yard at this hour?"

"I–I'm on an errand for the princess." The rain fell harder, dripping off his forehead.

Gripping his lance tighter, the guard squinted at him in the wet gloom. "Come closer. I don't recognize you. You a foreigner?"

Neil took a step closer. "I came only today. By the princess's command, I'm to begin playing for the queen tomorrow."

The guard grunted, wiped the rain from his brow. "Just this once, I'll let you pass. But tomorrow, I'll ask Lutz whether it's permissible for you to run errands at night."

"You'll have to take that up with Princess Uta."

The guard scowled, backed under the shelter of the entryway, and waved him on.

Neil turned back to the yard and hunched against the rain. He continued to the forge at a run.

The door to the shop lay open. He pushed inside and found the wood still popping and flaring in the furnace. The blacksmith must have lit it for him before going to bed. He breathed in the familiar smells of iron and clay, walls layered with wood smoke. After adding more wood to the blaze, he fired it hot with the squeaking bellows, and then searched for what he needed.

He found clay, pushed some into two mold boxes. After preparing plaster, he poured a thick layer into each mold. He removed the chain and picked up the pendant.

The familiar feeling of cold, prickling energy ran up his arm, far weaker than the one fashioned especially for him, yet still captivating. Shaking his head, he pressed the device into the first mold and fixed the second mold on top. He fired the combined boxes in the furnace until the water sizzled away. When he pulled them out, he let them cool and separated the boxes.

He pried the pendant loose. The mold was nearly perfect. With wire, he bound the molds tightly together.

Next, he heated the pendant in a ladle until it melted. Then he poured the molten silver into the new mold. As he did so, a black, oily vapor rose from the mold, hovered for a moment as if in anger, then vanished.

After the mold cooled, he broke the new pendant loose. He touched it and smiled. The spell was gone.

He filed and rubbed the edges smooth and reattached the chain.

Back outside, the rain had quit. He crossed the yard, nodding to the entrance guard as he reentered the palace.

When Neil returned upstairs, the guard outside Hedwig's room appeared to be sleeping more soundly. Good. He eased open the door and padded through the receiving room into the queen's bedchamber.

She lay flat on her back, breathing lightly.

As he walked to the bedside, the furs surrounding her bed deadened his footfalls. He lifted the chain out of his pocket. Her hand lay open on top of the blanket. Carefully, he dropped the pendant beside her fingers.

She shifted position, rolled toward him.

He waited until he was certain she was still sleeping.

Then he noticed the poodle at his feet. It had moved to this side of the bed. Looking up at him, the dog wagged its tail. He backed up so he could pet it. But as he knelt, he bumped into something behind him.

He whirled. The bust of some ancestor—it was tipping off its marble stand.

He lunged to grab it. But his fingers only pushed it farther away.

The bust and its high stand were falling. Time seemed to slow. The bust dropped away from him, tipped out of reach, headed for the hard floor beyond.

When it hit the marble floor, it shattered.

The crash was deafening. Pieces flew in all directions. The stand rolled and ground heavily over the shards.

He reeled like someone had slammed a mace against his head. Spinning on his heels, he raced for the receiving room.

"Stop, thief!" the queen's voice bellowed from behind. The poodle began barking.

He pushed through the outer door, slammed it open. The guard raised his head. Sprinting, Neil burst down the hallway.

"A thief. In my chambers. Stop him!" The queen's voice, filled with outrage, followed him down the hall.

Halfway down the corridor, the guard's heavy footsteps thudded behind him. How was he ever going to reach his quarters without being recognized? So far, no one had really seen his face. When the bust fell, he'd had his back to her.

At the stairwell, he took the steps two at a time. But on the second landing, his foot missed the last step. He fell forward. To break the fall, he put his hands out before him. He slid across the marble, stopping only when his hands reached the steps.

Heavy footfalls approached from behind. "Stay, thief! Or my lance will find the other side of your gut."

Neil lay where he was, prone on the floor. If he could stand, he'd make a break for the bottom. But another set of footsteps echoed up from below. Even more guards clopped down from behind, joining the first man. All chance of escape—now gone.

From the top of the stairwell came Hedwig's voice, "Do you have the thief?"

"Ja, my lady. We've got him."

CHAPTER 34

THE PRISON

Stand him up. Let me see him." The queen's footsteps echoed down the stairwell.

The tip of a sword prodded Neil's back. "You heard her majesty. Stand."

Neil stood and faced her.

"The foreigner!" Hedwig scowled from the stairs above. "So Lutz was right. I should never have trusted you. What were you trying to steal from me?"

"Nothing, my lady." He bowed. "I . . . I was . . ." He shook his head. Nothing he could say would explain this. He was in deep trouble.

"You were trying to steal my pendant. Say it."

"Nay, my lady."

"Then 'tis the gibbet over the river for him." Her eyes narrowed to tiny slits. "As usual, leave the door open. Let the thief choose his own death. Let him contemplate what happens to those who enter the queen's bedchamber uninvited."

The one with the sword bowed. "As you wish, my lady."

She gave them her back and slowly climbed the stairs.

When she'd gone, the lead guard's spear again prodded his back. "On your feet. It's up the steps to the gibbet with you."

Still breathing heavily from the chase, Neil stood. The guard, followed by two others, led him up the staircase to the first landing, where they turned toward a door hiding in the shadows. Rusty hinges creaked.

Flickering torchlight revealed the gallows platform he and Caitir observed from the bridge. A chill breeze carried the roar of the falls, embracing him with a damp hug.

The guard pushed him through. "I'd rather lose my head to the axe than be hung over the river to starve or be picked to death by the birds. No theft is worth that. If I was you, I'd jump, give yourself to Golob's Maw."

"What's Golob's Maw?"

The guard laughed. "A foreigner you truly are. Does you hear that sound?" He pointed down the river.

"Aye."

"Why, my poor, ignorant lad, that rumble is the Great Falls. And all who jumps off this platform is carried away—no chance of swimming against the mighty Grauwin. All is swept down to the Maw. A hundred fifty feet straight down to the boulders, it is. And if that don't kill you, then it's the tumbling roil below. Sometimes, the bodies churn in the roil for days before they comes out downstream, all battered and crushed. Certain death it is to go over the Maw. But if I was you, I'd do it. Better than a slow death by starvation and being picked to pieces, day after day, by the birds."

Neil swallowed.

They prodded him toward an empty cage beside the gibbets' sole current occupant, the desiccated corpse. The center of each boom rested on a swivel, and now the guard pivoted the wooden beam until the cage swung, creaking and groaning, to the parapet.

"In you go, lad." He prodded Neil with his sword. "Think about my advice. I hates to see them starve away to skin and bone, giving weak struggle while their flesh is torn apart, their eyes and nose and lips picked away."

Neil shuddered. Then he stepped through an opening halfway up and wriggled down into the cage. He stuck his legs into the cage's lower half. The gibbet was only wide enough to stand up in. His jailer clanged shut the door but didn't lock it. To prevent anyone from climbing the chain to the boom while the door was open, a wide baffle of iron guarded the top.

The jailer gave the boom a mighty push, and with more iron complaints, it swung out over the river, dark and roaring below. Then he locked the mechanism in place. The cage creaked back and forth.

"Not even Wodan can help you now."

Neil tried to face the guards' platform. In the confines of the metal chamber, he could barely turn his upper body. The guards and his jailer watched him for a moment, shaking their heads, then left the platform. The iron slats of his small prison were spaced six inches apart, at its base, sides, and top. The device was constructed such that he could take only the one, uncomfortable, standing position. He pushed open the door to feel less confined and stuck out his arms.

A light rain began again. Out in the open, hanging over the river, he soon became soaked. Shivering, he tried to huddle, but found it difficult even to hug his arms around his chest. Then the rain quit, replaced by a cold wind.

What a mess he'd made of it! How could he ever free himself from this contraption except to jump into the river below? But as his eyes adjusted to the darkness, one look at the river's dark, swirling waters told him it was madness to try swimming against such a current. As the guard had said, it would surely sweep him toward the deep, angry rumble from Golob's Maw to the north. And to certain death.

He spent the rest of the night shivering, trying to preserve his warmth. He gave Elyon a fleeting thought but shook his head. His only hope now lay with Uta. He just hoped she would come soon.

With morning's arrival, he welcomed the sun's light and warmth. But soon the sun beat down so hard, he couldn't touch the hot iron slats.

For the first time, when he looked downriver, he saw a stretch of rapids before the falls, angry, roiling water breaking over huge boulders.

Beyond, a mist cloud boiled and churned high. The fall's thunder roared on and on.

By noon, clouds drifted overhead, cooling the metal bars. He was already weak from having gone without food or water for a day. He tried to sleep, found it impossible. Squawking crows landed on his cage, tried to peck him through the slats, but he squirmed and wriggled until they flew off. He grew more and more impatient that Uta hadn't come to him. Was she going to abandon him here?

Night fell again and with it another drizzling rain. He opened his mouth to catch as much of it as he could. Time seemed to stretch, and he lost track of it.

"Neil."

He jumped at the voice. He twisted his upper body enough to see Uta standing alone on the platform in the dark. "I'm sorry, princess. I've made a mess of it."

"No, you haven't. The magic has gone out of my mother's fiendish device. Yesterday and even more so this morning, sanity seems to have returned to her. She's quite the crank but lucid. Perhaps in a few days . . . ?" Did a smile flicker across her lips? "You've done what I asked. Now I must help you. I'm sorry I didn't come sooner. But Lutz suspects I helped you in some way. He's restricted my movements."

"Can you release me from this cage?"

She stared at him, at the cage, and then averted her eyes. "Since yesterday, Lutz has ordered my maid to follow me around the keep. And he's put another spy outside my door. Moments ago, I slipped away from both of them on a ruse, but I doubt it will work again. I must be quick. I cannot come back to you anytime soon."

"Are you just going to let me die here?"

"I'm sorry." She looked up. "I don't know what to do."

He thought a moment. "Can you contact someone for me? Perhaps she can help me?"

"Who?"

"A woman who came with me. Her name is Caitir, and if she followed our plan, she should be selling pastries by the palace gate."

"You have an accomplice in Beilzig City? Maybe there's hope for you yet."

"What hope?"

"Once I heard some men from the home guard boasting in the soldier's mess. One of them said that if ever he found himself hung in one of the queen's gibbets, he would jump into the river and escape the Maw."

"Is that possible?"

"His plan involved an accomplice—such as yours. His friend would station himself on the narrow spit of boulders hugging the far northern end of the palace wall. The rocks there are treacherous, but it's possible to find one's way to the end. Our soldier planned to have his friend watch for a shadow jumping into the river. Then he would throw a rope to the swimmer and pull him in."

"Do you think it would work?"

"His comrades had their doubts. The current is so strong and swift, it's swept every other jumper over the falls. Days later, we find their broken bodies downstream."

"Can you go to Caitir and tell her this plan? Also give her the map you promised me."

"I will go. But are you sure you want to do this?"

He gripped the bars. "What other choice do I have?"

She nodded. "When?"

"Tomorrow morning is too risky. We'd surely be seen. I'll not last many more days in this barbaric device. It must be tonight."

"Then tonight it is."

"How will I know if she's there?"

Uta shook her head. "I cannot return here. But no one will suspect if I make a trip outside the castle. I will find your lady friend today. I'll tell her what must be done. That's all I can promise."

Neil swallowed. Such an uncertain plan. "If I make it to shore, how can we get off the island without being seen?"

Uta frowned. "A hay wagon leaves the city empty each morning for the fields. It brings back feed for the castle's horses. I'll tell your friend where to find it. Hide under the tarp until morning. I'll tell the driver he's to carry you across without revealing your presence. I've done favors for him, so he will obey me. Or he'll be next in the gibbet."

"Thank you, my lady. If this succeeds—"

"It must. Thank *you* for freeing my mother from the druid's spell. Perhaps, in a few days or weeks, she'll return to her old self."

"Perhaps."

Neil spent the rest of the day hoping for clouds to blunt the heat of the iron slats. Several times, he waved off vultures who flew to the nearby cages, watched him, and waited. But the crows still found ways to peck at him through the bars.

"Go on!" he shouted, sending the birds to flight. "I'm not dead yet."

It was a misty, roaring darkness that blacked the sky, for the falls overshadowed even the night. He looked toward the spit of land downriver from the keep. What if Caitir couldn't get to that particular spot? What if there was no rope to buy? What if he jumped and the current was so fast he couldn't grab the rope and went over the falls? Uta's lack of enthusiasm for the plan wasn't encouraging. Her last plan hadn't worked well at all, had it? Why should this one turn out any better?

He waited and watched. Not knowing if Caitir was in position gnawed at his thoughts. How could he have agreed to a plan with such uncertainty?

Finally, he began crawling out of the cage's narrow confines. His calves rebelled. Both arms and legs ached from holding the same position for two days. He climbed through the door, and his movement sent the cage swinging. He clung to the outside and peered at the darkness below. The waters swirled and churned, broke into foam. From downstream, the continuous thunder of Golob's Maw declared its power.

He thought of the teachings of his people, before he'd heard of Elyon and Neavh. The druids had long taught that all who died went to the

Underworld, a place of dim light where Manannán mac Lir ruled. But Manannán was also the sea god, ruler of the deep where swam fell monsters. A god who was ever capricious and violent. How could his reign be good or kind? Where in that dark place would he find joy? Peace? Or hope? Nay, it would be a place of darkness and despair. It was for all eternity, and there did he greatly fear to go.

But this new teaching from Machar was different. If Neil trusted in Elyon—and after the visitation, how could he not?—then when he died, he would go instead to Neavh, a place of happiness without end.

If the Maw took him, was he then destined for Neavh, no matter what else happened?

He raised his eyes to the mist-laden darkness. "O Elyon, I don't know you well. I only know you created Erde and all that's in it. And that you spoke to me. So can you get me out of this? You've told me to bring back the Scepter. So, Elyon, please save this poor life. Let Caitir be there with the rope. Let me catch it. And let us both escape. But if I die, please take me to Neavh. Let that be my resting place, not the Underworld."

The prayer gave him strength. He took several deep breaths and let go of the cage. Wind roared in his ears as the river rushed up from below. He flailed his arms, tried to keep upright. His heart beat wildly. The castle walls flew by.

His feet hit the water with shocking force. Then he went under. Instantly, the cold began sucking the life from him. His face went under, and he kept going down. He kicked and struggled for the surface. But he kept going down.

Finally, he was heading up. The current wrenched him sideways—a cold, relentless force, hurtling him on. He kicked harder but made little headway. His lungs were near bursting. Where was the surface? He kicked and kicked. Then his head broke through, and he sucked in air.

But now the castle walls were racing beside him. Moving too fast. He swam toward them but made no progress. Where was the rope?

He passed the last section of wall. Still no rope. And no Caitir.

The current was carrying him straight to the rapids and Golob's Maw.

CHAPTER 35

CAITIR

Neil looked behind him to the receding castle walls. On the narrow shore hugging the fortress—only the shadows of large boulders.

The thunderous roar of the falls shook the air as if announcing his doom.

Something brushed his arm. Something thick and hairy. The rope? He grabbed for it. But the current carried him so fast, it slid roughly through his hands. He grabbed again, got only a handful of water. Then he reached as far as he could, slammed his arm over the water, and closed his fingers. But the rope slid along his palms, scraping flesh. He couldn't hold on.

Then his hand caught a loop at the rope's end. Caitir had made a loop! Quickly, he thrust his whole arm through. The current yanked his body straight, nearly wrenching his arm from his shoulder. Water broke over his face in a steady wave. But he held on.

The bank was thirty feet away. But how could he swim toward it? He was expending all his energy just staying where he was.

"Tristan!" Finally, Caitir's voice, weak and distant.

"Pull me in." He could barely raise his head high enough to shout.

"I can't. The current."

"Loop it, bit by bit"—he gasped for air—"over the boulders."

For the longest time, nothing happened. Then in one great leap, he was pulled a few feet closer to shore. The water was so cold, his feet and hands were going numb. Again, the rope jerked, and at that moment, he kicked with all his might. Two days without food or water in a cramped position had weakened him. With each yank forward, she was moving him left, out of the current, into calmer waters sheltered by the castle walls.

Finally, he escaped the worst of the current. A knee struck a submerged boulder. He grasped onto it, fumbled toward the next boulder. Then he stood on an uneven bottom and walked to Caitir. He collapsed at her feet, tried to catch his breath.

She knelt. "Tristan . . . I mean, Neil. You're shivering." She wrapped her arms around him and held him tightly.

"I . . . I don't know if I can go farther just now."

"Just rest. We don't have to leave yet."

Then she hugged him. He luxuriated in her warmth, in being able to stretch out his legs and arms, free of the cage. She produced a hunk of cheese, and he devoured it.

"Have I told you how glad I am you're here?" he said between bites.

"Nay. But you can say it again if you want."

He smiled. Finally, he felt rested enough to go on.

"I'm going to throw the rope into the current. If they don't see it, they'll think I jumped to escape a worse death, like all the others."

Freeing the rope from each rock, he came to where she'd anchored it firmly around a boulder. When he undid it, the river swept it away.

He returned to her side. "Did Uta tell you how to find the cart?"

She nodded and led them back through the narrow boulder field to a rocky beach beyond the castle. There she'd hidden their packs and weapons.

"Your quiver is full."

"'Tis that. In my spare time, I made some arrows."

Neil strapped on the baldric holding his sword and knife.

They left the spit of boulders and ascended stone steps leading up to the city. It was good to walk again, just to move his legs. Caitir led them down dark alleys and streets until they reached the musty, quiet warmth of the cart shed. They closed the door behind them and lay down on hay in the corner. Then Caitir produced a feast of bread, cheese, sausage, and wine. After Neil ate and drank his fill, he stretched out and slept a sleep, if not of the dead, then of one who'd come very close to it.

He woke to the shed door creaking open and a horse's neighing. He sat up. Daylight streamed through the open door.

"You'll get under that tarp now, right quick, and say nary a word." The gruff voice belonged to a black-bearded man dressed in ragged, torn clothes. He was hitching a dappled mare to the front. "If they finds you under there, it'll be both our hides. Someone discovered a rope this morning. Caught on the rocks just below the castle. Now there's soldiers out everywhere looking for you."

"Thank you, kind sir." Caitir jumped up into the cart, followed by Neil. "We'll be quiet."

"Fool thing, my agreeing to this. Do you have the coin?"

"The princess said you're to get it only after we're safely across the bridge." Caitir's words came slow and firm.

The man stared at them a moment, frowned, and then climbed into the driver's seat.

They pulled the tarp over their heads and lay still. The cart lurched away, clattering and bouncing over the cobbles. On the ride through the narrow streets, the driver seemed to hit every large stone and rut. At the drawbridge, he stopped. The falls roared louder here in the open.

"Late this morning, Oscar." The voice of one of the bridge guards.

"Ja. Missus had me doing errands."

"Your tarp's a bit lumpy. You're not hiding our prisoner under there, are you?"

Neil's heart leaped. He reached for his sword.

"A bit of refuse I forgot to take out," said the driver, now identified as Oscar. "My guess is the fool lost his grip on the rope and went over the Maw."

"No doubt you're right. No one's fought Golob's current and lived. All right, Oscar, get your ugly face across."

"And aren't you one to talk, with a puss like a horse's behind?"

Laughter erupted from the other guard.

Then came the strain of ropes and the creak of wooden cogs finding their grooves as the drawbridge lowered. The driver whipped the reins, and the cart trundled across.

Within moments, the cart found a quieter track, and the going was smoother.

A long while later, with the rumble of the falls far behind them, the driver's voice came again. "Here's where I dumps you off. No matter what happens, you never saw the likes of me, hear?"

Neil threw off the tarp and jumped out. "Your secret is safe with us."

Caitir handed the driver the number of coins the princess had agreed upon. "Thank you." She hopped down.

The man grunted, turned his cart around, and whipped his horse to a trot.

Here, they were beyond even the rock-walled fields of domesticated deer. Beside the path, the Grauwin's waves crashed and tumbled over boulders.

"We're north of Beilzig City. Do you have the map?"

Caitir reached inside her pack and drew it out.

When he saw the ink diagram over new leather, Neil beamed. At least they'd achieved one goal. After studying it for a time, he put it in his knapsack. "There's no other choice now." He spoke slowly. "You and I . . . must go for the Scepter. Without the others."

For a moment, as Caitir's eyes widened, he imagined fear darkened their green to a deep emerald. "But the Horn . . . we canna free Ewan and Machar without it."

"Ah, but I learned from Princess Uta that it, too, lies inside Schwarzburg Castle. So that is where we must go."

A smile slowly raised her lips. "Next time I ask to go on an adventure, slap me good and hard, hear?" She thrust her hands on her hips.

"Then 'tis on to Schwarzburg we go. We'll get the Scepter, Tristan, just you and me. And the Horn. I ken it."

Neil smiled, grasped her hand, and wrapped his arms around her. She had pluck.

"But you must call me Neil. Even here. Lest you start to forget."

She nodded. "While you were inside, I took a nice piece of leather in exchange for a pastry. And I made something for you."

He cocked his head. "What?"

She pulled from her pack a leather armband, oiled and etched with interlocking swirls. After slipping it up his arm, he smiled. "Why, 'tis beautiful. Thank you, Caitir." He leaned over and kissed her on the cheek.

She blushed. "Had to do something with my time."

He glanced at it again. What did it mean, this armband? When a woman gave a gift like that to a man, it meant something. Didn't it?

When they parted, she looked at the sky. The morning moon hung low, already in its first quarter. "We haven't much time to free them before the moon—"

"I know," he said. "The map says we're to take the same trail we arrived on but turn west at the 'sign of the scarecrow'."

"I do not remember such a place."

"Nor I."

"Then we'll have to watch for it carefully."

He led them the two leagues up the path until they were abreast of the island with the two boulders and Egon's notched tree. Retrieving the bone whistle, he blew it several times.

"What if they don't come?" Caitir's brows dipped.

"We'll keep trying. We need the elch to protect us from the wolves and make good time."

All the rest of that day, they tried unsuccessfully to call their mounts. As night fell, they found a bed in some soft grass away from the trail. "I need to sleep," he told her. "We'll risk the wolves just this one night."

"Just like a man." She smiled and knelt beside him.

"Something tells me the wolves don't often come here. But, Caitir?"

"Aye?"

"I'm glad you're safe. Before I entered the castle, I felt a premonition that something bad would happen. I feared it was going happen to you."

"But nothing happened."

"Aye. Still, you don't know how much just the sight of you there, safe in the moonlight, warms me."

A smile lifted her mouth. Then she sat back on her furs.

Neil drew his own furs up to his chest and tried to sleep. But then he started and opened his eyes. Caitir was kneeling above him, staring at him. But her eyes were moist. Were those tears he saw?

When she realized he was awake, she drew her fingers gently across his cheeks, then over his lips. He was aroused. She leaned down and kissed him on the lips. Her tears wet his cheeks. He pulled her close and returned the kiss. Warmth coursed through him.

"I do love you, Tristan mac Torn."

He sat up and held her at arm's length, his heart pounding. "And I . . . love you, Caitir."

Her eyebrows scrunched. "Really? Do you really?"

"Really. And I've realized it for some time. But tonight, I think we should not do anything until . . . until we're married."

"Married?"

"Aye, lass. I hadn't planned on saying this right now. But aye, I'm asking you to marry me."

He gazed into her eyes, and though she was smiling, her eyes were still moist. A tear ran down one cheek.

"Marry me? This can't be happening. *Me?*"

"Aye, Caitir, you."

Much to his surprise, she began sobbing. He hugged her and whispered in her ear, "What's wrong? We'll be all right."

She pushed away, hit him lightly on the arm. "Silly lad, you do not ken a lass at all." She fell into his arms, and they kissed again. When they parted, she whispered, "I'm crying because my answer is aye."

"Aye? I don't understand. But that's grand. That's wonderful. That's—"

She put a hand to his lips and just rested her head on his shoulder.

Neil smiled. For some time they embraced each other. Finally, he said, "We must get some sleep. We've a long ride ahead of us tomorrow."

"Aye, future husband." She lay down next to him. "Only sleep."

The next morning Neil called the elch again, but to no avail. "We can't enter the forest without them. Let's walk down the river path a ways."

"Will that thing also call the wolves?"

"I hope not."

They'd gone maybe half a league, blowing the whistle occasionally, when they heard the parting of underbrush ahead. Neil whirled and drew his sword from its sheath. Caitir readied her bow.

Two elch appeared ahead and shook their heads.

They spent the rest of the morning coaxing the elch back to the trail junction, then trying to saddle and bridle the hulking beasts.

When Caitir finally sat atop her mount, she faced him. "That was like—well, it was like trying to saddle an elch."

Neil smiled, and they started down the trail into deep forest.

As they rode, he pondered how the Company of the Scepter had been whittled from eight to four and now to two. He would miss Machar's knowledge in all things Scepter-related. That and his fighting skill. Ewan, too, was sorely needed.

He was charged by Elyon himself to do this. But the more he thought about it, the more foolhardy their quest appeared.

His enemies were Faolukan the Grim and the Deamhan Lord. They faced a great darkness, as ancient as Erde itself, spreading out with unstoppable force from Drochtar in the east.

And what stood against them?

A mere blacksmith and a cooper's daughter.

Part VI

Chapter 36

The Stream of False Steps

Neil and Caitir retraced their original route from Hochnest, watching all the while for the "sign of the scarecrow". As before, the forest silence, dark and deep, hovered above and settled down around them, broken only by the occasional chattering of a startled squirrel.

"Tristan, look behind you." Caitir's voice came sharp and fearful.

He shifted in the saddle. Ten wolves as large as ponies paced back and forth across the trail, eyeing them. His elch caught their scent and whirled, lowering and shaking a set of pointed antlers nearly eleven feet across. The wolves stopped their advance. The elch shook its head again, dug antlers into the forest floor, pawed at the ground, and threw up clods of needles and dirt. The wolves sat on their haunches. Then the elch returned to the path. After a time, the wolves stopped following.

They'd gone perhaps six leagues when they came to one of the forest's rare islands of light, where rock outcroppings and clumps of grass replaced giant oaks. There Caitir called out, "That tree. Is that what we're looking for?"

In the center of the rocks stood a dwarf oak, shrunken, its bare, white trunk standing stark and lonely atop the outcropping. All but two limbs were gone. Now these branches stretched out, like bent arms, extended with long, twisted fingers.

"It must be." Neil pointed. "Look. There's a trail beyond the rocks."

He led his elch over the slate onto the hidden southern trail.

For the next two days, they rode, sleeping each night in a tree. They saw no more wolves, only the Waldreich's ever-present gloom. In midafternoon of the third day, Neil stopped to rest and again examine the map. "There's something ahead called The Stream Of False Steps."

"Uta mentioned it to me." Caitir frowned. "Said something about needing to step on the right rocks, in the right sequence."

"Or what?"

"Or we can't cross."

"What kind of deviltry is this?"

"She said a druid bewitched the stream."

They continued in silence. Neil didn't think it possible, but the farther they went, the darker and deeper the forest became. Under the forest canopy, all was quiet and dead. Late in the afternoon, they came to a meandering stream. It trickled at the bottom of a deep streambed. Rocks dotted the middle. On the opposite bank, the forest thinned.

Neil pulled his mount to a halt. "'Tis only a wee brook. No more than twenty feet across. And shallow. I could wade across and not wet my knees."

"Aye, this canna be the one. Let's cross."

Neil urged his elch down the bank into the water. Caitir rode beside him. But his elch's back feet had barely entered the stream when the water on all sides rose up as if on command. What had been a quiet, gurgling brook now became, within an eyeblink, a raging torrent with waves crashing over his head. Its power threw Neil from his mount. Both were suddenly in fast, deep water, being carried swiftly downstream. Then a wave tumbled and rolled him roughly up on the bank.

Nearly as fast as it had come, the waters slid back into the quiet stream they'd observed only moments before. Caitir was twenty yards below him, as were both elch, climbing the banks beside her, shaking themselves off.

She joined him, and they sat and stared at the brook. "Who would have expected *that*?"

"You say we'll find rocks that are the key to crossing this?"

"Aye, 'tis what the princess heard from those who knew. But that's all she told me."

They grabbed the elch's reins and returned along the bank. As they passed some berry bushes, the elch decided to stop and munch. With difficulty, Neil drew the beasts back to where they started.

"There." He pointed upstream to a grid of flat stones, three to a row, leading to the other side.

"'Tis a puzzle." Caitir cocked her head. "We must step on just the right stones, in just the right sequence."

Neil threw up his hands. "And how, in Erde, are we to do that?"

"There are fifteen rows. This shouldna take long."

"You want to do this by trial and mistake?"

"Aye, laddie." She gave him a wry grin and walked down to the first row. She planted both feet on the middle rock and waited. Nothing. She shot back a wide smile. "See. This should be easy."

She stepped onto the far right stone of the next row. In another eyeblink, the waters reared up and washed her off the rock, hurtling her downstream. Neil ran along beside the raging water, fearful she'd hit a boulder.

When she found herself back on the bank, he put a hand on her forehead. It was bleeding.

She shook her head. "This is going to be harder than I thought."

"Even if we succeed, we'll never be able to take the elch across."

"You're right. We might as well release them now."

They unsaddled the beasts and let them go. The animals headed straight for the berry bushes. Neil found a hiding place high up in a tree for the saddles and bridles. But after he came down from the massive trunk, something told him to climb back up and secret a goodly cache of bread and cheese. He returned to Caitir.

"It's getting dark." He frowned at the water coursing around the rows of stones. Besides the worry of the wolves, he remembered how quickly night descended on the Waldreich. "Let's solve this riddle tomorrow."

Caitir nodded. They climbed into the high branch of an oak. But no sooner had they settled in comfortably, than Caitir squeezed Neil's arm and whispered, "Look."

On the opposite bank, two lehbrágan approached the rows of stones. Both wore short green tunics with red hats and knapsacks. The first hopped out onto the stones.

"Remember which rocks he chose," Caitir whispered.

When the first sprite was on their side, the second began skipping from stone to stone after him. Neil thought to climb down and greet them, but before he'd even lowered a foot, they were gone.

"Quick." Her voice was earnest. "We must write this down."

"Do you remember their footsteps?"

"I've got the second through sixth stone."

"I only remember the first three."

Neil removed the only parchment he had—the map. "He stepped first on the right."

"Then it was center, left, right, center, center, right, right."

By the dying sun, he scraped the combination on the back of the map with his knife. Then Caitir nestled against him, and they slept as best they could, leaning against each other and the trunk while the darkness thickened around them.

With the morning light, they ate, and again approached the rows of stones.

"Now we only have to figure out eight rows to get to the ones we know will work." Caitir flashed a bonny grin. "Sure, and that's better than fifteen."

Neil handed her the map and his knife. "Let me take the brunt of this today. Write down what works." He jumped onto the middle of the first row then examined the next. His feet found the far left rock. Nothing happened. He looked back and smiled. "So far so good."

His next step on the third row landed in the center. Instantly a giant wave rose up and surrounded him. If possible, the water raged even more violently than yesterday. It carried him much farther downstream before it threw him up on the bank. He flopped onto the sharp pebbles, smarting from bruises and panting from the effort to tread water in the swift current.

"That was brutal." He lay on the bank, trying to catch his breath. "How are we going to figure this out before I'm injured or killed?"

Caitir helped him up, and they returned to the puzzle. Neil stepped out again on the first two stones when she called out, "Wait!"

"Wait?"

"Come back and look at this."

He returned to the bank.

"Do you see how the moss on one stone of each row is different from the others?"

Neil stared. Indeed, the lehbrágan's crossings had marked each stone. "Aye! You've solved the puzzle. 'Tis plain as day."

He jumped back onto the second row and examined the stones of the third. There, less moss coated the far right. He landed on it. Nothing happened. He grinned back at Caitir. They retrieved their packs then made their way safely across to the opposite bank.

"Thanks to you, we did it."

Caitir smiled from ear to ear. "Sometimes, a wee bit of wit is better than a heap of brawn."

"And glad I am your wit saved me another pounding." He withdrew the map again. "This says we've now left the Waldreich."

"That's the best news I've heard in days."

"And we're only a day or so from Schwarzburg."

"Lead on, future husband."

Neil smiled, liking the sound of that. He turned to the trail ahead, and they left behind the Stream Of False Steps.

They hadn't gone far when he realized they'd entered a different kind of forest. Here, the trees grew smaller, and in numerous places, sunlight streamed through leafy branches. Pipits in the treetops sang a continuous, high-pitched melody. Once, a boar broke from the underbrush, turned, and bolted into a thicket. Well-behaved brooks trickled across their path. The trail sometimes led through open fields where roe deer bounded through tall grass.

Joy surged through Neil's chest, bringing with it an urge to sing. This was a forest of life. All the rest of that day, they luxuriated in a forest as it was meant to be, under sun and fresh breezes.

But as they passed what looked like farmsteads, he never saw anyone about. Indeed, weeds had taken over every field. The entire region appeared abandoned.

The farther they went, the more uneasy he became. They passed long-abandoned villages, where the huts had become homes for badgers and owls.

Soon the woods themselves began to die. A tree here. Another there. Until every third tree was a leafless, dead trunk.

Toward evening, they topped a hill and overlooked a valley. Below them, everything changed.

"Wh—what happened?" Neil gaped. "'Tis a forest of death."

"Aye. Something's sucked the life from all the trees."

CHAPTER 37

DIETER JÄGER

They camped that night back among the living trees near a deserted roundhouse, its roof partially caved-in. Neil chopped logs for a fire as Caitir scrounged for more wood.

"Neil," she called, in a voice thick with alarm. "Come here."

He dropped his flint, unsheathed his sword, and ran to her.

"Look." She pointed under a tree. Two skeletons. One an adult, the other a child.

"Someone or something killed them." Neil nodded toward the adult. "That one's skull was crushed. And look. It's missing an arm."

Caitir shuddered.

Behind him, from the direction of the dark building, feet scuffled over hard ground. He whirled.

A woman, her tunic torn and ragged, stepped out from the structure. An emaciated face stared at them. She pointed toward the dead valley and shook her head. Then she raced for the shadows. A child of about six ran after her.

"Wait!" Neil called. But both of them slipped into the forest.

"What was she trying to tell us?" Caitir asked.

"I don't know."

Caitir shrugged and hurried her armload of firewood back to camp.

The next morning, they descended into the valley. Where the sunlight had occasionally burst through the leaves the day before, a gray haze now clung to the sky. The few living trees beside the trail gradually gave way to fallen limbs and leafless trunks. As they descended, their feet crunching brittle branches, neither hare nor squirrel nor mice crossed their path. The wind itself seemed to stop, until, by the time they attained the valley floor, a deathly silence reigned.

Black scarecrow trunks grasped dead fingers toward a metal-gray sky. The fallen carcasses of once-great oaks occasionally barred the way. White moss and fungi devoured the fallen. Not a green blade or red flower broke the gloom.

They walked through the ruins of one abandoned village after another. When they peered inside open windows, past desiccated vines, they saw even more skeletons. He had glimpses of a few lone survivors, but as soon as they saw Neil and Caitir, they fled behind locked doors. All attempts to hail them failed.

"What could have caused such a disaster?" Caitir blinked at him, her eyes wide. "And why will not anyone talk to us?"

"Fear and desolation have gripped this land. Surely, 'tis the result of the Deamhan Lord and his evil."

They trudged up a barren hill devoid of grass, then down into a black valley thick with dead and rotting vegetation. Branches crunched under their feet. The pungent smell of mold and decay accosted Neil's nostrils.

They had only gone about a league from their morning camp when they topped the last hill. There below, without doubt, lay the object of their quest—Castle Schwarzburg. It commanded a hillock in the center of a barren valley. Its sheer black walls rose stark and ominous from the ruined landscape. Four square towers climbed the corners. A squat keep with battlements dominated the center. Beyond the castle on the valley's far end sat a small town. But no smoke rose from its chimneys. No livestock grazed the brown fields nearby. And no one crossed, or even peered out, from the single lane dividing the town in two.

"It looks abandoned. 'Tis as if Elyon himself cursed this place." Neil shook his head. "But do you feel that?"

"What?"

"Something from the castle. A faint undercurrent of—despair, fear . . . hate."

Caitir faced him with a raised eyebrow. "You've a sense I do not have."

Neil nodded then just stared at the way ahead. "I don't know what to do next. We've come all this way, and—I've no plan for how to get inside. I know nothing about this place, only that some horror has beset it, may be inside it."

Caitir put a hand on his shoulder. "What did Machar say to do?"

"He said to trust in Elyon, didn't he?"

"Aye, but how?"

Neil shrugged, but as he glanced again at the devastated scene before him, he prayed silently to Elyon to show him the way.

Suddenly, he felt better. Then he led them down the trail, past the cadavers of trees, some fallen, some standing. But the farther they went, the more anxious he became. The skeletons of deer, horses, and men littered the woods. Death lay all around them.

Two hundred yards from the castle, as they passed through an area of small earthen mounds, he slowed the pace. Some mounds had iron grates barring their openings.

Wait until tomorrow.

What was that? A voice inside his head. He brought them to a halt. He edged Caitir off the trail behind one of the knolls.

"What are we doing?" Her glance scanned the knolls around them.

"Something just told me we shouldn't go any farther today."

"What told you?"

He shrugged. How could he tell her he was hearing voices in his head?

He walked in back of an earthen mound hidden from the castle's view. Facing him and standing open was a wide door of iron grillwork. Neil peered within. Cut stones, fitted tight together, lined the walls and ceiling. Along one wall, an empty shelf led in about ten feet. It was wide enough to hold—what? A coffin? The grate was open. It squeaked on its hinges. When he pushed it shut, the lock clicked. He rattled the door several times. Locked. He withdrew the two tools he always carried, inserted both into the mechanism, and within moments had unlocked the door.

"We'll be safe in here." He motioned for Caitir to come inside but left the door open.

"Safe from what?"

"I don't know. I only know we must wait here until tomorrow morning."

"I do not ken what you're doing, but I believe you. This whole valley is cursed." Caitir inspected their tiny prison. "This was once a tomb, wasn't it?"

"Aye."

She shuddered then slumped down next to him on the bench.

All that day they talked, made short ventures outside to gaze toward the castle, returning always to their refuge. Once, as he faced the town, he thought he saw quick, furtive movements, but it could have been his imagination. The cloud cover dissipated, and a pale sun occasionally peeked through. Caitir took a nap nestled against him on the bench. When the shadows of bare trunks and earthen mounds stretched long across the landscape, Neil pulled the door shut and locked it.

As night fell, they ate from their dwindling store of sausage and cheese. They still had a full skin of water but no wine. Then they lay down beside each other, but Neil slept fitfully, with dark dreams.

It was late when he woke and sat up straight as a staff.

"Wh–what's wrong?" Sleep thickened Caitir's voice.

Motionless, Neil squinted through the bars toward the next mound, outlined by moonlight.

"The feeling of dread—it's back. Strong. Very strong."

"What does that mean?"

"Something's out there. Something evil. And it's close."

Caitir slid closer and grasped his arm. He shot her a glance. She was clenching her jaw.

Just out of sight, claws scratched over rock. Then a shadow inched into view, sniffing around the corner of the tomb. Huge clawed feet. A vaguely human face, but instead of a nose a blunt snout, roughly wolf-like. Then it saw them. It opened its mouth to reveal long incisors.

Caitir slunk to the back of the tomb. But Neil sat unmoving and stared at the creature, his hand sliding toward his sword.

It growled, stuck a furred arm through the bars, and reached for him. The claws grasped and struggled, trying different holes in the bars. But it couldn't get any closer.

"What is it?" Her voice quavered, near panic.

"A púca. Don't worry. It can't get us."

At the sound of his voice, the creature growled and stuck a claw in the lock. But it couldn't release the mechanism.

Suddenly, a feeling of dread a hundred times worse pressed down upon him. The púca stopped its efforts to get into their cell, quieted, and cast its glance toward the nearest tomb. Then even it cowered on the ground and tried to bury its face in the dirt.

Neil moved to the back of the cell beside Caitir and held her close. "Sssshhhh," he whispered. "It's coming."

"*What's* coming?"

"I don't know. Something far worse than a púca."

"How's that possible?"

"Sssshhhh."

Something black, huge, and humped moved ever so slowly into their field of vision beyond the bars. It paused. Then the moonlight dimmed and darkened. Neil peered at the clearing outside. Heavy shadows draped every object.

Fear sliced through him like a knife. His heart thumped wildly. What was it? A mass of darkness, nothing clear or distinct about it, as if the night had distilled, taken vague form, and come alive. The only sharp features were its eyes—two pinpricks of red surrounded by swirling black circles.

He froze. Caitir gripped a hand tightly around his.

Then the eyes looked elsewhere. And the darkness lumbered off.

Outside the cell, the púca whimpered.

Neil shut his eyes, breathed deeply, and opened them.

"What was it?" Caitir was shaking.

"The barghest."

She didn't answer. For several moments, her breathing came fast, too fast. Then she whispered, "Will it return?"

"I don't know. But look." Neil pointed to the ground just beyond the bars. Where the púca had been only moments ago lay a man. He was naked, huddled in a ball, and shivering. Neil reached a hand through the bars and shook him, but he appeared to be in some kind of trance.

Neil unlocked the door and eased it open. He gazed down at the man.

"What are you doing? What if he turns back?"

"But look at him. Right now, he's not a threat to anyone. And if that thing comes back—he might be killed."

"Maybe that would be better."

"Still, right now he's a man, is he not? When he wakes, perhaps we can learn something from him."

Neil dragged him inside the tomb. But the man remained curled on the floor, his arms wrapped around his legs, shivering. Neil covered him with his own cape.

All the rest of that night, they waited inside the tomb with the door locked, always keeping the man on the floor in sight. Neil tried to stay awake but fell asleep late.

Near morning, he woke again to a feeling of deep dread that rose to a crest then receded, as if the barghest had again passed nearby.

Soon, a gray light broke over the landscape. Neil knelt at the man's side.

His face had not the features of a longtime shapeshifter. He was young, about Neil's age, with flowing black hair. Neil shook him hard.

The man opened his eyes, stared wide-eyed at his two cellmates. He examined the cape wrapping his naked body. "I have no clothes," he whispered. "It's happened again."

Neil rummaged in his pack for the extra loincloth he always carried. When he held it out, the man pulled it on. "Thank you," he said, standing now.

"Who are you?" Neil stepped back.

The man stood up straight. "I shouldn't tell you. I should leave."

"How did you end up a shapeshifter?"

He raised one eyebrow as if puzzled. Lifting an arm, he examined it, and then patted his face. "That *is* what I've become, isn't it? A shapeshifter. It's why I keep finding myself outside, naked, with blood on my hands." He gripped his head with both hands and shook it. "You've said the words, put a name to it, and you're right. I knew it but couldn't accept it, could never name it. And who would I speak the words to anyway?" He closed his eyes and shook his head, again and again. "Oh, what have you done to me, you evil man?"

"Who? Who did this to you?"

He looked up. Tears wet the corners of the man's eyes. Pain, loss creased his face. "The druid. Ever since he arrived, nothing's been right. Look around you"—he waved at the landscape—"at the trees, our beloved trees. When I was a child, this was a lush forest. I used to love the forest. Our town—it once held a thousand souls. Now all that lives here are scarecrows, frightened women, broken shadows of men . . ."

"I repeat. Who you are?"

The man frowned. "You might as well know. What does it matter now? I am Dieter Jäger, captain of the guard of Castle Schwarzburg. Or what's left of it."

"How did this happen to you?"

"About a month ago . . . The druid—he's away now—came to me with a proposition. He'd give me immortality, he said, if only I would drink his potion and pledge him my service. King Brandt gave his approval. But the king is . . . addled, not himself. His kingdom is . . . gone. But can you imagine? Eternal life? Never to die or grow old. So I drank the potion. And then the nightmares began."

"What was the druid's name?"

"Faolukan."

Neil closed his eyes. When he looked up again, he put a hand on Dieter's shoulder. "You are not the first to succumb to his wiles. He's brought many others to ruin."

"But who are *you*?"

"I am Neil mac Connell. And this is Caitir. We are travelers from Ériu."

"*Ériu*? What a far country, indeed! But why are you here?"

"We came to end Faolukan's rule and bring peace to your land."

Dieter's jaw slackened. "How can you fight one as powerful as the arch druid? What can anyone do against him and his spells?"

"We can return the Scepter—the one he stole, that's in his castle—to its rightful place back in Ériu. That, we believe, will bring Elyon's peace once again to all of Erde."

"The Scepter?" Dieter gulped. "You would steal Faolukan's greatest treasure from him? This treasure the castle has held for millennia?"

"'Tis because the Scepter sits in your king's palace that Faolukan is able to do what he did to you. And to this land."

Dieter nodded, eyed the ground, then Neil. "I believe you. Perhaps because you saved me from his barghest. Had the shadow creature returned and found me huddled in human form, it might have killed me. Sometimes when I dream, I wake like this. That must be when I change form.

"I've had nightmares of how it stalked me and how I fled. I also believe you because you said that name—Elyon. I don't know who that is, but I sense power in it. The very sound of it is comforting. And I believe you because everything the druid has told me is a lie.

"He's done a terrible thing to me, Neil of Ériu. Every time I wake like this, I'm different from the day before. Today, I'm not the same person I was a month ago. One day, I fear I'll wake and be someone else entirely. Someone who will bow and slaver at the druid's feet. Like others I've known. Like a few of the guards under my command. Aye, that's what he's doing to me. Turning me into one of his slaves."

"He has others like you?"

"At least six at Schwarzburg. But he is gathering an army, Neil of Ériu. Men from Drochtar arrive daily, rest a few days, and then march north. That's where he went when he left—to go to their encampment, wherever that is."

Neil shuddered. This only made the capture and return of Elyon's gift even more urgent. "How can we enter the castle unseen and steal the Scepter?"

Dieter glanced at each of them in turn. "I will help you, but first hear my advice as someone who owes you my life: Go not into Schwarzburg. Instead, flee from here now. As fast as your legs can carry you. For all who enter uninvited, Castle Schwarzburg is a place of death."

Neil shook his head. "Our mission compels us to go in."

Dieter thought a moment. Then he smiled. "Then you will become my revenge on the druid. There is a secret way in. But it's dangerous. Not only for you, but also for me."

CHAPTER 38

SCHWARZBURG CASTLE

Dieter gave them instructions for how and when to enter the castle. But as he spoke, a growing unease gripped Neil. Dieter whispered of caves, tunnels, and dark underground mazes. How was he going to get through this? Just hearing of these things sent a chill across his shoulders.

Dieter finished with, "My friends, you must arrive at the tunnel exactly at sunset, before they release the barghest. Come too early and the guards may see you. Come too late, and well—he may find you. And after I let you in, I must become again the captain of the guards and perform my duty, even if it means ordering your deaths. Do you understand?"

Neil nodded. "Will there be a guard on the battlements?"

"Perhaps at sunset there will be an urgent task that distracts him, no?" A sly smile twisted Dieter's mouth. "I hope you accomplish your mission. I hope it ends what's been happening here." He shook their hands. Then he left, wearing only the loincloth.

For the remainder of the day, Neil and Caitir waited again inside the tomb, sleeping as much as they could. As evening approached, he became more and more anxious. Theirs was a risky plan. To take the Scepter from the very throne room of King Brandt was brazen. How to get past the creature guarding it also preyed on his mind.

As shadows lengthened across the devastated landscape, he caught Caitir's glance and swallowed. "'Tis time."

"Aye, laddie, 'tis time. We must do what we came all this way . . . to . . . to . . ." But though her words were brave, her face was now ashen. The reality of what they were about to attempt hit them both.

"We'll get through this, Caitir. Somehow."

Her attempt to smile failed.

He didn't know how to comfort her. It was all he could do to keep his own fear under control. He reached out with both hands, pulled her close, and they hugged.

They emerged from the protection of the earthen mound and walked out into the dead forest. Following Dieter's instructions, they kept off the road and slipped between the lengthening shadows of tree trunks. Their feet scraping over bare rock, they gained the base of the castle hillock. Above them loomed the massive, iron-banded castle gate. But they didn't ascend.

Instead, they circled to the left, hiding in the shadows at the hill's base where the guards couldn't easily see them.

Though it was cool, Neil's forehead sweated, and moisture slicked his palms. A quarter of the way around the perimeter, they approached a large gate dug into the hillside. Thick iron bars, spaced a foot apart, criss-crossed a twelve-foot high opening leading deep into the hill. Beyond lay heavy darkness. A smell as of some rank, unwashed animal seeped through the bars.

Now the same wave of despair, fear, and hate from the previous night washed over him. Somewhere beyond the iron grill lay Thrag, the shadow creature. Soon the guards would come to let him out.

"This is madness. We're supposed to go into its lair?" Caitir peered through the bars into the blackness.

"Aye." But he just stared into the dark tunnel. "Let's look for the cave." Even as he said the words, a lump formed in his throat.

Halfway up the incline, a small hole, just big enough for a man to squeeze through, opened in the hillside. Neil stared at it. Dieter had said it only went in a few feet, deep enough to hold both he and Caitir. Yet he couldn't make himself enter. By now, the sun's light was fast fading.

"The fear of caves again?" Caitir put a hand on his shoulder.

He nodded.

She smiled and crawled in ahead of him. "It's cozy in here"—her voice echoed from the darkness—"room enough for two. Come on in."

But he didn't move. Maybe he could just wait here?

Creeeeak.

Jolted, he spun toward the angry creak of great iron hinges. The feeling of dread hit him again full force. It was coming. He threw himself into the hole and scrambled to join Caitir.

They lay beside each other on the cool, wet rock. His breathing slowed. With Caitir beside him, it wasn't so bad in here, was it? Finally, they heard Dieter's signal—three clanks of iron on iron.

"I'll leave my bow and quiver here," said Caitir. "Too bulky in narrow cave passages."

He nodded, and they left the tiny cave. Beyond the hillock, an amorphous black shape lumbered across the landscape. It moved within its own circle of darkness. Was it heading toward the living trees a league away? Only now did he realize the danger they'd faced two nights ago when they'd camped beside the farmstead. Was this what the emaciated woman was warning them of?

Convinced the creature wouldn't return soon, he walked back down the hill to the now-open gate. Much to his relief, a torch burned in a holder just inside the opening. He picked it up, exhaled as the oppressive darkness receded. As instructed, they climbed the stone steps on the right. At the top, a much less imposing iron gate stood open. A cluster of torches burned in the antechamber beyond.

He remembered Dieter's words, "Normally, the guards' gate is always shut, and we lock the main gate after it's gone out, reopening it again just before dawn. Tonight I will perform this task myself and leave both gates open. You must lock both of these behind you. I trust you won't fail in this."

Neil had solemnly promised he would.

Just inside the small chamber, a heavy chain wound around the control wheel, out through the rock wall, over a pulley, and down to the main gate. He passed the torch to Caitir, gripped the wheel, and began turning. The hinges complained and creaked. The outside doors moaned, ground against stone, and then shut with a boom. Next, he shut the barred gate that protected the guard who performed this twice-daily act.

He caught Caitir's glance and smiled.

"That wasn't so bad." The torches' light helped push back the gloom—and his fear.

Then they began climbing the tunnel steps. Back and forth it wound, climbing up through the bowels of the hill. It ended at a closed wooden door.

Neil breathed deeply. "We're there."

They hid their packs in a niche behind the door but took their weapons. They'd pick up their packs on the return. He shoved the torch into a wall sconce. Opening the door, he peered into a long, torch-lit hallway. They were inside the castle.

"Now what?" Caitir glanced in both directions.

"Now we find the storage room Dieter described. Then we wait."

He led them down the hall, past three darkened rooms, and turned left at the junction with the next hallway. Footsteps echoed from the passage ahead.

"Quick," he whispered, "into one of those rooms." He backtracked and led Caitir into a darkened side chamber.

They pressed up against the room's outside wall and listened.

"He's coming back tonight, he is," said a voice from the hall. "And we're to prepare our best venison."

"Harrumph." Heels clicked loudly on stone. "And how are we supposed to get venison when the nearest live deer is two leagues distant? Everything in and around Schwarzburg is dead and dying."

"A squad is bringing it in now. Keep talking that way, and you'll be next into the maze."

"As if the thing hasn't killed enough and . . ."

When their voices trailed off into faint echoes, Neil peeked out into the hall. Empty. He motioned to Caitir, and they resumed their slow traverse of the route Dieter had described. Two more turns and a curtain blocked the way.

Neil peered out through a crack into the king's presentation hall. Schwarzburg's throne, covered with red velvet and gilded arms, sat empty. Beyond was a great room big enough to hold hundreds. Off to the right was the cage.

Behind bars of shining steel sat an enormous cat, bigger than any he'd ever seen or heard about. From its jaws sprang two enormous, curved fangs, each longer than an arm. Now it paced back and forth within a thirty-foot wide cell. When Neil caught a glimpse of what waited beyond, his heart leaped.

The Scepter.

Shining golden in the torchlight, it rested upright in a metal vase fashioned to receive it. Colored jewels festooned its crown.

No other treasure was visible. Voices approached from the hall's far end. Neil slid back behind the curtain.

"It's there—the Scepter. Now all we have to do is wait for everyone to go to bed."

"Where's this room where we're supposed to hide?"

Neil led them back a dozen yards, found the battered wooden door Dieter had described, and they entered a storage closet filled with brooms, wooden buckets, and bristle brushes. They sat on a pile of musty carpet and waited.

As the night wore on, Neil's heart raced. So much depended on what happened next. All their efforts so far had brought them to this point. The Scepter—this device that would bring peace and joy and hope to so many—was only dozens of yards from where he sat. As was the giant cat guarding it. He tried not to think about what would happen if he failed. Or why he hadn't seen the Horn of the Reich that would free his friends.

When he guessed it was near midnight, Neil creaked open the door. With Caitir behind him, he retraced their steps to the throne room. Only two crackling torches now lit the huge space, both beside the cage. No one else was about.

They approached. The saber-tooth beast saw them, rose on its haunches, and lowered its head. Its eyes seemed to grow larger, to gleam. A deep growl rumbled in its throat.

"Are you going to play for it, Neil?"

"Aye. But not yet." He looked to the nearest wall, and there found the set of keys on a hook, just as Dieter described. He gave them to Caitir.

"When I nod, open the door, and I'll go inside."

Caitir swallowed but nodded in agreement.

Then he removed his bone whistle, fitted it to his lips, and began to play. The song was soothing, lulling, and the great cat responded almost instantly. But the notes echoed too loudly in the cavernous space. He hoped no guard would hear. Still, he played on, weaving a melody of peace, calm, and serenity.

The cat slumped down on its forepaws and began to close its eyes. It lay just to the right of the Scepter, only a yard away. He nodded to Caitir.

She fit the key in the lock and turned it. The mechanism clicked. Loud. Too loud. She yanked the door open. Neil stepped inside. The cat opened its eyes a crack but didn't seem to notice him. He walked as he played, stepping ever so slowly toward the Scepter.

When the artifact was in front of him, he halted but continued playing. The cat's eyelids closed. He played a few more notes.

While one hand gripped the flute and his lips blew a last few notes, the other hand reached out. He grabbed the Scepter. He stopped playing. And bolted for the door.

"It's seen you!" shouted Caitir. She held the door open. He was half-way there.

"It's leaping!" Caitir nearly screamed.

Neil lunged, jumped through the opening.

She slammed the door shut behind him. But he heard no click. He spun and rammed his shoulder against the door until he heard it lock. He fell back onto the marble floor just as the great cat crashed into the bars, one paw snaking through the gap, claws scraping the marble floor. The cage shook as if the bars themselves would rip from their mounts. Then the beast let out a deafening roar.

Everyone in the castle would be able to hear that roar.

He picked up the Scepter and started to run for the curtain.

But as soon as he grasped it and squeezed, he knew something was wrong. Caitir kept running, but he stopped.

The Scepter—the jewels' colors appeared cloudy. One seemed loose. He squeezed the metal tube between thumb and forefinger. A gem popped out. It wasn't a jewel at all, only colored glass.

He examined the metal baton. He squeezed harder. The metal crumpled.

"That's right, my foolish lad." The words echoed across the hall. The voice shot through him like a sword through his gut. "Do you think I'd be so foolish as to leave the greatest treasure of the age—or should I say abomination—in so obvious a place?" Faolukan's caped form glided over the floor toward him.

Neil whirled. Soldiers were pouring into the great room. They'd already blocked Caitir's escape at the curtain. He spun back to Faolukan, his heart thumping, feeling like he was going to be sick.

Five yards away, the arch druid stopped. "You made enough noise to be heard in Beilzig City."

Stunned, Neil let go of the imitation Scepter. It clattered to the floor, glass beads flying in all directions. He slid his sword from its sheath but knew it was too late.

"Drop it, or we'll kill you both," a familiar voice—Dieter's—resounded behind him. He'd warned them what would happen if they were caught, hadn't he?

The guards held bows, arrows nocked and aimed at him and Caitir. With a sickening, lightheaded feeling, he dropped his sword. It clanged over the marble.

"Take that flute from him." Faolukan's voice carried the note of triumph. "He'll not be needing it where he's going."

Dieter himself rummaged in Neil's tunic and snatched the flute.

Another figure, an old man in a nightdress, shuffled in. He rubbed bewildered eyes and stifled a yawn. "What's happening, Faolukan? What's all the commotion?"

An instant smile transformed the druid's face, and a soothing tone entered his voice. "Nothing to concern yourself with, your grace. Just some interlopers we will quickly deal with."

The king blinked stupidly. "As you say, druid. As you say." Then he pulled a crescent-moon pendant from beneath his gown and began to fondle it.

After the king had ambled back down a hallway, Faolukan again faced Dieter. "Now search them for any other bit of magic they might possess."

As one guard searched Caitir, another shoved the point of a sword against Neil's back. Dieter himself ran his hands up Neil's legs, inside his crotch, then up his chest. When he touched the pouch with the hidden gem Machar had given him, he stopped.

"Remove your tunic." Dieter's harsh voice grated, nothing like the frightened, thankful wretch they'd rescued only last night.

Neil doffed his tunic and handed it over. He stood now in only his loincloth.

Dieter untied the strip of leather holding the pouch in place. He searched the rest of Neil's tunic then threw it back to him.

While Neil dressed, Dieter passed the find to Faolukan. "This was well hidden. Perhaps it's important."

Faolukan took the pouch and cocked his head. Then he gave it back. "Open it for me."

Dieter undid the bundle and lifted out the gem. Its clear yellow crystal gleamed bright by torchlight.

"Ah, a precious stone." Faolukan's eyes brightened. "Give it to me."

Dieter placed it in the druid's open palm. Instantly, Faolukan winced and whipped his hand away. The gem clattered across the marble.

"Elyon's foul work!" Faolukan shook his hand as if it was injured. "Throw both abominations into the hole where no one will ever see them again. Throw in their weapons as well. In case more spells are at work there."

Dieter bowed and picked up the gem. Then he walked to what looked like a stone well, topped by a round metal cover. He lifted the lid on its hinges and dropped all their belongings into the hole. A long while later, from far below, came the echo of metal on stone and a splash.

"That's right, Neil mac Connell, high prince of Ulster. Your magic toys won't help you now. Your quest is over. You should have taken the offer I made at the inn in Áth Cliath. But it's better this way. My barghest's hunger is never satisfied. He's killed and eaten far more than I'd anticipated." Then Faolukan addressed Dieter, "Captain of the guards, you will wait until Thrag has returned and is locked inside the tunnel. Then you will put these two in his path."

Neil stared at Faolukan, a cold numbness creeping over him. They were sending him to face Thrag, the shadow creature. He who extinguished all light. Without the charm Machar had given him. He began to shake.

Was there a fate worse than this? He couldn't think of one.

"My lord, there are also these." Another guard, younger than Dieter, held up Neil and Caitir's packs. His jutting forehead and deep eye sockets revealed he'd been a longtime púca. "I found them just inside the tunnel leading to the barghest's gate."

Neil's heart pounded.

Faolukan nodded. "Ernst, throw their packs down the hole as well."

The guard did as instructed.

Now Faolukan stroked his thin beard with one hand. "In the guards' tunnel, you say? That brings up an interesting question: How did our two thieves know about a passage that guards have pledged their lives to keep secret?" Ever so slowly, his glance shifted toward the men.

Meeting his stare were blank looks, ashen faces, shrugged shoulders.

"Was it not your duty, Ernst, to release the creature and secure the tunnel?" He spoke to the same púca who'd found their packs.

"Aye, but not tonight. Dieter asked me if he could take my place."

Faolukan raised an eyebrow. Like a viper about to strike, his head shifted again, but now toward Dieter. "Is that so?"

Dieter swallowed and nodded.

"Is that your usual practice?"

"It is not, my lord."

"How then, did they discover the way in? Can you answer that question?"

Sweat formed on Dieter's pale face. The guard shook his head but said nothing.

"You can't answer me because you told them, didn't you? Perhaps because they found you outside, reverted to a man's body? When you are hunting and danger approaches, you cannot keep your form, can you? That's a sign of a weak character, Dieter. You have not become the púca I wished you to be."

Dieter opened his mouth, but he couldn't respond.

"Speak, man!"

"I did." Dieter's face seemed drained of its blood. "I showed them how to get in." Then his hands formed into fists at his sides, and he stared at the druid. "You ruined me, Faolukan. You tricked me into drinking your potion, turning me into one of your half-man, half-animal things. Just like you abused King Brandt, giving him the fiendish device that's addled his mind. Just like your foul creature's presence has ruined everything that once thrived around Castle Schwarzburg."

Faolukan stared for a time then addressed Ernst. "Ernst, you are now captain of the guards." A brief smile fled across his lips. "Your first official act will be to put Dieter with these two in the maze. That's the penalty for treason."

Ernst bowed, but his face, too, seemed to grow pale.

Dieter grasped his head with both hands as his own guards came to relieve him of his weapons.

Then they came for Neil and Caitir.

CHAPTER 39

THRAG

The guards led Neil, Caitir, and Dieter down a different set of steps cut from the rock. Down, down they went, their feet reverberating hollowly in the narrow tunnel. The air cooled and moisture glistened from every wall. At length, they arrived at a large chamber with a door, covered all in iron and rising the height of a man.

Ernst ushered them at sword-point into a holding cell cut from the rock beside the gate. He looked at the torch in his hand, hesitated, then passed it to Dieter. "I'll allow you to spend your final hours in the light. I'm sorry, Dieter." Then the door closed with a deep thud.

Dieter dropped the torch into a wall sconce then slumped to the floor in one corner, holding his head and shaking it.

Opposite him, Caitir nestled up against Neil. He grasped her hands. "Everyone was counting on me. Now, what hope do we have?"

"None, my friend." Dieter raised a wincing glance to them. "No one's ever escaped Thrag's maze. Here is what will happen now. Ernst will wait until the creature returns from his nightly roam. As soon as he's locked inside the tunnel, they'll push us into the path before him. When Thrag catches our scent, it will only be a matter of time. He's slow but relentless. And wherever he goes, the light fails. Torches"—he gestured to the one in its wall sconce—"are useless."

Tears formed at the corners of Caitir's eyes. Neil caressed the backs of her hands with his thumbs while facing Dieter. "How many years ago did Faolukan bring Thrag to this place?"

Dieter cocked his head. "Within the last thirty years. But it's only been fifteen since the druid started releasing him at night. The creature's appetite is insatiable, and no one could provide him enough to eat. That's also when the trees began dying. Before that, our valley held villages, farmsteads, orchards—all filled with life. Everyone paid tribute to King Brandt. Now, his subjects have fled or been killed. The kingdom is dead, and the king has become nothing but Faolukan's slave."

"Aye," said Neil. "We've seen the same thing happening elsewhere. Only here it's far, far worse. He's trying to gain control of every ruler and country in Erde. But before Thrag—was anyone down here? Surely, someone once explored these passages?"

"I've heard rumors. The castle has harbored the Scepter for a long time. Though no one living has ever seen them, they say the warren of tunnels crisscrosses and intersects so many times, it's impossible to remember where you've been. The guards are afraid to go in, even when Thrag is roaming outside. But it doesn't matter. When the barghest returns, we'll see nothing but darkness. We'll stumble around until he corners us and takes us. When they first push us into his path, he will come from our left. So our only hope is to turn right and—in the dark—run and find some small crevice to hide where he can't enter."

"Then what?"

"Then wait to die from starvation or thirst. For in the dark, we'll never find our way back out through the maze."

Neil shuddered.

"I must warn you of something else." Dieter's eyes narrowed as he sought Neil's gaze.

"What?"

"I may change again. Then you will also be at risk from me."

"Can you not control it?"

"Not always. The others have complete command. But it's new inside me and seems to come and go on its own. I'm sorry. But as Faolukan said, when threatened, I revert to a man. I would never have made a good púca."

Neil nodded. How could things get any worse? Then he did the only thing he knew how to do. He prayed.

"O Elyon, creator of all that is, save us this night from the creature, Thrag. We are in desperate need of your help. We have lost the Scepter, with no hope of finding or recovering it. We simply ask you now for our lives."

When he'd finished, Dieter looked toward him with wide eyes. "That was most comforting. I've never heard anyone say a prayer like that."

"The Scepter is Elyon's. Long ago, he gave it to our people to keep it safe. But we failed. We let Faolukan take it."

"And you say this Scepter once held back his evil?"

"Aye. And everyone thought it was in the great hall upstairs. Even the ancient texts said so."

"We thought so, too."

Then Neil's eyes opened wide, and he sat up straight. "What if he threw it down the hole? Everything of Elyon goes down the hole, doesn't it?"

"Aye, Neil." Dieter smiled. "Faolukan cannot abide the presence of anything belonging to Elyon. Long ago, he might have thrown the Scepter down the hole." Then he frowned. "But that knowledge will do you no good."

"Why not?"

"Because the hole is not connected to the maze. It's simply a well, dug ages ago, straight down through solid rock."

Neil slumped against the wall. Every doorway seemed to have closed. His one protection against the barghest was the gem Machar had given him, a light against Thrag's darkness. Now it languished at the bottom of an inaccessible pit. Along with the Scepter.

As they waited for dawn, no one slept. All through the night, Neil prayed silently for deliverance.

When a key clicked in the lock, and their cell door finally opened, Neil's heart began beating wildly. Was it time already?

"Into the passage, now." Four guards flanked Ernst. He was taking no chances. "Dawn is almost here."

After Ernst led them to the tunnel gate, he and a helper slowly creaked open the iron-banded door. It was at least a foot thick, covered inside and out with iron. Ernst waved toward the passage with his spear. Neil, Caitir, and Dieter stepped in. The smell of something rank and feral hit Neil's nostrils.

Back in the chamber, the new captain of the guards shook his head and held up a hand. "Wait. Keep the door open."

While the other guards exchanged puzzled looks and pointed their spears at the prisoners, Ernst disappeared. When he returned, he passed the prisoners six torches, three of which were lit. "I never do this. But I liked you, Dieter. At least these will light your way for a few moments and give you something of a chance."

They each took a lit torch and a spare. Ernst returned to the safety of the main room, and the access door creaked shut. Wet stone glistened like the insides of some rock creature's bowels. Far down the tunnel echoed the outside door clanging shut. Now the tunnel gate itself slammed closed with heavy finality. Only their torches lit the passage.

Dieter looked to his new companions, fear twisting his face. "Run. As fast as you can, run!"

They turned right and broke into a sprint.

As Neil ran, the dark walls bounced up and down by torchlight. Caitir raced beside him, fear contorting her face. Was it just him or were the walls swirling, narrowing, turning black? His old fear of dark holes in the ground. But now he had to run, to flee. The only thought he dared hold now was escape.

They burst into a room where enormous teeth of dripping, wet rock stretched down from above. Claws of slimy, sharp stone reached up from the floor. Skeletons, bones, and rotting tunics lay strewn everywhere. Without torches, how could Thrag's victims have ever gone farther?

Five trails led away from the room. The left passage climbed. The central passage widened. The two right ones fell. Dieter started across the cavern toward the central tunnel. They clambered over even more skeletons. The stench of old death, trapped down here, was overpowering. Neil gagged.

Now he felt Thrag's presence, strong behind him. A deep despair, a silent, brooding hate, tore at his soul as if it were alive inside him, as if cold, dead hands were throttling his inner being.

Suddenly, the torches dimmed—their light decreased by half. His heart began beating wildly. The darkness, the sense of evil behind him combined to twist and tighten his insides. Even though the cavern was cold, sweat dripped down his forehead. He wanted to scream. Instead, he ran faster. Their footsteps reverberated down the tunnel.

Dieter tripped over a pile of bones and went down. Neil stopped to help.

Dieter tried to stand, but as soon as he put his weight on one leg, he crumpled again. "Go on." His voice was contorted, frightened. "Something's wrong with my ankle. You can't help me now."

Neil gave him one last look then ran down the central passage where Caitir had already fled. The tunnel joined three more. He stopped, breathed heavily, his glance bouncing over the options. "The middle one. It's been well trod."

So they took the central tunnel. For some time, they followed where it led. Now they encountered the remains of fewer men. Then the tunnel split in three again. Neil stared at three more choices.

From far behind came screaming. The sound wrenched at his stomach.

The central passage showed three-toed footprints in the slime. It widened and went straight. The left trail was also well trod and veered sharply left. But the right trail narrowed and dropped down.

Farther away now, the screams continued behind them. Desperate, agonizing, endless screams. Was the creature eating Dieter alive?

Neil took a few steps down the right passage, stopped, and held up his torch. "Maybe it will narrow enough so the barghest can't follow? Few have ever come this far."

"What difference does it make?"

They started to run. But to avoid the sharp fingers of ceiling rock, they had to stoop and drop to a walk. Without warning, the path steepened and slickened with mud. Neil's feet slid out from under him. He fell onto his back. Then he started sliding. Down the passage he went, still holding his torch high, until he spread his feet and slowed his descent. Caitir came sliding down behind, her feet crashing into his back. The two slid farther as the way steepened and constricted even further. Then he thought, what if the passage became nothing but a chimney, a hole too tiny for them to go through, too steep to climb back out?

But the tunnel widened and dumped them into another echoing, cavernous room where they stopped at the base of a rock mound.

"Oh no." Caitir moaned and pointed. "Look."

Three trails exited the room. Two of them showed the telltale signs of the barghest's travels.

"There. We'll take the one he doesn't use." Neil nodded to the narrower way, also leading down. But the moment he said it, their torches dimmed. And a feeling of dread hit him so hard he staggered. "It's coming. It's close."

"How is that possible? We've traveled so far already."

"I don't know. It's moving faster in these tunnels. And it knows where it's going."

They ran down the path. For a time it climbed, but then leveled off. Then it, too, emerged in another cavern. Here, they saw no skeletons. Six trails went off in six directions. Neil's head spun. The creature was nearing. Their torches were darkening. For no particular reason, he picked the far right trail. He led them down, but it quickly dead-ended.

They scrambled back to the main room. Now the torches barely gave enough light to see by. He raced along the next passage to the left. It widened then began to rise. It climbed steeply and slowed their momentum. Then he felt the dread, strong and close behind. His torch barely lit a circle around him.

He saw Caitir's face and barely recognized her, so dark with shadow, so smeared with mud and contorted with fear it was. Finally, the way leveled off, and they sprinted through a straight passage. They came to yet another dark cavern with five tunnels leading off in all directions.

Neil stopped, staring at the mud and skeletons before them. "We've been here before."

"Oh no, you're right. I see our footprints."

"Which way haven't we gone?"

"There, to the left."

He ran where Caitir pointed. Both were breathing heavily now. Sweat was dripping down his forehead into his eyes. The torches dimmed. No matter where they went, it seemed the barghest sensed and followed.

They ran on and on. They passed two, three, four more junctions and took trails at random. He knew now he'd never be able to find his way back. They'd only survived so long because Ernst had given them torches. Soon even those would be useless.

Then they found themselves in a tight passage without footprints of men or barghest. They followed it for some time and entered a room. He stopped to catch his breath.

From here, three paths branched off. Two led up. The right trail led down.

"Let's try the middle route." Caitir panted. "It's smaller. Perhaps it willna follow us there."

Their torches started to dim. Neil felt the barghest's presence coming down the tunnel as a lead weight on his soul.

To the right.

The voice again. "No, we must go down."

"Down?"

"Aye. To the right." And he led them down.

But it was too wide. The creature would easily be able to follow.

Moments later their torchlights became so weak, Neil could barely see the floor ahead. Close behind now, they heard its raspy breathing, the shuffling and scratching of clawed feet over wet stone. Neil tried to hurry, tripped, and went down.

Caitir helped him up. They continued on, but slower.

Now his torch was so dark he could barely see Caitir and the way ahead. The path dumped into a small room. By the dying light, Neil searched for an exit. But the chamber had no exits. In one corner rose a pile of rubble, testifying to some kind of cave-in where part of the ceiling had given way. Halfway up the mound of rock debris was a narrow, dark slit. But did it go anywhere? And was it big enough to crawl through?

His torch died farther. Now it carried only an outline of dark flame. Was it still lit? He passed his hand through it. He winced as the fire burned his flesh. Yet its light was gone.

Thrag's clawed feet scratched on the floor behind them. Total darkness filled the room.

CHAPTER 40

AN OVERDUE DISCOVERY

He wanted to scream. To run. To fight. But he could none of those. They dropped the torches. Useless now.

"Go up the mound." He fumbled for Caitir's arm, grabbed it, and pulled her along in the dark. Together they scrambled up the pile of broken slabs, hunks of ceiling rock. Her breathing echoed, heavy and frantic.

Behind them, Thrag's shuffling and scratching drew nearer. Its hate, anger, and bloodlust pressed on his mind like a tightening vise. He was breathing too fast.

Clambering over rocks in the dark, he stubbed his fingers. He cut a leg on a crag. Still, they rose higher.

Thrag's clawing scattered stones from the pile below. It, too, was climbing. Stones shifted under its weight. The whole mound slid down a few feet. Then the sliding stopped.

Neil grasped the next rock, lunged higher, hit his head on something in the dark. Caitir climbed up beside him.

The pitch leveled out. He stuck his fingers toward the remembered opening, the narrow slit. Was it wide enough? Did it go anywhere?

His fingers grazed the rock above him, slid down the sides, encountering a horizontal chute, barely the width of a man's chest. "Go first," he whispered.

"Nay, Tristan." Tension throttled her voice.

"Aye, go on." He pushed her through.

She struggled, her feet kicking. But she seemed to make progress. Moments later, her voice came back through the chute. "It's wide enough. There's room for us both."

At the bottom of the pile, Thrag was clawing his way up. A rank, musty odor, as of some feral, unwashed creature, fouled Neil's nostrils. He scrambled faster toward Caitir's voice.

Something sharp and heavy hit his leg, knocked him sideways. Then a jolt of pain. Warm blood ran down his calf. It was upon him. He kicked, hit something soft, and then wriggled into the hole. A foul, hot breath, reeking of corruption, swarmed around him.

But he was inside.

Then came the sound of claws, scratching ineffectually on stone. A howl of frustration and anger roared around his ears, followed by a fell breeze. It filled the air with the stench of rot and the metallic scent of fresh blood. He scrambled farther into the passage. It widened enough to sit up.

"We're safe." His chest heaved as he tried to catch his breath. But pain gripped his leg.

Caitir reached for him, drew him close, and broke down, crying. He hugged her, kissed her neck, and laid his cheek next to hers. "It can't follow us in here."

"B—but how are we going to get out? What's to become of us?"

"I . . . I don't know." He'd told her they were safe, but that was a lie, wasn't it? What kind of safety had they achieved? They were trapped underground with no chance of escape.

They crawled farther. The chute opened up and led down a gentle slope into a larger area of some kind. From a far corner, came the echo of dripping of water. Here, they stopped, fearful of continuing in the dark. For a long while, the barghest continued to howl back at the far entrance, but the sound receded into the distance. Then it fell silent.

They just held each other. Neil felt for the place where the creature had clawed his leg. The bleeding had slowed. The wound cut deep and throbbed, but he had nothing with which to bind it.

Exhausted from the long chase and being up all night, they fell asleep in each other's arms.

⸎

When Neil woke, he wondered how much of the day had passed. He heard Caitir's quiet breathing beside him. He sat up and opened his eyes. The darkness in the cave was total. He listened to the echoes of dripping water.

When he stood, his wound sent a jolt of pain up his leg. What if it festered? But what did it matter? He may never live that long. Reaching up, he couldn't touch the ceiling. He waved his arms but felt no walls.

Then the darkness appeared to come alive. Tiny lights burst before his eyes. The dripping water reverberated like thunder in his ears. He could hear his heart beating wildly, the blood rushing through his head.

He'd survived the ordeal in the tomb of the Aeshitha, hadn't he? Yet this was worse. Far worse. Now again, he was trapped underground. They'd lost their torches. Even if they returned from this dead-end cavern and avoided the barghest, how would they ever find their way back? How many junctions hadn't they passed through? And many looked alike. His heart beat faster. Sweat streamed down his forehead.

Even Elyon seemed to have abandoned him now. Neil hadn't cleared his name or restored his honor. He hadn't found the Scepter. He didn't even know where the thing was. Everything he'd done had been for naught. There was water here, somewhere, so they could drink. But if someone didn't help them now, they'd soon die of starvation.

Then he remembered what the siòg had said. If ever he was in desperate need and called her, she'd come. How could there be a more desperate situation than this?

"*Malavhìn!*" he called in a loud voice. "Malavhìn, I need your help. Please come."

He repeated her name several more times then waited.

"Who did you call?" Caitir was awake.

He explained what the siòg had promised.

"But how can she come to us, when we're trapped down here and she's in some far distant land? I do not understand."

"Neither do I. But I don't know what else to do. I have no idea how we're going to get out of this."

He told her about his wound.

"Oh, Tristan. What can we do about it in the dark, without salve?"

"Nothing."

Then she fell silent, and the only sound was dripping water.

He pulled her close. They lay in each other's arms until they dozed again.

When Caitir shook his arm, he awoke. He opened his eyes to a dim glow. Light? From where? Though the light was faint, he now saw they were in a small cavern. He was facing the spot where they'd entered. Then he smelled sweet, mountain snowbells, fresh mountain air.

"Turn around," Caitir whispered, surprise lifting her voice.

When he faced the other way, he saw her.

The siòg. Malavhìn. She'd come.

He shot to his feet, winced from the pain, and took a step toward her.

A soft glow emanated from the siòg as she hovered over the middle of the cavern. On all sides, glistening rock needles reached down from the ceiling and up from the floor. He now saw that the room had no other exit but the way they'd entered.

"Why did you call me, Tristan mac Torn?" Her voice soothed and comforted but carried a hint of reproach.

"Because we are in terrible difficulty. A barghest has trapped us in this cavern. Even if we can escape him, we're lost in a warren of tunnels. I didn't know who else to turn to."

She frowned. "You already have what you require. You did not need to call me. All you lack is trust in Elyon. And is this not what someone has already told you? The only help I will give you now is to heal your wound." She drifted close and touched his injury with one hand.

Warmth flowed into his leg and settled. Instantly, the pain vanished.

"Trust in he who made you. And press on to the end." Then she floated up through the ceiling and was gone.

Instantly, total blackness returned.

"That was it? That was all the help your magical friend could offer?" In total disbelief, Caitir's voice rose in pitch, echoing in the dark. "I do not understand."

"I'm only just beginning to." He sat down and tried to control the fear returning with the darkness. Elyon had created Ereb, the sun, the moon, and the stars. And hadn't he appeared to Neil back in the palace of Ewhain Macha?

"O Elyon," his prayer began, "here I am again, asking your help. I've made a mess of it, haven't I? Everyone, including you, put their trust in me to do this task. And I've failed miserably. How can I ever restore my honor now? How can I ever prove my worth and gain the respect of all those who've despised me since birth?

"But here I am thinking of myself, and they say the future of Erde rests on this quest. If you didn't send me to return the Scepter to Ériu, then why am I down here? Why is Caitir with me? Why have you let us go all this way into the very bowels of Schwarzburg? I don't understand. Without your help, there is nothing left for us here but to die. Then the Deamhan Lord and Faolukan will win. Is that what you want? I don't think it is. Help us, Elyon. Please help us."

Then he dropped his head into his hands and closed his eyes. The darkness around him was complete.

A moment later, Caitir's fingers found his shoulder and squeezed, hard. "Look!" she breathed.

He opened his eyes to a dim light filling the chamber. Not the kind of light from the siòg. Sharper, brighter—even though still dim—and coming from the floor by the opposite wall, where the dripping water fell.

Standing, he took slow steps across the slippery rock to a ridge blocking the light.

When he stepped over it, his heart leaped. The light surged.

On the ledge beyond the pool lay their packs. Lying half-unsheathed with the blade resting in the water was his sword. He knelt. The pool held only a few inches of water. Machar's yellow gem glowed and lit up a clear bottom.

Then he saw the object beside the gem. And it took his breath away.

The Scepter.

It gleamed golden in the ethereal light. Its gem-studded crown sparkled with red rubies, bright green emeralds, and shimmering moonstones. No imitation this, he sensed its powerful presence even from here.

He reached down and lifted the Scepter from the pool. It was heavy.

Energy and light coursed through him. The Scepter itself began to glow.

Then, just as on the balcony back in Ewhain Macha, Elyon's presence filled him. A powerful essence roared out of the device like a supernatural wind. It carried the promise of love, kindness, and mercy. Joy lifted him so high, he wanted to shout and clap. He felt hope—hope that the darkness would be defeated, hope that good would triumph over evil.

He also felt a strong undercurrent of power, a tide of undelivered judgment, and a restrained anger so deep, he shuddered. A just anger against all the evil now befouling the world.

Now he understood how important the Scepter was. Not only was it a symbol of obedience, it was a reservoir of holy power locked inside a physical object. It was a means for mortal man, as a race, to prove its love for the words and commands of the one who made the world and everything in it.

A fleeting thought crossed his mind that, with the Scepter in hand, anything was possible. Any deed. Any project. Any war. Now he also realized the great danger it held. The holder of this device possessed in his hands the power to rule, to build, or to destroy. The Deamhan Lord, being spirit and not flesh, would have difficulty using it. But in the hands of someone like Faolukan it could, for a time, further the cause of great evil. Yet, just as Malavhín had warned him with Elyon's other gifts, those who used the Scepter's holy power for their own ends would eventually be destroyed by it.

Now he wondered: Why had Faolukan abandoned it in the bottom of a well? For millennia, it had lain there, unused and untouched. Did Faolukan know it could destroy him? Or was he saving it for some great and terrible deed, some brief but gargantuan feat of villainy that would further his power, yet not lead to his undoing?

But any such act would be risky, indeed. Only the man chosen by Elyon, who could further Elyon's goals, would be able to safely wield the Scepter. Even there, in the chosen one, lay great danger. For in such great power lay even greater temptation.

All this Neil knew intuitively, just by holding it.

He faced Caitir, beaming. Words failed him.

She was standing now, gaping at him with open mouth, smiling eyes. The Scepter's light washed over her, lighting her green eyes, illuminating even the individual strands of her hair.

He stooped to retrieve the gem Machar had given him. When he lifted it up and put the chain around his neck, its glow brightened, filled the cavern. The wet daggers of ceiling rock glistened red and yellow and white. White crystals embedded in the walls sparkled and twinkled. The whole room seemed to come alive with light and shout for joy.

One more treasure lay nearby. Poking out of the pool was a long alabaster horn with a shining gold mouthpiece. The Horn of the Reich? He nestled it in his knapsack.

Yet another item caught his eye—a metal tube, bent, corroded and resting in a rock crevice. He pulled it out, turned it over. It weighed little. He shook it. Something inside bumped against a tightfitting cork at one end. This, too, he tucked in his pack. Anything thrown down here must be important. He also collected his sword, knife, and bone whistle.

From back up the passage, the barghest howled, as if in pain, perhaps sensing the Scepter's presence in his hands. Then it howled again.

"Our salvation was here all along." Breathless excitement rushed through Neil's voice as his eyes focused on the golden rod still in his hand. "The Scepter, the gem, our weapons. It wasn't until I put my trust in Elyon that his light showed us the way."

"Just as Machar had said."

"And the siòg."

"Now what do we do?"

"Now we get out of here."

CHAPTER 41

ESCAPE

So what's your plan?" Caitir put her hands on her hips and gave him a half-smile. "You *do* have a plan?" Her words bounced off the stone and continued long after she stopped talking.

He gazed at the hole in the ceiling far above, the bottom of the well leading from the castle. Too high. Even if they reached it, they'd never make the long climb up such a narrow chute to the top. That left only one alternative. "The gem will light our way, and if the barghest approaches, it may even drive him back. But at dusk, he'll probably go to the gate. He's used to roaming the countryside each night."

"Then we can sneak out before they lock us inside again."

"Aye."

Filled with new hope, he placed the Scepter inside his knapsack. Both Horn and Scepter made for a tight fit. Yet even resting snug on his back, he felt its presence. It emanated far less power than when he held it in his hands. Still, it buoyed him up. With the gem's amber light showing the way, they climbed up the slope and entered the chute.

As the passage narrowed, a moment of doubt assailed him. Would the beast leave? Would he be able to control his fear? Instantly, the light dimmed.

"What's happening?" called Caitir from behind. "I can't see."

He breathed deeply. He must have faith in Elyon, whose power filled this gem. Was Elyon's power not greater than any creature's on Erde? The light returned to the gem, and they continued on.

The chute narrowed and brought them to the top of the debris mound in the adjoining chamber. Then his forehead began to sweat, and his palms became clammy. He thrust the gem aloft. Its light dimmed.

Be strong. Have faith.

The light's strength returned. While Caitir emerged beside him, he examined the room below.

"The creature's gone." She gave him a fleeting smile. But it fled from her face as soon as it appeared.

They scrambled down the pile. At the bottom, he used his flint to light the two unused torches.

Looking around him all the while, he crept to the room's center. The torches burned brightly. Here, he felt none of the creature's dread. He led them back up the wide passage where they'd fled only yesterday. But as they ascended the gentle slope, he wondered if, somewhere, the barghest lay in wait.

They emerged into the room with the two dead-end tunnels on the right. As soon as he stepped inside, the torches dimmed dramatically.

"There!" screamed Caitir. "In the corner."

Not only did the torches dim, but so did the gem.

No, have faith! This is Elyon's gem.

The jewel's light increased. The barghest was a vague shadow, huge and black. The gem now revealed features he'd never before seen— clawed feet, huge paws, and a glimpse of dark brown bristles on a bulging shoulder. Its eyes were two pinpricks of red floating in pus-colored orbs. But a halo of swirling, churning dark hovered about it, and what was revealed one moment, was swallowed by a black cloud the next.

The shadow rose up, and a roar shattered every corner of the room. Its foul breath, reeking of rotting flesh, made him gag. Then the swirling black form crouched, as if about to strike.

Neil threw his torch to the wet floor. It hissed and went out. For light, he must now rely only on the crystal. He drew his sword. The metal sheath vibrated, the sound echoing off the ceiling. His heart beat wildly. The gem's light dimmed.

The creature rushed at him.

Gripping the hilt with both hands, he swung his blade sideways in an arc.

Thrag hurtled back, avoiding the blow. Then it lunged forward with a long, shadowy arm. All Neil saw was claws. He thrust up with the blade's point and pierced a paw.

The barghest howled and lurched back. Red blood dripped onto the floor.

Real blood. It could bleed! That meant that, like any other creature, it could die. Hope surged within him.

The gem's light increased. The shadows around the monster swirled black and gray and angry. It crouched.

Its lunge caught Neil by surprise. He backed up and jumped to the side. The barghest struck out with a paw and—Neil sidestepped just in time. The claw was so big, it could easily have cut him in half.

Breathing heavily, he backed into Caitir, almost knocked her down. She'd circled to keep Neil between her and the creature. Behind him, her feet scuffled off into a corner.

Thrag raised its shadowy head and howled again. Its two pinprick eyes glowed red. For a second time, it lunged. But too slow.

This time, Neil was ready. He leaped aside, let it pass, took a quick step toward the creature's back. Straight at the center of the blackness he thrust his sword. The blade broke through hide and cut into flesh.

The barghest jumped back, staggered. It howled again. Then it backed up.

Now Neil could hear its rasping breath. Blood dripped from its wounds, pooling in two spots on the stone floor.

The gem's light pulsed, flooded the room.

The barghest retreated several steps. Then it turned its back and fled down the central passage.

Caitir's torch burned suddenly brighter. When she caught his glance, a smile broke her face.

Neil sheathed his sword.

She ran into his arms, and they hugged. "You've beaten it," she whispered.

"Perhaps. But now we must follow it to the gate. Its blood will show us the way out."

He retrieved his dropped torch and relit it. Then they followed its trail.

Thrag seemed to be making straight for the gate. The blood trail led through chambers where they'd been yesterday and through some he didn't recognize.

Soon, they entered the familiar large chamber filled with skeletons where lay Dieter's body, the flesh gnawed from his bones. Neil shuddered, and Caitir let out a short cry. Quickly, he pulled her past what was left of the corpse. Then they gained the tunnel leading to the exit. They passed the iron-banded access door, now closed, where, yesterday, they'd been pushed into Thrag's path.

A small circle of dim light shone from the end of a long, straight passage—the outside gate! Beyond it, the sun was setting. Just seeing that distant, tiny circle of red and blue sky filled him with hope.

But between here and there, two hundred feet from the entrance, Thrag lay crouched and waiting, creating its own, swirling circle of darkness.

"He's waiting for the gate to open." Neil stopped them. "So here we too must wait." He extinguished his torch on the wet stones and sat by the wall.

Caitir put out her light, and they waited.

Now he shielded the gem with his hands. Machar had said it could only be used for the space of one day. Now it shone even through the flesh of his cupped fingers.

They didn't have long to wait, for soon they heard the massive doors creaking on rusty hinges.

"Quickly, now." Neil jumped to his feet and shoved the gem into his pocket.

They ran down the passage, their footsteps echoing loudly on the stone.

Ahead, Thrag had risen and was lumbering toward the open doorway. But they were still a hundred yards behind him. If they came too close, would he turn and attack? Neil didn't want to find out. He slowed their pace.

But he'd misjudged the distance between creature and gate. Suddenly, it was through—the doors were already closing! And they still had a hundred feet to go.

"Oh no," Caitir breathed. "We'll be trapped."

They ran faster. Would the guards hear their footsteps? The iron hinges were loud, but so was the clopping of their shoes on stone.

Without torch or setting sun to guide their way, the tunnel darkened. But the smooth floor offered no obstacles.

Only fifty feet now. Here, the noise of the creaking hinges was deafening. The tall slit to the outside world was narrowing, would soon shut completely.

He slipped through, scraping his chest on the grate. Caitir was behind him. He pulled on her arm. Her tunic caught. He pulled harder. It ripped, and then they fell to the ground outside just as the iron bars clanged together.

Quickly, he led them off to the side where no guard could see them. Then they fell into the dirt, catching their breath.

A surge of joy energized him. They had escaped the tunnels and caves. Above him, the moon shone, bright and silver, in a cloudless sky. He breathed deeply, tried not to think about how close the moon was to being full. Only a few more days and his friends would be given to Wodan.

But tonight, he could see the moon. And tomorrow, they'd see the sun again. And that was a reason to rejoice.

Down on the plain of ghost trees, the barghest's shadow lumbered toward the horizon. Then it appeared to stop. Neil withdrew the gem. It had ceased shining. Its magic was gone.

"Is it still moving?" He peered through the moonlit night.

"I don't think so. There's only a lump on the ground."

Neil squinted across the moonlit plain. Then the shadow swirling above it disappeared. Now all he could see was a large black lump, lying motionless.

"Did it bleed to death?" asked Caitir.

"Maybe. But if someone else also sees what we do, they'll suspect something's wrong. Faolukan may even search the caverns. Then he'll know we've escaped."

"Then we must make as much distance as we can."

"Aye. They've got horses. And we don't."

They retrieved Caitir's bow and quiver from the small cave on the hillside. Then Neil led them across the bleak landscape, slinking from one dead tree trunk to another.

But when they reached the top of the far hill and took one last look over the dead valley, his heart skipped a beat.

Two riders were leaving the castle, headed for the spot where Thrag had fallen.

PART VII

CHAPTER 42

FLIGHT

Neil and Caitir left Schwarzburg's dead valleys and entered the living forest. They passed abandoned farmsteads, their tumbled bricks standing ruined and lifeless in the moonlight.

Despite the air of abandonment, it was good to breathe again the scent of new leaf and loam, to hear crickets chirp and nightingales sing. They had entered a land mostly untouched by Faolukan's evil, not yet oppressed by the Waldreich's gloom, and their spirits soared. The life around them—and possibly the Scepter in his backpack—gave Neil renewed energy.

Caitir, too, seemed to feel it. She ambled beside him, humming, sometimes skipping, often holding his hand.

For too long had they fought for their lives in Thrag's oppressive cave. Now they embraced the illusion of safety and could forget, even if only for a wee bit, who followed them.

After another league's travel, they paused to eat the last of the cheese in their packs. But it had become hard and stale. At a pool below a frigid, bubbling brook, they filled their waterskins and washed the cave grime from their bodies. They marched on at a rapid pace. He didn't know how long it would take Faolukan to determine their corpses weren't among the cavern's dead. Maybe not until morning. Still, they needed to make haste.

All night they hiked, scattering deer from grassy forest clearings, surprising foxes in their nightly haunts, hearing the hoot of an occasional owl announcing its nocturnal hunt.

Neil reveled in the defeat of Thrag, and of being free of the dungeon. The power of Elyon's Scepter resting against his back buoyed him.

As dawn filtered through a leafy ceiling, they arrived again at the Stream Of False Steps. Quickly, they leaped from stone to stone, stepping only on the places where footsteps had worn away the moss.

Once again, they stood at the edge of the Waldreich.

He found the tree where he'd hidden their gear and brought everything down to the water and the light. Facing both ways along the stream, he blew the whistle several times.

"Do you think they're still here?" Caitir peered through the massive trunks into the darkness beyond.

"If you were an elch, would you want to go in there?" He pointed into the Waldreich's gloom. "Or stay near the water?"

She smiled. "I'd go eat the berries upstream."

"Speaking of food, I've got a surprise for you." He pulled out the package of cheese and bread he'd stashed with their gear. The bread's hard outside crust kept it from molding. "Breakfast."

She beamed and they ate. As they finished, the elch appeared along the bank.

Then they began the long process of trying to saddle the first recalcitrant creature. But half the morning had fled, and they'd only saddled one animal. The second wanted no part of Neil's bridle.

His frustration boiled over. "You sorry excuse for a horse, come here." But it just stood its ground, blinking at him, shaking its antlers.

How long before Faolukan's soldiers appeared? He tried soothing words while hiding the bridle behind his back.

Still, it shook its head, gave him its hind end, and pranced ten paces away, only to turn and stare at him again.

Caitir came up beside him. "I wonder what elch steaks would taste like?"

At that moment, their attention snapped to the stream. The sound of hooves pounding on dirt announced a rider on a black horse galloping down to the far bank. He stopped, glaring at them in silence while his horse drank from the brook. Then he jerked on the reins and raced back the way he'd come.

"This is bad." Neil frowned. "That must have been one of Faolukan's scouts. The rest won't be far behind."

"At this rate, we'll still be here at sunset trying to saddle that thing. Why don't you try your flute?"

Smiling, he untied the bone whistle from its tunic pocket. He began to play a slow, soothing melody. Moments later, Caitir bridled the animal.

While she held the beast, Neil saddled it. "Why didn't we think of that before?" he said.

Once mounted, they entered the forest at a gallop. As before, the Waldreich's gloom and oppressive darkness bore down like a heavy-laden cloud. They rode until midafternoon. By then, neither could keep their eyes open. When they came to one of the rare rock clearings, they stopped to rest. They didn't unsaddle the elch, just tied them to a tree in the center and lay down in a patch of sunlight.

"We'll only rest a wee bit." Neil stretched out on the soft grass.

The events of the last two days—little real sleep, the chase, the fight, the long ride—all combined to send them both into a deep sleep.

Neil woke as Caitir gently shook him. "Wake up. We've slept overlong."

He opened his eyes. The sun was high above them. Was it already noon? The elch were edgy, their hooves scraping and pawing at the rocks where he'd tethered them. Even they knew it was time to move on.

On through the day and into another night, they rode. When the moon rose over the trees of another clearing, it was almost full. Only a few days now before Machar and Ewan would be given to the idol. They pressed on.

In the dark, they relied entirely on the elch to keep the trail. Neil also worried about the wolves. In this blackness, the predators might decide it was safe to attack even these fearsome beasts of burden, despite their enormous size and antlers.

Another morning broke, and they made a frightening discovery. In the night, the elch had left the main trail.

"I've no idea where we are." Neil looked around, but everything inside the Waldreich appeared the same. Their only guide through the forest's murk had been the well-worn path.

"Now what do we do?"

"We let the elch take us where they will."

Caitir frowned. "Do they know the way home?"

"I hope so. But have heart. Faolukan won't expect us to be here. He'll be following the main trail."

All that day, they let their animals lead them. As night fell again, they were too exhausted to go further, and they stopped in a clearing. After unsaddling the elch and letting them feed on tufts of grass, Neil peered up at the small circle of sky and the moon rising over the trees.

"I'm guessing we've only two days left."

Caitir stood beside him and gripped an arm. "Let's hope we're close."

They climbed a tree to sleep, and when dawn broke, they saddled the elch in record time while Neil played his flute. They started out again at a rapid clip. Shortly after noon, they crossed a trail heading north.

"Do you recognize it?" Caitir caught Neil's glance.

"Nay, they all look alike. We could be on the same path we took out of Beilzig City. Or not." He peered at the forest floor. "But this one has seen recent, heavy traffic. That's a good sign. I think."

Caitir nodded, and they continued on this new trail.

When they made camp that night, he cut some downed limbs for a fire with his sword. As they huddled around the flames, the eerie cries of a tawny owl, sounding like a lost, wounded animal, broke the stillness.

Neil wondered how they would ever find the Naz again and whether they'd be too late. Ewan's and Machar's lives were in his hands. He had the means to save them—the Horn of the Reich. All they had to do was bring it there in time. Long before the morning sun brought its dim light, he woke, and they set out in semidarkness.

"Tonight, the moon will be full. If we don't find the Naz by then . . ." Neil shook his head.

Caitir said nothing, only held his gaze. He saw the worry in her eyes.

Morning became late afternoon. Soon afterward, a dark form slunk through the trees beside him. But when he stared into the shadows for a better look—nothing. He glanced behind and caught a fleeting glimpse of another form, huge and black, before it too merged with the darkness.

"The wolves are back!" Caitir's voice startled him as he whirled to see another creature's form slink beside them.

"And even more of them than before."

"Aye. They're all around us."

She was right. The whole forest seemed alive with movement.

The further they traveled, the more numerous became the silent, looming menace around them. They continued on, keeping a close watch on the pack behind, beside, and now even in front of them.

But the wolves came no closer and even began to thin out, as if called away for some other purpose. Moments later, Caitir announced, "They're gone."

He looked behind them. No wolves. He scanned the trees on both sides. Nothing.

Then he heard the sound of drums, deep and low and distant. "Do you hear that?"

"It can only be one thing."

"Aye. We're nearing the Naz's place of sacrifice. And this trail seems headed straight for it."

"I hope we're not too late." Fear contorted her features.

"Aye."

Neil urged his elch to greater speed. The drumming grew louder, deeper. A chorus of voices, raised in chanting, now joined in. Through the trees, he glimpsed the towering flames of an enormous bonfire. Moments later, the trail opened into a clearing washed yellow with the fire's wavering light. It was the same place of sacrifice, where they'd found the woman chained to the deamhan idol.

"We've come in from the east." Neil pointed. "To the north is the trail we took when we first arrived."

They circled the clearing, weaving behind tree trunks, until they were beside the northern trail. They crouched in the shadows and watched.

On the field's far side, a growing pack of wolves sat on their haunches and stared with red, gleaming eyes at a gathering of men. Occasionally, one of the beasts raised its muzzle to the sky and howled. Each wolf-cry sent a shiver rippling down Neil's back.

But it was unlike wolves to sit like that. Something commanded them. And they were waiting for something.

Closer to Neil, hundreds of Naz gathered around the stone idol, beside the angry, popping roar of the nearby fire. A hundred feet away at the clearing's edge, dozens of elch, tethered to a long rope, pawed the ground and waited in the shadows.

But what Neil saw next sent his heart pounding and brought sweat to his forehead. Beside the elch and tied to two posts were the two men waiting to be sacrificed—

Machar and Ewan.

CHAPTER 43

AN UNHAPPY REUNION

Neil dismounted and gave Caitir his elch's reins. "I hope we're not too late. You'd better keep out of sight until I call you. And keep this safe." He passed her the pack containing the Scepter but took out the Horn of the Reich, wrapped in cloth.

The howls of several wolves sent more ripples across Neil's shoulders.

Fear crossed Caitir's features. "M–may Elyon go with you."

"Thank you." He smiled. It was the first time she'd ever said that name.

Leaving the woods, he crossed the clearing. He threaded his way through the back of the crowd. As men saw him approach, a path opened to the center. He headed straight for where King Veit, Egon, and lastly, Detlef, the chief druid, were standing.

Before the monarch of Hochnest, he bowed low. "My lord Veit, I have returned. And as promised, I've brought you the Horn of the Reich."

With a gasp, the king looked up in surprise. Silence spread through the assembly like a summer breeze through the upper boughs. Only the angry snapping of the bonfire disturbed the silence. A log slid from its pyre, throwing a rain of sparks into the sky. Questioning faces turned to their neighbors.

Slowly, Veit spoke, slurring his words. "Is thish true? You've brought back . . . that which was lost to us?"

"Aye, my lord. And when I did, you agreed to release my friends, did you not?"

Veit frowned, lifted a hand to scratch his chin. "You've brought the Horn?"

"Aye."

Veit's eyes seemed to have difficulty focusing on Neil.

"You're interrupting a sacred ceremony." Scowling, the druid Detlef now stepped forward, dressed all in white. "The sacrifice has begun. The foreigners have already been consecrated and promised to Wodan. You're too late."

Veit waved a hand at Detlef and edged around him. "Let me see the Horn."

Neil removed the wrapping. Like an exquisite jewel, the alabaster horn with its golden mouthpiece sparkled in the firelight.

The crowd murmured approval as King Veit, his eyes wide, turned it over. By the flickering flames, it shone amber and gold. His fingers caressed it, ran along an outer curve as long as a man's forearm, and then gently circled the mouthpiece. "Surely, this is the great Horn of legend. You have done well, Neil mac Connell."

But an item swinging from the king's neck now caught Neil's attention—a crescent-moon pendant. He felt his jaws tighten. What had transpired since they'd left?

Neil braved a smile and bowed. "The only thanks I need is for you to release my friends and send us on our way with all dispatch. I fear a powerful druid follows us."

Detlef stifled a smile and exchanged a knowing look with his monarch. "My lord, the ceremony cannot be stopped. Surely, 'tis wondrous that this long-lost artifact has returned to us tonight. But promises made to Wodan must come before any made to a foreigner, no matter what he's done."

Veit's glance shifted lazily from the Horn to the druid to Neil, as if uncertain what to do next. His free hand caressed the pendant.

"My lord, may I say a word?" Egon stepped between the druid and his king.

Veit's eyes began to close and his head to loll.

"My lord?" Egon frowned.

The king released the pendant and nodded at Egon. "You may . . . speak."

"With the great Horn again in our possession, we no longer need these sacrifices. You have but to blow on it, and all that was lost will be restored. For generations, this is what we've been told. It's what my father waited for, and my grandfather before him. This very night we can attack the wolves and drive them from our forests forever. With this talisman, this great Horn, they will fall away before us. That's what the legends promise. With the Horn's power, the Naz will regain the glory and honor it once had. All you have to do is blow on it."

A new voice, a familiar voice, spoke up from the back of the crowd. "I'd strongly advise against that." The words shot through Neil like an arrow. He whirled. Sliding through the crowd came Faolukan.

"That's right, foolish one. We meet again, and now for the last time. Detlef is right. Once consecrated, the sacrifices must be made." He faced Detlef. "But now we have another offering for Wodan, do we not? We must perform the ceremony again. From the beginning."

Detlef grinned. "At once, my lord."

Neil faced King Veit, hoping for a change of mind, but the king's sole concentration now focused on the pendant.

Faolukan approached the king. "I'll keep this for you in a safe place." His fingers wrapped around the Horn, and he pried it from the king's grip. Suddenly, he dropped it, as if the device had burned him. "Wh–what!"

Veit looked down, grabbed the artifact. "Nay, druid. I will keep it. Better yet, Egon will keep it. This Horn, so precious to the Naz, must never again leave our possession. Even into the hands of a druid as great as you."

Apparently shocked by what happened, Faolukan stared at it. "As you wish, my lord." He backed up a pace. "We can discuss this later."

Egon rushed forward, bowed, and received the Horn from his king. As he left, he flashed a smile at Detlef but avoided Faolukan's glare.

Detlef commanded the men around him, "Take the foreigner and tie him up with the others. Then resume calling the rest of the pack."

Four Naz gripped Neil's arms and nearly lifted him off his feet. They dragged him across the field to a stake at the forest's edge where Machar and Ewan were already bound. The Naz began tying him to the pole.

"Well, my lord." Machar was staked on Neil's right, and he gave Neil a wry grin. "This isn't the rescue we'd envisioned." Machar appeared fully recovered from his fever.

The druids who'd bound Neil headed back to the gathering with haste. Neil waited until they were alone then said, "He deceived us, Machar. I brought him Horn of the Reich, but Veit broke his agreement."

"You found it, did you? Well done. I'm impressed. But only yesterday, Faolukan arrived, and the king quickly succumbed to his magic. Now Veit cares for naught but his blasted pendant. Where magic and idolatry reign, honor, fair dealing, and common sense soon depart."

"Aye, Neil," Ewan called from the stake beyond Machar's. "We're in a bad way here. They haven't even fed us tonight. But where is Caitir?"

"Ssshhhh. She's still out in the forest."

One Naz strode toward them from the clearing and waved a spear. "I'll hear no more jabbering from you three."

As soon as he'd left, they quietly decided what to do when Caitir made her move.

While the Naz again beat on drums, resumed their chanting, and focused on their ceremony, more wolves filtered in from the forest to join a large and growing pack.

Just beyond the fire's light, Neil could make out Caitir's silhouette, a slender, shadowy form slinking from tree to tree, moving closer. She paused, readied her bow. He heard the twang of a string. The guard nearest them fell, clutching an arrow in his chest. Then she ran from the shadows, a knife in one hand, Neil's backpack in the other.

"Glad I am to see you, lass," whispered Ewan, as she cut his bonds.

"And I you. Both of you." She took her knife to Neil's stake then Machar's.

When they'd been freed, Machar and Ewan ran for the Naz's string of elch, still saddled and tethered to a long rope stretched between two trees. Machar separated two animals from the line with the guard's knife, while Ewan began cutting the longer string at both ends.

Meanwhile, Neil and Caitir grabbed handfuls of unlit torches where the guards had dropped them. Then they ran for the shelter of the forest where their own animals waited. Neil had just mounted when shouting rang out from behind. He looked back to see Machar and Ewan leading away the entire string of Naz elch. Racing toward their stolen animals, but not fast enough, were all the Naz. Their shouts of alarm filled the night.

Beyond sat the wolf pack, still waiting, watching.

"You'll not escape." Although they'd left Faolukan far back in the field, his voice boomed through the trees, drowning out all others, as if carried on some kind of spell. "I'll chase you to the farthest ends of Erde."

Neil led, taking them down the trail on which they'd originally arrived weeks ago. Behind him, Machar and Ewan led all the Naz's elch.

But when a dozen whistles screamed in the distance, the elch began to balk. Machar and Ewan tugged on the ropes as the lead animal lunged toward the sound and tried to pull the rest with him. The elch finally gave up the struggle.

While still sitting astride the saddle, Neil struck a flint on his knife. He lit one torch and held it high. He lit another and passed it to Caitir. Each torch would burn for a goodly length of time.

Mounted, they quickly retraced ground that had taken them far longer to cover on foot.

But hauling the string of elch slowed their pace. After a quarter of the night was spent pulling, cajoling, and threatening the recalcitrant animals, Caitir broke the silence. "Machar and Ewan have fallen far behind."

Neil shouted back, "Will the elch go no farther?"

"Nay, my lord." Machar's voice breached the distance. "We must release them." He paused, frowning.

He and Caitir rode back. Then the four dismounted and began cutting each of the animals loose.

"Each of you," said Machar, "take a spare mount."

After they had released the rest and tied leads to their chosen spares, Ewan spat on the ground. "Cursed, stubborn beasts. Can we not have one on a spit for supper?"

Machar smiled. "I'm sore tempted. But tonight, we have to make as much time as we can."

Ewan's face was downcast, but he nodded.

Machar addressed Neil. "I'm confident we've a good lead on the Naz and Faolukan and his wolves. Perhaps we can even lose them. But now we should make for Schwarzburg. You'll be glad to know I learned its location from Egon."

Caitir grinned and put her hands on her hips. "Neil and I have decided we do not want to go anymore to Schwarzburg."

"What?" Machar's eyes widened. "You've abandoned the quest?"

"Nay, my lord. Neil's already got it."

"Got what?"

Neil reached inside his pack and pulled out the Scepter. "This." Light, like the sun's filtered through a thousand prisms, split the forest darkness. Neil felt its power surge.

The elch around them averted their eyes and bent their heads low, as if knowing, instinctively, from whence came the light.

Machar's jaw dropped.

Ewan shook his head. Then he grinned. Then he slapped one knee.

"H–how? We thought you went to Beilzig City?" Machar inched forward, one hand outstretched.

"We did." Neil held the glowing Scepter as Machar's fingers gingerly touched it. "Princess Uta told me her mother had sold the Great Horn to Faolukan and that he'd taken it to Schwarzburg Castle. There's a lot more to the story. But in the end, she gave us a map."

Machar stepped back, his eyes wide.

The Scepter pulsed, casting a bright luminescence about the four, lighting up the giant trunks around them, dispelling the forest gloom.

"And then"—Caitir's voice was breathless—"they captured us and threw us into some dark caverns below. Neil led us to a dead-end cave where he found the Scepter and the Great Horn. Then he killed Thrag, and we escaped."

"You did all *that*? And you killed the barghest?" Machar gripped his head with both hands.

"Aye." Neil smiled.

Now both Machar and Ewan gaped at him as if a stranger had entered their midst.

"Then surely, you are . . . the Toghaí," Machar breathed.

"What does it mean—that I'm the Toghaí? You've never explained it."

Machar took two steps forward and bowed. When he again stood, he was smiling. "It means only *you* could have found Scepter. And you did. It also means that you, and you alone, must bear it. As the prophecies correctly foretold."

Now Neil's mouth hung open. How could this be? He wasn't flaith. He didn't meet the signs.

Machar's eyes were on fire. "We've got the Scepter. Now we must return to Ériu with all dispatch. But first, we must stop at Ard Cúl Dín. Much as we often disagree with them, they must learn of this event, take steps, and prepare for the return of Elyon's light into the world. Just as important, we need somewhere to stop, re-provision, and rest."

"Provisions and vittles—sounds good to me." Ewan nodded.

"But I fear we've tarried here too long." Machar cast a worried glance into the trees and mounted his saddle. "We don't know how soon the arch druid and his wolves will come for us. But come they will."

Neil returned the Scepter to his pack. Then he mounted his elch and held his torch high.

As they followed the trail's outline by torchlight, the sound of hooves, padding heavily on hard loam, continued through the night.

Morning broke, dim and gray, casting shadows from the pillars of hoary trunks, barely lighting the canopy of deep leaf above.

"My lord"—pain scrunched Ewan's face as he addressed Machar—"we've not had a thing for supper. And 'tis past time for breakfast. Have we not a wee bite of anything for a starving man?"

Machar waved in Neil's direction. "Have we anything to eat?"

"A portion of jerky, bread, and cheese. But it's about gone."

Ewan beamed, but Machar held up a hand. "We must ration it. This may be the last food we see until the High Refuge."

Ewan's face fell.

"But perhaps"—Machar winked at Neil—"a wee bite now will give us the energy to carry on through the day?"

Ewan's smile returned as Neil passed out some of their meager provisions.

"Do you ken?" asked Caitir as she took her portion. "Have we lost Faolukan and his wolves?"

"A good question, that." Machar looked back along the trail. "If he were going to catch us, I'd have expected him to have done so by now. But surely, there are other trails through these woods. Some might even be far shorter than ours. He could be ahead of us. So we must not tarry."

Neil exchanged worried glances with Caitir.

When they'd finished eating, they rode on through the day and well into the night, switching often to their other elch to give each animal a rest.

The dark of another night deepened around them. Despite all his efforts, the regular sound of the elch's hooves padding on dirt lulled Neil's eyes to close.

"Caitir!" Machar's shout brought him back to consciousness. "Wake up."

Neil glanced behind him. She was slumped forward in the saddle, in danger of falling off. She straightened, shook her head, and rejoined them.

"Machar, we must sleep. And these"—Neil held up his torch—"are nearly burned out."

Machar nodded, and they dismounted. So tired were they that Machar agreed they would simply tether the animals and sleep on the ground. "We've seen no wolf-sign and nothing of our pursuers. We must be a far piece . . . ahead of them," he said, his words slowing. "Enough maybe, so we can sleep until dawn."

As Neil's head hit the soft patch of leaves, he wondered if they had, indeed, left Faolukan behind.

Sleep fell upon him like a door shutting out the light.

CHAPTER 44

THE VALLEY

U p, everyone!" Machar's voice cut through layers of sleep, and Neil opened his eyes to the dim light of a Waldreich day. He stretched and stood. No telling how long they'd slept.

The crinkle and rustle of leather announced to the others it was time to eat. He pulled bread and cheese from his pack and distributed it.

Caitir was just opening her eyes.

"That's the last of our food," he said.

Ewan took his portion and chewed it with gusto. Then he looked at his empty hands as if he'd just been tricked.

Machar frowned. "I expect we've one more day until the western trail. Then it's only a quick hike across the valley and a short climb to Ard Cúl Dín. I've fasted longer and survived. So can the three of you."

Ewan groaned. "Maybe Caitir can shoot us a deer?"

Machar shook his head. "No time for hunting or cooking."

"Have we lost them?" Neil glanced back into the trees.

"I don't know. But I wouldn't expect the druid to give up." Machar's gaze followed Neil's. "If only we can gain the Refuge—he won't follow us there. For millenia, their great defenses and Elyon's veil have kept the Capulum priests safe from the enemy."

They mounted and rode again through what was left of the day. Too soon did dusk come, stealing what little light the Waldreich begrudged them. Now their original mounts became so exhausted, they were forced to free them.

Twice that night Neil thought he saw movement in the woods beside them. But when he looked again—nothing. Was exhaustion taking its toll?

The next day dawned gray and dim. Neil felt as worn out as his tunic, now ripped, torn, stuck with briars, and streaked with mud. They'd barely traveled a league through the morning gloom when a little-used trail branched off to the west.

"Ah, me laddies." Grinning, Machar brought them to a halt. "And of course, me lass. We've come to the way out. I think we've escaped our pursuers. 'Tis only a wee ride now, and we'll leave this accursed forest of gloom for the high country, fresh air, and the Capulum fortress."

Neil breathed deeply. "I'd be grateful for a long rest in a soft bed."

"A wee morsel or two from the pan would be grand, indeed." Ewan tried a smile.

"I'm sure, when the monks of Ard Cúl Dín see what we've brought, they'll put on the best feast that ever that place has seen."

Ewan's grin nearly cracked his face.

They turned west, filled with renewed hope and energy at the prospect of a respite from their travels.

Soon, the trees thinned, and sunlight burst all around them. Aspens and birch fought the oaks for the ground and won. The great oaks themselves now grew smaller, as if cowed by sunlight. Perched in a nearby sapling, a turtledove cooed. Whatever dark spell had gripped the forest behind them appeared to weaken, then die altogether.

They left the Waldreich.

On through the morning they rode, seeing occasional deer and squirrels, and once, even a badger. Still, Machar forbade them time to kill and cook a few hares, even though hunger rumbled in Neil's belly.

They climbed a rocky hill. In the distance rose a mountain range, stark and windswept. Below the peaks lay a valley forest, verdant and dense.

"See the high wall stretching between those far peaks? And the line of watchtowers?" Machar swept an arm toward two, distant, snowcapped mountains. "That's Ard Cúl Dín. The last refuge of the Capulum against the darkness."

"Why haven't we heard of it before?"

"Its existence is well known to many, but its secretive monks have worked hard to keep their location known only to a few. Long has Elyon's magic prevented Faolukan and his minions from seeing it. Beyond the gap, the mount of Beinn Siarach blocks the way. For hundreds of leagues, the Blue Mountains admit no crossing. On this side, the Waldreich bars all but the most resolute traveler. What better way to hide and protect a town in the mountains?"

As Neil surveyed the valley between here and there, a thick fog hovered over the center. From above, it seemed to roil and churn with an unnatural darkness. Bursts of light flashed from within, followed by the rumble of thunder. "Look." He pointed.

Machar's gaze apparently found it for the first time. "Strange. I've never seen a storm so deep and dark clinging so low over a valley. But the weather here is unpredictable, so we'll just have to brave it. 'Tis only a short hike across and a wee climb to the refuge."

Machar led them down the slope. At the bottom, they entered a narrow tunnel through the trees. Its left side bordered the rock face of the mountain. On the right, brush, vines, and trees tangled close together.

"It's grown wild here. Not many travelers come this way." Machar swept a hand. "But 'tis only a short ways across."

They rode on. Soon an overhanging fog closed above them, and the trail became almost as dark and oppressive as the Waldreich. An unnatural thunder reverberated ahead.

"I don't like this." Machar frowned. "'Tis an unnatural storm, this."

Now, mist closed all around them, but it was unlike any fog Neil had ever seen. On all sides, wave upon wave of black vapor churned and roiled. From within the gloom, light flared, followed by low, angry rumblings.

"Something's moving beside us." Fear quavered in Caitir's voice. "The whole forest—'tis . . . *moving*."

Neil peered into the heavy mist. Fleeting movement. Dark shapes as tall as a pony.

"Wolves," called Ewan. "Hundreds of them."

"Faolukan's wolves." Machar drew his sword. "'Twas too good to be true. 'Tis a trap!"

Ewan reached for his sword but found only the stolen knife. "I've naught a proper weapon to fight with."

Neil threw him his sword and pulled out his bone whistle. He began to play.

But the wolves didn't respond. They continued massing and running alongside the travelers. Neil played and played, but today, the music had no effect on them. Occasionally, they turned muzzles in his direction and growled. He put the flute away. Now he had only his knife to fight with.

Above and beside them, the fog deepened. Lightning exploded in great bursts. Thunder rolled through the tumbling vapor. All combined to send icicles of fear shooting down Neil's back.

"What's happening?" He stared into the mist, at the lightning, the wolves. "I've never seen such a fog."

"Sure, and 'tis driven by a spell to keep us from our goal." Machar brandished a sword toward the wolves. Yet his voice wavered. "We must . . . keep on."

Ahead, the cloud darkened and roiled and became the blackest of nights.

The elch came to an abrupt halt. Neil kicked his mount, but it wouldn't budge. Neither would the other beasts go on. He glanced behind. More wolves gathered there.

"We must dismount." Machar slid from his elch. "We can't fight from atop these animals. And they won't go on."

Neil and the others followed his lead.

The fog in front parted slightly to reveal dozens of figures in black capes, each riding a misshapen wolf. But their faces! These riders weren't men at all. They were púcas—men with the heads and upper bodies of bears, wolves, and even lions. Then the group gave way to a figure even greater than they, a man surrounded by a halo of darkness—Faolukan. Neil felt his presence as if icy, slithering insects were scampering over his arms, legs, and back.

He whirled to look behind him. They were surrounded on three sides, trapped against the rock ledge on their left.

The shapeshifters emerging from the fog growled and bared their fangs. The men who accompanied them leered and readied their swords. The smell of feral, unwashed beasts befouled the air.

When Faolukan spoke, his voice thundered with unnatural power and menace. "You have escaped for the last time. But I give you one final chance to redeem your lives. Surrender to my master and join my army."

Neil fought the urge to obey. The arch druid was using another powerful word spell. Neil swallowed. Then he answered for all of them. "Nothing could convince us to join you or your army of evil. Not even death."

"You will not win this fight." A smirk lifted the scar on one side of Faolukan's face. "You're not even properly armed."

Machar spat on the ground. "Our prince speaks for us all. We'll die fighting with what we have, rather than become one of your shape-shifting horrors."

"Then so be it." Faolukan signaled with his hand.

Their teeth bared, their throats growling, their fangs outstretched, the beast-men charged from the mist. The men and their púca allies kicked their wolf-mounts and joined in.

The four travelers retreated to the rock wall. Unable to flee, their elch backed up beside them. Neil's elch lowered its antlers, shook a warning at the predators, and emitted a deep-throated, multi-chorded bellow.

But the numbers arrayed against them were . . . overwhelming.

Caitir's bow twanged as three arrows flew in rapid succession. Two men and one wolf-púca fell. But the downed shapeshifter regained its feet until another missile ended its struggling.

Machar's blade swung wide and cut the jugular of an attacking bear-beast. Backed against the wall, Machar's elch swept down with its antlers and smashed one ravening púca hard into the rock wall with a crunch of bone and flesh. It dropped, lifeless, to the ground.

Another elch lowered its head and grappled with a predator whose fangs had locked onto its horns. Quickly, two, then three, then more wolves attacked the elch's legs and sides and brought it down. Growling, their teeth ripped into flesh and tore into its throat and back.

Neil had only a knife. He started to reach for it.

Use the Scepter.

From nowhere came the words, as if written in light inside his head.

Hold the Scepter. Raise it high!

His fingers fumbled inside the pack behind him and brought out the Scepter. In the moment he touched it, hope and power surged through him. Gripping it with both hands, he held it high.

At once, a bright light encircled him. It pulsed with multicolored brilliance, sending out piercing ray after brilliant ray, its luminescent circle growing larger and brighter with each thrust outward. A pure, glorious white light, it contained within it all the colors of the rainbow. But nay, each color somehow multiplied into thousands more, so that the light sparkled and glinted with an ethereal, holy glow on everything it touched.

Simultaneously, power coursed through him, stripping away his exhaustion, filling him with energy and hope. He felt his thoughts being magnified and focused on the adversaries before him. *Stop your attack*, he thought. *Flee*! *Run and hide*! *Leave and never come back*!

All the attacking púcas, men, and wolves—all except Faolukan's mount—stopped their advance, blinked, and cocked their heads.

"By the power of Elyon"—from nowhere the words seemed to tumble from his mouth—"I banish you from this place!"

A púca, fangs bared and almost upon Caitir, halted its lunge and stood as if frozen. It pawed at its wolf-face. Then it began morphing back into a man. In moments, bristles melted away and flowed back into human skin. Its wide nostrils closed in upon themselves, and its wolf-snout squeezed into the form of a human nose. Claws shrank and became fingers and toes.

The same thing began happening to all the púcas.

Cowering, the wolves whimpered and backed up. Then, as one, the animals bolted.

The fog itself began to calm. The thunder stopped. The churning roil ceased. The mist began to thin. A slim ray of sunlight burst down from above.

"Nay!" Faolukan cried, desperation in his voice as he realized, for the first time, what had happened, what he faced. "Thief! You've stolen it. How . . . ?" He shook his head, gaping in apparent disbelief. "This will not—*must* not—stand." But he neither approached nor withdrew.

Holding the Scepter high, Neil began walking toward him. "I command you to leave this place. *Now!*"

Fear distorted Faolukan's face, now pallid and sweat-streaked. As if the Scepter's blinding light were shooting needles of pain through him, he raised his arms before his eyes and winced. He backed his wolf-mount a few steps.

The shapeshifters—now all changed back into men—stood naked, blinking, and defenseless. Bare-bottomed, they turned and sprinted for the trees.

Neil never stopped striding toward the druid. The Scepter's light kept increasing, shining now with the brilliance of ten thousand torches concentrated in a single point. Its power radiated, pulsed, and threw itself outward in wave upon wave of golden, blinding, otherworldly light, a light carrying the breath of Elyon and the essence of all that was holy, good, and right.

The fog thinned then seemed to evaporate before his eyes, burned away by the Scepter's radiance. Sunlight burst down from above. Only Faolukan and one black-clad man remained. Then the lone man at the arch druid's side turned his wolf, kicked its sides, and he, too, fled into the trees.

Faolukan stood alone.

Again, the druid backed his wolf-mount. Even as his wolf retreated, Faolukan grimaced and held up a hand to shield his face from the Scepter's growing light. "There is nowhere you can hide, Neil mac Connell." Tight and hoarse, as if each syllable caused great pain, the words strained past his throat. "I will find you. And when I do . . . you will regret you ever laid eyes on Elyon's foul device."

Then he spurred his wolf's ribs, twisted the beast around, and the forest swallowed him up.

Neil let out a long, slow breath.

He stared at the place where Faolukan had gone. He searched the way ahead and behind. Everywhere, the fog had evaporated, the enemy, departed.

"They've gone." Caitir breathed the words.

"Aye." Ewan looked with widened eyes at Neil. "My lord, you chased them off like a dog after a herd of mangy sheep."

Neil lowered the Scepter, its light already dimming. It wasn't him. He'd only obeyed the voice inside his head. He returned the device to his backpack.

Machar came up beside him, his mouth open. "The power I felt . . . coming off you! How did you know to raise the Scepter? Who told you to speak those words?"

Neil shrugged. "I think you know."

Machar stared at him. "You continue to amaze me, Neil mac Connell. You surely are the Toghaí. Three months ago, if someone had told me this was how we would push back the darkness, I would never have believed it."

Then Machar did something that took Neil's breath away. He pulled out his sword and knelt at Neil's feet. This leader of men, this pillar of the Capulum, bowed his head and, with both hands, lifted his sword. "You've done what no one has ever done before. Surely, you are the Toghaí. You have borne yourself with honor and truth and bravery. I am proud to call you my lord. From this day forward, I pledge to you my fealty and my sword."

Before Machar's speech was over, Ewan had also bowed before him. "Honor is the word, my lord. You've carried out your task with honor, true and certain. My sword is also yours. Always has been." Ewan lifted his knife, the only weapon he had.

Gently, Neil's fingers tapped each of Machar's shoulders then Ewan's. But when they rose, Neil could barely see them. Tears filled his eyes and streamed down his cheeks, so touched was he by their gesture.

But who were they honoring? Tristan mac Torn? Or Neil mac Connell? Instead of lifting him up, their honor and their pledge of fealty tore at his insides. Aye, he'd taken the Scepter from the bowels of Schwarzburg, but hadn't everything he'd done since leaving Hidden Pines been a deceit? Ewan knew this. It was his scheme that got Neil into this. But what if Machar learned the truth? Would the warrior still be bowing before him then?

He tried to turn away, but Machar hugged him. "You did well, Neil."

Ewan patted him on the back. "I'm proud to be your squire."

But he wasn't flaith. So how could he be the Toghaí?

"Cheer up, my lord," said Ewan, smiling. "Why such a long face?"

"I'm thinking our lord Neil doesn't know how to receive honor." Machar was beaming. "But accept it, Neil. 'Tis yours. Aye, my grand Company of four. We owe Neil a great debt. We have the Scepter. But let us not forget, our journey is far from over. We've yet to return it safely to Ériu. And who knows what trials yet await us?"

"After what we've been through," said Caitir, "'twill be as easy as making biscuits."

"Do not talk of biscuits unless you've got some to share." A frown briefly won over Ewan's smile. "Or I do not ken if I can ride another league."

Neil tried to smile, but he didn't share their joy.

Caitir approached, wrapped her arms around him, and kissed him hard on the lips. "He's something, is he not? My husband to be?"

"Husband?" Machar's jaw dropped.

"Aye, did we not tell you? When we return to Ériu, we're to be wed."

"Then let me be the first to congratulate you." Machar rushed forward, shook both their hands, then hugged Caitir. "A marriage between commoner and flaith is sure to start tongues wagging back in Ewhain Macha. But Neil is the Toghaí. So perhaps he can break all the rules."

Neil winced. If Machar only knew who he really was.

"And I'll be the second to congratulate you." Ewan approached and hugged them both.

Their affection and the lingering glow of Caitir's kiss finally won him over, eking out a smile. Beside him, Caitir held one of his hands and squeezed.

They mounted, but since one elch had died in fight, Caitir slipped up behind Neil. He waited for Machar to lead them on.

Machar's animal was ready to lunge ahead, but the Capulum warrior jerked back on the reins. "'Tis only fitting, my lord, that you lead us now."

For a moment, Neil sat motionless.

"Do it," Caitir whispered in his ear. She tightened her grasp around his waist.

He kicked the sides of his elch and rode to the front. As he passed Ewan, the squire beamed from ear to ear. Machar nodded gravely.

Yet, as they left the valley forest and began the ascent, he wondered when the day would come that he could tell Machar who he really was. And afterward, would the Capulum warrior still be willing to follow him?

He tried to put aside his doubts. They'd achieved their goal. And soon he could look forward to going home, back to Hidden Pines, to becoming just a blacksmith again. And also—he smiled—to marrying Caitir.

Washed by rays of sunlight, buoyed with new hope, Neil led them up the bare, rock-strewn slopes of Beinn Siarach.

Crisp mountain air filled his lungs, brushed his cheeks.

Somewhere beyond the city's high defensive wall, a hammer struck thrice on a heavy, metal gong. The clangor reverberated like thunder off the mountain walls.

Ahead rose the iron gates of Ard Cúl Dín, the last refuge of the Capulum against the darkness.

OTHER BOOKS BY MARK E. FISHER

The Scepter and Tower High-Fantasy Trilogy from Extraordinary Tales Publishing:

Quest For The Scepter
Into The Druid's Lair (Coming May-June 2019)
Return To The Tower (Coming July-September 2019)

Historical Fiction from Lighthouse Publishing of the Carolinas, Heritage Beacon Imprint:

The Bonfires Of Beltane
The Medallion

To learn more about Mark's books, please visit:

www.MarkFisherAuthor.com

SHARE WITH OTHERS

Let others know what you thought of this book by leaving a review on Amazon.

ACKNOWLEDGMENTS

In the beginning, the making of a work of fiction is a solitary affair. But after the author has exhausted his last run-through, made his "last" edit, and put it aside, he must then bring in other eyes, other perspectives, to catch what he didn't. Thus do I thank the following folks for reading through my initial document and giving me invaluable advice:

Sam Graber, whom I met at an ACFW conference, another fantasy enthusiast.

Melody Graber, Sam's sister, whom I have never met, but whose incisive analysis and comments greatly enhanced this work.

Becky Isaacs, a longtime writing associate and one-time collaborator, who read through and commented on yet another of my novels. Thanks, Becky, yet again.

I also thank Mike Kalmbach and the Rochester Minnesota Authors group, whose advice greatly improved Chapter One, always the most difficult part for me.

I must also thank my editor, Deirdre Lockhart, of Brilliant Cut Editing, for her fine-tuning, overall comments, and line editing.

Finally, I thank my wife, Barbara, for putting up with this compulsion that makes me sit, hour after hour, day after day, in front of a glowing screen, banging out stories that I hope will bring some light into a world that is all too often dark.

Glossary

- Albion—the great island to the east of Ériu. (Britain) But it's surrounded by a wall of black mist. It's rumored a great evil lies there, but since time began, no one knows what.
- Ard Cúl Din—[Ard Cool Deen] the High Refuge, a secret fortress town of the Capulum in the Blue Mountains, west of the Waldreich.
- Armorica—country of northwestern Ereb
- Áth Cliath—[Ah CLEE-ah] main port town of Ériu.
- Aeshitha—[Ay-SHEE-tha. From aes sídhe, or aos sí] A supernatural race similar to fairies, but here they are the lantern folk, or will-'o-the-wisp, who hover over bogs and swamps.
- Beilzig Stadt—[BALE-zig Shtat] city of the Pruss where Queen Hedwig rules on the River Grauwin, archenemies of the Naz.
- Beinn Siarach—[Ben Shee-RAHK] the mountain below which Ard Cúl Din was built.
- Bothach—[BO-hak] lowest group on Celtic class system with no property rights: criminals, unskilled laborers, and indebted farmers.
- Burgundia—country of southwestern, central Ereb
- Cairt Mhór—The Great Charter, wherein the five realms of Ériu united as one country under the Alliance of Kingdoms. The charter also changed the means of selecting their high king or queen. When the process of electing a high king from

the realms' high flaith became so fraught with bribery, fraud, and abuse, they forever bequeathed the office to the Conn royal family of Ulster.

❖ Capulum—secret organization of scholars, warriors, and priests, who for millennia have been dedicated to the preservation of ancient knowledge and the recovery of the lost gifts of Elyon.

❖ Cathair Duvh—[CA-hair Duv] remote capital of Drochtar, site of the Deamhan Lord's base, lying in a mountain valley of Drochcarn. (Irish: Cathair Dubh)

❖ Crom Mord—the dread idol inside which the Deamhan Lord now resides.

❖ Curragh—[COOR-ah] An ancient Irish boat, composed of a wooden frame covered with hides and tarred. From six to seventy feet long, with one to possibly three sails.

❖ Hidden Pines—Tristan's small village in Ulster, east of Ewhain Macha.

❖ Deamhan—When Elyon cursed the rebel siòg under Faolan (later to become the Deamhan Lord), he banished them from Neavh. They became the Deamhan, incorporeal demon spirits who inhabited stone or wooden idols, or who possessed the bodies of foul beasts.

❖ Drijvendby—[DRY-vend-by] the country and city of "islands" of northern Ereb, protected by the Great Sea Wall.

❖ Drochtar—far eastern land of barren, windswept plains, and molten rivers, now living under the cloud of The Deamhan Lord's evil rule.

❖ Drochcarn—the mountain of shadows in Drochtar, whose high, dead valley holds Cathair Duvh.

❖ Elch—a species of large moose, with sharp, pointed antlers, standing eight feet tall at the shoulders, with an antler-span ranging up to twelve feet, native only to the Waldreich.

❖ Elyon—God.

❖ Ewhain Macha—[Ewhen Maha] the largest town of Ulster and capital of Ériu. (Irish: Emain Macha)

❖ Erde—the world containing the continent of Ereb and the islands of Ériu and Albion.

❖ Ereb—the mainland continent of Erde, a vague echo of Europe.

❖ Ériu—[AYR-yoo] a Celtic country similar to Ireland.

❖ Etrucsa—a country of south-central Ereb

❖ Faolan the Traitor—[FOOL-an] Once Faolan was leader of the siòg, but Elyon banished him from Neavh. Now he's the Deamhan Lord, a foul spirit who lives within the idol Crom Mord.

❖ Faolukan the Grim—[FOOL-oo-kan] The Deamhan Lord's arch druid. Once a monk of Ériu, he was turned to the Deamhan Lord's service and given immortality on Erde.

❖ Fell Bogs—a stretch of swamp and mire that once held the great nation of Saxia and the city of Überhort. During the Great Upheaval the land sank and the rivers flowed in, creating the bogs.

❖ Feighn—an extended family unit that all lives in a single roundhouse. (Irish: fine)

❖ Flaith—the highest social class; nobility.

❖ Golob's Maw—the great falls below Beilzig City on the River Grauwin.

❖ Goivhniu—[GOIV-niu] Celtic god of smiths. (Irish: Goibhniu)

❖ Grauwin—the raging river that flows over the great falls of Golob's Maw and protects Beilzig City.

❖ Great Lands, The—another name for the continent of Ereb.

❖ Great Purge, The—the seventy-five year period in which the Deamhan Lord's servant, Faolukan, ravaged Erde and purged both enemy and innocent, alike.

❖ Heyerrah Bosch—The Good Tower that the legendary Patrick built in Sarkenos to imprison the Deamhan Lord and Faolukan.

❖ Hochnest—forest city of the Naz, high above the treetops of the Waldreich.

❖ League—a distance of about three miles.

❖ Lehbrágan—[LEH-brak-ahn]—(Orig. leipreachán, or leithbrágan) sprites, leprechauns, or "the little people". In this story, a race that separated from the siòg and lost their spiritual gifts. Standing only four foot high, the men are bearded. They work as shoemakers, leatherworkers, or clothiers. They wear red or green. Descended from the Tuatha Dé Danann, they once lived underground.

❖ Lost Era, The—the two-thousand-year period after the Scepter and Elyon's second gifts were stolen during which Erde entered a dark age and civilization declined.

❖ Manannán mac Lir—[ma-NA-nan mac lir] the sea deity, also ruler of the Underworld.

❖ Mam Giorag—The dread pass that leads over the mountains to Drochtar, the only known way in.

❖ Naz—the secretive forest people of the Waldreich.

❖ Neavh—[Nev] heaven. (Irish: Neamh)

❖ Pneuma, The—the Spirit of God.

❖ Pruss—the people living east of the Naz by the River Grauwin, archenemies of the Naz.

❖ Púca—a shapeshifter. In Irish mythology, a type of fairy that could change into terrifying shapes such as wolves, bear, crows, and ravens. In this story, they are followers of the Deamhan Lord and Faolukan.

❖ Roamers (also called the Sheachranahk [SHAK-rah-nach])—a wandering tribe of gypsy-like refugees from Erdelstan who long ago took up residence on Ériu.

- ❖ Roundhouse—A communal round house from twenty to forty feet in diameter, built of a wicker frame covered on the outside with thatch and on the inside with furs.
- ❖ Saxia—the country that once occupied the Fell Bogs before the Great Upheaval.
- ❖ Schwarzburg—a kingdom and castle hidden deep in the Waldreich.
- ❖ Sfarsit Mountains—The high mountain chain that blocks the way into Drochtar.
- ❖ Sheachranahk—see "Roamers" (Irish: Seachranach)
- ❖ Shuderrah Bosch—the Deamhan Lord's Dark Tower near Samotun where he ruled Sarkenos.
- ❖ Thrag—a barghest in Faolukan's service, in whose presence all light dims and goes out. Some say he's like a bear or dog walking on hind legs, but no one has ever seen his true form.
- ❖ Toghaí, The—[TO-hai]—the one chosen by prophecy to find Elyon's missing gifts and end the darkness.
- ❖ Tower of Dóchas—[Do-HASS] the great tower beside the palace of Ewhain Macha, rumored to have once held the Scepter.
- ❖ Tuath—[TU-ah; *pl.* tuatha] A Celtic clan composed of many feighns.
- ❖ Überhort—Name of King Lange's castle in lost, ancient Saxia.
- ❖ Waldreich—[VALD-rike] The great, dark forest that occupies the south, central section of Ereb. Home to a secretive forest people, wolves, and dark magic.
- ❖ Wodan—Forest god whom the Naz worship.